The Seal Cove Theoretical Society
S.W. CLEMENS

Also by S.W. Clemens
With Artistic License
Time Management, a novel
Evelyn Marsh

For my neighbors,
who know the difference between a lie and an interpretation, or should

"No one is useless in this world who lightens the burdens of another."
— Charles Dickens, *Doctor Marigold's Prescriptions*.

"But such is human life. Here today and gone tomorrow. A dream — a shadow — a ripple on the water — a thing for invisible gods to sport with for a season and then toss idly by — idly by. It is rough."
— Mark Twain, "Closed Out" sketch, included in San Francisco letter to Virginia City *Territorial Enterprise*, 1/28/1866

From Emily Abbott's Notebooks
The Ocean

People take solace gazing at water. I don't know why this should be so; it just is.

The ocean is always changing. On a calm, clear morning when the rising sun is still hidden behind the mountains, the high pale blue sky subtly changes to pale green and yellow and pink, and the sea is pink except in the blue wake of fishing boats. When the sun clears the mountains and floods the ocean with light, the wake of boats gleam white and the water turns cobalt blue in the deep water, and jade green in the shallows. Later the water takes on a duller shade of blue, a French blue. On overcast days the sea is grey and at times slate green, and in the afternoon, when the sun is past its zenith, the ocean is like a million mirrors reflecting the light so intensely that you have to look away. And then there are the sunsets. On cloudless days the horizon blazes orange with yellow bands sandwiched between the pale blues of sky and sea. On days when the cirrus catches fire, the sea seems to burn, changing from orange to purple as the darkness comes on. And at night the moon sparkles in its mysterious depths.

And it isn't only the colors that change, but the surface of the water. It's said that the people of the Arctic have a hundred different words for snow. The English language is inadequate to describe the textures of the sea — calm and oily, choppy, whitecapped, crinkled, windblown and storm-tossed. You can read the wind and currents on the face of the water. And then there are the waves, cold and dreary lines crashing against the cliffs, eating away a little of the land with each assault, or big combers rolling into shore, white horses racing toward land with manes blown back in an offshore breeze.

Chapter One
Rumrunners - 1928

"Tell me another story."

At six-years-old Derek loved listening to Grampa Ed's bedtime stories, particularly stories that were real.

"Just one more, I have to get to sleep myself. How about the one with my dog Rex in the snow?"

"No, tell me about Grampa Frank."

"Okay, that would be my grampa, so that's your great-great grampa. Back in the day, that would be back in the 1920s, almost a century ago now, a lot of people in this country decided that drinking alcohol was a bad idea, and they passed a law called Prohibition. Do you know what 'prohibition' means?"

"Tell me." Derek snuggled down in his blanket with a smile.

"To prohibit is to forbid or prevent people from doing something."

"And we don't like prohibition. We want people to do what they want."

"Well, it all depends. It's complicated. You wouldn't want people driving through a stop sign would you?"

"No, but it's nobody's business what we do in our own homes."

"Who told you that?"

"Dad says it all the time."

"At least he comes by his opinions honestly. I'm afraid he got them from me. Anyway, where were we?"

"Prohibition."

"Yep, there was Prohibition. The teetotalers were in control and they forbade the sale of alcohol — wine, whiskey, beer and the like. But there were a lot of people who liked to relax after work with a glass of beer or whiskey..."

"Like Dad."

"He does like his Scotch."

"And champagne."

"He has good taste. So, there were a lot of people who didn't agree with this law, and they were willing to pay a lot of money to people who would sneak booze into the country."

"Booze is alcohol."

"Booze is alcohol, yes. So my grampa, Grampa Frank, he didn't like that law, and he knew there could be good money to be made by a little smuggling."

"Like pirates," Derek exclaimed excitedly and waved his arm as if swishing a sword.

"Well...not exactly like pirates. Smugglers don't think the government has any business telling them what to do. That was your great-great-grandfather. At the beginning of Prohibition, the government's jurisdiction ended three miles offshore. So all the smugglers had to do was to anchor outside that boundary and let small boats come out to them. On the west coast ships came down with loads of whiskey from Vancouver, and on the east coast the smugglers brought rum up from the Caribbean, which is why smugglers of that era are known as rumrunners."

"Rum is booze."

"Rum is booze made from sugar cane. Very sweet. Makes good mixed drinks, like rum and coke, or daiquiris."

"Momma likes daiquiris."

"Yes," Grampa Ed said with a sigh. "Yes, she does. A little too much sometimes, but it's not my place to ..."

# # #

"Emily!"

For a moment Emily Abbott tried to hold on to the vision of Grampa Ed and the real hero of the story she was writing, the little boy who would grow up to be Derek Law, the dashing reporter who mixed as comfortably with the riffraff as with the gentry. She pushed away from the desk and sighed.

"Emily!" her mother called again. "I made a pot of tea. Did you buy cookies at the market?"

The vision evaporating with the demands of the moment, Emily Abbott closed her laptop and started downstairs, leaving what she thought of as her shadow life. It wasn't important, she told herself. She would come back to it later. Someday all of her time would be her own. Until then caring for her mother was a solemn obligation. It was the right thing to do, and she'd promised her father.

The Abbotts had lived in the pale-yellow two-story duplex on the corner of Ellendale and Seacliff since Emily was four-years-old. At first the elder Abbotts, John and Mary, lived on the upper floor with a view over the top of the Birminghams' small red bungalow that sat on the edge of the cliff where Spanish Creek flowed into the tide pools. Emily was relegated to the in-law unit on the bottom floor. Later, after John's first heart attack and Mary's stroke, the elder Abbotts moved downstairs, and Emily moved to the brighter rooms upstairs.

Emily loved reading or writing in the study in her wingback chair by the window, or on the deck overlooking the rocky tide pools and the sea. The view was always changing. The sea could be calm and peaceful as a bay, or choppy and whitecapped. Wind sculpted and textured its surface. The color too was constantly changing, from cobalt to palest blue, from slate green to slate gray, from sparkling silver to blinding white. And there was always activity. Birds chased above its surface — cormorants and pelicans, gulls and grebes. Sailboats and fishing boats cut white wakes across its face. Tankers and container ships slid along its horizon. And now and then humpback, or blue, or gray whales blew steam and arched their backs into the sun before sinking out of sight.

Mary Abbott peered up from her wheelchair as Emily descended the stairs. "What were you doing up there?"

"Nothing, just reading," Emily said. She was glad that infirmities prevented her mother from going upstairs. What her mother didn't know couldn't hurt her — couldn't hurt either of them.

"What are you reading?"

To Emily, it was a loaded question. Mary Abbott had never allowed "trashy" books in the house. No romances, no thrillers, no potboilers, and nothing with even a suggestion of bad language or sex. If Emily wanted to read, her mother instructed, there were the classics (by which Mary Abbott meant anything written prior to 1940) or non-fiction.

"The biography of Robert Frost," Emily lied. If Mary Abbott could have found a way upstairs, she would have been appalled by the comfortably cluttered rooms and shelves stocked full of "trashy" romances and thrillers.

"I made a pot of English Breakfast tea, if you'd like a cup," Mary Abbott said, "but I don't know what happened to the cookies. You didn't eat the last one, did you?"

"No, of course not. I'd know if I ate the last cookie, wouldn't I? I'd put it on the list."

Emily searched the pantry, the cupboards and the drawers. Her mother rolled in her wake, closing doors and drawers as she'd been doing ever since Emily was a toddler. Mary Abbott often said reprovingly, "There are door openers and door closers, and you Emily are a door opener."

"No cookies," Emily confirmed. "Have you had breakfast?"

"There's nothing to eat."

"I just went to the market," Emily said, opening the refrigerator. "There's milk. You could have cereal."

"I don't like cereal."

"There's fruit."

Mary shook her head. "Upsets my stomach."

"Eggs then. I could whip you up an omelet."

"Oh, I don't want to be a bother."

"I have to make myself something anyway."

"With mushrooms and artichoke hearts?"

Emily took out two eggs, Parmesan cheese, and mushrooms. Then she went to the pantry. "We're out of artichoke hearts."

"Oh," Mary sighed with disappointment. "That's okay, really, I'm not hungry anyway."

"We don't need artichoke hearts. I'll make a mushroom omelet."

"No, that's okay."

"You have to eat something."

Mary Abbott closed the pantry door. "I wanted cookies."

"You can't subsist on cookies."

"I like fig Newtons. Fig Newtons have fruit."

"I'll go to the little market after breakfast."

"The tea will be cold."

The tea could be reheated, she could make a new pot, but Emily knew better than to deny her mother's will. "Alright, I'll be back in fifteen minutes," she said. The little market was only three blocks away.

"But you're not going out like that!" Mary cried with alarm.

"Like what?"

"In those clothes."

"What's wrong with my clothes?"

"Nothing," Mary Abbott said, wrinkling her nose. "Nothing, they're just so...frumpy."

"I'm not going to a beauty pageant; I'm going to the market."

"You always want to look your best when you go out; you never know who you might meet."

"Prince Charming doesn't shop at Coastside Market."

"Well, I suppose you know best."

"I'll be back in fifteen minutes."

"Don't forget the list."

Chapter Two
Seal Cove Brewpub

The point on which the town of Seal Cove is built, shelters a small harbor on the south, and a series of lovely secluded coves on the north, one of which lends its name to the town. Locals affectionately and sometimes grumpily call the town Fog Beach, in complaint of the fog that blankets the coast during the summer months.

Tom and Daisy Birmingham were a fixture in Seal Cove. They'd lived in the little red bungalow on the edge of the cliff overlooking the tide pools for thirty-five years. Everyone liked the Birminghams. They were naturally friendly, cheerful, honest and forgiving. Daisy taught kindergarten at Farallone View Elementary School. She knew most of the children in town and a good many of their parents. Tom had built a small company importing some rather wonderful, though esoteric, white wines from Alsace and Germany. The Birminghams' only regret was that their son Douglas had grown up, married and he and his wife had moved to Bellingham, Washington, as housing in the Bay Area was beyond their means.

Like most people, the Birminghams had grown into their eccentricities over time. What began as youthful affectation, had now become a solid part of their natures. Tom's sense of style was informed by black-and-white movies. Often when the weather was warm, he wore an ivory flannel suit and a Panama hat, which gave him a stylish if crumpled appearance. When the weather was cool, he wore tweeds, a vest, and a trilby hat. He often carried a walking stick. Daisy, flamboyant in her own way, favored bright colors and richly embroidered clothes, with a variety of hats and jewelry to match any outfit. Together or apart they stood out in a crowd.

On their last day together in Seal Cove, the blue sky was streaked with contrails and mares' tails. It was Presidents' Day holiday and Daisy was accompanying Tom as he called on his coastside accounts. Their first stop was the Seal Cove Brewpub, formerly known as Rick's Roadhouse, overlooking the cove. In coming up with a name, the owners had originally wanted to call the brewpub Smuggler's Cove, the local moniker since Prohibition, but that was too long to fit gracefully on the label of a bottle of beer. In the end, they named it Seal Cove Brewpub in honor of the town, and the various beers all bore the Cove insignia — Cove Amber Ale; Cove Pale Ale; Cove Stout; Cove Porter, etc.

The brewpub has a long mahogany bar, dining room with wrap-around windows, and a downstairs terrace where guests enjoy drinking and dining under propane heaters or sitting around the fire pit. The food isn't much to speak of, but the beer and wine are plentiful and reasonably priced, and the view of the cove is sublime.

Before sitting down for lunch, the Birminghams first went to the end of the bar where Tom set down three bottles and took off his Panama hat. Gene Price finished mixing a Negroni for a young blonde and came down the bar with a jovial smile.

"Mr. B, Mrs. B, what have you got for me today?"

"Two Alsatians and a Mosel. I'd like to know what you think. If you're interested, orders need to be in by April — we're planning to ship at the end of May."

Gene Price picked up a bottle to examine the label as Tom slid a spec sheet toward him.

Daisy nudged her husband. He looked at her with questioning eyes.

"Aren't you going to tell him?" she whispered.

He shook his head. "Not yet."

Gene had acute hearing and couldn't help asking, "Tell me what?"

Tom looked from one to the other. "Mrs. Birmingham is retiring at the end of the school year."

Gene's face broke into a spontaneous grin. "That's great news! Congratulations!" He'd been one of her first students and had always had a soft spot for Mrs. B.

But she was still looking at Tom. "And...?"

Tom arched an eyebrow and ran fingers through his white hair. "Nothing's settled yet," he said. There was an awkward silence before he added, "She's got me to promise to retire too. But not before the next shipment and all of the existing inventory is consigned. So I'll be retired by the end of the year, most likely."

"Who's taking over the business?"

"It's a one-man operation, so there's no one to take over."

"I might be interested, if you'd be willing to show me the ropes. I have a little money saved up."

Each May and November Tom traveled to Europe for three weeks of wine tasting and convivial meals with old and new friends in the wine trade. It was a niche market, and one he'd personally cultivated over many years. It had never made him wealthy, but it had afforded him an enviable lifestyle. "That's tempting. We should talk numbers."

At that moment an elegant redhead in tight jeans pushed back from a table in the barroom. She grabbed her purse, lowered her sunglasses, and leaning over the table toward her male companion, declared, "You're so full of it, I don't even know where to start!" Then she turned on her heels and headed for the exit.

Steve Wexler stood up, undecided whether to follow. The redhead didn't look back but held up a middle finger for his benefit as she pushed out the front door. Wexler stared after her, dumbfounded. "What a bitch," he mumbled, oblivious of anyone else in the bar except the pretty young blonde with the Negroni in hand who started toward the stairway to the terrace. Wexler watched the sway of her hips as she passed and held up an index finger to catch Gene Price's attention. "I'll have whatever she's having," he said, tossing his long hair over his shoulder as he nodded towards the blonde.

"You don't want to go there, mate; her husband is in the restroom."

"Crap," Wexler said. After a moment's hesitation, he hurried out after the redhead.

"Guy'll never learn," Gene said shaking his head. "He still thinks he's a celebrity."

"What's his story?" Tom asked.

"I thought you two were neighbors."

"He lives around the corner, but the only time we speak is when I ask him to turn down the music. Do you know what he does for a living?"

"Nothing, now," Gene said. "He was the bass player for Totally Wrecked."

Tom looked blank.

"Rock band? You remember, had a couple of hits — sixteen, seventeen years ago."

Tom shrugged.

"*Add Fuel to the Fire*? *Like Walking in Circles*? No?"

Tom shook his head. "Not my kind of music."

"Anyway, he's got plenty of money. Not much sense, but plenty of money."

# # #

Tom and Daisy took a table with a panoramic view from the cove to the horizon. The ebb tide had exposed part of the reef, and gray harbor seals lay sunning themselves on the exposed rocks.

"That was interesting," Tom said. "You learn something new every day. How old do you think he is?"

"Our neighbor? Oh, late thirties I guess."

"Can you imagine? Thirty-something and already retired?" They both studied their menus for a minute. "Was he a student of yours?" Tom asked.

"No, I'm sure he didn't grow up here."

"It can't be good to have so much success so early. Doesn't leave any goals to shoot for."

"Better early success than no success at all. He's lucky."

"I guess. But what would you do with the rest of your life?"

"It doesn't seem much different than any retirement," Daisy observed. "Maybe he can give us some pointers."

"I doubt that very seriously. He doesn't seem particularly happy."

"As we all know, money doesn't buy happiness, although it does buy security."

"I don't know if security is all it's cracked up to be. I don't think it's healthy. There've been studies of lottery winners. Five years after they win, most of them are unhappy or broke or both. Adversity builds character."

"Adversity causes stress, which isn't good for the mind *or* the body."

"No," Tom admitted.

They studied their menus in silence for a minute.

"What would you do if you won the lottery?" Daisy asked.

Tom smiled and looked into her blue eyes. "I already hit the lottery when I married you."

"No, seriously."

"I don't think I'd change a thing. Maybe remodel the house."

Daisy thought a moment. "I'd buy Dougie a home close by."

"His job is in Bellingham."

"He could get another job. I just wish he would find something he liked, a career, something better than testing video games, something that gives him long-term satisfaction. Some incentive to get out of bed in the morning. He seems so rudderless."

"It could be worse. I read that a third of all eighteen to thirty-year-olds in the U.S. live with their parents."

The waiter placed two champagne flutes on the table. "Compliments of the house," he said.

Tom looked toward the bar where Gene Price was giving them a thumbs up. Tom raised his flute in acknowledgment. Then he and Daisy clinked glasses. "To retirement," he said.

"To retirement." They sipped their champagne. "Are you going to consider Gene's proposal?"

"About mentoring him? I'll think about it."

Daisy closed her menu. "What are you having?"

"I'm torn between the fish tacos and clam chowder."

"Get the chowder and I'll get a crab Louie and we can split them."

"That works for me," Tom said. "What were we talking about?"

"Millennials. Jobs. Douglas. I always thought Douglas would make a good doctor."

"His grades weren't good enough for med school," Tom said, remembering how hard it was to cajole their son into doing his homework assignments. "Anyway, it's too late to go back to school. I wish he'd take over my business, but he shows no interest in it."

"I just want him to find something he's passionate about."

"He's an adult. He's going to have to find his own way. Besides, how can we advise him, when we can't even imagine the world he's going to be living in? Could you have imagined *this* world when we were kids? There were three TV channels. There were no personal computers, no wifi, no internet."

"No buying online," Daisy added.

"No email. No texting. No ATMs or cell phones. No fax or scanners."

"No digital music."

"Or digital cameras," Tom said. "No GPS or self-driving cars."

"No video games or robots."

"Or DVDs or solar power."

"When we were kids no one could have planned to write code for a living — there was no such thing."

"I worry about him," Daisy lamented.

"I worry about his whole generation. It's a lousy time to grow up."

"I miss him," Daisy said.

"Me too," Tom said wistfully, not thinking of the man, but of the boy.

"There's something I look forward to in retirement. If I get to missing him too much I'll just fly up to Washington for a few days."

"You can video chat for free."

"It's not the same. And it wouldn't cost much. The only expense would be airfare. They have an extra bedroom."

The waiter came back with a basket of fresh, warm bread and took their orders.

"Just think," Daisy said, buttering her bread, "when we're retired we can do this every day. Everyday will be a holiday."

"We never did it when you were on summer break."

"We were always busy. You were, anyway. Will you miss the traveling?"

"A little bit. I enjoy getting away, meeting old friends. But then I get to come home to *this*." He gestured a circle with his champagne flute. "I get the best of both worlds."

They sat up to take in the view. It was the same old view. It was the same and glorious. Dark cypress perched on the bluff eighty feet above the white crescent of Seal Cove. Small waves broke and rolled out white carpets of foam one after the other. The fishing fleet was out, little white specks on a sparkling blue canvas stretching all the way to the horizon. Just beyond the reef, a single crab boat bobbed on the swells as a crabber hauled in his pots.

Chapter Three
Gary Myron

Miss Behavin' drifted with the current off Seal Cove, nudged shoreward with each swell, a half-mile offshore in that thin band between the inner and outer reefs, just beyond the kelp beds, in 75 feet of water.

Gary Myron, the captain, gave the idling throttle a little nudge to compensate for the current. This was his first season on his own boat after spending a decade as a deckhand. Only twenty feet from stem to stern, Miss Behavin' was small for a crab boat, but he still felt a certain pride that comes with ownership.

Jessie Barber, his swarthy deckhand, snagged a crab buoy with a boat hook. Then he attached the line to an electric winch and began winding in the line. He was looking over the side when the winch began to labor, then screech. "God damn it," Barber swore. He hit the red kill switch. "Line fouled the winch again."

"Wouldn't happen if you kept your eyes on the spool," Myron said. He spoke in a high pitched nasal twang that precluded a career in politics or the law.

"I did, it just jammed."

"You'll have to haul it up by hand then. I'll pull her forward and take some tension off the line. At least it's not deep."

Myron gave the throttle a little more thrust.

"Hold it! There, that's good," Barber yelled, pulling up the blue line hand over hand. "It's awful light."

Gary Myron cut the engine.

When the stainless steel and wire trap, or pot, was hauled over the side he eyed the meager catch with concern. Eight crabs clung to the wire. He opened the trap and began sorting. The females and undersized males were thrown over the side. Barber put the rest into a water-filled storage locker along the port gunwale. "Four friggin' keepers," Myron said. "This isn't

working. We'll barely make expenses at this rate. We'll have to go deeper."
He knew Dungeness crab preferred a sandy bottom where the tidal current
wasn't too strong, which meant out past the outer reefs at two to six miles
offshore where the competition was fierce.

"How deep?"

"150, maybe 200 feet."

To account for tides and swells, a pot in 150 feet of water needed a line
of 190 feet. He had 100 pots spread between Pedro Point and the southern
edge of Half Moon Bay. He had 25 off of Miramar Beach where the take
was a little better on most days, but for the past week gray whales had been
moving through the area. They passed in groups of three, the mother, her
calf, and an aunt, hugging the coast on their northward migration, and he
was obligated to keep his distance, which made tending the pots problematic.
So those pots would have to be moved as well. If he took all of them out
to deeper water, he'd need almost 20,000 feet of line. He calculated the cost
in his head. "It won't be cheap, and it'll take some time, but I don't see an
alternative."

"How much time?"

Myron shrugged, pushed the bill of his cap up and spat a wad of
bubblegum into the water. "Time is money. We'll have to do it in stages." It
was a simple fact that he could barely stack sixteen pots on the deck of Miss
Behavin', so it would take several roundtrips to gather all the pots. Taking
them back out would take longer, as each 1,200-foot bale of crab line took
up as much room as a pot. "I don't know. We might get it done in three days.
Maybe it would be best to do half and see how it goes." He'd figured his small
boat would have a competitive advantage being willing to crab in shallower
water than the big, deeper draft boats cared to go, and he'd done well enough
the first couple months of the season. But the crab count was dwindling.
Now he'd have to compete with the big boys.

Barber wiped a sleeve across his forehead. "I suppose this is a bad time to
ask for an advance."

Myron rolled his eyes and let out a small, mirthless laugh. "No time is a
good time."

"Because the thing is, you know Bill Fix? He's leaving for Oregon, so
there's a spot opening up on the Morpheus."

17

The Morpheus, Myron pointed out, paid deckhands only eight percent, while he was paying fifteen.

"Yeah," Barber acknowledged, "but eight percent of a lot, is a lot more than fifteen percent of nothing."

"So you're jumping ship?"

"I didn't say that. There are other guys want the spot. I just don't want to turn down any opportunities." Barber shrugged without apology. "I need some cash to pay rent."

"I thought you were living with your parents."

"I am, but Pop's asking for rent now."

Gary Myron mulled this over. "Forgive me if I'm unsympathetic." He'd been living in the cramped quarters aboard Miss Behavin' for three months. "Now let's get as many of these pots pulled up as we can in an hour. Tomorrow morning we'll pick up the rest here and check the pots off Miramar. Then I'll go scrounge for more line."

Myron opened a water bottle and gulped a quarter of it. Then they set to work. It took twelve minutes to free the fouled line. It took another hour to pull up nine more pots, yielding just 53 keepers. Then, the deck piled high with empty crab pots, they sped southwestward through a jarring chop that slapped the bottom of the boat like a car driving down a washboard road, with the occasional pothole thrown in for extra measure.

Out to sea, he could see the tiny profiles of bigger boats out in the deep water where the crabs were plentiful. He longed for a boat that would make the whole process more efficient, more fun. He'd worked on such boats, boats like Morpheus that were multi-purpose vessels with wing-like poles that served as stabilizers, and for trolling when the crab season was over and the salmon season began. A man could make a good living with such a boat.

Chapter Four
Wexler's Rock & Roll Past

Steve Wexler followed the redhead out of Seal Cove Brewpub. Monique? Or was it Monica? He couldn't remember. Whatever. He had to dodge her car as she sped out of the parking lot, driving one-handed as she thrust her other fist out the window and gave him the finger. He watched her car top the rise and disappear. He had no clue what he'd done to deserve such wrath. She seemed to think he could read her mind.

He decided to walk back home through the cypress grove on the bluff. The path followed the curve of the cove for half a mile before dropping down to the marine reserve parking lot. From there it was just a two-block walk up Sea Cliff to his home.

Wexler (most people called him by his last name) had come to the coast in his freshman year of high school when his father took a job with the Odwalla juice company in Half Moon Bay. He played standup bass in the school orchestra, where he met three of his bandmates. In the summer between their freshman and sophomore years they formed a rock band because (hey, everyone knew it) music was like an aphrodisiac to teenage girls.

Andy Espinosa, the de facto leader of the band, named it Rampant Disturbance. It was a name that didn't stick. For a while, they were known as Stand Off. Then Wexler had the brilliant idea of calling the band Totally Wrecked. The name struck a chord with their audience. Andy would strut onto the stage, grab the microphone and shout, "Who wants to get Totally Wrecked?" The double entendre always elicited an eruption of cheers and hoots from wannabe rebels who frequented the raucous, dingy clubs in hopes of appearing worldly, dissolute, and older than their years. Then Noah Samuelson on drums would lay down a strong beat, Wexler on electric bass would lay down the bassline, and Clifford Cook on rhythm guitar would join in on an amped-up Martin Dreadnought. Andy, self-confident and charismatic, naturally took lead vocals and electric guitar solos.

They weren't half bad for a garage band, and the girls did start hanging around, gravitating to Andy and Cliff and Noah. If music was a chick magnet, Wexler thought he must have his polarities reversed, for he seemed to repulse girls. He'd been fooled a few times, seduced into the hope that a girl might actually be interested in him, only to find she'd used him as a stepping stone to get to Andy or Cliff. Had he been a different sort, he might have left the band, but Wexler (little Stevie as his mother called him) couldn't find it in himself to resent his bandmates' good fortune.

At first, they played classic rock-and-roll covers, then began writing original tunes that blended blues and reggae. When Cliff left for college he was replaced by a talented songwriter named Bill Morrison, a nineteen-year-old high school dropout whose previous band had occasionally shared the bill with Totally Wrecked. Morrison brought some jazz influence to the group and added ballads to their usually hard-edged lyrics. He also introduced Andy to hard drugs.

With Wexler occasionally switching to keyboards and Morrison alternating between rhythm guitar and flute, the music took on a polish that contrasted with their earlier, rougher tunes, and gave them an air of sophistication. With the hiring of a manager they graduated from dives to bonafide music clubs, touring West Coast venues in Andy's old panel truck. Two halcyon years of sex and rock-and-roll. It was a step up for Wexler, though he had to privately admit that he was always the alternative. The girls would come to their motel after a show looking for Andy or Bill. Even Noah held a higher place on the totem pole than the gangly, pimple-faced bass player who was always in the background and never their first choice. He remembered a couple of girls coming late, finding Andy already occupied with two other fans, Bill passed out on the floor, and Noah's door locked, and only as a last resort did they settle for the bass player. If the girls couldn't have the Alpha male, they could at least accommodate one of his lieutenants. At times it felt like he was playing a part that was written for someone else. Not that he was complaining. Having groupies fawn over him was a young man's wet dream.

It was impossible to flirt with so many women without forming an attachment to at least one. There was one girl in Bakersfield that Wexler couldn't get out of his mind. Her eyes, her smile, the tone of her voice, the warmth of her skin all captivated him. She stopped by after all three of the band's shows. He might have followed up on that one if she'd given him a legitimate phone number.

At the end of their second year of touring, Totally Wrecked put out two studio albums. It was in the last gasp of the CD era and both sold well and brought in enormous royalties. Their two greatest hits, *Add Fuel to the Fire*, and *Like Walking in Circles* had been used in several commercials for pharmaceuticals, cars, and computers, and had cemented their place in the lexicon of the Millennial generation. They were, however, destined to become a mere footnote in musical history after Andy overdosed on heroin and Morrison, suffering a paroxysm of guilt, quit the music business. Noah joined another band, and with that Totally Wrecked was totally wrecked.

Wexler's father stepped in to direct his son's finances. With the cash they financed the house in Seal Cove and invested the rest in dividend-paying stocks. As long as Steve Wexler remained prudent, he didn't have to worry about paying the bills.

From Emily Abbott's Notebooks
The Coastside Market

Between Point Montara light and Pigeon Point light, a stretch of twenty-five miles, lie half a dozen small towns set at the foot of the Santa Cruz Mountains — Farallone City, Seal Cove, Princeton, El Granada, Half Moon Bay, and Pescadero. Interspersed among the towns are fields of Brussels sprouts, and artichokes, bright yellow mustard, fava beans, puny pumpkins, nurseries, Christmas tree farms, and greenhouses growing produce and flowers.

Seal Cove is a small town of three-thousand souls by night. By day the population is half that, as most of those who live on the San Mateo coast work on "the other side of the hill," as coastsiders call anything on the San Francisco Bay side of the mountains. The great migration begins early on weekday mornings. The gulls that spent the night resting on the beaches, awake at first light and begin their commute to Ox Mountain landfill. The great white ribbon of lazily flapping birds catches the morning sun as it peeks over the mountains. Soon thereafter cars stream out of the coastal towns by the dozens, bound for San Francisco and Silicon Valley.

When the commuters have gone, Seal Cove is inhabited by the retired, by housewives and househusbands, by students and feckless adult children, middle-class drug addicts, artists, postmen, monks, dog walkers, and the proprietors of the town's few businesses — a yoga and pilates studio, a brewpub, a wine bar, a taqueria, a bed-and-breakfast inn, a massage parlor, a gas station, and a market. And, of course, the Russian Orthodox monastery.

For more than a century the monastery has been hidden in the shadows of a dark stand of windswept cypress across the street from the Coastside Market. No one ever sees the monks, save for one day a year when they come out of their compound, dressed in black cassocks and holding aloft a golden cross and pennant. Then the bearded monks march solemnly in procession around the block and file back through the gate, and no one will see them again for another year. No one but Gibson, who delivers their groceries.

Gibson is the owner of the Coastside Market. No one knows his last name, or what part of India he came from, but he's owned the market for thirty-some years. It's one of those old-fashioned neighborhood markets built before the advent of supermarkets, and within its four walls you can find most anything — sweatshirts and caps, coffee, beer and wine, produce and canned goods, bread and tortillas, frozen pizza and sausages, hamburger, chicken, Cornish game hens, eggs and dairy products, fruit juice and sodas, ice cream, kitchen utensils, bubble wrap, cardboard boxes, cleaning supplies, sundries and party favors, even flowers and greeting cards. From behind the counter you can also buy tobacco and lottery tickets, canisters of propane and, according to some, the finest selection of Scotch whisky between San Francisco and Monterey.

Chapter Five
Emily Abbott

That Emily was a mistake, a mid-life miscalculation, was a secret known only to her mother, who had assumed she could forego birth control at 44. Her father, who was 10 years older than her mother, was delighted. He was unaware that his wife even used birth control, and considered himself blessed to become a father at last. John Abbott doted on his daughter and Emily's happiest moments of childhood were outings alone with him. He indulged her whims and did not believe in any rule but the Golden Rule, which he practiced religiously. Mary Abbott made up for his laxity by imposing a rule for every occasion. There was a right way and a wrong way to do everything. Her husband would smile blithely and turn a deaf ear to her edicts. Less willful, Emily suffered her mother's criticism with a despairing heart.

Throughout her school days, Emily had but three friends, and only one that stuck, and that was Linda Murphy. For a long time, they played only at Linda's house. Emily had never brought anyone home, for though she adored her father, she was vaguely ashamed that her parents were so much older than all the other kids' parents. When she eventually allowed Linda to visit, Emily prepared the way by declaring that, "You know, they're not really my parents; they're my grandparents. You see, my parents were killed in a plane crash when I was just a baby, and my grandparents took me in. Grandmother insists I call them Mom and Dad. But I guess it's no worse than being adopted." The story got around and all the other children looked on her with pity.

Pity, however, did not make her any more popular. Among their classmates, everyone but Linda considered Emily an odd duck. Pale lips and thick black bangs that covered her forehead gave Emily a severe no-nonsense air. She had no sense of style, nor would her mother have indulged her if she had, and while her classmates made reference to contemporary music and television and video games, Emily had to feign indifference, for her mother only allowed classical music in the house, television was restricted to educational channels, and video games were not tolerated. As a result, Emily became a bookworm, but even her reading was curated by her mother, who dismissed popular contemporary novels as "potboilers and trash." When Emily's ninth-grade English teacher assigned Rainbow Rowell's *Eleanor and Park*, Mary Abbott paid a visit to the school to voice her objection. Emily was embarrassed, but not deterred. Many a school lunch break was spent in the library reading forbidden books — Romances by Karen White, Thrillers by Nora Roberts, Mysteries by Michael Connelly and Jeffrey Deaver, and Horror stories by Stephen King. Reading and writing were her great escapes.

# # #

Wheeling her basket back from the market she thought how nice it was to be out of the house, if only for a few minutes. She tried to pretend how it would be if she had no one waiting for her, no obligations restraining her, chaining her to the house, her time entirely her own. It was an odd feeling. She couldn't keep up the pretense for long, because the image of her father walked beside her, chiding her discontent. She remembered him lying in the hospital bed after his first heart attack, when she was a senior in high school. He'd said, "I wish you would be more patient with your mother. I know she doesn't always show it, but she does love you." Later, after her mother's stroke confined her to a wheelchair, he'd said, "You've always been a good girl, always done the right thing. I know I can count on you to care for your mother when I'm gone." Emily knew what was expected of her. Often she imagined conversations with her father. She could still remember the timbre and intonation of his voice, and she knew what he would say: "It's all in your head, lollipop. You can be as happy as you choose to be. You live in a nice home free of room and board. Who could ask for more?" The second heart attack, the fatal one, came on a beautiful spring morning of her sophomore year of college. Her mother sank into a dark, listless depression. She had loved her husband, and felt cheated that he had been taken from her. Emily dropped out of school, figuring she'd go back when her mother passed away. At the time she didn't think her mother would last a year without her father, but they were coming up on the sixth anniversary of his death. *You have to roll with the punches*, Emily told herself, and if she were honest she would have to admit to a certain pride in her sacrifice. She knew her father would be proud.

Chapter Six
The Dog that Ate Crab

Carl Olmsted came west from Wisconsin to work for an internet startup in San Francisco in 2007. The first year and a half he lived in a little tenement in a dilapidated Victorian in the Mission District, for which he paid the princely sum of $3,000 a month. Its only advantage was that it was within biking distance of work. But that also meant that all of his free time was spent in a dump. Its disadvantages, besides the cost, were occasional gunshots that disturbed his sleep, old plumbing, and bars on the windows, which ruined the view of the telephone pole and the tenement across the street. Once the novelty of living in San Francisco had worn off (that is, after his bicycle was stolen) he began looking for a place that was safer, more affordable, and within commutable distance. He found a house rental in Seal Cove in 2010. A twenty-minute drive, followed by a fifteen-minute ride on Bay Area Rapid Transit, deposited him a couple of blocks from his office. The commute was longer, but the change of habitation gave him a beautiful and restful place to spend his evenings and weekends.

When he'd been living in Seal Cove for almost two years he bought a mutt for company. The mutt was a presumed cross between a Kerry Blue and a Soft-coated Wheaton Terrier. He named the mottled dog Roscoe. On weekday evenings after work, he walked Roscoe out by the lighthouse, and on the weekends he walked him on the bluffs overlooking Pillar Point Harbor. One Saturday afternoon he made the mistake of continuing down to the harbor, where he sat at an outdoor table at the Careless Crab and ate clam chowder, a BLT and french fries. Patrons at adjacent tables dined on hamburgers and crab and fresh fish. The air was heavy with the heavenly scent of food. Roscoe whimpered. It was enough to drive an otherwise sensible dog crazy.

The house Carl rented had a dog door that led out to a small enclosed yard, so while Carl was at work Roscoe could sleep in the comfort of the house or run around the gopher-pocked lawn as he pleased. It might have been a nice life for a tired old dog, but Roscoe still had some bounce in his step. He felt cooped up and lonely, and when he slept he dreamt of the Careless Crab.

Each weekday evening Carl looked forward to his homecoming. Roscoe would jump up and wag his short tail enthusiastically and smile and turn circles until Carl knelt and ran his hands down the soft fur of Roscoe's back, and scratched behind his ears. Carl had never been so warmly greeted by a human being. Then one day Carl came home to a quiet house. His call for Roscoe was met with silence, save for the hum of the refrigerator. In the backyard, he discovered that Roscoe had dug a hole under the fence and was gone.

Carl was bereft. He walked the immediate neighborhood, then took to his car to cover more ground. He checked with his neighbors and he checked with the Sheriff. He filled in the hole and left the front door open just in case Roscoe decided to return in the middle of the night. That turned out to be a mistake, as two raccoons decided to investigate the pantry. It took Carl nearly an hour to chase them out the door with a broom. The excitement kept him awake 'till dawn.

That morning he called in sick and spent the day making up posters with Roscoe's picture, address, and phone number. He tacked the posters to telephone poles all over town, and on cork boards at the Coastside Market and the Post Office.

Carl fretted for three days before receiving a call from one of the waiters at the Careless Crab. It seemed that Roscoe had been begging scraps from diners at the outdoor tables. He'd already finished off half a crab sandwich and a bread bowl saturated with clam chowder before a waiter chased him off. But all Roscoe did was to go around back. A waiter on a cigarette break heard a crunching, scraping sound from the yellow dumpster. He peeked cautiously over the rim and saw Roscoe gnawing contentedly on a steak bone. The bartender found Carl's phone number on Roscoe's collar.

Carl retrieved him, but a few days later Roscoe was back at the back door of the Careless Crab. He couldn't help it. The temptation was too great for his doggy conscience. Each time Carl filled in a hole, Roscoe dug another. And when Carl came home to an empty house, he knew just where to find him. He spent a good deal of time at the Careless Crab over the next six months. Finally, Carl resorted to an electrified wire that stretched around the perimeter of the yard, which did the trick but made Roscoe disconsolate.

Eventually, fed up with the coastal weather, Carl moved to Millbrae above San Francisco Bay. He wasn't particularly surprised when Roscoe escaped under the cyclone fence at the new house, but this time Roscoe left his collar behind, caught on the bottom of the fence. Carl checked all of the local restaurants and tacked posters to telephone poles to no avail. He never could have imagined that Roscoe would find his way unerringly up the hill, under the freeway, and over the mountains to his favorite restaurant.

Chapter Seven
Gary and Tom Meet

Roscoe was there, sitting patiently by the back door when Gary Myron with a plastic crate of live crabs, and Tom Birmingham with three bottles of wine, arrived simultaneously.

"After you," Tom said with a smile.

"If you wouldn't mind; I've got my hands full."

Tom tucked a bottle under his arm and knocked on the door.

"Your dog?" Tom asked.

"Nope."

"Looks fat and happy."

"And dirty."

Tom knocked again. This time Red Ramsey, tall and freckled, answered the door. Ramsey was the daytime bartender of the Careless Crab's Harbor Bar, which connected to the restaurant. He took in the trio and said, "Just a minute." He ducked back inside and came back with a steak bone and a half-eaten crab sandwich for the dog. "Never seen a dog that loved crab so much."

"He a stray?" Tom asked.

Ramsey told them the story of Roscoe, as far as he knew it. "I used to call his owner. Dog had a tag with the phone number. Now he's lost his collar and I don't know who to call. He's a nice dog. Been here for three weeks this time. I feel bad when it rains."

"You ought to adopt him," Tom said.

"Me? No, the missus wouldn't approve."

Tom looked to Gary. "How about you?"

"Can't. I live on a boat."

Red asked, "What've you got for me, Tom?"

Tom passed over the three samples and some spec sheets. "All three are great with seafood. I'm bringing them over in May, so if you want any, I'll need your order by April."

"Ok, good," said Red Ramsey, then to Gary said, "I'll get José."

Ramsey left the door open. They could see down the dim length of the bar. Ramsey set the bottles on the bar and went through the swinging doors to the right.

"Looks heavy," Tom said, indicating the crate.

"It is," Gary said and set it down. Roscoe came up to smell the crabs that bubbled and made skittery sounds in the blue plastic crate. Gary shooed him away.

"Do you sell wholesale off your boat?" Tom asked.

"On Thursdays, Saturdays, and Sundays."

"Got a card?"

Gary took a wallet from his back pocket and passed over a card.

"Thanks," Tom said. "I'll be seeing you."

Gary touched his forehead in a casual salute as Tom turned to go.

José Rivas came to the door wiping his hands on a white apron and glanced at the crate. "Ah good, we're runnin' low. How many you got?"

"How many you need?"

José nodded at the crate. "How much is that?"

"Fifty-nine pounds."

"That'll do for now. You want to talk to Maria?"

"No, she gets off shift in fifteen minutes anyway. Just tell her I stopped by."

Chapter Eight
Best Intentions

Highway One bends its two lanes around the point on which the town of Seal Cove is built, effectively dividing Seal Cove heights from the flats. The houses spill down the hill and jump the highway and spread out along the flat for a quarter of a mile to the coastal bluffs, where they run out of continent and sit gazing westward at the distant and unbroken horizon. Every house is different, but all are built of wood to withstand earthquakes, and many are two stories high, with decks situated on the ocean side to take advantage of the view.

Now the streets on the flats aren't technically flat. They run shallowly downhill toward the Marine Reserve parking lot and the coastal bluffs. But Emily Abbott still strained to push her 140-pound mother in a 40-pound wheelchair in the uphill direction, which she did with cheer if not enthusiasm on sunny afternoons. Mary Abbott liked a little fresh air and looked forward to getting out of the confines of the house whenever Emily had the time to push her. They were at the end of a block of rising ground and Emily was puffing when they passed a portable elliptical trainer with a FREE sign on it.

Now, those whose jobs take them away from the coast to sit behind desks on the other side of the hill have very little time to enjoy outdoor activities or the benefits of natural exercise, so they often succumb to the allure of gym memberships and exercise equipment. More often than not their good intentions go for naught. The memberships lapse and the equipment gathers dust in junk rooms and garages until their owners face reality and drag them to the curb in hopes of passing their good intentions on to others. The elliptical had originally been purchased by Chris Cordner who, after watching a late-night infomercial promising renewed youth and vigor, plunked down the first of three easy installments. He never actually took the thing out of the box, and three years later left it at the curb, where it was picked up by an enthusiastic Peggy Hazenstein, who in turn pawned it off on the unsuspecting Roberta Bergerson, who left it for the curious Randy

Rasmussen (who used it every day for a week before retiring it to the garage for two years); followed by Louise Lewandowski, in front of whose house it now stood as good as new, except for a thin layer of dust on its black surface. Mary took note as they passed and suggested her daughter could use such a contraption. "It would be good for you to get some exercise," she commented helpfully. "You spend too much time shut up in the house." Emily, whose brow glistened with drops of sweat from pushing the wheelchair, said nothing, but in her darker thoughts she imagined stepping away from the chair and watching it roll back down the street, picking up speed as her mother's expression formed a silent scream to rival Munch's. It was only a passing thought that she immediately regretted, and Mary was, as has been amply illustrated, entirely and blissfully oblivious.

The upper story of the Abbotts' house comprised a small kitchen, a living/dining area, a bedroom, and a study. Emily had the run of the place, but she spent most of her time in the study. It was a space of carefree, purposeful clutter. On the windowsill and desk and on top of the bookcases were shells and sand dollars, and inexpensive but beautiful glass paperweights, a geode, an agate obelisk and a piece of petrified wood that had belonged to her grandfather. Books and journals filled the shelves and lay stacked on the floor and the filing cabinets and on the edge of the desk. Emily reveled in the disorder. That her mother would have been appalled only made it that much sweeter.

Emily was a slow but avid reader and a closet novelist. Having no romance or mystery in her real life, she indulged a particular passion for romance and mystery novels. The heroine of one series so caught her imagination that she couldn't wait for the next installment. In anticipation, she wrote a fan fiction knockoff and posted it online for free. It was only a short story and took a different storyline than intended by the series' author, but Emily received so much encouragement from other fans that she wrote a full-length sequel. With the third, she struck out on her own, with original characters and storylines cobbled together from all the romances she'd yet read. Six years and seven self-published ebooks later, she was secretly pleased with her progress. She wrote romances under the pseudonym Margaret Pennypacker, and because she found it entertaining to masquerade as a man, she wrote mysteries under the pseudonym Robert Cole. Both pseudonymous "authors" had developed a small following. Each had a website and a blog.

After lunch, Mary Abbott took a nap while Emily retreated upstairs and took up the story of young Derek Law and his Grampa Ed where she'd left off that morning. She wasn't sure where the story would lead, and she was excited to see how it unfolded.

# # #

Grampa Ed paused for a moment to take a sip of water and look at the dark shapes in the room lit only by the night light that glinted in his grandson's open eyes. "Where was I?"

"Rumrunners."

"Yes, rumrunners. My Grampa Frank was a rumrunner. Ships full of booze would anchor just past the three-mile mark. This was called the rum line. Fishing boats would take a shipment and hide it under their catch. But the Revenuers and the Coast Guard soon caught on to what was going on, so the rumrunners had to come up with all sorts of ingenious ways to get the booze ashore."

"Grampa Bill was a Revenuer."

"Yes, your mom's great-grandfather Bill."

"Did Grampa Frank and Grampa Bill ever meet?"

"Yes, but it was long after the repeal of Prohibition, on the occasion of Bill and Eydie's fiftieth wedding anniversary — they even shared a toast!"

"I like toast with jam."

"No, no, to share a toast means to share a drink to one's good fortune."

"So they liked each other."

"By that time they were both more enlightened."

"Go on."

"I remember Grampa Frank saying for a while they used to load cases of booze onto a raft at night and cover the raft with seaweed and float it toward shore on an incoming tide, but sometimes the rafts capsized."

"Sunk."

"Yeah. Anyway, after a few years, the government extended the international boundary to twelve miles to make it harder for small boats to get out to the ships. At first Grampa Frank was the captain of a boat disguised as a fishing boat. He would load up from the mother ship, then run in to half a mile offshore and make the exchange with skiffs that rowed out from the little coves that were hidden from the Revenuers, who spent most of their time examining boats that entered the harbor. Later on, he commanded a speedboat that would rendezvous with smaller boats at night."

"Tell about the speedboat."

"It was near dawn and the Lady Gay was barely moving through the water. He had to find his way by dead reckoning because the fog was so thick he couldn't even see the light from the lighthouse. He could hear a fog horn off to his left, and the sound of distant waves in the direction of the shore. They dropped anchor and waited a long time, listening for the sound of a motor or the rhythmic stroke of oars. For a while, he worried he'd made a miscalculation and they were in the wrong place. Then through the gloom, he saw someone strike a match to light a cigarette (everyone smoked in those days), and he heard a whistled tune that was their mutual signal. He whistled back. In a few minutes, a skiff pulled up alongside and shipped its oars, and after some pleasantries, the crew began passing over cases of Canadian whiskey. Now the dawn was really breaking. The fog turned pearly grey and pink and began to recede from the shore, revealing Rick's Roadhouse on the bluff above Smuggler's Cove, so he knew his dead reckoning had been on the money. They were almost through making the exchange when the fog suddenly pulled back, leaving them in the open like sitting ducks, with a Coast Guard cutter approaching from half a mile to the north, and a Revenuer coming around Pillar Point a mile to the south. There was only one thing to do, and that...."

#

"Emily? Emily!"

Emily shut her laptop, once again caught between her two worlds. The dark bedroom, the grandfather and the grandson slowly faded away, and she was suddenly looking out on a bright blue ocean and gulls riding the air currents above the cliff's edge. She opened the French doors to clear her head.

"Emily!? Did you buy ice cream? I don't see any ice cream! Emily?"

Chapter Nine

An Accident

"Where to from here?" Daisy asked as Tom slid in behind the wheel of the Civic.

"Sam's Chowder House, Miramar Beach Inn, Pasta Moon, and the Ritz Carlton. Are you getting bored?"

"No, it just gets warm in the car and I was thinking about a gelato. But that's all right, we probably shouldn't, we don't need the calories."

"I don't mind. We have the time."

"If it's no bother, I was thinking of Mezza Luna Café. We could sit outside."

It was pleasant on the terrace, unseasonably warm for February, and thankfully calm after three months of torrential rain. They sat at a metal table under a red umbrella, and shared an affogato and a pistachio gelato, and talked about the season's unusually high tides and subsequent erosion of the coastal bluffs. "I'm worried about our front yard," Daisy said. "I think we've lost two feet this year."

In the thirty-five years since they'd moved into their bungalow, they'd lost more than fifteen feet to erosion. Originally theirs had been a corner lot fronting on Pacific Street, but that street had long since crumbled to the beach, and their front porch now sat just thirty feet from the cliff's edge.

"I wouldn't worry about it," Tom said fatalistically. "We'll be dead before it reaches the house."

"Don't be unpleasant."

"It's just a fact. You worry too much."

"You don't worry enough."

"You worry enough for the both of us."

"We could live to be ninety. What then?"

"Worrying about it won't change things. Whatever is going to happen will happen."

"We could move," Daisy suggested.

"Where would we move to?"

"I don't know, a tropical island would be nice, where the water is warm and there's no fog in the summer."

"I've never thought about moving. I like it here."

"The house is paid off. The housing market is crazy. We could probably sell our house and buy a condo in the tropics and have a lot of money left over."

Tom was nonplussed. "It never occurred to me that you'd want to move."

"It's just it's such a nice day, and I was thinking how dreary the summer will be — all that fog."

"I guess we should sit down and make up bucket lists and see if we have any matches."

"I don't believe in bucket lists."

"That's like saying you don't believe in dreams."

"Don't let's argue."

Tom ate some ice-cream. "I guess I've never thought about what we'd do in retirement."

"Anything we want," Daisy said brightly, "within reason."

Tom didn't know what to say to that. He'd been content with the life they'd built. He didn't really want it to change. Of course, change was inevitable, but up to now it had always been incremental and positive and planned. They'd built careers, raised their son, done the responsible thing day after day, and it had brought them to a state of contentment. At least Tom thought they were content. He'd never considered that Daisy might have plans that conflicted with his own.

The light turned green as they approached the intersection of Capistrano Road and Highway One. Sam's Chowder House was a right turn and two hundred yards further south.

"The next few stops will be pretty quick, but you might want to come in when we stop at Celadon. Parking there is always a bitch, and I have to hand-deliver the samples to the manager. Otherwise, they tend to disappear."

"We should stop at the market and pick something up for dinner."

Tom began to make the right turn onto Highway One and the world came apart at its seams. There was an intense thump and jerk as the airbags hit him full force like a punch to the face so powerful that it felt as though his skull had turned to jelly. He tasted blood and for a moment the whole

38

world was contained within the sound of metal on metal and shattering glass. A sharp pain shot through his ribs. He thought *We'll be waking up in the hospital,* and a fraction of a second later thought *No, we'll be dead. This is it.* Everything slowed. Daisy seemed far away. The world was a spinning maelstrom of ear-splitting sound that seemed to go on and on. Then for a moment, they were weightless in a silent cocoon, as if riding a barrel over Niagara Falls. A tremendous jolt wrenched them in the opposite direction. They came down like a twig broken over a knee. His breath left him. He struggled for air. Nothing mattered but the next breath. His ears rang. And then it stopped. A dull numb feeling stole over him like a shroud being pulled over a corpse. *This is bad* he thought. *This is very bad.* At that moment his diaphragm twitched and he sucked in a teaspoon of air, then a cupful, then great, painful lungfuls of wonderful, glorious air that he welcomed even as each breath sent an intense stabbing pain through his ribs and spine. He felt faint. Everything went white, then began fading to black.

The pain suddenly ceased. He could see how serious it was from his vantage point above the wreck. As would be reported the next day, an appliance delivery truck had run the red light. The driver, arguing with his assistant, had simply missed the change of lights. The truck had struck the driver's side door, flipping the spinning car onto its roof before slamming it a second time on the passenger side and sending the Civic flying into the light standard on the median island. It was a nasty looking accident. Tom watched the aftermath like a morbidly interested bystander. People who were stopped at the light got out of their cars, cellphones to their ears. Someone was taking pictures. *That's helpful for insurance purposes,* Tom thought, *and for the highway patrol.* Only then did it dawn on him that he was observing the proceedings from the top of a telephone pole. *Oh,* he thought, *I'm having an out-of-body-experience. I've read about those. So it's true.* He felt cloaked in serenity. There was no pain. *I do hope Daisy is okay,* he thought, though it didn't seem likely given the twisted state of their car. *So much for retirement.* He looked around in hopes that she might be hovering somewhere nearby, but she was nowhere to be seen.

A minute later he heard approaching sirens. Then he was rushing backwards, sucked into a dark tunnel. The wreck retreated and diminished. He turned his gaze upward, craning his neck to see the light that shone brightly at the other end of the tunnel. He had always hoped that consciousness might survive death. Of course, it was possible this was just his brain hallucinating as it died, but he felt lucid. Even so, it wasn't in his nature to blindly accept anything. Belief systems were always open to revision as the facts changed. But so far this experience was progressing as previously reported. If this was the afterlife, it wasn't so bad. It wasn't scary. But still, he had to wonder if consciousness could survive more than a few hours without a body. Could all of this be counterfeit? A product of oxygen deprivation, of a dying body grasping for the last morsel of life? His body lay mangled in the wreckage. His mind, however, was free and content, even joyous. Not that he wanted to die. Life was a treasure beyond reckoning. It was such a privilege, such a blessing, that it couldn't be fully comprehended. He didn't want to let it go, but he didn't think he had a choice in the matter. The end of the tunnel was approaching. The light was getting brighter. *Bring it on,* he thought, with great and hopeful anticipation.

Chapter Ten
Gary and Maria

After they'd delivered crab to the local wholesaler and taken the empty pots to the staging area, Jessie Barber finished washing the deck and tossed the hose onto the dock. Gary Myron sat on the transom, took a sip from a bottle of beer, and passed an unopened bottle to Jessie. The deckhand drained a third of it in one gulp.

"If you decide to jump ship, give me some warning."

"Sure," Jessie said. He took another gulp and belched. "I gotta get going. See you tomorrow."

"Ask around about crab line. Somebody might have an extra bale or two in storage. It would save me a trip over the hill." It was unfathomable to him how a working harbor with 369 berths had no chandlery in the vicinity, but such was the case.

He watched his deckhand stroll away down the dock. Going up the ramp to the pier Jessie sidestepped Maria Hernandez. Maria had dark brown hair pulled into a bun, and dark eyes. She wore black slacks and a black short-sleeved shirt with the Careless Crab logo emblazoned in red above her left breast. Gary helped her over the gunwale.

"José said you stopped by," Maria said.

"Just dropping off crab. Tired?"

"My feet hurt. They always hurt after work."

"Kick off your shoes, I'll give you a foot massage."

She leaned back against the starboard gunwale and kicked off her running shoes. Not that she ran, but the shoes had cushioned insoles and arch support for a day spent waitressing. Gary knelt and massaged a foot while she wriggled her toes and sighed.

"How was your day?" she asked.

"Lousy. We're going to have to go deeper, and that means more line. If we splice onto existing line, we might get away for as little as 2,000 bucks, but it's going to take time."

"I don't know why you don't just get a regular job."

"You sound like my parents."

"You work too hard for too little. It's not steady."

The thing that she didn't understand, that none of his friends or family understood, was that the money was incidental. He needed it to stay in business, but it was the business that was important. It was grueling and physically punishing work, but he loved nothing more than being out at sea. Each day was a treasure hunt with the crab as treasure. Each day was a surprise. He felt far luckier than his older brother Dave, a radiologist who spent his days under florescent lights in a closed room that smelled of antiseptic wipes, taking pictures of bones of arthritic, injured, and sometimes hysterical patients. Others he knew sat at desks, pushing paper. The money he made crabbing might be inconsistent, but the work was real and timeless. People on this coast had been gathering crab and eel and mussels and abalone from the tide pools, digging clams from the sand and fishing for salmon for six millennia. Fishermen today were more efficient in their methods, but the activity was essentially the same — the gathering of food for the community. Despite all its discomforts, he enjoyed his days on the water smelling of brine and seaweed, at the whim of tide and weather, with all of his senses alive and attuned. At the end of the day, he brought in his catch. What could be more elemental and satisfying? He couldn't make Maria understand, so he remained silent. He massaged her other foot and asked if she wanted a beer.

"It would put me to sleep," she said.

"We could go into the cabin and lie down," he suggested hopefully.

"I'm not making love on a boat."

"What's wrong with a boat?"

"You got no bathroom. It smells like fish."

He would have protested, but for the fact that it smelled even worse than fish. It smelled of bilge water and marine toilet and gasoline.

"Besides," she said, "I can't even stand up in there. It's too cramped."

"What about your house?"

"Are you crazy? With my sisters hanging around? Besides, Mama doesn't approve of you."

"What?" He was flabbergasted. "What'd I do? I've said all of three words to the woman."

"It's nothing you said. She just doesn't like that you're not Catholic."

"My grandmother on my mother's side was Catholic. Doesn't that count?"

"Be serious."

"Is it a problem for you?"

"It would be easier if you were Catholic."

"Is that you talking, or is that your mother?"

"Never mind," she said. She didn't want to argue. She slipped on her shoes. "Maybe you could get another apartment."

He hadn't always lived on the boat. It had only become a necessity when his landlord raised the rent on his studio apartment. The $361 a month live-aboard permit was a fraction of his old rent, though living on a small boat had its challenges. The cabin was tiny and the amenities rudimentary. He had a propane stove to cook on, and a battery-powered lantern. The marine toilet was available in case of an emergency. Otherwise, he used the public restroom at the foot of the pier or walked to the far end of the parking lot to take a shower.

"I have Friday off," she said.

"You want to come out on the boat?"

"I get seasick."

"Since when?"

"Since forever."

"How come I never heard about this?"

"You never asked me out on the boat before."

Gary looked at her angelic face with dismay. They'd been going out for five months now. It had never occurred to him that a girl he was attracted to might not share his love of the sea.

Chapter Eleven
Gary and Dave

When the sun sank below the horizon the sky's fire reflected in the calm waters of Pillar Point harbor. Gary was debating whether to heat a can of soup or walk over to the Careless Crab or Crustacean Station for a bite to eat. A bowl of soup at one of the restaurants was cheap and came with a bread basket and free refills of coffee or iced tea, and on nights when they weren't busy he was welcome to take a table for the evening. The restaurants were warmer, the atmosphere convivial, and the light better for reading. Having no television on the boat, Gary was an avid reader. If he ever got the urge to watch a basketball or baseball game on TV, he would install himself in the Harbor Bar and nurse a beer or two, but most evenings he spent reading. A few civic-minded citizens up the hill in El Granada had erected Little Free Libraries in their front yards, where anyone could exchange books for free. Each library was just a little bigger than a microwave oven. Gary rooted through them for thrillers and mysteries and horror stories — books by Stephen King, John Connelly, John Grisham, James Patterson, Craig Johnson, Martin Walker, and a host of other writers who knew how to grab his attention and keep him turning pages to the end.

He'd about decided to spend the evening at the Careless Crab, where he could sit in a corner by the woodstove, when he heard footsteps on deck. Kyle, his twelve-year-old nephew, appeared in the companionway. "Hey, Uncle Gary. Can I come in?" A product of his brother's second marriage to Deborah Brown, Kyle got his dark hair and brown eyes from his mother and his high cheekbones from his father. Gary pushed some clothes aside on the bunk to make room for Kyle to sit.

They heard heavier steps above. A moment later Dave Myron asked facetiously, "Permission to come aboard, sir?" Without waiting for a reply, he came down the four steps. He was taller and older than his brother and had to crouch to keep from banging his head. "My god, how do you live in here? It's claustrophobic."

"Out of necessity," Gary answered.

"What did you do with all your stuff?"

"I don't have a lot of stuff, and what I can't fit in here I keep in my truck and a storage unit."

"Took us forever to get here. There's a big accident somewhere on Highway One. It was beep-and-creep for miles. We had to come the back way by the airport."

"We saw whales," Kyle said enthusiastically.

"The Grays are migrating," Gary said. He turned to his brother. "What brings you over the hill?"

"Kyle and I have Presidents' Day off. I thought we'd stop by and take you out to dinner."

Gary knew there was more to it than that. Dave didn't often stop by unannounced, and he had never offered to pay for anything before. But why refuse a free meal? Gary grabbed his book in case his visitors had to leave early. The threesome walked up to the Careless Crab. A bitterly cold north wind had sprung up and from the recreational marina came the cacophonous clicking and clanking of loose halyards slapping aluminum masts.

The restaurant's teak doors were adorned with stained glass insets depicting a lighthouse on the left door and a setting sun on the right. The interior walls were decorated with oars, a wooden ship's wheel, an aquarium on a shelf, a couple of model boats, paintings of the harbor, and dozens of framed photos of local commercial boats. They sat down in a corner by the woodstove.

"Where's Leslie?" Gary asked. Leslie was Dave's third wife.

"She's skiing with some girlfriends."

The waiter came and took their orders. Instead of his usual soup or salad, Gary ordered a cup of clam chowder, the seafood platter with French fries, an appetizer of fried artichoke hearts, and hot chocolate. There was no sense being frugal when someone else was paying the bill. Besides, he figured Dave had come to ask a favor and the meal was his cost of entry. They engaged in small talk for a while. Then Dave started talking politics. The country, he lamented, had elected a dishonest, bombastic, narcissistic, self-serving imbecile. "He's a demagogue, and he can't even form a coherent paragraph! You can't ignore it. You should be outraged," he said.

"I try not to focus on it."

"You *ought* to focus on it. Every responsible citizen ought to focus on it. You should be concerned."

"I am concerned," Gary said, "but there's an old Chinese proverb: 'Heaven is high and the Emperor is far away.'"

"What's that supposed to mean?"

"It's out of my hands. I've done what I can. I voted."

The talk was clearly boring Kyle. "Can I go out on your boat sometime, Uncle Gary?"

"That's up to your parents."

"Anytime," Dave said.

"Do you ever see whales?" Kyle asked.

"All the time."

Dave looked at his son. "Kyle, don't you have to go to the bathroom?"

"Not yet."

"Why don't you go wash your hands then. I want to talk to your uncle alone for a minute."

Gary caught Kyle's eyes, then lifted his chin and jerked his head to the left. "Through the swinging doors into the bar, on your left."

Kyle left them for a minute. Dave looked at his plate and cleared his throat. "I was wondering if you might be able to take Kyle during Spring Break. Leslie and I are going to Hawaii. She wants to have a second honeymoon."

It seemed to Gary like they'd just finished their first honeymoon. "What about Kyle's mom?"

"Deborah was never very maternal, and Kyle doesn't like her current boyfriend."

"What about Mom and Dad?"

"They'd rather not. Since they moved to the condo there's not much room, and there's nothing for a kid to do. I thought maybe he could help you out on the boat. He'd think of it as an adventure."

"I'm barely scraping by as it is, Dave. I'd have an extra mouth to feed, and he's bound to slow me up. I don't know if I can afford it."

"Well, here's the thing: I need your help. Kyle is...." Dave sighed deeply, gathering his thoughts. "You see, he's not like other kids. Other boys. I can't seem to get him interested in anything, you know? I've tried getting him into baseball, but he can't focus on the game. Basketball, same thing. He doesn't like sports."

"Neither did I."

"Because you were puny."

"No, because I didn't want to compete with you."

"Good luck with that."

"That's what I mean. What would've been the point? You were always bigger. You were always picked first. Who would want to compete with that? Maybe Kyle feels the same way."

"Naw, he never saw me play. And it's not just sports. He's not into Boy Scouts or camping. He doesn't have any friends that I can see. I mean, he's a good kid, but he's...I don't know how to put this...he's odd."

"Come on, he's a nice kid."

"I know, of course he is."

"His grades are okay?"

"Yeah, oh yeah, he's a wiz at school."

"So what's the problem, bro? He seems normal enough to me. Does he spend too much time on the computer? Is he a video game geek?"

Dave took a sip of coffee. "No, he's not even into games that much. I mean he plays video games, but mostly he's on the computer reading about animals and plants and insects and shit like that."

"Maybe he'll be a vet."

"I don't know, I just think he needs to get out and do boy stuff. You know, like fishing. I think it would be good for him."

"Has he ever been on a boat?"

"The ferry."

"I mean on the ocean. What if he gets seasick? I can't stop working if he gets seasick."

"If he gets sick you can take him back to his mother."

"I don't know, Dave. It was one thing when I was in an apartment, but..."

"I'd be willing to pay. I wouldn't expect you to foot the bill. We'll only be gone a week. I could pay maybe a hundred and twenty-five a day. That's eight hundred and seventy-five for the week."

Gary mulled it over. He could use the money, but he wasn't sure it was worth the added headache. It might even cost him money if Kyle was uncooperative. "I'm not a babysitter," he said.

"What if I upped it to a thousand?"

"Make it twelve hundred, and he'll have to work for me. I'd pay him twenty-five a day. If you cover that expense too, then we got a deal."

When Kyle came back to the table his father said, "We have a business proposition for you."

Chapter Twelve
Tom Meets His Fate

Tom Birmingham burst out of the tunnel, like a clown from a cannon, into a place of bright light. It was, he thought, a perfect bookend to his birth.

Standing together not far away were pillars of light he knew (though he didn't know how) to be the spirits of his parents and sister and grandparents, and his best friend who had died in his twenties, and many others. Before him was another glowing spirit whose features were so indistinct that it was impossible to say if it was young or old, man or woman, and yet it might have been any and all of those things at once. Tom waited for the spirit to speak, and when it didn't he thought, "*You seem different than the others. Do I know you?*"

"You've always known me," the spirit said in Tom's own voice, not the voice the world heard, but the voice in his own head.

"Where did we meet? Where did you come from?"

"Where we all come from — consciousness, the dark matter of the universe that binds everything together and gives us Time."

"Are you God, then?"

"No more, nor less than you," the spirit answered enigmatically.

"What are you, then?"

"Your Fate."

"My guardian angel?"

"On occasion, when needed. Mostly I'm in charge of the big picture."

"I thought God was in charge of the big picture."

"I'm in charge of *your* big picture."

The spirit made a sweeping gesture, if one can be said to make a gesture with light. Images from his childhood flew through his mind like the faces of playing cards being shuffled, and yet each distinct and grounded in its own time between one image and another, so that his whole childhood sped by in a second, but was fully comprehended nonetheless. Then in succession came his early adulthood, his middle age, and beyond, like the movements of a symphony. It was almost too beautiful to contemplate. When it was over and no more than a fading nostalgia, Tom gave the slightest deferential bow and said with as much gratitude and humility as he could muster, "It's been a great ride, an amazing life. I've been so blessed."

"You've made it easy. I think we work well together. Sometimes characters and Fates are at cross purposes. Some Fates like more drama than others. Some like comedy, some tragedy, some have a penchant for epics. Some like to keep it short. You're one of my favorite characters because we're on the same wavelength — 'Moderation in all things, including moderation,' as Oscar Wilde said."

"I have very few regrets, thank you."

"You're welcome."

The few regrets he did have came unbidden to his mind, lapses of character, times he had hurt someone else's feelings, and he brightened. "Ha! I just thought of something. If you control everything, I don't have to blame myself for my shortcomings. It's all your fault."

"I wouldn't say I control *every*thing. You did some of it on your own. Isabelle Highacre was all your idea. Or, actually, she was one of my colleague's ideas, and I let him borrow you."

"So it *was* you!"

"It didn't seem to affect your story much, just gave you a bit of guilt, added a layer of complexity."

"I wasn't very mature back then," Tom lamented. "I didn't treat her well."

"No, you didn't. You were a jerk. But that's what she needed at the time."

"We're just puppets then?"

"I wouldn't say that exactly."

"Do I have any free will at all?"

"Of course, I'm not a micromanager. I don't control every little thing. You're always a work in progress. I just guide you based on your natural traits. Those traits produce natural consequences. Some of these stories you can run on autopilot — they're so logical. But every once in a while we Fates get surprised. I've been lucky. So far I've avoided those characters who change their name and reinvent themselves. That's why I stay away from Hollywood. There's a lot of reinvention going on down there, but with few exceptions, actors aren't half as interesting as the characters they play onscreen. When they do that, they're like a character playing a character playing a character."

"Fascinating. So you don't like people reinventing themselves?"

"It can be fun, but other times it's just illogical, or it messes with the whole story. When a character hijacks the story and takes off in a direction I didn't anticipate, I either have to go with it, or throw some obstacles in the way. You remember that girl in college, Melanie somebody-or-other? I could see that wasn't going to end well, so when you took her to a party I made sure you ate bad shrimp. While you were puking your guts out in the bathroom, she met Steven Furniss and the rest is history. Don't I get credit for that?"

"Yeah, sure. Thanks, I guess."

"You guess? You'd never have met Daisy if you'd still been pursuing Melanie. So there you have it. The one hand taketh away, while the other hand giveth. Anyway, you're not my only character. You know Mrs. Cavendish, at the sandwich shop in Half Moon Bay? She's one of mine. And the dentist — Colton (the secrets I could tell!). There's Gary Myron, a crabber. And Hanna at the hardware store (she used to have a secret crush on you when you were younger). I have a lot of different threads going in a lot of different directions. It's not always easy keeping track. Sometimes those threads get tangled up. Sometimes I lose track."

"You drop the ball."

Fate shrugged. "Nobody's perfect. It's not always my fault. Once in a while it's the character's fault. I get bored with them. Or they get to whining. I hate whiners. One of my colleagues just loves whiners. She gets a kick out of nebbishes. She thinks they're funny. The more bumbling they are, the more they complain, the better. I prefer characters who genuinely appreciate what they've got. I'll put up with a whiner for a while, but if they keep it up I might have to remind them how lucky they really are by throwing a bit of bad luck their way. If they still don't get it, I might turn my back for a while and let them muddle through on their own. I get annoyed just like anyone else."

The whole time they were talking Tom was vaguely aware of another connection far below them — the wrecked car in the intersection, a fire truck, an ambulance, highway patrol cars with lights flashing, EMTs and police and bystanders. "And this crash? This was your idea?"

"Well, no. Sometimes one of my colleagues steals a scene, needs something to happen to one of theirs. I was busy with another story or I might have intervened. But there are worse ways to go, and you've had a good run."

"I have. I appreciate it. I really do. It was a blast. It's just I was looking forward to retirement with Daisy. I guess that's out of the question now."

"I think so. I'm not sure yet. It's not all up to me. Daisy's not one of my charges. She's usually a recurring character in your story, but not every time."

"Usually? You mean we've done this before?"

"Oh yes. I traded for you about a millennia ago."

"Traded for me? Like baseball cards?"

"No, certainly not. Cards are just a representation of people. We manage the actual people. We build a team. We trade players."

"No kidding?"

"No kidding."

"Well I'll be damned."

"Oh, I hope not. Not on my watch."

Chapter Thirteen
The Pickup Artist

The path through the cypress grove, with its view of the ocean through twisted branches, was a pleasant walk during the day, a wild and beautiful and romantic stroll with a girl by his side. But at night Steve Wexler found the trees dark and foreboding, the wind through the branches cold and menacing. At night the trees swallowed the moonlight and evil seemed to lurk behind every trunk. Since he knew he'd be coming back after dark, he drove out to the highway, traveled the three blocks to Cypress Avenue, and followed it out past Seal Cove Inn to the brewpub. He could have walked it almost as fast.

Wexler drove a classic 1958 aqua blue Corvette with whitewall tires. It was his father's idea. If you wanted to look prosperous and current, you had to drive a new car. But buying or leasing a new car every three years was an expensive proposition. Each year you lost a hefty chunk of change to depreciation. By buying a classic you were making a statement that you were above petty posturing, above keeping up with the Joneses. You were a collector. It had only cost him $50,000, and he'd been driving it for fifteen years. What's more, every year that passed made the car more valuable. He also kept an old Ford F150 pickup in the garage for practical transport.

He walked into the brewpub at a quarter past five o'clock and surveyed the crowd.

"The usual, Gene."

Gene Price chuckled and shook his head. It was their private code. There were still empty stools at the bar and Wexler chose one, leaving an empty stool between him and a long-haired blonde who wore dangling earrings, bright red lipstick, and smokey eye shadow. She looked to be about twenty-eight or twenty-nine and was half way through a vodka tonic, looking decidedly bored. Gene Price turned over a tumbler in front of Wexler, added ice, a maraschino cherry on a toothpick, and tea with just a splash of Cointreau for flavor. Wexler had learned early on that drunk women in bars, didn't like drunk men in bars. It was another of life's inequities. It was also easier to direct the action if you had your wits about you.

He watched the blonde out of the corner of his eye as she went through her drink. As she was up-ending the tall glass he asked, "Can I buy you another?"

She gave him an appraising look with raised eyebrows. "It won't get you anywhere."

"All I'm looking for is the pleasure of your company. I haven't seen you in here before."

"You spend a lot of time here?"

"I live nearby. What's your name?"

"Linda. It means 'pretty' in Spanish."

"How appropriate," Wexler said and signaled Gene Price to make her another drink.

He waited for more information, and when none was forthcoming he asked, "Where are you from, Linda?"

"Sausalito."

"Do you like it?"

"It's expensive."

Most people loved to talk about themselves. Linda was as closed as a clam. Gene Price placed a napkin and another drink on the bar in front of her. When he'd moved down the bar, Wexler continued.

"What do you do, Linda?"

This was usually the place in the conversation where the girl would tell him she was a student, or a waitress, or a nurse, or a secretary, or a mid-level manager with some high-tech company. Then she'd ask him what he did. A decade earlier he would have quickly led the conversation around to Totally Wrecked, which more often than not impressed the subject of his attention. These days fewer women remembered the band, or worse, remembered only the commercials.

"I'm a marine biologist," she said.

When she didn't elaborate, he asked, "With...?"

"The Marine Mammal Rescue Center."

She sipped her drink and stared at her reflection in the mirror behind the bar. Wexler ate his maraschino cherry. Trying to engage in conversation with this woman was like pulling teeth. He turned to Gene Price. "I'll have another," he said, and muttered to Linda that he'd be right back. He turned the corner at the end of the bar into the short hallway toward the restroom. It was occupied. He leaned against the wall waiting his turn. A minute later he heard Linda's voice at the bar. "The old guy's paying."

When he returned she was gone.

"She stiffed you for her first drink," Gene Price said. "I didn't think you'd want to make a fuss about it."

"Put it on my tab," Wexler said. He picked up his iced tea and slid off the stool. "Could you have a crab sandwich delivered on the terrace?"

"Fries or slaw?"

"Fries." He knew he shouldn't, his weight had been creeping up this past year, but coleslaw gave him gas.

A cold breeze raked the terrace. He sat down in a chair by the fire pit, across from a couple of young ladies in jeans who shared a blanket laid across their laps. One was mousey and slightly built. Her companion was a brunette with gorgeous, sparkling, hazel eyes that picked up the light of the lowering sun. She had intriguing lips that made a bow when she was thinking and turned up at the corners when she smiled. Their empty glasses sat on the wide lip of the fire pit. Wexler smiled like a cat eyeing a couple of canaries. If he'd had a tail it would have been twitching.

"It looks like you ladies need something to drink. Can I buy you something?"

The girls looked across at him, then at each other, and started giggling. The mousey one said, "No, no, no, no. I've had enough, more than enough. Too much. We've had too much."

"Speak for yourself," the brunette chided. "Come on, one won't hurt. It'll warm you up."

"No, no, I've got to get going. I'll see you tomorrow."

The brunette twiddled her fingers at her departing friend, then pulled the blanket around her shoulders. The waiter came with the crab sandwich. Wexler offered her half.

"Maybe just a little," she said.

55

The waiter hovered on the other side of the fire pit. "Can I get you anything to drink, Mr. Wexler?" He knew Wexler always gave him a good tip when he remembered to address him as Mister.

Wexler turned to the girl. "What would you like?"

"Champagne?"

To the waiter, he said, "Two champagnes, Alessio. Tell Gene I'll have my usual, and put it on my tab." It was code for one champagne and one sparkling water with angostura bitters. He was no teetotaler, but he was in no mood to get wasted tonight. He thought he might get lucky.

She asked, "Do you own this place or something?"

"No, I'm just a regular. I live down by the Marine Reserve."

Her name was Nicole. She was practically a local, hailing from Pacifica on the north side of Devil's Slide. She was either a very good actress or she held her liquor well, for she did not appear to be in the least intoxicated. When the champagne arrived they clinked glasses sociably, and she smiled at him in that way that always made him melt with tenderness and sympathy for the opposite sex. She directed the conversation, peppering him with questions and giving him no time to ask any in return. When it came around to his being a musician, she said, "My father says I have a 'tin ear.' He used to play in a band in high school. He's an accountant. What do you play?"

"Bass and piano, a little guitar."

"Do you play any gigs around here?"

"Not anymore. The band broke up," thinking *I may not be in a band anymore, but at least I'm not an accountant!* He was saving the big reveal for later in the evening, when he'd nonchalantly gesture toward the two gold records on the wall and say, "Oh, yeah, that was my band." Even if she didn't remember the band, she would surely be impressed by the gold records, the stand-up bass, electric bass, three guitars, and the baby grand piano that he could play well enough to serenade her. She paused to sip champagne, leaving him an opening. He said in as casual a manner as he could muster, as though he didn't care one way or the other, "I'm going back to my place to watch the sunset from my deck. Why don't you come along? We'll have more champagne."

She cocked her head and thought about two seconds.

"Okay."

She was suitably impressed by the Corvette, prancing around it like a cheerleader around a quarterback. "Hop in," he said, turning on the engine. It made a throaty burble at idle.

"I've got my own car," she said. "I'll follow you."

She walked across the parking lot and got into a new BMW. Wexler felt the air leaking from his evening plans. This had happened to him many times before. They would drive out to Highway One, he'd turn left, she'd turn right, and that would be the last he'd see of her. He contemplated another lonely night in a dark humor. It was true that most of his pickups ended as one night stands, but a night of small talk, warm skin and tactile pleasures dispelled the blues for a few days. Often the phone numbers the girls gave him were bogus, so he had no way of following up on a second date, but he had from time to time had relationships that lasted a month or two, and he'd once dated the same girl on and off for almost two years before she gave up on him. He longed for the days of his youth when he was the pursued, instead of the pursuer, even if he had been the second or third choice of the groupies who flung themselves at the band.

He was wondering what to do with the rest of his night as he turned onto Highway One. He accelerated and glanced gloomily in the rearview mirror, surprised to find that she was still following him. Perhaps she would just keep going toward Pacifica when he turned, he thought, but as he signaled and turned left on California Avenue she followed suit. The promise of a convivial night lifted his spirits as he drove a block, then turned right on Ellendale, and left on Sea Cliff. His was the third house on the right. He pulled into his garage. Nicole parked behind him in the driveway. This was shaping up to be a good night.

Chapter Fourteen
A Shocking Discovery

Wexler and Nicole entered through the front door. The bedrooms were downstairs. They took the stairs up to the kitchen. There wasn't much food in the refrigerator, but there was a fine selection of white wine, champagne, vodka, gin, tonic, juices and sodas, jars of olives, pearl onions, maraschino cherries, and limes. There were also fancy cheeses, spaghetti sauce, and frozen pizza. He made up a cheese and cracker plate, opened a bottle of Mumm champagne and poured a couple of flutes. A sliding glass door let onto the deck that overlooked a rectangle of lawn that stretched sixty feet to the cliff's edge.

They sat in Adirondack chairs under a propane heater and chatted amiably as the sun sank into the Pacific. She was a poised and articulate young woman, and Wexler enjoyed listening to her voice. There were no awkward silences, the conversation just flowed. They talked of cars and travel and new inventions, and the disruption to the economy that would come with robotics, and when the stars began winking on Nicole talked of astronomy and the possibility of life on other planets. The breadth of her knowledge made him feel a little inadequate. This was the most entertaining conversation he'd had in months. Here was a sexy girl with brains and curiosity. What a find!

On the ocean, squid boats turned on their bright lights to lure the squid to the surface. Two doors down, lights came on in the Abbotts' house, and in the houses on the other side of Spanish Creek. A dog began to howl mournfully in the moonlight.

Wexler and Nicole went back inside for refills of champagne. Then they passed through the living room into the music room. The baby grand was tucked into a corner. The walls were hung with musical instruments, pictures of the band, and the two gold records. "Oh wow," she said. "I didn't know you were famous!"

He demurred. "We were never that famous," he said, falsely modest. "But it was a good band."

He put his champagne flute on the piano and began to play chords. He may have been in a rock band, but he knew enough to play a classic ballad to woo a woman. He played and sang the first few stanzas of *These Foolish Things*, while she took in the room and marveled at the shrine to his illustrious past. He was playing the instrumental coda when she barked, "No way! No fucking way! You were with Totally Wrecked?"

"That was us," he admitted, beaming. Here was a young lady who knew her music.

"I can't believe it. Really? Totally Wrecked? *Like Walking in Circles*? That Totally Wrecked?"

"Yep," he said proudly, playing a blues riff.

"Then you must know my dad. That was my dad's band."

"Huh?"

"That was my dad's band!" she repeated.

"No, I don't think..."

"Clifford Cook?"

"Cliff? Oh fuck."

"I know, right?"

"Clifford is an accountant?"

"Yeah, he always said he left the band at the wrong time, just before you hit it big. My mom used to play your stuff all the time, 'til my dad had enough of it."

Visions of a romantic evening vanished before his eyes. He was hitting on Clifford's daughter. He felt disgusting. "Wait a minute," he said, doing the math in his head. "How old are you?"

"Nineteen."

"Nineteen?! How the hell were you buying drinks at the brewpub?"

"I didn't say we were drinking alcohol. We had Shirley Temples."

No wonder she didn't look intoxicated, he thought. "Oh my god, Cliff's an accountant."

She was taking in the photos of the band. Most were of the later band with Bill Morrison, but she paused before one of the early photos. "That's him. That's my dad."

"Yeah, well tell him hello for me."

"He's gonna flip out when he hears."

"I'll bet."

"This is so cool. Can I have another champagne?"

"I think maybe we've had enough. I wouldn't want you to get into an accident."

"We've got all night."

"No, I don't think that would be a good idea. I could get in trouble for influencing a minor."

"I'm not a minor. I'm nineteen."

That was true. What would the law have to say about that? Too old to be a minor, too young to legally drink alcohol.

"We could smoke some weed," she suggested.

"No, I don't think that would..."

"We could...you know...?" The way she hung that sentence and winked lasciviously left little to interpretation.

"Ah, no. I think.... No." In his own mind he had stopped aging at twenty-three, but being in the presence of a teenager brought him back to reality. "I'm old enough to be your father."

"I know, right? Is that weird or what?"

"Yeah, definitely weird. Hey, I think maybe you should get going. Tell your dad hi for me. Tell him we should get together sometime soon."

He saw her out to her car as graciously as he could. A hoot owl asked "who, whooo?" from a nearby cypress. Wexler watched Nicole's tail lights diminish and turn the corner, and went back upstairs feeling let down, old and a little sleazy. The dog took up its mournful howl again.

Chapter Fifteen

Tom and Fate Continue Their Conversation

While Tom and his Fate talked in the bright place, the scene below changed. They were now hovering over a wailing ambulance, trailing along in its wake like water skiers behind a speed boat. Tom felt quite removed from the scene below, entirely serene, in stark contrast to the urgency suggested by the siren and the speed at which the ambulance bellowed its way through traffic.

"Wait a minute," Tom interrupted. "You say I've lived other lives? Why don't I remember them?"

"Would you like to?"

"I think so. I'm still trying to wrap my mind around it. How many lives have I lived?"

"I don't remember; I've lost track."

"Were they all as good as this one?"

"You thought they were at the time. That's what I like about you."

"What?"

"Your attitude. You're content no matter what I throw at you. You're easy to work with."

"Thanks, but I don't know if I can take credit for that. I'd probably have a rotten attitude if I was homeless and cold and living under an overpass. Or if I was sick (I'm a lousy patient)."

"Don't underestimate yourself. Things didn't always go smoothly for you in this life. What about your mother's cancer? Your father's Alzheimer's? Your best friend's death?"

"I'd rather not think about them," said Tom.

"Some people wallow in that sort of tragedy. They let tragedy define their whole lives. You let it go, like water off a duck's back."

"There's no point in fixating on bad stuff. Besides, there was nothing I could have done to prevent any of it."

"How about Pat Fitzgibbons, the bookkeeper embezzler? You didn't let that gnaw away at you."

"We couldn't have recovered anything; she'd spent it. Besides, Daisy reminded me that there's no sense in holding onto negative energy. Sometimes you just have to let it go and move on."

"See? That's what I mean. You have a good attitude. You appreciated your life. It *was* pretty sweet, wasn't it?"

"It was incredible. I couldn't have written a better scenario. But it begs the question — Why me? What did I do to deserve all this?"

"You're not complaining, are you?"

"Heavens, no! I just have to wonder what I did in those past lives to justify such good fortune this time around."

"It's all in your head, Tom. To live is to learn, and each time you retain a little more. You're not born a blank slate after all."

"So we learn from our past mistakes?"

"I wish it were that easy. Everyone is on a different path and it's not always a straight line. There are some lessons you seem incapable of learning. It's frustrating watching you make the same mistakes over and over, life after life, but then I have to remind myself, you're only human."

"What mistakes?"

"For one thing you let your libido get the better of your common sense sometimes. Too often in fact."

Tom was taken aback. "You must have me mixed up with someone else."

"Oh really? Your fascination with the female sex has derailed more than one of my story lines. Desire wrecks havoc on logic. Of course, I could make you more risk-averse, but then you wouldn't do all the interesting things you've done because you ignore the consequences."

"I never ignore the consequences. How else do you think I could stay faithful to Daisy for forty-five years? It came from being fully aware of the consequences. It was mind over matter. It sure as hell didn't come naturally!"

"And who do you think is responsible for that?"

"Don't tell me you're going to take credit for my self-control."

"Oh please, I figured this time around you needed my help. So I made you a little too willing to please when you were young (women don't trust a man who's too eager), and I made you unable to read their come-hither cues for a change."

"For a change?"

"In your past lives you haven't been known for stellar self-control."

"I have to take your word on that," Tom replied peevishly. "I don't remember a thing."

"Here, let me show you." The Spirit touched his forehead, and Tom had a glimpse of a parade of girls and women he had known and adored and disappointed. It made him sad. Then the spirit shrunk back. "Do you see now?"

"Yes. They were all so lovely."

"It's a fault in your character to think so, I'm afraid. It was messing with my storyline."

"Don't blame *me*," Tom said. "Apparently, I have no say in the matter. I'm at the whim of you and my hormones."

"Not always. Sometimes you act independently, although I have to say it gets you into trouble more often than not."

"Are you finished complaining about my shortcomings?"

"Who's complaining?" Fate asked.

"You are."

"I thought I was explaining things."

"And I thought heaven was supposed to be bliss."

"Who said this is heaven?"

"I assumed...."

"Just one of the reception rooms, I suppose."

It wasn't so much a room, Tom saw, as a brilliant white, horizonless space, rather like being inside a brightly lit cloud. The spirits of the dead remained at a distance, emanating warm, loving thoughts, and suddenly he sensed the presence of Daisy. Turning, he saw her not twenty yards away in deep conversation with a spirit of her own.

"Later," Fate said, "she's busy. What were we talking about?"

"My failings."

"You do have your faults."

"I thought I was 'easy to work with.'"

"You are, but guiding your overarching story is like herding cats. You're easier than most, but you're a work in progress. We're still working on it."

"Anything in particular?" asked Tom.

"It's a sad fact that your greatest strength is also your greatest weakness. Your insistence on seeing the best in people is one of your most endearing traits, but it makes you too trusting. You let people take advantage of you."

"I'd rather be trusting than suspicious."

"It's unrealistic."

"It's hopeful."

"Your hope is misplaced," Fate said. "Establishing dominance is as natural to human beings as breathing."

"Yes, I've noticed. Some real stinkers make out like bandits."

"But stinkers are rarely happy, you know. They're always driven, never satisfied."

"They're successful," said Tom.

"It depends on how you define success."

"They get things done."

"But at what cost? Don't tell me you'd rather be one of them?"

Tom thought about that for a long moment, thought of all those who, for better or worse, moved society forward. There were the creators (inventors, scientists, visionaries, artists — rule-breakers all). There were the destroyers (warriors, dictators, demagogues, ideologues, and religious zealots — rule-makers all). And there were the enablers (the leaders, politicians, marketers, and captains of business — opportunists all) who brought both the creative and destructive visions to bear on the masses. They were the builders and destroyers who made history, but were they happy? Was happiness even the ultimate goal?

"I think it would be gratifying to have an impact," Tom said. "I had a really good time in this life, but I didn't make much of a difference, did I?"

"Don't be stupid. No one lives a full life without having an impact. Everyone has the power to make those around them happy or miserable, satisfied or frustrated. What more do you want?"

"A story worth remembering, I suppose."

"Don't tell me you're dissatisfied."

Tom smiled. "Not at all. I've been very happy. Very happy. I just wish I could have made more of a difference, that's all."

Fate sighed and gave him a kindly smile. "You have a lot to learn. We're going to have some good times together."

Chapter Sixteen
Buddy Howls

Margaret Pennypacker and Robert Cole were Emily Abbott's alter egos. Sometimes she wrote as Margaret Pennypacker, and sometimes she wrote as Robert Cole, as the mood struck her. Over the past six years, she'd written three romances as Margaret Pennypacker, and four mystery/thrillers as Robert Cole, which she published as ebooks online. At first, the romances outsold the thrillers three to one.

To try to drum up interest, Emily maintained a blog for each pseudonym. Each blog had a few hundred followers. Writing a blog post as Margaret shortly after publishing *The Spirit of the Law,* a Robert Cole thriller, Margaret had praised the novel and hinted at an attraction to its author. Sales for both went up slightly. She stepped up the compliments, and Robert Cole answered back on his own blog, admitting a secret admiration for Margaret Pennypacker.

Soon the fans of each blog were following the developing love story between the two authors. Margaret then wrote her best romance to date, about two authors who fall in love with each other's work before falling for each other in "real" life, entitled *A Mysterious Romance* — heavy on the romance, light on the mystery — written in the first person from her protagonist's point-of-view. She followed it up with a novel by Robert Cole entitled *The Girl by the Silver Sea*, a mystery with a side of romance from protagonist Derek Law's point-of-view.

According to their respective blogs, Robert and Margaret were currently engaged and vacationing on Majorca. Every few days they ostensibly sent a postcard to their mutual friend, Emily, who posted it on one of the blogs or filed it away for the next installment of the series. It might have landed her on a psychiatrist's couch if she'd been of a different mind.

Emily had no illusion that her stories were high art. But they were entertaining and life-affirming. And the more she wrote, the better her writing became. Her ebooks had won her a smattering of fans, some as far away as Australia. Lately, she'd self-published paperback editions of her novels, available to print-on-demand, and she'd left copies in all of the Little Lending Libraries on the coastside to build up a local following.

After cleaning up from dinner, she sat in an easy chair in her study, writing Robert Cole's blog post from Majorca. She called up a satellite view of the island on Google Earth, then a street view that showed a quaint bed-and-breakfast inn. The inn's website displayed pictures of the rooms, a list of things to do in Majorca, as well as a little of the island's history. By the time she'd finished her online research, she could write a credible and authentic-sounding post. For an hour or more she took a little trip in her head. It was almost as good as being there.

She had written a couple of paragraphs when the Birmingham's dog began to howl. Buddy was a black Lab, and he seldom barked unless urging Tom Birmingham to throw a ball. She had not heard Buddy howl since he was a puppy. She went out on her deck. The bungalow below was dark, and she could just make out Buddy's form in the tiny, enclosed backyard. She called out, "Hey, Buddy! Don't worry, everything is okay. Are you hungry?" The dog cocked his head and stopped howling. He woofed questioningly. "It's okay. Your master will be home soon. Just lie down." Buddy woofed again and she could see him in the gloom, trotting in circles.

She went back to work and in a little while Buddy began howling again. Then her mother called up the stairs, "Why is that dog howling?"

Emily was tempted to say, "Gee, Mom, I don't know. Why don't you go ask him yourself?" But she knew what was expected of her. She was supposed to investigate and get the dog to stop.

To give a sense of urgency, her mother added, "I can't hear my T.V."

Emily gathered a flashlight and the key to the Birmingham's house. They had traded house keys in case of emergency, though Emily had never had occasion to use it. They had never spelled out what emergencies might require them to enter one another's homes, but the unspoken insinuation was that there might be a fire, one or both of them might be incapacitated and unable to call for help. Emily let herself in through the kitchen door.

She called out, "Is anyone home? Mr. and Mrs. Birmingham? This is Emily. Are you all right?" She turned on the lights. She would have been more worried if Tom had been on a business trip and Daisy all alone, but she'd seen them both that morning. So it stood to reason that they were unexpectedly detained. They may have had car trouble, or decided to go to a movie.

With the lights coming on, Buddy had stopped his howling and was scratching at the back door. She let him in. "Come on, Buddy, Come on boy." He came bounding in and woofed a greeting, wagging his tail with relief. She knelt and petted his head and scratched under his chin. "Are you hungry? I'll bet you're hungry." She looked into the pantry, found some kibble and poured a couple of cups into the empty dog bowl. He devoured it in less than a minute, while Emily briefly looked into each room, just to make sure there were no bodies to be found. She left a note on the kitchen counter, found Buddy's leash, turned off the lights and led Buddy to her house. When she came in the door her mother had a few words to say.

"You can't bring that dog in here! I'm allergic to pet dander."

"I'll take him upstairs."

"He'll shed all over the place. His claws will scratch the hardwood!"

"I'll have him curl up on a rug."

"Put him out on the deck. Who does he belong to? Why are you bringing him here?"

"It's Tom and Daisy's dog. He was hungry. I gave him some kibble."

"Where are they?"

"I have no idea."

"It's irresponsible to leave a dog alone like that. It's no wonder he was making such a ruckus. Don't you think they'll be worried when they come home and there's no dog?"

"I left them a note."

"The sooner you take him back the better. I'll be sneezing for a week."

Emily led Buddy upstairs. That's another thing she would do someday when her mother was gone, she'd get a dog for company. No sooner did the thought pop into her head than she reproved herself. She wasn't wishing her mother dead. Not really. She just wished she could be free to do whatever she wanted, whenever she wanted, and not to be at her mother's beck and call day and night. She loved her mother, she told herself, she really did. Mary wasn't a touchy-feely kind of mother. She was contentious by nature. But if there was little warmth or humor in her, she was still family, and you always did what needed to be done for family. Even so, in an ideal world Emily would have had a dog or a cat.

A half moon hung over the horizon when Emily heard a car door close. Buddy raised his head and perked his ears. Thinking it must be the Birminghams, she opened the French door and stepped onto the deck. The dog followed. There were flashlights at the side of the bungalow. In the dim moonlight she could see the array of lights, dark now, atop the SUV and realized it must be the sheriff. She confined Buddy to the deck and went to investigate.

Outside she heard one of the officers knocking on the front door and saw another shining a flashlight through the living room window.

"Hello?" she said. "Are you looking for the Birminghams?"

The taller sheriff stepped off the front stoop. The shorter one shined a flashlight at Emily, who squinted against the light.

The short one asked, "Do you live here?"

"Next door."

"Your name?"

"Emily Abbott."

"Do any other family members live here besides Mr. and Mrs. Birmingham?"

"No, just the Birminghams and their dog."

"We haven't seen a dog."

"He's next door with me. What's going on?"

"The Birminghams have been in an accident. Do they have family nearby?"

"Not that I know of. Their son lives in Washington."

"Would you happen to have his number?"

"I do, actually. Are they...? Was it a bad accident?"

"I'm afraid we can't discuss the details until we talk to the next of kin."

When Emily opened the front door her mother said, "What's going on? Why did you go out?" Then she saw the sheriffs standing outside. "Oh dear, what's the matter?"

"Not now, Mom, I need to find Dougie Birmingham's number." She had written it in her address book and hoped it was still current.

She copied the number to an index card and gave it to the short officer whose name tag read E. Wong. She asked if he knew which hospital the Birminghams were at.

"Seton, I believe," officer Wong said, "in Daly City."

Emily closed the door. "That's so awful," she said more to herself than to her mother. "I hope it's not too serious." She hoped it, but she didn't believe it. Mention of "next of kin" sounded ominous.

"Horrible, just horrible," Mary Abbott said. "You should call the hospital."

"They won't tell us anything. We're not family. I'll text Dougie tomorrow morning. The sheriffs should have broken the news to him by then. He can fill us in and let us know if we can do anything to help."

"What are we going to do with that dog? We can't be taking care of a dog for god knows how long."

"I'll think of something in the morning," Emily said, and went upstairs with a heavy heart. She'd seen both of the Birminghams just that afternoon. They'd been in good spirits. Mrs. Birmingham had been so excited about retirement.

Chapter Seventeen
Of Fate and Future

Time seemed suspended in the bright place where Tom and his Fate lingered. He thought he might have fallen asleep for a while, because he now saw far below them doctors and nurses busily working on his body in an operating room.

One of the nurses who was monitoring his vital signs said, "Blood pressure is dropping. We're losing him, doctor."

"Any time now," Fate said soothingly. "Patience."

Tom was feeling a bit intoxicated in the presence of his Fate. Fate seemed his best buddy. What a great guy, or gal, or...? What a great Being. *What a great life I've just lived,* Tom thought. How could he be other than eternally grateful? But no sooner had he felt this outpouring of gratitude, than he felt that something was wrong, something counterfeit about this whole situation. He turned around to see Daisy, but she was gone now. He turned back toward the spirits of the dead. They were still there, still emanating an aura of goodwill, but there was definitely a paradox here.

"Wait a minute," Tom said to Fate. "How many lives have I lived?"

"I don't know. Dozens."

He was suddenly wary. "It doesn't make sense. If we keep being reborn, why are my parents still here, my sister, my best friend, my grandparents? Why haven't they all gone on to other lives? They're still stuck here. Is this some sort of purgatory?"

"Oh, you noticed. You're very perceptive."

"You're devious."

"Not really. These are the pieces left behind to greet newcomers. Your loved ones have all gone on with the next phase of their journeys. All but your grandmother. She actually made it all the way."

"All the way to what?" asked Tom.

"The highest level."

"So she sits in the clouds singing hosannas in a choir? Is that the highest level?"

"Where do you get these ideas?"

"The Bible. You know, I thought it was supposed to be like sitting around God's throne in the clouds."

"Don't confuse religion with Nature, or Nature with religion. They're two different things," said Fate.

"All right smarty pants, you're the one with all the answers. *You* tell *me*."

"Well, I suppose what you'd call the highest level depends on your viewpoint. It's different for different people. A wise man once said something like 'the kingdom of heaven is within you.' It's not necessarily a physical place. It's more of a mental and emotional dimension."

"So what does that mean? That my grandmother is in some mental dimension?"

"Oh no. She's one of us."

"Of who?"

"I guess you'd say she's sort of a provisional Fate, or a Fate in training."

"You mean she directs things...lives?"

"Yes, like me. Like you, eventually."

"It doesn't sound like much of a life, or should I say death?"

"It has its rewards," said Fate.

"How long have you been at it?"

"I don't know, thousands of years, I suppose. No one has ever asked me that before."

"What comes after for you?"

"I don't know. Sometimes one of us disappears. We don't know where they go."

"Doesn't that scare you?"

"Why would it? It is what it is, even if I don't understand it."

Tom felt pity for his Fate. "That puts a whole new spin on things."

"It's just a part of the mystery."

"So what now? For me, I mean. Where do I go from here?"

"You get to choose another life."

"*I* get to choose?"

Fate paused a moment, considering. "With some guidance."

"Okay. So what are my choices?"

"Do you want to come back as a human being or another species?"

71

"I have a choice?"

"Of course you have a choice. If you've ever wondered how it might be to live as a dolphin, or an octopus, or a bird, now is your time to speak. But wait — before you say anything, I should mention that I don't really do other animals very well. Their stories are often short and brutal, and my heart's not in it."

"It's hard to know what to pick without knowing what I've done before. Can you show me all of my past lives?"

"It's not recommended."

"Humor me."

"Okay, brace yourself."

Tom closed his eyes and waited for the flood of images and emotions that hit him a second later like a freight train rolling over a penny. It seemed to go on forever, and when it was over it took several minutes to regain his composure. He'd seen it all and all of it was exquisite, and savage. It left him feeling elated and at the same time inexplicably melancholy.

Fate asked, "So have you decided on the species? Would you like to be a bird, or a fish, or a sloth? What's your pleasure?"

After a moment's hesitation, Tom said, "Human."

"I'm curious as to why."

"Music, literature, architecture, painting, movies, photographs. People have the gift of imagination and the impulse to share it. In a way it allows us to live more than one life at a time."

"Yes. Humans are complicated. Less content, but more interesting."

"I was a bird once."

"Before I knew you."

"I love flying, and birds inherit a lot of practical memories, but they still live only one life."

"So human it is. Male or female?"

"Male."

"Are you sure? I thought you might choose female this time."

"It comes down to whether I'd rather be bewitching or bewitched, to pursue or be pursued. I'm feeling like I have a lot of love to give, and women are so wonderful, so easy to love."

"Oh gad," Fate exclaimed, "here we go again! I'll have to throw some obstacles in your way."

"Do I get to pick the time period?"

"No, we're always working in the present. Why do you ask?"

"I was just thinking; I don't have a lot of regrets, but there are times in my life where making a different decision, even a small one, might have made a big difference to some people I knew. It might be interesting to see how things might have turned out differently, that's all."

"Well, it's not against the rules. Some of my colleagues play that game endlessly. They just change the names and the players do it all over again. But I'd rather cover new ground."

"Oh. Okay," Tom sighed.

Fate caught a note of despondency in his voice. "Aren't you excited about the future?"

"I don't know. I have mixed feelings. It's getting a bit crowded."

"Yes, we've noticed. It's a controversial subject among the Fates at the moment. More is not necessarily better, but that's a discussion for another.... Uh oh."

"What?"

"Change of plans. You're going back." Fate began to shimmer. "Don't worry. This is good. It'll give us a chance to tie up some loose ends."

"What loose ends?" asked Tom.

"You'll see. You can help me out. You might even learn something along the way. See you soon enough."

Fate was fading. The kindly spirits receded. Tom was sucked back into the tunnel like a flea into a vacuum cleaner. He closed his eyes, gasped, and felt a jolt of pain shoot through his fractured ribs.

"We've got a pulse!" the nurse cried.

"Crap," Tom thought.

Chapter Eighteen
Of Dogs and Crabs

On the day after the accident, the sky was clear, and the wind blew cold out of the northwest, kicking up whitecaps on a dark blue sea. Loose halyards made a racket in the harbor, and the red, triangular, small craft warning flag flapped stridently atop the flagpole above the Harbor Master's office. Most of the boats would remain in port. It was a day Gary would have preferred to stay in port, because windy winter days were biting cold, and the chop made holding position problematic.

Gary waited until an hour after sunrise before calling Jessie Barber. It was obvious from Jessie's voice that the call had awakened him.

"Wha', what? Who's this?" Jessie mumbled.

"It's Gary. Are you coming?"

"What? You're not seriously thinking of going out in this blow...." Barber said.

"It's not so bad. The anchovies have moved off the point and the whales have followed, so we can pull those pots off Miramar."

He didn't want to leave the crab pots another day, as crabs will turn cannibal once they've finished dining on the bait.

"Listen, Boss, I'm not going out in this shit. It can wait."

Gary felt the urge to harangue his deckhand, but didn't see the point. The man was not going to take no for an answer. He was consistently unreliable. "All right, fine, screw it. I'll go out alone. Go back to sleep."

"That's what you ought to do. There's no sense in getting blown around the ocean for a few crabs."

Gary ended the call. Then he fired up the engine and made himself a strong cup of coffee before motoring out of the harbor. He would haul up the pots, distribute his catch, and drive over the hill in the afternoon to round up more lead line so they could crab in deeper water.

Gary worked the pots off of Miramar beach, taking the brunt of the blow that came stumbling over the bluffs at Pillar Point. The first few pots came up without a problem, but as he moved toward the next buoy the engine sputtered and died. He swore, walked back to the outboard, and looked over the side. A tangle of floating yellow polypropylene line had wound itself around the propeller. He tilted the engine back to bring the prop out of the water, detached a marlinspike from the carabiner at his belt, and set to work. Fifteen minutes later he had all of the line cleared but a small length that had wound its way around the shaft and into the housing. Experience told him that reversing the engine might free the line, but it would require rotating the engine back into place so he could pull the starter cord. In the meantime the wind had pushed Miss Behavin' southeastward and closer to shore, forcing him to set the anchor. Once that was done, he worked in vain to restart the engine. Buffeted by cold wind and porpoising in the swell, he fitted the emergency auxiliary outboard to the transom and putt-putted back to harbor with his tail between his legs. It was just another day at work.

# # #

The wind whistled around the eaves of the Abbotts' house and snuck in under the French doors. Emily awoke early, put on a robe and slippers, and made a fire in the little woodstove. Then she went downstairs to turn on the electric wall heater in the living room before her mother got out of bed. Buddy followed her, hopeful of a handout. Emily gave him a piece of cheese and a slice of chicken. Then she ate a tangerine, made a cup of coffee, and went upstairs to shower and dress, while Buddy lay contented on a rug before the fire.

The dog on her floor was a constant reminder that something terrible had happened the previous day, and though she tried to work, she found herself staring out to sea, mulling over the possibilities, and wondering about the accident.

At half-past nine, Emily heard the thunk of a car door and peered out the window to see a middle-aged woman walking around to the front of the Birminghams' bungalow. Emily intercepted the woman as she returned to her car.

"Can I help you?" Emily asked.

"Oh, I don't know. Maybe. I'm looking for Mrs. Birmingham. I'm from the elementary school. She didn't show up for class this morning. I've left messages, but she hasn't returned my calls."

"I'm afraid the Birminghams were in an auto accident yesterday. I don't know much about it, but I was told they're at Seton hospital."

"Oh my god! How awful! Oh lord, I better get back and arrange for a substitute. Oh my!"

Emily texted Doug Birmingham: "Hi Dougie, sheriffs said your parents were in an accident, yesterday, but didn't give us any details. I've taken Buddy to our house. Let me know what their status is when you get a chance. Let me know if there's anything I can do. Hoping for the best, Emily."

He never responded to the text. Instead, Emily saw a rental car pull to the curb beside the bungalow shortly after 1:00 pm. She met him at the front door before he had a chance to knock. It was obvious from his somber expression that the news wasn't good, but before he could speak Buddy came bounding out, nearly knocking Emily off her feet. Doug knelt and took the dog in his arms. "Hey, Buddy, calm down now. Everything's all right. Take it easy." The dog squirmed and wriggled and licked and mewled.

"Yeah, yeah," Doug said, "nice to see you, too, Bud. Stop it. Enough! Enough!" He stood and held his hand on Buddy's head. "Stop it! Sit!"

Buddy sat, still squirming, still whining, his tail thumping the ground. Doug turned his attention to Emily. "You wanted to know what's going on." He took a deep breath before going on. "Well, Mom didn't make it. Dad's in intensive care. He'll be okay, but he has some broken ribs, a collapsed lung, concussion, bruised spleen, and a broken leg. He'll be in the hospital for another couple of weeks at least."

"Oh, Dougie," Mary said from the entry. "I'm so sorry to hear that. It's just terrible."

"It sucks," Emily added. "Is there anything we can do?"

"Not right away. I've got to see to Mom's cremation, notify people, get Dad to sign a Power of Attorney so I can deal with insurance companies and all the bureaucracy. But I do have to be back in Bellingham no later than Sunday evening. I can take care of Buddy 'till then. If you could take him after that, just until Dad gets back...." He left the sentence hanging.

"Of course, we'd be happy to," Emily said.

When Doug Birmingham left with Buddy at his heels Mary turned her glare on her daughter and hissed, "You shouldn't have volunteered to take that dog! I thought I made that perfectly plain last night."

"It's only until Mr. Birmingham comes home. Besides, it's the right thing to do."

"What am I supposed to do about my allergies?"

"I'll keep him upstairs. You won't even know he's here."

"Fat chance," Mary muttered.

# # #

Gary sat alone at his table at the Careless Crab, sipping hot chocolate and thinking about the wisdom of the bargain he'd struck with his brother. If he'd had time to think about it he might have refused. He liked his nephew well enough. Kyle was actually remarkably well-adjusted for a kid whose parents seemed to regard him as an afterthought, a pawn in their marital drama. But the cabin of Miss Behavin' was barely big enough for one person, let alone two. Gary had no doubt that the novelty of it would keep Kyle happy and occupied for a day or two. But a week? And how much did a twelve-year-old eat? What was he physically capable of? If Kyle should prove obdurate or incompetent, he could slow down the operation and cost more than he was worth. On the other hand, the money Dave was paying would help defray the cost of the crab line Miss Behavin' so sorely needed. The more he contemplated the need to go deeper, the more the problems multiplied. Where would he drop his pots? Given the competition, what were his chances of making a go of it in deep water? How long would he have to live on the boat? Could he count on Jessie not to jump ship?

After high school, Gary had spent the summer as a deckhand on Minerva, fell in love with the sea, and stayed on while most of his erstwhile classmates followed the path his parents had always assumed he would take — community college and university to prepare for a white-collar job. He was far from stupid, but academics didn't interest him. That first summer he found himself excited to get up in the morning and go to work, and by the end of the salmon season, he found he had made a decent living and even banked some money. He calculated that over the five or six years it took his former classmates to get through college, he'd put aside a nice nest egg, while they had run up substantial debts. It remained to be seen how all of that would play out in the long run, but he figured he'd now spent a decade doing a job that made him feel alive, and that was worth a great deal more than money. It wasn't always comfortable. But it was real. He wouldn't have known a better way to express it.

His parents were disappointed in his choice of profession. They never declined an opportunity to point out how well his older brother Dave was doing, and how Gary could always go back to school, get a "decent education" and a "real" job.

"But I have a real job," he would counter.

"It's not a career," his father insisted. "It's fine for a youngster like yourself, but you're not getting any younger, you'll be thirty soon. Look at the long term. It's physically demanding and dangerous, and you'll never save enough to retire. You can't expect to be doing this in twenty years. And then what? Don't expect us to bail you out. Hell, we'll probably be in a nursing home in twenty years, and you and your brother will be paying for it."

Gary didn't expect much from his parents, but he might have expected moral, if not economic, support. He understood their concerns. As with all jobs, the owners stood to make the lion's share of the profits. He acknowledged that. He had never expected to remain a deckhand forever.

But when he asked for a loan from his parents to buy a boat, they'd adamantly refused. They were willing to pay to continue his education, but they wouldn't loan him a cent to continue fishing, even with interest. He'd been obliged to take out a loan from the bank. It had taken him all he had saved and then some. It was an expensive proposition. There was the down payment on the boat, interest on the loan, vehicle registration, insurance, maintenance, gas, slip fees, live-aboard fees, crab pot license, fishing license, crab pots, buoys, and line. There was a never-ending list of expenses. He knew one misstep and he might find himself back on another boat as a deckhand, earning eight to ten percent of the profit, instead of the lion's share. His initial calculations had depended on him having a competitive edge by taking crab from shallower water. However, the crabs weren't cooperating. They liked the bottom better in deeper water. And the simple fact of the matter was that crabbing in deep water was better accomplished on a bigger boat. And bigger boats were also better equipped to fish for salmon when crab season was over. For the moment, however, he had to make do with what he had.

He swallowed his pride and called his parents. "Hey, Pop," he said.

"Hey, Gary! Your brother just called. I'm so glad you could take Kyle. Really, we don't have room for him, and besides, I don't think your mother has the energy to deal with a teenager."

"He's only twelve, Pop."

"Close enough. He wouldn't be happy here. We don't have anything to entertain him."

Gary chuckled ruefully. "You think I have? I don't even have a T.V.!"

"Well, I'm sure he'll be happier with you. You're closer to his age."

"Yeah, well, you gotta take care of family. Speaking of which, I was hoping.... I was wondering... if you could give me a loan. I'll pay one percent more than you'd get from the bank."

"I told you not to buy that boat. Did it break down already?"

"No, I just needed a little work done on the engine, and now I need more line. I don't want to put the line on the credit card; the rates are too high."

"So you want us to be your bank."

"Just for a few months. This extra expense just comes at a bad time, but I ought to be able to pay you back by the end of the season."

"You should have thought about unforeseen expenses before you spent all of your money on that boat."

"I can give you more than you'd make in a bank."

"We don't have any money in the bank. Everything we have is in the stock market. I'm not risking our nest egg on a fishing expedition. Now, if you want to go back to school, maybe we could help out with a student loan."

"Student loan? You paid for Dave's entire education."

"He had a direction. He knew where he was going. And that was before we had some setbacks. Besides, you know what I think of this fishing business. It's feast or famine. It's a gamble, a black hole, a money pit. I'm not throwing good money after bad. We've got to be frugal if we want to retire before we're dead." Then, as though to put a permanent exclamation point to his opinions, he changed the subject. "You still going with that Mexican gal?"

"Her name's Maria, Pop."

In the background, Gary could hear his mother asking who was on the line. His father mumbled something and then his mother was on the extension. "Oh, hi dear, I hear from your brother that Laura is back in town."

"I know; I saw her."

"He said she's single again. What is she doing now?"

"I don't know, Mom. I saw her across the street and turned the other way."

"I always thought you liked her."

"I did, before Dave stole her away."

"Oh, now don't you go blaming your brother. How's a girl to know you like her if you don't tell her."

"I don't blame him, believe me. He did me a big favor."

"I bet she'd like to see you again."

"No thanks. She has two kids from two different marriages. As far as I'm concerned, I dodged a bullet."

His mother sighed. "Ah, well, I guess there are other fish in the sea. I just wish you'd find someone suitable."

The clear implication was that neither of his parents thought Maria was suitable. *Who knows*, he thought, *maybe they're right*. Maria wouldn't make a suitable daughter-in-law, and, apparently, he wouldn't make a suitable son-in-law. But he still thought that in matters of the heart, third parties were not welcome at the table.

From Emily Abbott's Notebooks
Native Americans

Before the Americans, before the Spanish, Native Americans lived on this coast for six millennia, comprised of approximately fifty tribes. The coastside had a plentiful supply of food and fresh water, and a mild enough climate that little clothing was needed to protect the natives from cold. They made tule huts, and tule boats, wove tule baskets, and harvested mussels, oysters, abalone and eel from the tidal flats, dug for clams on the beaches, fished the creeks and ocean, hunted sea birds, seal, deer and raccoon. They gathered seeds and nuts, herbs and plants along the creeks and in the mountains. At the shore they gathered seaweed for food. They practiced shamanism and other nonsense common to the human species in every age, and left nothing behind but arrowheads, stone scrapers, and middens of shells and bones. It was a sort of paradise. It still is.

Chapter Nineteen
Walking the Dog

A footbridge crosses San Vicente Creek a hundred yards before the creek empties into the Pacific Ocean. On the west side of the bridge the path forks, the right fork climbing steeply seventy feet up to the bluff top, in the midst of a cypress grove. The left fork rises more gently southward along the edge of the grove. On Monday under low, scudding clouds Steve Wexler strolled up the left fork without a thought in his head. He was comfortable in the brisk weather, bundled into a warm coat with a knit cap pulled down over his ears. His breath blew steam. He serenely marveled at the gnarled trees, some living, some dead, that towered a hundred feet overhead. Pale green-gray Spanish moss hung from some of the branches, and the air was filled with the cacophony of croaking frogs that lived in the pond below Seal Cove Inn.

While no one would have accused Wexler of being a deep thinker, many holy men might have taken his instruction on how to clear the mind of chatter. His mind was like a tuning fork sounding just one pure note. He didn't stop to examine his motivations, and rarely considered consequences. He simply did what felt right in the moment. It was at once his greatest strength and his greatest weakness. It was his strength because he never worried about what could be, or what might have been. It was a weakness because his lack of self-awareness also made him less sensitive to the feelings of others. He couldn't imagine worrying about things over which he had no control, though those around him seemed to make it their life's work.

He would have freely admitted to being a hedonist. He loved physical pleasure, be it food, wine, liquor, or sex. But what he really craved was the lasting warmth and admiration of a woman. He'd spent more than half his life searching for a mate. Someone he didn't have to work to impress. Someone who loved him without regard to his past accomplishments, if you could call playing bass guitar an accomplishment (sometimes he had his doubts). The women he charmed into his life soon grew bored with his past and drifted away.

In the middle of the path ahead two women with dogs had to chat. One, Wexler observed, was a tall, auburn-haired beauty ～ジ～ jeans, hiking boots, a red, form-fitting turtleneck sweater that accentuated her stunning curves, and a cute newsboy hat. The other he recognized as his plain Jane neighbor, Emily Abbott, whom he knew well enough to say hello to, though they'd never had a proper conversation.

Now, as has been previously noted, our musician had a vigorous libido and on casual inspection categorized women into two broad groups — those he would want to sleep with, and those for whom he had no sexual interest. Lumped into the latter group were the infirm, the homely, the overweight, and jail bait. These distinctions had always been immediate and automatic. Women in the first group were instantly fascinating. Women in the second group might as well have been marble statues. He assessed the stranger with genuine interest, observing her bright green eyes and lovely smile, and calculated that she was neither too young nor too old. He slowed and stopped when he came abreast of the two women who interrupted their conversation as the dogs came forward with wagging tails to nose Wexler's crotch.

"That's not for dogs," he quipped, but received no chuckles in return. It wasn't a woman's kind of joke.

"I ought to be going," the lovely stranger said, and started back the way he'd just come.

Wexler absently petted Buddy and watched the pleasing sway of the woman's hips as she sashayed down the path. "Who is that?"

"Laurie Hunt," Emily said. "She lives on Reef Point Road. Her husband is a dentist."

"Ah, too bad," he said. He'd had three affairs with married women over the years, and had given up the practice after an irate husband threatened him with a gun. He enjoyed the thrill, but it wasn't worth the risk.

"I didn't know you had a dog," he said.

"We don't. This is Buddy, the Birminghams' dog."

"The little red house?"

"Right. You heard about their accident?" she asked, and when he admitted he hadn't she began filling him in. A moment later her phone chimed. She held it to her ear and rolled her eyes. "Can't it wait?" she asked. "But he hasn't pooped yet. Oh, well, hold it; I'll be right back." She looked perturbed and said, "That was Mom. She's got her wheelchair stuck in a doorway and she needs to get to the bathroom. Would you mind taking Buddy? I've got to rush back. He's an old dog. He doesn't need much exercise, he just needs to — you know — do his business." She handed him the leash and a green plastic bag. "For the poop," she explained.

"But I'm going to the brewpub."

"They allow dogs on the terrace."

Then she turned and jogged down the path, calling "Thanks!" over her shoulder.

Wexler looked at the dog and sighed. He'd never been able to refuse a woman. "Come on Buddy, let's take a dump."

On the way to the brewpub, he stopped to talk with two other dog walkers, both nice looking women. There was something about a dog that invited trust. A woman with a dog felt safe talking to a stranger, and a man with a dog was automatically judged to be empathetic and responsible.

On the terrace, women were drawn to Buddy as to a magnet. It turned out that pets were a conversation starter, as men and women thought nothing of striking up a conversation with a complete stranger to inquire after the dog's name, age, and breed. They all seemed to have pet stories of their own to tell him. Buddy was a friendly dog and strained against his leash to check out other dogs on the terrace, which naturally led to other friendly encounters. With a dog in tow, Wexler found he didn't need a pickup line. He even exchanged phone numbers with another dog owner that first day, which mitigated his disgust at having to pick up warm, gooey poop.

When he delivered Buddy back to Emily he said, "That was fun. Can I borrow him tomorrow?"

Mary Abbott rolled into the entry. "Why borrow him? Why not just take him until Tom gets out of the hospital? I'm allergic."

Emily turned a reproving eye on her mother. "Mom, I don't think he's volunteering for..."

"I don't mind," Wexler interjected. "How long before the old man comes home?"

"A couple of weeks, I think," Mary said. "It would be such a help. Emily is so busy, and I really am terribly allergic to dogs."

"Sure, no problem." He was eager to explore this new angle on how to attract girls. "What do I need to know?"

Chapter Twenty
It's About Time

That season the coastside seemed a vortex of misfortune. The portents of doom began with the confluence of storms and monster tides that pummeled the coast throughout the winter, biting off great chunks of the coastal bluffs like a ravenous shark. In January Seahorse Ranch experienced two catastrophes. The ranch provides escorted trail rides down to the beach and back. Horses waiting for hire were saddled and tied up in a line in the shade of a corrugated iron canopy. A rare thunderstorm sweeping in from the south brought with it a bolt of lightning that struck the canopy, electrocuting six horses. Not long after, a usually docile trail horse threw its rider and ran onto the coastal highway, where it was struck by a southbound car, killing both horse and driver. Those who believe bad things happen in threes were at a loss to explain the continuing calamities that followed. At the neighborhood badminton court on Stetson Street Warren Bateman stepped in a gopher hole and broke his ankle. A falling branch obliterated Maddie Hodge's playhouse. Christine Blaylock found an aborted gray whale fetus on Montara Beach. A mountain lion carried off the Dewars' hound. And then came the Birminghams' horrific accident. Everyone was waiting for the next shoe to drop. The whole coast seemed to cower under a cloud.

A couple of weeks after the Birminghams' accident Emily was upstairs when she heard her mother calling from the bottom of the stairs, "You've got a FedEx delivery!"

Emily went down the stairs, trying to remember if she'd ordered anything online.

"It's heavy," Mary Abbott said, eager with anticipation. "Is it my birthday present?"

"No, Mom, I haven't ordered anything yet."

"What is it then?"

Emily took it from her mother's lap. It was only about five pounds. She looked at the return address: Bergan and Olson. "I don't know, let's see." She found a knife in the kitchen and slit open the cardboard FedEx box. Inside was a brown plastic box with a lid that was taped shut. She cut the tape and lifted the lid, and immediately snapped it shut.

"What?" Mary asked.

"Never mind."

"What is it? Tell me, what have you got in there?"

"Nothing that concerns you."

"This is my house," Mary Abbott snapped. "Everything concerns me. What are you hiding?"

"Nothing, Mom."

"Then why won't you tell me? What are you hiding? What are you ashamed of?"

Emily found her mother's persistent meddling annoying and decided to tell her.

"It's Daisy."

"Daisy?"

"Birmingham."

Mary Abbott crossed her hands over her chest looking apoplectic. "Oh, lord! What are they doing sending her here? How dreadful."

"It's just ashes, Mom."

"I don't even want to think about it. Take her away! Why ever did they send her to *you*?"

"Sorry, I forgot. Doug called last week and asked if I'd hold the ashes until his dad comes home from the hospital."

"I don't want them here. It's bad luck."

"It's not bad luck," Emily chided. "Don't be so superstitious."

"I don't like it," her mother said, because she always had to have the last word.

Which, ironically, is exactly what they were — her last words. The next time Emily came downstairs she found her mother seated in her wheelchair in front of the television tuned to The Nature Channel. Emily thought she was sleeping and went about making them both chicken sandwiches for lunch. When she discovered the truth, she lost her appetite.

As anyone can imagine, Emily was stunned. It's not that she was unaware that death comes to us all sooner or later. It's just that it rarely comes when expected, and it's so final. It comes as a profoundly disruptive shock. For the departed, it's the end of the story. For the living, it signals a change of direction, and sometimes a change of heart. It's the end of a familiar era and the beginning of the unknown era to follow.

Death also puts an exclamation point on final words. It seemed entirely appropriate that Mary Abbott's last words had been, "I don't like it." It summed up her World View. And Emily's last words to her mother had been, "Don't be so superstitious." Under the circumstances, she had to admit that her mother may have had a point.

Emily knelt and put an ear to her mother's chest, just to make sure. She held her breath, listening for the faintest murmur of life, but all was silent. The ticker had stopped ticking. She gazed into her mother's flaccid face and reflected on all the mean thoughts she'd directed toward her mother over the years. She tried to feel guilty, but she couldn't. In the end, she had to confess that she'd never known her mother particularly well, had never understood her motivations or attitude. Mary Abbott had never shared her hopes and dreams, had never reminisced fondly about her childhood, nor had she ever cared about the wants of others. Theirs had been, Emily privately acknowledged, a sad excuse for a relationship.

Emily poured herself a cup of coffee and went to the toilet before calling 911. Then she sat down at the kitchen table with pen and paper and started to make a list. First, she wrote, *Fulfill Dad's last wish*, and checked it off. There was a lot to think about.

#

Steve Wexler stared out to sea in a funk, wondering how he had grown so old without noticing. That he was old enough to be the father of a woman to whom he was attracted was a horrifying thought. The CD changer cycled from Thelonious Monk's Round Midnight to Oscar Peterson's solo album. Did anyone buy CDs anymore? It seemed everyone was downloading music these days, or streaming genres, but he didn't get it. Listening only to your favorite tracks was to take the music out of context. There was a cohesiveness to a good album. The songs stood in relation to one another to form a whole impression. There was also the advantage of liner notes, so you could see who the personnel were, and when the album was recorded.

He sat at the piano trying to riff with Peterson, but soon gave up. His own piano playing would have earned him a gig in a hotel lounge, but it would never be his strong suit. He took his standup bass and played along with Peterson's piano, losing himself in the music for half an hour. The acoustic sound of the standup bass filled the room with mellow tones in a way that an electric bass could not. Each had its place, but he had to admit that he preferred playing standup, and when the album came to an end he felt even more depressed. He had become so out-of-date that he was listening to his grandfather's music and enjoying it.

Cliff's daughter was cute, damn it, and half his age, which was a little creepy now that he thought about it. He stood in front of the mirror and turned from side to side, assessing himself. He'd never been particularly good looking. His nose was too sharp, his chin a little weak, his upper lip too thin. His chestnut hair, shoulder-length and parted in the middle, was his best feature. It was a declaration that he was young and he wasn't from the corporate nine-to-five world. The unkempt style had cost him $50 at the hairdresser's. He tossed it casually over his shoulder with a practiced jerk of the head. When he bent forward it hung before his eyes giving him an air of mystery. It was healthy and shiny. It was...his eyes went wide with surprise and he leaned into the mirror for a closer look...yes, it was — a streak of grey at his left temple! He turned his head and there it was on the other side as well. He made a quick mental note to buy some hair dye. Could he really be getting old?

He stood back from the mirror and tried to see himself as others might see him walking into a bar. He'd always been lanky, but now turning sideways he noticed a slight bulge around the middle. He pulled in his stomach. *My god, I've let myself go,* he thought. *I have to get back in shape.* It wasn't too late. He lay down on the rug and began to do sit-ups. It was easy — one, two, three, four, five, six, seven, eight, nine. He felt his stomach muscles tightening. Ten, eleven, twelve, thirteen. His muscles began to ache; his exhales came with a wheeze. Sixteen, seventeen, eighteen — he felt like someone was punching him in the gut. At twenty-two he paused and took several deep breaths, determined to make it to thirty. At twenty-eight, he lay panting and closed his eyes for a minute. He resolved to work up to it slowly, one day at a time. He would begin the very next day.

Then he got up and went to the kitchen. He poured himself a tumbler of Lagavulin, gave it a dollop of water and sat down on the couch in the living room. The Scotch had a salty tang to it. He stared out at the whitecapped ocean and settled down to a quiet afternoon of reading. Romances and Erotica were his guilty pleasures. He thought they gave him some insight into the inscrutable mind of Woman.

Chapter Twenty-One
Grief Comes in Many Forms

Tom found himself sitting on a bench in a park overlooking the ocean. It was a balmy morning, rather warmer than Seal Cove, semi-tropical. The bench sat on a lawn under a tall cypress, along a path bordered by a profusion of orange nasturtiums and neon purple ice plant. He was blissfully content, perfectly in tune with everything around him, as though he were part of the trees and the plants and the waves that pounded the rocky shore. It was a timeless space. He'd been there for a very long time and felt no wish to be anywhere else. Yet something kept trying to pull him away. His sense of self, as separate from the whole, would bubble to the surface of his consciousness where he was aware of a bright white room, a beeping machine, and a wheezing and distant groaning that may or may not have been issuing from his own throat. Then, like a deflating balloon, he would settle back down again, back on his bench in the park, where a picnic basket appeared beside him. He pulled out a red checked table cloth and spread it on the lawn and lay down and closed his eyes, listening to the waves and feeling a gentle breeze caress his cheeks and stir his hair. For a long time, he simply was. He didn't think or speculate or plan. He existed there in that place in that time and he was part of it, and it was part of him, and he was content to simply be.

He fell asleep and when he woke he was gagging on an intubation tube. A nurse hurried in, put a pillow behind his back and told him to keep calm and the doctor would come soon. The doctor, when she came, had the intubation tube removed. A nurse gave him a drink of water. His throat hurt.

"Do you know where you are?"

He nodded, a little annoyed by the question. It was obvious. He was in a bed in a hospital, on white sheets, in a space separated by white curtains, surrounded by white machines, under florescent tubes. The atmosphere was cold and sterile and business-like.

"Do you know *who* you are?" asked the doctor, whose name tag read Christine Larson, M.D.

He nodded again, pretty sure he knew who he was. He was himself.

"Do you know what year this is? Try to speak, if you can."

He was about to tell her how stupid the question was when he realized he couldn't answer the question. Not only did he not know what year it was, the concept of what a year represented eluded him. He knew it was something important, and he knew he should know it, but what it was wouldn't come to him. In every other way he felt his mental faculties were functioning normally. This gap was disturbing.

He shook his head. "No idea. What is a year?"

"You've been in an accident. You've had serious injuries, including a concussion." Doctor Larson turned and gave orders to the nurse: "Let's take his blood pressure again. And get me an iron count as soon as possible. Cognitive impairment could be the result of internal bleeding, or he may have had a stroke. If the bloodwork is normal, we'll schedule an MRI."

Addressing Tom once more she asked if he remembered the accident. Tom closed his eyes and nodded again. Of course, he knew it all. Or most of it. He cleared his throat and rasped, "Car accident. A truck hit us."

"Yes. Okay now, we're going to do a few more tests, and you need to rest. We'll talk again in the morning."

Tom closed his eyes and in a moment he was back on the bench overlooking the ocean, and he forgot about the doctor and the accident. Occasionally they would wake him and a couple of times they rolled him about on a gurney.

When he awoke he was in the white room again, under florescent tubes that flooded the room with unnatural light. Doctor Larson was looking benignly down at him. "How long?" he asked. "What day is this?"

"You've been with us for four days now. You've had a couple of operations. How do you feel?"

"Empty."

"Of course. Understandable." Doctor Larson said, and looking sympathetic said, "Your wife.... I'm afraid your wife...she didn't survive the crash."

"I know. I saw her on the other side."

"Ah."

Tom sensed skepticism in the response. "What's that mean?"

"What?"

"'Ah' — what's that mean?"

"Nothing, nothing at all. Patients often report...going to another place. It's common enough."

"Do they?"

"Some do."

"I did."

"Well, don't let it worry you. It's — perfectly normal."

"I'm not worried. I know she's okay."

The doctor's expression displayed something between a smile and a grimace.

"You don't believe me," Tom said.

"It's not my place to believe or disbelieve. You believe it, and that's enough. "

"Is it?"

"My patients believe a lot things. It doesn't change my prognosis or the treatment regimen. So what I believe is immaterial. If your beliefs serve you, so much the better."

This wasn't the answer Tom was looking for. He wanted corroboration, or at least an acknowledgement that he wasn't off his rocker. "But you say it's not abnormal?"

"It happens occasionally. "

"I know, it happened to me. I was there. But you're obviously skeptical."

"Let's just say I'm undecided. I think it's just as likely to be hallucinations that accompany oxygen deprivation. But as you say, you were there, I wasn't. So who am I to disbelieve?"

"Right, but you nonetheless do — disbelieve I mean."

"It's not my place to dictate beliefs, Mr. Birmingham, and if that makes you uncomfortable, I apologize."

"No, it's good to have another opinion. But like you say, you weren't there."

"I'm sure we all hope she's in a better place."

"I don't know if it's better. It's just different. And it's there. It's really there."

"You may be right." Doctor Larson smiled indulgently and added, "Would you like to talk to a psychiatrist?"

Tom could tell from her tone that she was just trying to humor him. It was obvious she thought he was delusional, but it didn't matter. She'd know for herself soon enough. "No, thanks; I don't think it's necessary," he said. There was no point in debating what couldn't be proved without first dying.

Once when he opened his eyes he saw Douglas in a chair looking down at the phone in his hand. Tom closed his eyes, too tired for a conversation. The next time he opened his eyes Douglas was gone. And the next time he was there again. "How long have you been here?" he asked.

Douglas perked up. "Hey, Dad! How do you feel?"

"Tired. Drugged, I think. Weak."

"I don't doubt it. You know about Mom...?"

"I know. Don't worry, she's in a nice enough place. It seemed nice, anyway. There were Fates."

Douglas nodded and grunted a noncommittal "Mmm."

"How long have you been here?"

"Since Tuesday. I came as soon as I heard."

It was a reply that meant nothing to Tom, as he didn't know what day of the week it was, nor how long he'd been there. "You'll be going back soon."

"Tomorrow, I'm afraid. But I'll be back next weekend."

"There's no point, really. I'm not much company under the circumstances. I'm tired."

"I could call instead. Would you rather I called?"

"That would be better."

"I have some papers for you to sign, so I can pay bills and take care of Mom's...arrangements."

"She wanted to be cremated."

"I know."

"Me too. Oh, you should know all the important papers are in the safe under my desk. The combination is your birthday."

# # #

94

As the days passed, he thought of his adventure with Fate, of Daisy's loss, of his future, and of the future they'd dreamed of that was no longer an option. No one he'd talked to had taken him seriously when he mentioned his near-death-experience. They all seemed to regard him as delusional. As far as they were concerned, the tale he related was merely an hallucination. His doctor scheduled three sessions of grief counseling before his release. Even the psychiatrist, ostensibly a neutral party, seemed to be humoring him. He said, "Whatever floats your boat."

That Tom had hovered above his own body and had a conversation with Fate didn't frighten him half as much as the oblivion of going under anesthesia. Several days after the accident his bruised spleen had ruptured and he'd been rushed into the operating room. The next thing he knew he was waking in the ICU, loopy as a drunk, with no memory of the intervening time. Not even a dream. It was simply lost time, and it scared him, because if he was wrong about his near-death-experience, then there was no future, no afterlife, only nothingness.

Chapter Twenty-Two
The Burden of Freedom

Emily didn't know what to think of her mother's death. Because she felt so little emotion, at first she assumed she was in shock. She held her breath, an ear cocked to hear the squeak of the wheelchair, waiting for something else to occur, as if her mother might spring back to life and declare, "I'm not ready to go! You can't make me!" That so indomitable a force could be quieted by something so mundane as death seemed impossible. But as the hours passed and no demands issued from downstairs, Emily realized that she was beyond her mother's constant criticism. She wanted to feel sad. It was only right. It was expected. But in truth, her mother had been an impediment her whole life. Emily had dreamed of the day when she would finally be free from obligation, and now that it had come, she was lost. Unfettered, she didn't quite know what to do with herself. And it didn't seem to matter that her mother wasn't there; she was still in Emily's head telling her the right way to do everything.

Being a duplex there were kitchens on both floors, but Emily was so used to going downstairs to cook for her mother that she did so now without thinking. There she noticed a chef's knife she'd left on the counter and her mother's words came back to haunt her — "Wash that knife and put it in the drawer where it belongs. It's not safe leaving knives lying around like that for anyone to cut themselves on." Emily stood there for a long moment. She almost reached out to pick it up, and caught herself. She didn't have to comply with her mother's rules anymore. She could make her own rules. She left the kitchen, but returned a minute later, the knife still beckoning to her. "Come wash me," it said. "Put me away, so no one can cut themselves."

"Why ever would I cut myself?" she answered. "I know the difference between a handle and a blade."

She left it in place and went upstairs. She tried to read, but she couldn't concentrate. Instead, she sat in the wingback chair and gazed at the ocean, where tall spouts marked the stately migration of whales.

96

In the afternoon she went downstairs to make a pot of tea. The knife was still there, looking at her reproachfully. "I'm dangerous," it said. "Wash me. Hide me away." Instead, she impetuously plunged her hands into the knife drawer, pulling out all of the knives and tossing them willy-nilly in a heap on the countertop. She felt a string snap, as a marionette come to life might break away from its puppeteer. She could hear the echo of her mother's voice remonstrating, "You can never be too careful." *Oh yes you can,* Emily thought. *You can too be too careful.* She wanted to be reckless for a change.

She put the water on for tea, then reached for her mother's favorite teapot. It wasn't Emily's favorite. It wasn't even a close second. She took a deep breath and tossed the pot into the trashcan. God, it felt good! It felt so good in fact that she took it out and threw it into the can again, this time with enough force to break the spout.

Far from granting her freedom, her mother's death had saddled her with the boring but necessary work of administering the will, obtaining death certificates, meeting with her parents' lawyer, being appointed executrix, dealing with Social Security, searching for insurance policies, safety deposit keys, investment accounts, recurring payments and the like. For all her dependence on her daughter, Mary Abbott had never delegated the banking. She had a pathological distrust of anyone where money was concerned. Emily had always assumed her mother's frugality was simply the byproduct of a stingy personality. It was weeks before she understood the full extent of her mother's precarious finances. The one saving grace — the house was owned free and clear.

#

For the first couple of weeks, she was consumed by the legal paperwork and notifications that accompany any death. When she wasn't filling out forms, making appointments, calling the lawyer, or fulfilling items on her to-do list, she found it difficult to concentrate. Her focus was scattered. Even reading took too much concentration. She would read three pages and forget what she'd just read.

Then came a day when she had no appointments or obligations. She spent the morning staring out to sea, thinking of nothing, and after a while she sat down at her desk, opened her laptop, and picked up the story where she'd left it. Grampa Ed was saying:

"There was only one thing to do, and that was run, but they couldn't just gun the engine and make for the open ocean. The skiff was heavy now and low in the water with the weight of the booze. Any sudden movement by the Lady Gay could swamp the smaller boat. They had to wait for the skiff to push off and the men to haul on their oars, while the Coast Guard and the Revenuers closed the gap like a crab pitching a minnow, ready to nab both Lady Gay and the skiff. As soon as the skiff was safely away, Grampa Frank backed the Lady Gay around and gave her the gas, but slow at first, trying to lure the Coast Guard away from the skiff, and sure enough, they turned toward the Lady Gay. Of course, they couldn't follow the skiff into shore because the skiff had a shallower draft even with the weight of the booze, and the Coast Guard would have to risk running aground on the reef. So instead, they set off in pursuit of Lady Gay, and my Grampa Frank waited until the Coast Guard lays a shot across her bow before turning on the gas. Man, that Lady Gay could go! She took off like a bat outa hell headed straight into the fog bank, and that was the last the Coast Guard ever saw of her. That was the closest he ever came to getting caught."

Grampa Ed leaned over the bed to kiss his grandson's forehead. He could tell by the steady breath that Derek was already asleep.

It was only when she had finished the scene that she realized how blessedly quiet it was. Her mother had not called from downstairs. The telephone had not rung. She took a deep breath and grinned.

Chapter Twenty-Three

Homecoming

Three weeks after the Birminghams' accident Doug Birmingham paid Emily a visit. She liked him. They'd never been chummy, as he'd been three years ahead of her in school, but he'd always been pleasant, had never teased her and had a self-effacing manner that left her at her ease.

"Hey Emily, I've brought Dad back," he said, his eyes cast to a spot over her shoulder, then down at his feet, and finally meeting her own quizzical gaze. "He's on the mend, still stiff, and his leg is in a cast, but he'll be okay. Physically at least. I'm a little worried about his mental state." He looked toward his childhood home and back at his feet, and back to Emily. "I'll be around for a couple more days, but I was wondering" — he looked down at his toes — "if you could check on him once in a while, and maybe phone me once a week or so, just until...." He left the sentence hanging and shrugged.

"Of course."

"He asked me to pick up Buddy and Mom's ashes."

"Oh, well, Buddy's not here. Come on in, I'll get the ashes." She then explained that Steve Wexler was caring for Buddy. "Mom was allergic to dogs, and I've been.... Oh," she exclaimed, clapping her hand over her mouth, "I forgot, you wouldn't know. Mom passed away last week."

"Oh my god, Emily! I'm so sorry!"

This litany of woe came with the prescribed calls and responses, and while they commiserated Emily felt like a fraud. She could hardly say, "about time," or "finally," or "what a relief."

#

Buddy knew his permanent masters were a man and a woman. Most days they disappeared for a few hours at a time, and occasionally the man would go away for several days. But he'd always come back and Buddy had faith they would both come back soon, though it had been a long time now and he was getting worried. Buddy rested his chin on his paws and looked up at his new (and he assumed temporary) master. This temporary master was friendly and often took him to a terrace where there were people and dogs and food that smelled delicious. The people there sometimes shared bits of food, and the air was redolent of crab and fish and beef, clam chowder, cooking oil, garlic, French fries, and sourdough bread.

Buddy gamboled around the lawn at the cliff's edge, barking at passing gulls that silently glided by so tantalizingly close but out-of-reach. Buddy jumped and turned in circles and wagged his tail and barked some more. He seemed to be enjoying himself despite his inability to actually catch one of the birds.

Steve Wexler sat on the back deck watching Buddy and noodling around on an acoustic guitar, experimenting with different riffs. He came up with a flourish that sounded something like burdle-di-dum-diddly-oh-ti-wang, where he bent the wang into a plaintive bluesy sound. On an electric guitar that wang would have sounded like someone stepping on a cat's tail, but it sounded pretty good on an acoustic guitar. He'd always preferred acoustic instruments, though professionally he'd only played an electric bass and occasionally an electronic keyboard.

His mother had enrolled him in piano lessons when he was ten and from then on he'd found his calling. He was a decent pianist and he'd excelled at the bass, but he'd never been more than a mediocre guitarist. Nonetheless, he found that Buddy liked the sound. When he strummed the guitar and sang a few lines the dog came to lie at his feet.

Buddy was an easy dog to care for. It helped that he'd been well-trained. He never jumped up on people, never got up on the sofa or the bed, never ran away or got into fights, and he came when he was called.

Besides the social advantages afforded by a dog, with Buddy at his side Wexler was no longer afraid to walk through the woods at night, and while Buddy didn't hold up his end of the conversation, he was a great listener.

The previous day they'd gone on their afternoon walk on the trail that skirted the cypress forest, past the frog pond and Seal Cove Inn to the Seal Cove Brew Pub. It was a dead calm day. The flags hung limp on the flag pole by the pub. The place was packed. It turned out to be some sort of anniversary (of the establishment, the building, or the founding of the brewery he wasn't quite sure) and all of the drinks were half price. Humans and canines filled the terrace to capacity. Blackbirds perched at the periphery looking for an opportunity to swoop in at the drop of a crumb. The dogs were all on the lookout for scraps and sniffing each other's butts. It was a convivial atmosphere for all. It was a mostly local crowd and Wexler saw several dog walkers he knew. Buddy was fond of a chocolate Lab owned by an elderly man who had been in the import/export business. While they talked and the dogs visited, Wexler glanced about the crowd with a less predatory eye than usual. There were a few women who were obviously single, whom he looked at appreciatively without planning his approach. Buddy provided a more organic endorsement and introduction, no come-on lines required, and when the women struck up the conversation first they were much more relaxed and fun to talk to, even if it hadn't yet scored him a date. A photographer from the Half Moon Bay Review was recording the event. Wexler treated himself to a couple of flutes of champagne (the real deal, not his usual ersatz sparkler), and felt a warm glow in the camaraderie of the patrons, both human and canine. Just after sunset he struck up a conversation with the owner of a golden retriever, a woman near his own age, he'd seen before from a distance. She wasn't his type, but Buddy and her dog seemed to hit it off. The woman wore no wedding ring, and Wexler asked if she might like to stop by his place for a nightcap. She declined, but seemed to leave the door open for another time, and Wexler and Buddy walked home through the cypress forest in companionable and contented silence.

The next day, as Buddy lay on the deck listening to his temporary master humming a tune and strumming his guitar, the front doorbell rang. Wexler wouldn't have heard it if Buddy hadn't raised his head and perked up his ears. It was a Saturday and he expected to find Mormons or Jehovah's Witnesses at the door. Instead he found himself looking at a man about his age wearing jeans and a flannel shirt, not the usual suit and tie of evangelicals. He gave the man a quizzical look, but before he could ask his business Buddy bolted into the arms of the visitor with a wagging tail and a happy whine, by which Wexler understood the situation.

"I'm Doug Birmingham. Dad's home now. He's anxious to see Buddy and to thank you for taking care of him."

"Sure," Wexler said, feeling a bit let down. "It's been a pleasure. Buddy's a good dog. Let me get his leash."

"No need, he'll follow," Doug said.

Wexler accompanied them around the corner to the Birminghams' bungalow. Tom Birmingham sat in a wheelchair with a cast on his lower leg. Wexler didn't know him well. They'd only met a few times out by their respective mailboxes and on the few occasions that Birmingham had come over to ask that the music be turned down. He hadn't been petulant about it, framing the request as a question — "Would you mind turning down the volume a bit? My wife is trying to sleep." Wexler had always complied without rancor and they'd parted amicably, so there had never been hard feelings between them. But the brevity of their encounters had also guaranteed a degree of anonymity. They were, at best, acquaintances, having nothing in common but the neighborhood.

"Ah, there he is," Tom said, as pleased at seeing Buddy as Buddy was at seeing *him*. "I've missed you, Buddy." He scratched the dog behind the ears and thanked Wexler for taking care of him.

"Oh, he was a pleasure. I enjoyed it," Wexler said, and gesturing to the cast on Tom's left leg said, "You won't be able to walk him for a while."

"No, that's a fact. They tell me three to five more weeks before the cast comes off, and then there'll be physical therapy."

"I'll be happy to walk him for you until you're up and about," Wexler offered hopefully. Then realizing he had a rival he added, "I think he's a handful for Emily."

Tom turned to Buddy. "What do you say Buddy? You want Mister Wexler to walk you for a few weeks?"

The use of the honorific 'Mister' reminded Wexler how little they knew one another. The only other person who referred to him as Mister was Alessio, the waiter at the brewpub, and he only did it for the tip.

"I can walk him today and tomorrow," Doug interjected, "but I have to get back to Washington Sunday night."

Wexler gave Tom a card with his number on it. "Just call me when you want him walked. I can come anytime."

Doug saw Wexler out to the street. "Thanks for that. That'll be a big help," Doug said. "And here's my card, just in case you have to get in touch with me for any reason. Emily will be keeping an eye on Dad too."

"I'm sure he'll be fine. He seems to be in good spirits."

"I'm not so sure; I think maybe he's taking it all a little *too* well. Mom's death doesn't seem to have sunk in yet. It's like he thinks everything is okay, and it's not. I'm worried he'll wake up one day and it will hit him all at once."

"I'll keep an eye on him," Wexler promised.

Returning home, the house seemed too quiet. Not that Buddy was a noisy dog, but somehow his very presence made the house seem more alive. His leash hung on a peg by the front door. His bowls sat forlornly on the deck. The yellow tennis ball, with which they'd played fetch, lay neglected on the green lawn. Rather than feeling freed of an obligation, Wexler found himself feeling lonely.

The following Monday he picked up Buddy for a morning walk around the block and came back in the late afternoon to walk Buddy to the brewpub.

The bungalow at the end of Ellendale Street was an anomaly for an oceanfront home in Seal Cove, with its right side facing the street and its front door facing the water. Coming back from the brewpub close to sunset, dog and man found Tom sitting on the front porch staring across the water at the mist-shrouded Marin headlands twenty-five miles distant. He wore a sweater and had a throw spread across his lap. His cast rested on a footstool. Beside him on a small table were a tall green bottle and two glasses. He greeted Buddy and gestured Wexler into the second chair as he poured two glasses of wine.

"You were out a long time. Where'd you go?"

Wexler laid out his route and their stop at the brewpub. "There are a lot of dogs there. You know, dog owners are a kind of subculture I never knew about until I started walking Buddy. It's amazing. Anybody will talk to you if you have a dog."

"You know Buddy likes beer," Tom said.

"Not really."

"Oh yes. I don't give it to him often, don't drink much beer myself, but Buddy likes it."

"I'll keep that in mind." Wexler took a sip of the wine. "Hey, not bad."

"It's an Alsatian Pinot Gris. They have more character than most. Oregon and New Zealand have some good ones."

"I mostly drink champagne," said Wexler.

"Champagne taste on a champagne budget."

"What?"

"You've heard the expression — He has champagne taste on a beer budget?"

"Oh, yeah, sure."

"If you mostly drink champagne you must have a champagne budget."

"I'm not really extravagant. I mostly drink the California stuff, which is a lot cheaper."

"I'm aware. Extravagance is relative."

They sat silently for half a minute watching the sun descend toward the horizon. Wexler was thinking how the Adirondack chair seemed to pull him into it as though wrapping him in a hug. "I'm sorry about your wife," he said. "Were you married long?"

"Forty years."

"I can't imagine."

"Have you ever been married, Mister Wexler?"

"Mister Wexler is my father. My friends just call me Wexler."

"You don't look like a Wexler to me. Wexler sounds too much like a butler or chauffeur. What's your first name?

"Steve."

"I'll call you Steve then."

"Suit yourself," Wexler said and picked up the bottle. "Do you mind?"

"No, no go ahead."

Wexler poured himself a splash. He was getting comfortable. He scratched Buddy's back as the sun sank below the horizon and lit the western sky a bright orange and purple.

"You seem to hit it off with my dog," Tom said.

"Buddy's good company."

"You know you never answered my question."

"What question?"

"Have you ever been married?"

"No." He almost said the most obvious cliché, *I haven't found the right girl yet.* But wine is a kind of truth serum, and instead he said, "I haven't found a woman who'll put up with me."

"Well, Steven, we'll discuss your shortcomings another time. For now I'm going to make myself some dinner. I'll see you tomorrow then?"

"Yeah. Usual time."

"Help me get out of this chair."

So began a routine that would last a long while.

# # #

On the fourth day after Tom's homecoming, Wexler and Buddy returned from their afternoon walk after sunset and found Tom talking with Emily.

Tom patted Buddy on the head and invited Wexler to sit on the stoop. "Steve, do you know Emily?"

"We're acquainted."

"You want a glass? Grab one out of the cupboard." Tom turned his attention back to Emily. "How was your mother's funeral?"

"She didn't have one," Emily said.

In truth, she didn't know who to invite. The only member of the older generation she knew of was aunt Lilly, who upon hearing the news, asked, "What'd she die of?"

"Stroke," Emily had informed her.

"Well, I'm not surprised. I'll have to watch my blood pressure. Give my regards to your dad." By which Emily understood that Aunt Lilly and her mother had not spoken in over eight years.

Now Emily told Tom, "She wanted to be cremated, like my dad."

Her father's ashes rested in an urn on her mother's dresser.

"Daisy wanted her ashes scattered at sea."

"Mom never made arrangements. She thought she'd live forever."

"Then you haven't...?"

"No. I haven't really given it a lot of thought."

Mary Abbott's ashes were on the shelf in the coat closet.

"Maybe we could scatter them together," Tom suggested, "unless you have other plans."

"No plans. What date were you thinking of?"

"Grab the calendar in the kitchen. Let's take a look."

It turned out that April first was not only a Sunday, but Easter, as well.

"I think Daisy would appreciate the symbolism, it being Easter and all," Tom said.

Emily smiled, not because of Easter and the hope of Resurrection, but because April first was also April Fools Day. "That works for me," she said.

Chapter Twenty-Four

Of Boats and Ashes

Gary Myron looked back over his shoulder, regarding his nephew in the pre-dawn gloom as they motored out around the reef off Pillar Point. Kyle sat on the transom locker, legs bouncing nervously, face shrouded by his hoodie, hands clamped tight between his knees.

"Cold?" Gary asked. There was no response. "Kyle!" he called more loudly. The kid jumped to his feet then, and Gary motioned him forward with a jerk of his head. The kid looked half asleep, but he wasn't complaining. "The fumes back there can make you sick. Better stay up here. Are you cold?" The hood bobbed. "Go down in the cabin for a few minutes and warm up. There's a thermos of hot chocolate. And look in the locker under your bunk — I think there are some extra gloves and a knit cap."

His brother had dropped the kid off the night before and announced a change of plans. Spring Break, it turned out, was two weeks long, so he'd decided to extend their Hawaiian holiday to ten days.

"Or maybe twelve. We're not sure, but Deborah will pick up Kyle before we get back. So you won't be stuck with him for the whole two weeks."

"I thought Kyle didn't like Deborah's boyfriend."

"He doesn't, but he can't always have his way."

Gary wondered if his nephew ever had things his way.

Kyle came out of the cabin as the pink glow of dawn spread above the eastern mountains. He had on fleece gloves and a knit cap and looked revived.

"You feeling all right?" Gary asked. "Warm enough? You're not seasick, are you?"

"No, I'm good."

"Great, because as it is I need your help, if you're willing. Are you okay with that?"

"Sure, Uncle Gary."

"Good, because I'm shorthanded today." Jessie Barber had called in sick, but Gary suspected it was just an excuse. "I need you to take the wheel while I bait some pots. Try to keep it on this heading, with the buoy to your right."

Kyle brightened with the prospect of new experience and responsibility. Today they were relocating six pots into deeper water off Ross Cove and checking the pots already in place off Whaleman Harbor.

"What do you use for bait?" Kyle asked.

"Sometimes I use squid or mackerel. Today it's chicken legs. Crabs love chicken."

"So do I. I like buffalo wings and teriyaki chicken the best," Kyle said, and as an afterthought added, "And Cashew chicken. That's my favorite Chinese food."

"Crabs aren't so sophisticated. They like it raw."

Gary finished the baiting, washed his hands, and went below for a cup of coffee. When he came back topside he looked around, pleased with their course, and said, "Head out toward those boats, and tell me when the depth sounder reads 100 feet."

"Uncle Gary?"

"Yeah?"

"My dad thinks you.... I mean, he says that no one can make a decent living fishing. So...why do you do it?"

"He says that?" Gary wondered how to respond without insulting his brother. "Well, he's no expert on fishing. There are families here in Half Moon Bay who've been fishing for generations. So it can be done. We land over two million pounds of crab a year, worth more than seven million dollars, out of this harbor. I just want a piece of the action. It's not an easy way to make a living, but it's honest, and I'd rather do this than work in a hospital like your dad. To each his own, I guess."

"I don't like hospitals either."

"Of course, they're necessary, and they help people. Your dad helps people every day. But what works for one guy doesn't necessarily work for the next. I would feel claustrophobic indoors like that all day."

"Dad says I should go to college and be a doctor. He says that's where the real money is."

"He's probably right about the money, but you couldn't pay me enough to be a doctor. I'd hate it. First, you don't get out of school until you're thirty-something. You start off in debt up to your eyeballs. The hours are awful. You're always on call. You work in tiny enclosed rooms. You never see the sun. And you're around sick and injured people all day."

"I don't think I'd like it either."

"You never know. Your father seems to. Anyway, you're only twelve. You have plenty of time to decide yet. What are you interested in?"

"I like animals and flowers. I think I want to grow lavender."

"Why lavender?"

"I don't know. I just like it. It's pretty. It smells nice. They grow it around the Mediterranean and India, and there's a farm in the Sierras where they grow it, and they make soap and moisturizers and perfume and stuff like that. It's easy to grow, because insects don't like it. You don't have to use insecticides."

"That's handy."

"It's a good mosquito repellent. The dried flowers are used in flower arrangements, and it's used in cooking and baking, and you can make lavender tea. Mostly though, you make money selling essential oils."

"Sounds like you've done your homework."

"If you keep bees, you can harvest lavender honey. It's really good honey."

"I'll bet. It's nice to do something you really love to do."

"Like fishing?"

"For me, yeah. It's not for everyone. It can be rough. You're out in the weather a lot and it's dangerous. Edge out around those boats and let's cut the power some — we don't want to leave a big wake."

"Maybe I could work for you."

"That's what you'll be doing this next week."

"I mean when I grow up."

"What about the lavender?"

"I don't know. I haven't made up my mind. I like lavender, and bee keeping. But maybe I'd like fishing."

"Lavender smells better than fish."

"All I know is I want to work outdoors. I don't want to work in an office. Why'd you decide to fish?"

"It wasn't really a decision. I just sort of gravitated to it. I've always liked boats. I'm going to get another cup of coffee. You okay taking the helm alone?"

Kyle tried to look nonchalant, but couldn't suppress his enthusiasm. "Easy Peasy," he said.

"Don't get cocky. I guess I'll have to give you some lessons in navigation and the etiquette of the sea."

Off Ross Cove they pulled up pots, throwing back the undersized crabs and females, tossed the keepers into a water-filled storage locker that passed for the center well that you'd find on a proper crab boat, refreshed the bait, and relocated the pots to deeper water. They did the same off Whaleman Harbor, which was really no harbor at all, but a beach under the bluffs where Portuguese whalers had launched their longboats more than a century earlier.

By mid-morning the sun was warm on their backs, countering a cool westerly breeze. They motored northwest to a mile off Gray Whale Cove, well beyond the reefs, then turned and crept shoreward. "We want to take it in to about twenty fathoms and work out from there."

"What's a fathom?"

"Six feet."

When he cut the engine, he took a GPS reading and made a note in the log, then spread out a navigational chart.

"What are you doing?" Kyle asked.

"Making sure we know where we drop the pots. We have 100 pots to keep track of. Everybody has different colored buoys, so it's easy to tell them apart. Ours have alternating white and red and yellow stripes. So if a storm, or a strong current drags the pots, or a passing boat snags one of our lines, it's still possible we could find our pots again. I also mark them on the chart, the old-fashioned way, just in case the GPS falls overboard, or we lose the log. It's always good to have a backup." He handed a pair of binoculars to Kyle. "Now let's triangulate our position on the chart. Take a sighting off the lighthouse. See the window at the bottom of the viewfinder? How many degrees does it read?" Gary noted the compass reading in the log. "Now take a sighting off the radio tower on the top of Montara Mountain. What's it say?" He noted that reading. "Okay, now come on down to the chart table and I'll show you how to plot that triangulation. Then we'll see how close we come to the GPS numbers."

When they came back on deck after five minutes below, another boat bobbed ten yards off their stern. It was Marauder, a large, wide, yellow boat with trolling poles, stacked crab pots and a properly enclosed wheelhouse.

A tall, red-bearded man in a sock hat called out. "Hey, Myron! What are you and that bathtub doing out here?"

"Trying to catch crab, Randy, same as you."

"I thought you were working the shallows."

"I'm just following the crab."

"You know my territory," Randy yelled back, the accusatory tone loud and clear.

"I don't see any of your buoys."

"Just stay out of my way, Myron. Find your own spots! I didn't train you to steal my catch."

"Far as I know, no one owns the ocean, Randy, and the crab are up for grabs."

"A puny boat like yours, you're just making a nuisance of yourself. Stay out of my way, little man."

Gary snapped to attention, saluted sarcastically, and called out, *"Jawohl mein Käpt'an."*

Randy Rasmussen grinned, held up his middle finger and opened the throttle. The yellow boat seemed to crouch down at the back and spring forward like a cat, leaving a trail of frothy white foam and a wake that rocked Miss Behavin'.

"Who was he, Uncle Gary?"

"Guy I used to work for. Randy Rasmussen."

"He doesn't seem very friendly."

"He won't win any congeniality contests, but he knows his stuff. Most of what I learned about crabbing and fishing I learned from him. Now let's drop some pots."

"Won't that guy be mad?"

111

"Let him be mad; he doesn't own the ocean. Besides, Randy is more bark than bite."

Then they began laying out the pots 100 yards apart in line with the current, starting at a depth of 135 feet and continuing until the last pot was dropped in 200 feet of water. Having the pots in line with the current made certain that the scent of the chicken drifted from one trap to the next in line and drew crab like ants to bacon.

Kyle, it turned out, was a better conversationalist than the usual deckhands Gary worked with, men who were by turns taciturn or grumpy. As they laid the pots, Kyle kept up the patter by asking questions, sometimes about crabbing, sometimes about the family.

"What was Dad like when you were growing up?"

"I don't know, your dad was four years older than me, so we didn't play much. He was an okay big brother, but he was a hard act to follow. He was better at school, better at sports, and better looking. I admired him, but mostly I tried to find ways to be different from him, because I didn't want to compete."

On their way back to the harbor Gary let Kyle steer and opened up the throttle. The bow lifted and the boat shot forward, fairly skimming over the swells and throwing up a light spray with each jounce. Both uncle and nephew thought it more exhilarating than a carnival ride.

Somewhere off Montara State Beach the engine backfired, faltered and died. Gary swore like a sailor, then looked sheepishly at Kyle. "Sorry, don't repeat that. Your parents wouldn't be pleased."

"Dad swears worse than that."

"It's not something to be proud of. Your grandmother used to wash our mouths out with soap when we used that kind of language."

"This is the twenty-first century, Uncle Gary. Everybody swears."

"Well, you better not swear around me. Do as I say, not as I do."

"That's hypa...hyper..."

"Hypocritical."

"Yeah, that."

"It probably is, but I don't like hearing kids swear. It's a bad habit."

"Damn straight," Kyle said.

Gary was about to scold Kyle, when he got the joke. "Yeah," Gary said. "Damn straight."

It took ten minutes of pulling the starter cord to get the engine fired up again and Gary wished, for the tenth time, he had the wherewithal to buy a brand new, 200 horsepower outboard with an electric starter. A mere six grand. It really wasn't much, but it was more than he could currently afford.

# # #

While Buddy and Wexler were on their walk, Emily went to Tom to get his advice about scattering her mother's ashes. They sat on Tom's porch looking out at the tide pools, which were fully exposed now at low tide. Half a dozen people were looking into the pools, crouching down to peer at tide pool blennies, eels, starfish, urchins, anemones, mussels, limpets, and hermit crabs.

"I wonder why they bother," Tom observed. "It's a Marine Reserve. They're not allowed to take anything."

"I used to like looking in the tide pools when I was a kid," Emily admitted. "Each one is like a little aquarium, with hidden recesses and surprises."

"What kind of surprises?"

"I found a baby octopus once."

Tom nodded his head. "That would be a surprise all right." He deliberated for a minute, then said, "We could just scatter the ashes out there."

"It's possible," Emily said, "but it's illegal. I checked. Federal law mandates ashes be scattered three nautical miles offshore. On the other hand, California law only calls for 500 yards."

"What's the fine?"

"I don't know, I couldn't find out."

"Who's going to notice?"

"The Park Ranger, maybe."

"Are you feeling lucky?"

"I don't want to pay a fine, if that's what you mean," Emily said. "Besides, it would detract from the ceremony."

"Ceremony? You don't strike me as the ceremonial type."

"Shouldn't there be some…" Emily paused to find the right word. "Some solemnity to disposing of the remains?"

"You know I loved my wife."

"I know."

"I miss her terribly. But she's not here. What was left of her body sits on the shelf in my closet. Her spirit is elsewhere."

Emily had always felt that way about her father's ashes — his spirit was elsewhere. The urn didn't hold any significance. He had wanted to be cremated he said, 'just in case the spirit is in any way connected with the body, I don't want to be stuck in a box underground for eternity.' She wondered if he liked it any better stuck in an urn on his wife's dresser.

"What about Doug? What would he want?"

"You're right. I hadn't thought about that. I shouldn't be thinking of myself. Douglas wouldn't understand if I didn't ask him. But I don't think he'd want her scattered three miles offshore. He'd rather have her closer to home. So let's go by the State standards — 500 yards offshore — and screw the Feds."

"We'll have to wait until you get your cast off. You can't get on a boat like that."

"Hold on a minute," Tom said, and called his son in Bellingham. When he finished he turned to Emily and smiled. "There, that's settled then. I don't have to be on-board. Douglas will do it. I'm flying him down next weekend. Can you make arrangements for the boat?"

So it was that Emily found herself at the harbor that afternoon in search of a boat. The Harbor Master wasn't any help, except to say that most boats would take on the job if the price was right. There were over three-hundred boats berthed at Pillar Point Harbor, but most seemed deserted. The few fishermen she saw on the boats or on the docks looked rather scruffy and intimidating. It wasn't a profession that rewarded sartorial expression. Toward the end of the pier, she saw a woman hosing off the deck of the Queen of Hearts and inquired if the boat was for charter. The woman, whose demeanor suggested authority (she might have been the captain), turned off the hose and said, "We're always happy to take a private charter. What did you have in mind?" But when Emily explained where and when she wanted the ashes scattered the woman said, "We do plenty of burials at sea, but we don't go that far. We just go straight out from the harbor. It's a matter of time and fuel cost. And also, you're talking about a weekend. A lot of these boats here are charter boats, but you won't find many willing to take you on a weekend. Weekends we're fully booked with sport fishing and whale watching trips. You might try one of the crabbers."

Emily walked back down the pier, scoping out the boats that showed signs of life. There were a few men on the docks and onboard various boats, but they were a rough-looking lot, and while she knew they were probably perfectly upstanding individuals, she was reluctant to approach them. She frankly didn't have much experience with men and worried that they might ogle her, or take advantage of her obvious naiveté and overcharge for their services. They certainly didn't look like the roguish yet gallant rum runners of her fantasy world. Then on G dock, she saw a boy helping to hoist a banner that read CRAB FOR SALE. The young man with him (his older brother, perhaps?) was about Emily's age, and the presence of the boy markedly diminished her wariness. She went down the ramp to the dock, and with a facetious smile asked the boy if he was the captain.

Kyle smirked and called out, "Uncle Gary!"

Gary appeared from behind the wheelhouse to find a young woman in a dark blue cardigan, jean skirt, and dark hair pulled back in a ponytail. He sized her up in a moment — plain Jane, unmarried, tomboy, all business, no-nonsense. For her part, she saw a young man about her age, of medium build, disheveled sun-streaked hair, and a two-day growth of beard, who looked too eager by half.

"Looking for some crab?" he inquired hopefully.

"Uh, no, actually. I was wondering...." She explained where and when she wanted to scatter the ashes.

"You want to scatter all three in the same place?"

"Yeah."

"Does it have to be Sunday?"

"My neighbor's son is coming down from Washington Saturday afternoon."

"And exactly where again?"

"A little south of the lighthouse."

"That's off the Marine Reserve. That could be a problem. I don't know what the rules are, but..."

"It has to be there. That's where we live. The husband of one of the deceased will be watching from shore. Can you do it?"

Gary weighed the pros and cons. He could use the money, and he didn't want to disappoint this earnest young woman. On the other hand, Sundays he tried to be in port by 11:00 AM to sell crab off the boat to tourists. It was only about three miles in a straight line, but it would take half an hour to motor out of the harbor and out beyond the reef before he made the turn northward. How fast they could make the trip north and back depended on the weather and the sea. He figured twenty minutes or so for the solemnities. Two hours should be more than enough.

"I guess I could do it, if we can get an early start."

"How much would it cost?"

This was the tricky part. Gary hated haggling, and he didn't want to scare a good client away. "I don't usually do this. Actually, I've never done it. But just figuring time and fuel, I'd have to charge $350."

"Okay," Emily said without a blink. She and Tom had thought it would cost closer to $500.

Gary immediately wished he'd asked for more. "Can you be here as early as 8:15 Sunday morning?"

"I don't think that will be a problem."

He took her contact information.

"I should have your phone number," she said, "in case you sleep in, or get a flat tire."

"Not an issue. We live onboard."

Emily looked more closely at the boat. It didn't seem big enough to accommodate one person, let alone two. "Must be a tight fit," she observed.

"We're packed in like sardines," he smiled. "I lost my lease awhile back, and there aren't a lot of apartments on the coast. But we make do."

She glanced at the boy. It didn't seem right to bring up a boy on a boat. She wondered where he went to school. "I should still have a phone number in case we have a change of plans."

He rummaged in the cabin and came back with a dog-eared business card. "The address is old, but the phone is the same," he explained.

His smile set her at ease. "We'll see you Sunday then."

Chapter Twenty-Five
Dust to Dust

Kyle was easy company during the day. He held up his end of the conversation. He was curious and eager to learn. But Kyle was a kid, and kids crave entertainment.

As the sun sank behind Pillar Point Kyle asked, "Where's your TV?"

"In storage. There's no place for a TV on a boat."

"What do you do all night?"

"First, I'm going to take a shower. Then I'm going to get into some clean clothes and go over to the Careless Crab for some dinner."

"Then what?"

"I usually read and go to sleep. We have to get an early start tomorrow."

"I didn't bring a book. I don't read much."

"What do you do when you're at your mom's?"

"Do my homework. Play video games."

Gary sighed. "I don't have TV or video games. The only public TV is at the Harbor Bar, and they only tune to sports channels."

"I like the Warriors."

"The bar is no place for a kid. Get a change of clothes. I'll show you where the showers are. I'll think of something to do later."

A cinderblock building close to the pleasure boat docks at the far end of the parking lot housed restrooms, showers, and laundry facilities. Once the pair were clean and dressed they crossed to the Careless Crab.

After dinner, they went back to the boat. The cabin was hardly bigger than a truck bed. "Throw your dirty clothes behind the steps there." Gary scanned the few paperbacks on the shelf. "I don't have a lot of books kids would like. But since you like video games, you might like this." He handed Kyle *Ready Player One*. "Have you read it?"

"No," Kyle said, eyeing it skeptically.

"You'll like it."

They both lay down on their bunks with their books and were both asleep by ten.

Saturday the booths and tables were packed with tourists. People were waiting for tables. Gary caught the hostess's eye. "Hey, Monica, two for dinner. And can you tell Maria I'm here? I want to introduce her to my nephew."

"Maria went home early. She said to tell you she would see you tomorrow."

"Ok," Gary said, puzzled. "Did she say anything else?"

"No, just that she was looking forward to seeing you tomorrow." Monica winked. "Hot date?"

"No, I don't think so." He racked his brains but could not remember asking her on a date. She didn't really like to eat out after working all day in a restaurant. Maybe she wanted to go to a movie. What was opening that weekend? Gary couldn't remember.

# # #

Sunday morning was cold and grey. The flags above the Harbor Master's office hung limp and the water was smooth as glass, as Emily and Doug arrived on schedule. Gary passed around the lifejackets. "Coast Guard rule. Don't take it off. There's an old saying, 'one hand for the boat, one hand for yourself,' which means you should always be holding onto something. You wouldn't want to take a swim in these waters without a wetsuit. If anyone wants to use the restrooms, speak now or forever hold your bladder. The head on this boat is pretty primitive."

"The head is the toilet," Kyle explained.

The inner and outer harbors at Pillar Point are enclosed by riprap. The inner harbor shelters the docks and Johnson's Pier. The outer harbor, where boats can drop anchor or hook onto mooring buoys, provides protection from the open ocean. Ingress and egress are through a gap in the riprap at the southwest corner, where a tall, white foghorn beeps every 10 seconds.

Once they were out of the harbor a long, deep swell rocked the boat, coming first on an angle to the stern, then at an angle to the starboard bow as the boat first turned west to clear the reef and the treacherous break at Mavericks, then on the port bow as the little boat turned north. The result was a constant corkscrewing motion that had Doug Birmingham looking green at the gills. He stood staring stoically at the horizon, lips clamped shut, occasionally dabbing at his nose with Kleenex.

Emily sat on a little bench in the other corner, sheltered by the semi-open wheelhouse. Watching Gary at the wheel she was reminded of her nascent story that began with Dereck Law's rumrunning great-great-grandfather, and wondered where the story would go from there.

She caught Kyle's eye and patted the seat beside her. "I'm afraid we haven't really been introduced. I'm Emily."

"I'm Kyle."

"How do you like living on a boat?"

"It's fun. It's kind of like camping out all the time. Every day is different. Mostly we fish for crabs."

He glanced at the box at her feet and the urn in her lap. "Who died?"

"My parents. And Mr. Birmingham's mother."

"Oh."

"We're neighbors. Or we used to be. He moved to Washington state."

"I've never been to Washington."

"No, I haven't either. I haven't been much of anywhere, actually. My parents weren't travelers. What about your parents? Are they travelers?"

"They got a divorce."

"Oh, well, it happens. Sometimes people just don't get along."

"I don't like my mom's new boyfriend."

"What about your dad?"

"He's in Hawaii."

"Do you like Hawaii?"

"I don't know. I've never been."

Ah, thought Emily, *that's why he lives on the boat. He's lucky to have an uncle to take him in, but it's not much of a home for a boy. He can't have many friends, living in the harbor.*

"I'd like to travel someday," Kyle said. "I'd like to go to Provence."

"Why Provence?"

"They grow lavender there."

"You're young yet. You have plenty of time. What grade are you in?"

"Seventh grade."

"I thought you might be. Do you like school?"

"I like Social Studies. But I don't like Math. I don't get it. "

"I always liked school myself. Especially English. I like stories."

"English is okay. My English teacher is pretty nice."

They chatted like old friends until Gary cut the engine five hundred yards off the tide pools. They could see the small red bungalow and the pale yellow duplex looming behind it. Doug Birmingham called his father's cell phone. A minute later the front door of the bungalow opened and they could see the tiny figure of Tom sitting in the open doorway in his wheelchair. They waved and he waved back.

The boat wallowed into the troughs and was buoyed up to the crests of a series of big, smooth swells. At the stern Doug swayed like a drunken sailor, as Emily ceremoniously shook ash from the marble urn. Grey dust and white and black and yellow bone fragments chittered into the clear water, drawing fish that darted at the pieces as they fluttered like leaves toward the perpetual darkness of the ocean floor. Then she opened her fingers and let the empty urn drop into the water and disappear. She had said goodbye to her father long ago and it seemed an empty gesture. Next, she opened the box of her mother's ashes and poured them after her father in a single movement, like emptying a vacuum cleaner of its contents.

Looking decidedly pale, Doug stepped forward and scattered handfuls of ash over the water. The sea breeze blew some of the finer particles into his face. He sneezed, tossed a memorial wreath onto the water, then leaned far over the side and vomited violently. Gary grabbed the back of his life jacket to keep his client from falling overboard, and when the retching finally stopped, he pressed a cup of coffee into Doug's shaking hands and made him sit down for the return trip to the harbor.

# # #

121

Coming back to their berth, Kyle rushed around dropping fenders and tying off the bowline. *The kid is really getting the hang of this,* Gary thought.

Maria was waiting on the dock. Gary knew something was wrong, because she was wearing a formal suit and hat and high heels, and she looked furious. Gary wondered what he'd done wrong, and he also wondered how she'd walked down the gangplank and dock in high heels. He was grateful she held her anger in check until he'd helped Emily and Doug off the boat and saw them on their way. Then she let loose.

"Where the hell were you? You made me look like an idiot!"

"Whoa, hold on..."

"Who were those people?"

"Clients. We were scattering ashes," he explained. He thought it sounded like a good excuse for whatever he'd missed. Who could complain about being interrupted by such a solemn event?

She shook her head. "My parents and sisters went to the early service. I had to make excuses for you."

"What are you talking about?"

"You promised me!"

"What? Am I missing something?"

"Easter."

"What about Easter?"

"Today is Easter."

"Oh crap. It's April first?"

"Yes, it's April first! I reminded you two weeks ago."

"Jesus, I thought it was next week."

Then she looked toward the boat and seemed to see Kyle for the first time. "And who is this?"

"My nephew, Kyle."

"You just have time to get ready for the 11:30 service. Get into your suit. I guess my parents will forgive you if we say you were at a funeral.

"I can't go."

"What do you mean, you can't go?"

"My suit is in a storage unit, and I can't leave Kyle here alone."

Maria checked her watch. "I have to go. Be at the church at 11:30."

"I can't. I already told you."

"If you ever expect my parents to welcome you into the family, you'll be there!"

At that, she stomped off in a huff down the dock. She'd about reached the gangway to the pier when her right heel stuck between two boards and snapped off. She spun around with such a fury that Gary thought her head might explode. She screamed in frustration, yanked the shoe off her foot and threw it. It bounced twice before plopping into the water.

When she was gone Kyle asked, "Who was that?"

"Maria. My girlfriend."

"She wasn't very happy."

Gary let out a deep sigh. "No, I don't think she was."

Chapter Twenty-Six
Steve Gets Nostalgic

While Emily and Doug scattered ashes, Wexler was minding his own business having a crab and artichoke omelet in the Careless Crab, under a painting of Barbara's Fishtrap. It was a cozy spot on a dreary day, and there were no single women to impress except Bonnie, a cute waitress who was fun to flirt with but too busy to entertain a seduction. Doug had taken over the chore (if you could call it that) of walking Buddy that weekend, so Wexler was all alone. There wasn't much running through his mind (there rarely was), and he found himself eavesdropping on the desultory conversations of the other patrons, when his ears perked up at the mention of Totally Wrecked. It didn't happen often these days, but occasionally he'd be aware that someone was trying to place him — "Don't look now, but isn't that the guy who was with that band? What was the name of it? You know, *Add Fuel to the Fire* and...didn't they have a second hit? A long time ago?"

Out of the corner of his eye he saw two scruffy men in their mid-twenties sitting in a booth not ten feet away not even trying to be discreet. Among other comments, he heard "one-hit-wonder," and "has-been." Now Wexler was never quick to anger, but his indignation was definitely piqued and he stewed over these slights as he finished his breakfast and paid the bill. On his way out he paused by their table long enough to say, "Better a has-been than a never-was, losers." The acerbic comeback didn't give him much satisfaction. Their comments still stung, and his response felt small and sophomoric.

At home, he retreated to his music room and sat down at the piano, but soon gave it up, too agitated to play. Has-been! It stuck in his craw. He comforted himself by thinking that those twenty-somethings were probably just a couple of wannabe rock stars. Critics were a dime a dozen. Everyone had an opinion. But such thoughts didn't help much. No one likes criticism, especially if there is a grain of truth in it, and Wexler had to admit that the band's music was passé. Success was ephemeral. Tastes changed. Then again, how many bands ever made it? Their music had been heard by millions, and that should count for something, shouldn't it? It did, he knew it did, but that didn't change the fact that the band's brief flirtation with fame had faded with time. Today's successful acts weren't bands, he judged, but individuals with attitude and dance moves and pyrotechnics on stage. Lyrics were often spoken, not sung. The rhymes were forced, and where was the melody? The truth was he didn't really like the new music, an admission that made him feel as old as he actually was.

He put on *Wrecking Yard*, the second of Totally Wrecked's two CDs. He'd always been proud of the little-remembered track, *Stuck in the Mud of Love*, for which he'd supplied the bridge. The album was solid, and his bass gave the music its drive. Listening to it now for the thousandth time, he took a turn around the room studying each picture and reminiscing. Moving down the wall from one photo to the next he inevitably came to the mirror and stopped. The man in the mirror wasn't the youth of the photos, but there were similarities. He would never be handsome. He still had a pointy nose and his eyes were set too close together. On the other hand, his skin had cleared up, he wasn't quite so skinny, and his face was less angular. But the youth in the photos had more enthusiasm and hope.

This train of thought set him to thinking about high school and the music that had inspired the boys to form the band in the first place. He pulled out three CDs from his collection and put them on to play randomly. The songs brought back memories, and as he listened, he Googled the bands to see what had happened to them. Two of the three had slipped into obscurity. The third still toured under the same name, but with different personnel. He searched the internet, tracing the course of the original musicians, and found several had gone on to a succession of lesser-known bands, a few had gone into producing, and a couple had died. Of the musicians with whom Totally Wrecked had shared the bill, his favorite had always been Mark MacDonald, lead guitarist of Loaded. MacDonald had always been quiet and focused, though personable. They'd sometimes hung out together before performances. After Loaded had disbanded, he'd toured with a few short-lived bands before settling into the role of studio musician working in the background on more than a dozen fairly well-known albums, playing guitar and clarinet. He'd even put out an obscure eponymous album.

Wexler had MacDonald's number. In a fit of nostalgia, he called it, but before the phone was answered he hung up. They'd spent some pleasant times together, but that had been long ago. Would MacDonald even remember him? He decided to text him instead, then realized a shocking fact. From 1999 through 2002, when they'd been acquainted, neither of them had had a cell phone. He couldn't text a landline. For that matter, did anyone have a landline anymore?

He let the urge simmer for a while, then redialed the number. This time a woman answered.

"Hi," Wexler said brightly, "I know this is a long shot, but I'm looking for Mark MacDonald. This used to be his number."

There was a pause before she asked cautiously, "Who is this?"

"Steve Wexler. I used to...I...I was with Totally Wrecked?" There was a long silence. "I'm sorry, I must have the wrong number."

"Who were you with again?"

"I was the bass player for Totally Wrecked."

"Another musician?"

"Yes."

"Oh, well this is his mother. What do you want him for?"

"I was just wondering what he was up to, is all."

"He doesn't live here anymore, but I'll be happy to pass on a message."

"Tell him Steve Wexler from Totally Wrecked called."

"Your number?"

He gave it to her, though he was beginning to think this was a bad idea. Who called out of the blue after so many years?

# # #

Returning from their Sunday afternoon walk, Wexler brought Buddy around the succulent-lined path to the front porch where Tom sat beside a bottle of Alsatian Gewürztraminer and two glasses set on a grey-bitten three-legged stool.

"Pull up a chair, Steve," Tom said.

Wexler sat in one of the Adirondack chairs. Buddy flopped down at his feet, exhausted. Tom poured two glasses of wine.

"You like your whites," Wexler observed.

"I like reds, too, but I prefer whites. They're more subtle."

Wexler examined the label. Printed in tiny letters on the back label he read, 'Epicurean Imports, Seal Cove, California.' "That's you?" he asked.

"That's me. I was all set to retire after the next shipment. Now, I don't know. I'm not sure of anything anymore."

Wexler remained silent. What could you say to a man who had just lost his wife?

"How about you?" Tom asked. "Gene Price tells me you're a musician."

Having struck upon Wexler's favorite subject, Tom soon knew all there was to know about his neighbor. The more Wexler talked, the more Tom refilled his glass. Wine had a wonderful way of promoting camaraderie and loosening tongues.

During a lull, Tom said, "So I take it you enjoyed the fame."

"Of course. Who wouldn't?"

"I can think of a lot of people who would find it artificial. What's the best thing about it?"

"You know," Wexler said with satisfaction, "it's like that Dire Straits song, 'Money for nothin' and chicks for free.' I won't say the money was for nothing (it took a lot of work), but the chicks were sure free. Good times!"

"Anyone special?" Tom asked.

"Oh man, there was this one gorgeous chick in Bakersfield about wore me out. That was a good week."

"I'm not talking about getting laid. Anyone can get laid. I mean have you ever been in love? With all these girls jumping into your bed, haven't you ever found someone you wanted to spend the rest of your life with?"

"Me? No, well, yeah, twice. The problem is they didn't want to spend the rest of their lives with *me*. They left."

"And why do you think that is?"

"I don't know. I've never figured out what women want."

"Well one thing is for sure — you must not be giving it to them, or one of them would have stayed."

Wexler was taken aback. "Thanks for being so brutally honest," he replied sarcastically. "Damn."

"Just pointing out the obvious."

After a while Wexler asked, "How did you and your wife know you were right for each other?"

"You'll know if you've found the right one, when you care more about her well-being than your own."

With that bit of wisdom Wexler, pleasantly tipsy, walked back to his house, pausing at the bank of mailboxes on the corner to retrieve his mail. There were bills, clothing catalogues, brochures advertising luxury travel, supplications from various charities, banks offering low interest rates, and the Half Moon Bay Review.

Perusing the weekly paper after dinner he saw a photo of the brewpub terrace the day of its twentieth-anniversary celebration. He recognized Buddy in the photo and looked for himself. It was a mystery. He didn't seem to be there, and yet he knew he must be. He scanned the faces and profiles. Buddy's leash was held by a man with his back to the camera, a man with a little bald spot on the back of his head. Then to his horror, he recognized the shirt and knew it to be his own. In a panic, he hurried to the bathroom, found a hand mirror and stood so he could see a reflection of the back of his head in the vanity mirror. There was no doubt. A silver-dollar-sized bald spot had appeared where luxuriant locks should have sprouted. He'd always worn his shoulder-length hair parted in the middle. Now he combed it back, hoping to hide this embarrassment, but that only seemed to call attention to it. He was crestfallen. There was something pathetic about a balding man, particularly a longhaired balding man. Especially when it was himself.

Chapter Twenty-Seven
Money Troubles

Emily had so looked forward to solitude, to a quiet space where she could read or write without interruption, where she could play the music she wanted, as loud as she wanted, where she could eat when she wanted –– in short, to do whatever, whenever she wanted without fear of the inevitable criticism –– that she was disconcerted when her wishes were finally granted. The house was too quiet, the freedom too complete. As much as she hated to be at her mother's beck-and-call, her sense of duty had given life purpose. Now everything had changed. The time for dreaming was over. It was time to make of her life what she would, and that was a daunting ambition. She was paralyzed by indecision.

To make matters worse, as the bills began arriving on April second, she soon discovered that civilization doesn't come cheap. There were bills for water, gas and electric, trash disposal, home insurance, medical insurance, auto loan and auto insurance, phone, cable television, groceries, the estate lawyer, and the crematorium. Without her mother's monthly Social Security check there was no income, so it was necessary to tap the savings account. And taxes were right around the corner. At this rate the savings account would last her only three years, four if she was particularly frugal. She needed income. What could she do? Where would the money come from? Far from feeling free, she felt trapped.

She watched Wexler come and go with Buddy. She watched the cormorants and gulls. She watched the tide ebb and flood, and she watched a red-shouldered hawk patiently eyeing the ground for a gopher as he perched in the cypress tree on the other side of Spanish Creek. All the while her mind was spinning. What was she good at? How would she make a living? She wasn't stupid. She had potential. But she also acknowledged her limitations. In school, she'd struggled with Math, Chemistry, and Biology. She'd excelled at English, History, and Art. Since leaving school to care for her mother, she'd written some fan fiction and had self-published a few romances and two mysteries. Collectively they'd sold just less than two thousand copies

— a respectable number for a hobbyist, but it certainly hadn't brought in enough money to live on. To make a living she'd have to crank out a new book every six months, a task made that much more difficult by the time spent administering her mother's estate.

She had assumed that when she finally had the time the stories would just flow out of her. Instead, her ideas seemed forced and derivative. How could they be otherwise? When she drew from the well of life her bucket was dry. When it came to experience, be it romantic or adventurous in nature, she was a rank amateur. While her classmates had been playing sports, sneaking off to parties, getting high, climbing into backseats for some carnal exploration, or backpacking around Europe, Emily had been dutifully at home doing her homework and helping her mother through her father's decline and death. She'd done the responsible thing, and in doing so she'd neglected her social education. All she knew of real life derived from books and movies. It was a start. It was better than nothing. But it wasn't authentic. What did she know of love? What did she know of romance? What did she know of adventure? How could she remedy her situation?

She decided to talk to Mr. Birmingham, who was the next best thing to a father figure she knew. She grabbed a sweater and walked around to the Birminghams' front door. It took a minute for him to answer. She was surprised to see him standing on his cast, leaning on a cane.

"Doctor says it's good to get upright, put some weight on it, but it hurts. Come on in. Would you like a cup of tea or a glass of wine?"

Wine sounded tempting, but when she looked at her watch, she saw it was only four-thirty. "I really..." She started to decline, and realized the thought spoke in her mother's voice. Her mother was always critical when she brought home wine, and a second glass was likely to elicit the obligatory passive-aggressive question — *Haven't you had enough liquor for one evening?* So Emily said, "I'd really love a glass, thank you."

Tom hobbled to the refrigerator. "It's a white. I hope you don't mind. It's about all I drink these days."

Despite living next door she'd never really spent any time inside the house. Her interactions with the Birminghams had been along the lines of trick-or-treating at Halloween, or delivering cookies at Christmas. The living room was rustic, with cedar walls and ceiling and a trussed roof. There were gaps around the doors where the wind leaked through, the glass was single-paned, and there was no insulation, but a crackling fire warmed the room. The old fireplace had been constructed of round stones gathered on the beach over a century before, and on the mantel were a shell, a posed photograph of the Birminghams, and an anniversary clock under a glass dome. Above the mantel hung a still life of a violin. The TV stood on a table in one corner, and an antique upright piano in the other.

Once they were ensconced in the stuffed chairs in front of the living room windows, Emily took a long sip. She let the crisp liquid slide over her tongue and spill down the back of her throat. "That hits the spot," she sighed.

"Hard day?"

Emily nodded but checked herself. It would be petty to complain to a man who'd just lost his wife and was still recovering from injuries. "I can't complain, considering."

"Considering what?"

"Oh, nothing really. I'm young. I have my health. What more could I want?"

"I don't know; you tell me."

She sighed. "I don't know. I guess I'm just tense from all the paperwork to do with mom's passing. And bills coming due with no income."

"You must miss your mother."

"God no," Emily blurted, then clapped a hand over her mouth. "Sorry, that just slipped out. I'm being uncharitable. Am I terrible?"

Tom stifled a chuckle. "Well, it wasn't the response I expected, but at least you're honest."

"I don't mean to speak ill of the dead, but she was a hard woman to please. Dad was always an ally. Mom is (was) more an adversary."

"Daisy's mom was like that."

Emily leaned over and patted his arm. "I'm sure you miss Mrs. Birmingham though."

"Terribly. She was so happy about retiring. We were going to go on cruises. I wanted to take her to some of my favorite haunts in Europe. And now I don't know what I'm supposed to do."

"Do you have a bucket list?"

"Not really. I've done almost everything I set out to do, seen most of what I wanted to see. The few things that are left I was looking forward to sharing with Daisy, and now I don't see the point." Tom sipped his wine and looked out at the fog bank that sat half a mile offshore. "How old are you, Emily? Twenty-four?"

"Twenty-six."

"You're getting a late start. Are you going to stay here?"

"I don't know. I've never given it any thought."

"The world's a big place." He poured himself another glass and topped hers. "Have you ever been to the tropics?"

"No. We went to Nevada once and Oregon once. My parents weren't travelers. It takes money to travel."

"Money and time, the two hardest commodities to come by."

They sat with their separate thoughts for a minute. Then Emily said, "I can't get used to the quiet. I've never been on my own."

"You could always get a dog. A dog's good company. I know I'd go batty without Buddy. He's not much of a conversationalist, but he's a willing ear!"

"I'm tired of obligations. Besides, a dog costs money I don't have."

"That's just an excuse when you're sitting on a cash cow."

"What cash cow?"

"You have a duplex. Rent out the bottom floor."

"But all of Mom's things are downstairs."

"So clean out the drawers and closets, give her clothes to charity, and rent it furnished. You'll have income and company."

The thought brightened her spirits. It was obvious. She'd been so focused on the details she hadn't seen the whole picture. "I don't know why I didn't think of that."

"You would have sooner or later."

In a little while, Wexler came up the walk with Buddy and let himself in after wiping his feet on the mat. He pulled off his sock hat, revealing a mop of tangles. "Phwooo! It's colder than a witch's tit out there."

"Pull up a chair," Tom said.

"No thanks," Wexler said, positioning himself in front of the fire. "I just wanna warm up. Do you have any hot chocolate?"

"'Fraid not. Did you take Buddy to the brewpub?"

132

"No, we walked the bluffs almost as far as the radar station. Mavericks is breaking huge today. It wasn't too bad going, but coming back we had the wind in our faces." He sniffled.

Tom turned his chair around to face the fireplace. Buddy flopped down at his feet and groaned.

"You won't have to walk him much longer. I get my cast off next week."

"Don't rush it on my account. I don't mind. Really."

Ever since he'd walked in, Wexler and Emily had ignored each other. Tom sensed a chill between them. "Steve, you know Emily, of course."

Emily peeked around the side of the wingback chair.

"Sure," Wexler said and raised a hand in greeting.

Emily wiggled her fingers back at him and stayed silent.

Tom heated a mug of coffee and added some Baileys Irish Cream. Wexler tasted it and smiled.

Tom asked him if he'd ever had a dog of his own.

"My brother had a cocker spaniel, but we never walked him. We lived on two acres out by Elkus Ranch. He just chased rabbits all day."

"Is your brother older?"

"Six years. My sister is three years older. They both live in L.A.

"Are they musical, too?"

"Not professionally. My brother plays guitar. My sister plays a little piano."

"Daisy played piano," Tom said, gesturing toward the upright instrument in the corner.

Wexler crossed the room and played a few chords with his left hand. He winced. "Yow! This piano is in serious need of a tuning. I'll give you the number of my guy. He's good and not too expensive."

"Hey," Emily piped up, "do you know of anyone who would like to rent my downstairs?"

"No, can't say that I do," Wexler said. "You ought to put an ad in the paper."

"I don't want to advertise; you never know who you'll get. They could be crazy, or meth heads, or political cranks."

"Or play loud rock music at night," Tom suggested, mischievously winking at Wexler.

"I don't want to rent to just anybody. I'd rather rent to someone who comes recommended by someone I trust."

Tom chuffed and almost choked on his wine. "Then why'd you ask Steve?" He laughed.

Wexler looked wounded. "Why not? I'm trustworthy!"

Tom shrugged. "You might recommend one of your musician friends. A drummer, for instance. Wouldn't that be fun?"

Emily stood and stretched and said, "Thanks for the wine, Mr. Birmingham, and the advice."

"No problem, but Emily? — I may have been Mr. Birmingham when you were eight, but you're an adult now. Please call me Tom."

"Okay...Tom. I ought to be going."

"Come back again, now. I'm here all day."

Wexler followed her out.

When they'd gone, Tom was all alone again. The house was quiet except for the settling of coals in the fireplace, and the foghorn to which every coastsider had so habituated that no one heard it anymore. It was always there in the background, repeating at 10 second intervals night or day, in fog or sun, in wind or rain.

Chapter Twenty-Eight
A Blast from the Past

Wexler was a competent cook. He'd developed a repertoire of a dozen or more recipes that could impress a date. He was just sitting down to a solitary dinner of risotto, shrimp in garlic-lemon-butter and a mushroom béchamel with grated zucchini, when his phone vibrated. He didn't recognize the caller ID but it was a Bay Area number so he picked it up with a desultory, "Yeah?"

"Hey Wex, long time no see, man." Wexler recognized the caller at once. Mark MacDonald was the only person who had ever called him Wex. "I thought you'd dropped off the face of the earth, and then you call out of the blue. So, what's up?"

"Not much," Wexler replied noncommittally, not at all sure that he wanted to have this conversation now. He'd been in a nostalgic mood when he'd connected with MacDonald's mother. Now he realized he didn't have a lot to say. Unlike MacDonald, who was now a studio musician with numerous projects to his credit, Wexler had nothing to show for the last decade. He'd been contentedly coasting. Now, he realized that resurfacing after so many years required an explanation. "I was just listening to some old CDs and came across Loaded and wondered, whatever happened to those guys?"

"Which album?" asked MacDonald.

"Loaded Questions."

"Man, I don't remember the last time I played that. It was pretty good, as I remember."

"One of your best."

"I'll bet there aren't many of those CDs floating around. We didn't sell that many. Nothing like you guys. Man, we were so jealous of you when you hit it big. Where have you been? We all thought you'd moved to the East Coast, or were sitting on a beach in the Caribbean sipping piña coladas."

It was only now that Wexler had an inkling of how MacDonald must view him. They'd played the same dingy clubs until Morrison joined Totally Wrecked and they'd graduated to better venues. Loaded never made it, but their music had been solid. And when Totally Wrecked had scored a couple of hits, Wexler had never looked back. "No, I have a place here in Seal Cove."

There was a long pause on the other end of the line, as though his last statement didn't compute, and he realized MacDonald must be pondering why, after all these years, he chose to make contact now.

"How long?" MacDonald asked.

He couldn't very well tell the truth — that after Andy's death and Morrison's departure, he'd moved back home with his parents for a couple of years before settling in Seal Cove, that he'd been living locally all these years without renewing their friendship, so he just said, "Oh, a few years now; I've just been keeping a low profile."

"Are you still playing?"

"Now and then," Wexler prevaricated. He didn't want to admit that the only music he played these days was to an audience of one.

"Still collecting royalties?"

"Oh sure." The checks were small, but they arrived quarterly.

"Must be nice," MacDonald said wistfully, "I don't think anyone gets in this business expecting to get rich, but it's always an inspiration when someone makes it. It's a hard business. With all the cheap and free downloads, there's no money in it anymore."

"I never could make sense of it. I never knew why those two songs took off, and all our others were just filler. We were just lucky, I guess."

"God we were such kids then. Do you still see any of the old gang?"

"No, but I ran into Cliff's daughter a few weeks ago — you remember Cliff?"

"Of course, he's my accountant, does my taxes."

"No kidding, really? No, I lost track of everybody after the band broke up."

"Yeah, we were all shocked when Andy OD'd. I ran into Noah at a few studio sessions. He's still drumming."

"I haven't seen Noah in years. When Morrison quit the business, we didn't see any point in trying to regroup; he wrote most of the songs."

"You know Morrison is up in Mendocino now — Boonville, making acoustic instruments. He plays in a Blue Grass band on weekends."

Wexler had often speculated about Morrison. Now he had some answers and they didn't jibe with his assumptions. He thought Morrison had quit the music business, and there were times when he imagined that he'd died of a drug overdose like Andy. Instead, he was alive and kicking and had a weekend gig playing American roots music. "Is he still using?"

"I don't think so. He was pretty shaken up when Andy died. Last time I saw him, must be three years ago now, he was just smoking pot, and not much of that. He has a nice business making dulcimers and acoustic guitars. He does beautiful work."'

"Are you still living on Kings Mountain?"

"My folks still live up there, but I'm up in Daly City. Hey, you know, we should get together. I have a recording session at Aural Sax in Half Moon Bay on Thursday. You should swing by."

"What time?"

"I'm supposed to be there around nine. We should be done by one or so. We could have lunch and catch up."

"That's the place we used to go to make demo tapes."

"The same."

"And Henry Hodge, is he still there?"

"He is"

"God, he must be ancient."

"A face like Mt. Rushmore, and the ears of an angel."

"I remember. He made the crappiest music sound professional."

"He's scoring documentaries now. I'll be laying down tracks for a PBS special."

"Do you like studio work?"

"What's not to like? It pays the bills, and if you make a mistake you just do it over. I don't miss anything about touring, except maybe the girls, and my wife wouldn't approve of that."

"I didn't even know you were married."

"Eight years. We have three kids now — eight, five and two."

"Jesus, you've been busy."

"Time slows down for no man," MacDonald said.

The problem was — time had stood still for Wexler. If time is measured by notable events, he had nothing to show for his time since the band broke up.

#

By the time the call ended, his dinner was cold. He reheated it in the microwave and sat down at the dining room table, uncharacteristically brooding over the conversation he'd had with MacDonald. Wexler was not given to introspection, but ever since he'd picked up Cliff's daughter self-doubt had begun to press in upon his thoughts. In order to understand the magnitude of this change, it's perhaps necessary to point out that a clear mind was his default setting. Steve Wexler naturally assumed the attitude that others spent years trying to perfect through meditation. Where other minds were cluttered with thoughts of what ifs, and should haves, with speculation and planning and regret and worry, Wexler's mind was a still pond. He could have taught a Buddhist monk how to be in the here and now.

Perhaps that's why he had been so content for so long. And then Cliff's daughter had shocked him into an awareness of passing time. He felt like Rip Van Winkle awakening after a long sleep. He didn't feel any different, but he and the world around him had changed. Somehow he'd jumped from twenty-two to thirty-eight, seemingly overnight, without the memories, wisdom, and experience one might reasonably expect to attain after the passage of so many years. Maybe it was the realization that he was getting older. Maybe it was finding that erstwhile bandmates and friends had been filling that time by getting on with their lives — marrying, having kids, building careers, making memories. Whatever the cause, Wexler now found niggling discontent and doubt creep into his thoughts.

He saw himself reflected in the dark glass of the sliding doors, a homely, middle-aged man, alone and without a plan. He had the urge to cancel his meeting with MacDonald. He could say he was sick, or something had come up. But MacDonald had his number now and would just call again. He imagined it would be an awkward meeting, as he didn't have much to bring to the table. Fragments of their conversation kept circulating in the back of his consciousness, and one point kept recurring — Cliff was MacDonald's accountant. What were the odds?

Thinking of Mark MacDonald and Clifford Cook together gave him an idea. He Googled Cliff's number and called before he had time to reconsider. The phone made a staccato burr to indicate it was ringing, and just as he was about to hang up, a man answered.

"Cliff?"

"No, hold on."

He could hear muted conversation, annoyance, then a business-like voice declared, "This is Clifford Cook."

"Hey Cliff, you won't believe who called today."

In an exasperated tone Cliff said, "We don't want any."

"What?"

"Whatever you're selling, we don't want it. And take us off your call list."

"I'm not selling anything. This is Wexler."

Dead silence for five seconds, then, "Holy cow."

"I was talking with Mark MacDonald today and he says you're his accountant."

"I don't believe it. Where the hell have you been? What have you been up to?"

He'd expected a cold reception after hitting on his daughter, but Cliff seemed genuinely surprised and happy to hear from him. It slowly became apparent that Nicole had probably thought twice about explaining why she'd gone to an older man's home alone, which was fine with Wexler.

"Was that your son who answered the phone?"

"Yeah, that's Robert. He's a junior in high school. Nicole, my daughter, is going to the College of San Mateo. What have you been doing? Are you married?"

"Not yet."

"Where are you living?"

"Not far, actually. I'm in Seal Cove."

"No kidding, so close? Man, I had no idea you were still around. You say you were talking to Mark?"

"Yeah, we're meeting at Aural Sax on Thursday. I thought it would be fun if you came too. We could go out to lunch and get caught up."

"Jesus, it's weird you calling like this. My daughter has been listening to your albums for weeks now. I'll check my calendar. What's your number?"

A few minutes later Cliff called back to confirm their meeting on Thursday. "You know I'm glad you called. I'm on the planning committee for our 20th Class Reunion. We're planning on getting together in August. It'll be fun to catch up. Wait'll I tell Jeannie."

"Jeannie?"

"My wife. Didn't I mention I married Jeannie Ward?"

"Taylor's sister?"

"Yeah, we ran into each other at San Francisco State. I'll tell you all about it Thursday," Cliff said enthusiastically. "Hey, man, thanks for calling. What a blast from the past!"

Wexler was relieved. Now all the talk wouldn't center around his lack of accomplishments. If he asked the right questions, he could get them talking about themselves, asking each other questions, and they might not notice he had nothing to say.

Chapter Twenty-Nine
Little Free Libraries

Few people are content to live the life of a hermit. The need to connect is too strong. If we can't find connection with an individual human being, we find it in a group. If we can't find it in a group, we find it in a pet. That connection doesn't even have to be positive. A bickering couple is still a couple nonetheless. Even at her worst, Mary Abbott had provided her daughter with that connection. Emily would no sooner have abandoned her mother than she would have robbed a bank, kicked a dog, or slapped a child. It wasn't in her nature. But now Emily found herself in an unfamiliar state. Aside from an estranged aunt in Sheboygan she had no one –– no parents, siblings, co-workers, or classmates. She'd lost touch with her one friend, Linda Murphy, when she left school. Connecting with anonymous readers was small substitute for the real thing. So it was perhaps inevitable that she looked for connection no further than her nearest neighbor.

She waited until Wexler took Buddy for his afternoon walk before heading next-door to visit Tom. Tom, of course, was of her parents' generation, but Emily was comfortable around him, as she had considerably more experience with older people than with people her own age.

She found him sitting in the dining room, if one could even call the small niche at the end of the galley kitchen a room. From the bay window he could see her approaching the front door. He gestured her in. Tom was looking over a photo album.

"Have a seat," he said. "Can I get you anything?"

"No, you're settled."

"There's tea."

She poured herself a cup and looked over Tom's shoulder. The album was open to a page of photos of Paris. There were several photos of a brunette in bell-bottom pants and a tie-dyed T-shirt. It took Emily a few seconds to recognize a young Daisy. Tom tapped the photo of the woman and a long-haired, bearded young man with large sunglasses.

"This was on our honeymoon," Tom said.

"You were hippies."

"It was the style."

Emily sat down and Tom slid the album over so she could get a better look.

"She was beautiful," Emily said.

"She was only 23. We lived in the Avenues then. She was finishing her teaching credential at San Francisco State, and I worked for a wine importer on Fisherman's Wharf."

"You were lucky, you both had direction."

"Oh, I don't know. I didn't get into the business to make a career of it. I answered an ad in the paper, I made contacts, and one thing led to another. I might've gone a whole other direction. Life's funny that way."

"What did you major in?" Emily asked.

"I have a degree in Psychology. There was a lot of competition in the field, and I was really more interested in Neurology."

"Why didn't you go into that?"

"It would have required more schooling and I was burned out by then –– anxious to get on with life. What about you? What did you major in?"

"I only spent two years taking general education courses before Dad died. I never declared a major."

"What did you want to do?"

"I never got that far. I might like to teach."

"Daisy liked teaching. She loved being around kids. She mostly taught kindergarten. She loved the little ones."

"Yes, definitely elementary school. I wouldn't want to teach junior high or high school –– too many hormones, too much attitude."

"Have you looked into renting yet?"

"I don't know what to charge."

Tom pulled a Half Moon Bay Review across the table and flipped to the classifieds. "Looks like you can get $2,000 a month or more."

"That's crazy. Who would pay that much for one floor? They must be drug dealers."

"Not everyone with money is a drug dealer."

"I wouldn't feel right charging that much."

They batted the idea around for a minute until the UPS delivery man dropped a package at the door. Emily retrieved it and brought it back to the table. Tom opened it, pulled out a book, looked at the cover and placed it cover-side down on the table.

"What is it?" Emily asked.

"Nothing."

The back cover did nothing to disguise the content. It was a book entitled *There and Back: Near-Death-Experiences*. "Did you have a near-death-experience?"

"I don't want to talk about it."

"Why?"

"It's personal."

"What was it like?"

"You wouldn't believe it anyway."

"Of course I would. Why wouldn't I?"

"Even my doctor thinks I'm nuts."

"Oh, I doubt that. Lots of people have had them."

"Not like mine, I think."

Emily leaned forward eagerly. "Tell me all about it."

# # #

Coastsiders are a literate bunch. Several civic-minded ladies have persuaded their less than civic-minded husbands to build and install Little Free Libraries, each the size of a microwave oven (or bread box if that's your frame of reference) where readers can pick up books to read, and leave books they'd like to share with their neighbors. There are two Little Free Libraries in Farallone City, four in Seal Cove, two in El Granada, and three in Half Moon Bay. Each library is a reflection of the interests of its particular neighborhood. There are travel books, histories, biographies, self-help books, books on religion, psychology, bird watching, and sea life. Fiction runs the gamut of popular genres from science fiction to mystery, thriller, fantasy, young adult, and all the sub-genres of romance –– contemporary, historical, paranormal, time travel, comedy and erotica. Once in a while a stray book of horror or classic literature finds its way into the boxes.

Emily's self-published e-books were available online and as paperback print-on-demand editions. Collectively the e-books, priced at $1.99, sold an average of three copies a day. The paperbacks, priced at $10.00, were a harder sell. She always kept a dozen paperback copies of each title on hand to give away for review purposes.

Every time she went to a bookstore she looked longingly at the space where her books might be, and though it was next to impossible to get an independently published book onto bookstore shelves, it didn't stop her from dreaming. What had begun as a way to escape her humdrum existence, had become a compulsion. The characters demanded to be heard.

So while Tom pondered his purpose, Wexler connected with old friends, and Gary and Kyle ate dinner at The Careless Crab, Emily sat down in her study before a stack of paperback editions of her latest two books. On the title page of each she wrote:

Dear fellow Coastsider,

If you enjoyed this book please do me the favor of leaving an honest review online. If you find any typos, or if you have any criticism, questions, or suggestions, feel free to email me at SealCove2@comcast.net.

Happy reading,

Then she signed Margaret Pennypacker to copies of *The Master of Glenoch Castle*, and Robert Cole to copies of *Lawless*. It was only after she finished that she realized she'd accidentally inscribed four copies of *Lawless* with Margaret Pennypacker's signature. These she put aside with the intention of cutting out the title pages at a later date.

The following morning she loaded her books into a backpack and set out to make a circuit of all the Little Free Libraries on the coast. Emily's expectations were modest. She thought of a story as a dialogue between the writer and the reader. A story without a reader was incomplete. She wrote with an imaginary reader in mind, someone with an equally mundane life who wanted, if only for a few minutes, to escape into another world. The overwhelming number of positive reviews mitigated the occasional negative remark, which only served to remind her that she couldn't please all of the people all of the time.

Of books she'd previously left at the Little Free Libraries, none remained, which either meant they were being read, or readers were keeping them. Either way, it was a connection. She only hoped that some of her readers would leave reviews online, because reviews drove sales, sales meant more readers, and readers completed the circle.

In Half Moon Bay she passed the Miller Dutra Funeral Home, which set her to thinking about the day she had scattered her parents' ashes, and she remembered Gary and Kyle Myron, who lived on that little boat in the harbor. *They might want to rent,* she thought. Having a youngster in the house would be a breath of fresh air. When she got home she found the card Gary had given her and called the number.

"I guess it depends how much," he said after she asked if he'd be interested in renting. "I'm saving a lot of money living on the boat."

Emily was flying blind. She had never even had an apartment of her own. Having no experience, negotiating didn't come naturally or comfortably. She didn't want to scare him away, and she didn't want to be taken advantage of. In her ignorance, she hadn't even considered a lease, liability insurance, or deposits for first and last months' rent. She hated dancing around the subject, jockeying for the dominant position. So she asked bluntly, "How much were you paying in your last place? Truthfully."

There was only a short hesitation before he lied, "Sixteen hundred for a studio apartment in El Granada, including utilities." It had actually been eighteen hundred, he'd had to share a bathroom, and he'd had to pay utilities separately.

Emily said, "I've got a duplex, two bedrooms, living room, kitchen, and garage. Fully furnished."

Gary sighed. "I can't afford anything that big."

"What if you paid the same as for your last place?"

"I guess I'd have to think about it. I'd want to see it first, of course."

She gave him her address and told him to come by any time to look it over. "I haven't advertised yet. I thought about you and Kyle on that boat and thought you might be interested.

He thanked her and said he'd swing by in the next couple of days. It was a ridiculously good deal. On the other hand living aboard the boat saved him a lot of money. On the positive side of the ledger the live-aboard permit only cost $366 a month. However, on the negative side he was paying another $150 for a storage unit, and eating at The Careless Crab cost way more than cooking for himself. The boat was cramped, the public toilets cold, and the showers a five-minute walk away. He wondered if the duplex had a washer and dryer. While he lived on the boat, he washed his clothes at the coin-operated laundry facilities next to the showers on the far side of the harbor parking lot, or he took them to his parents. The former cost him a few dollars and three hours of boredom. The latter cost him a lecture about the folly of his chosen profession.

Chapter Thirty

Buoys

A broken layer of stratocumulus blocked the sun and turned the calm sea a silver-gray.

"We better work fast today," Gary said. "We're likely to see some weather tomorrow."

"How can you tell, Uncle Gary?"

Gary pointed an index finger and glanced upward. "This kind of cloud formation usually comes a day before the rain, and sometimes the day after."

The air temperature hovered in the high 50s, though rents in the clouds let through random shafts of warming sun. They were both dressed in layers and wore sock hats to cover their ears.

They brought up the pots off Miramar Beach and proceeded northward along the coast. In each spot, they dropped the pots in a line from shallower to deeper water. So far the experiment was proving Gary's supposition — pots in deeper water were yielding more plentiful and bigger crabs.

They'd worked past the lighthouse and Montara State Beach, and were half a mile off Gray Whale Cove. Gary throttled back until they were barely moving. He scanned the area, perplexed. Then he checked the log. "There should be eight buoys here." He checked the depth sounder, then picked up his binoculars and searched the calm surface. Farther inshore he could see three of his buoys in a line. The other five were missing. He'd occasionally lost a buoy. A line could snap under a storm surge, or a pot could drag. A buoy could be pulled under the surface if the pot was dropped at low tide and he failed to account for the swell and tide change. But he was sure he had made the proper calculations.

He handed the binoculars to Kyle. "Keep looking. The current would probably carry south."

They motored inshore to the shallowest three buoys and brought the pots up. Everything looked in order.

It was possible but unlikely that the missing pots had been stolen. Drunken pleasure boaters had been known to plunder crab pots on occasion. But it was foolhardy to actually steal one. Each pot was tagged, and stealing a pot was considered grand theft. It was always possible a charter boat had blundered into the area and run over the buoys, cutting the lines. He'd lost buoys to careless boaters before, though not so many. There was an off chance that the new line was defective. It was also possible a pod of whales had become entangled in the lines.

Gary calculated the loss of equipment at over $700. The lost crab would potentially cost him much more until he could replace the pots.

"Uncle Gary? I think I see one on the beach. A buoy, I mean."

Kyle handed the binoculars to his uncle. Gary spotted a buoy at the south end of the beach, but at this distance he couldn't tell if it was one of his.

He handed the binoculars back to Kyle. "Keep an eye out for any more."

Their last stop was a mile off Pedro Point. There they'd left six pots. All were accounted for, but the two deepest pots had been relocated to shallower water. There had been no storm surge. This was obviously deliberate. He'd been known to move an amateur's trap himself, if it was interfering with his commercial operation, especially as amateurs so often used cheap polypropylene floating line that could foul a propeller.

After sorting the crab and freshening the bait, they repositioned the two pots that had been moved inshore. Lowering the last one to the ocean floor he saw, bobbing on the surface 300-yards to the northwest, Marauder's distinctive blue and yellow buoys. Gary knew Rasmussen wasn't above moving pots. If Rasmussen was indeed responsible, it was a pointed slap at Gary's commercial status.

Gary let Kyle take the wheel on the way back to the harbor, while he scanned the shore for orphaned buoys and wondered about the missing pots off Gray Whale Cove. That was still a mystery. He didn't think Rasmussen would be so rash or vindictive. It was a hard enough business without engaging in petty feuds.

# # #

After washing the boat and distributing the crab between the wholesalers and a few local restaurants, Gary and Kyle piled into the pickup and drove north past the Brussels sprouts fields, through Seal Cove and Farallone City, past Montara State Beach, to the parking lot above Gray Whale Cove.

The beach is small and secluded and clothing optional. There are 310 stairs from the parking lot to the sand. On this afternoon, under a cloudy sky, the beach was nearly deserted, and no one chose to disrobe, much to Kyle's disappointment.

The buoy was still there and it did indeed belong to Miss Behavin'. Attached to one end was three feet of aqua blue crab line, cleanly cut as though with a knife or garden shears.

Gary felt frustration, disappointment and rage bubble up in him. Someone had deliberately set out to do him harm, to rob him of money and time, and for what? What did they hope to accomplish? He was small potatoes, no threat to anyone. Not even Rasmussen, who might be annoyed, but would never cut another man's line. Or was he just being naive? Not everyone saw the world the same way.

Kyle looked at the cut line and at his uncle's face. "Sorry, Uncle Gary."

"You know, most people are good at heart. But it only takes one in a thousand to ruin your day. I have five pots sitting on the bottom out there, full of crab and no way to bring them up. God damn it."

Who would be so malicious?

#

On their return, Gary turned off the highway in Seal Cove.

"Where are we going, Uncle Gary?"

"The lady we took out last Sunday has an apartment for rent. I want to look at it."

In truth, he didn't want to go back to the boat. He'd spent all night and all day on the boat, and he was downhearted at the day's turn of events.

Emily was glad to see them and showed them through the bottom floor. There was a separate entrance from the garage, and pocket doors could close off the front hall for complete privacy from her half of the duplex, if that's what they preferred. She didn't want to advertise the vacancy because she honestly didn't want to rent to just anyone. She'd told Steve Wexler that she was wary of meth heads and political cranks, but the real reason was less politically correct: She didn't want to rent to old people. She wouldn't have admitted it in front of Tom, but the fact was that she had had enough of old people. It seemed that her entire life had been devoted to old people, and much as she loved her father, she'd had enough of it. She wanted to be young and to surround herself with youth before it was too late.

"This is a lot more than I need," Gary said. "More than I can afford, I'm afraid, but thanks for showing us."

"You don't know how much it's going for," Emily appealed. "I'm only asking..." And here she recalled his saying he'd paid $1,600 at his last apartment. "I'm only asking $1,500 a month." When he didn't immediately bite, she added, "Utilities included."

"Is there a washer and dryer?"

"In the garage."

Gary was baffled. It was too cheap. Something was wrong here. "Just to be up front here. What are the hidden charges?"

"Hidden charges?"

"You know, like cleaning deposit, first and last months' rent, references — all that stuff."

"I don't know, I haven't thought about it. I guess I'd want the first month's rent ahead."

It wasn't the response he expected. "When do you need to know?"

"A week?"

"Okay, let me think about it. I'll get back to you."

He'd been prepared to pay more for a studio apartment. This was far bigger.

From Emily Abbott's Notebooks
Point Montara Light

Note to self — good location for smugglers' story, maybe as a place to land, or where Derek Law can observe the boats near shore. Or maybe to tie the past to the present:

Point Montara defines the northern boundary of Seal Cove, where an unnamed creek separates Seal Cove from Farallone City. The thirty-foot high, conical, cast-iron Point Montara lighthouse first saw service in Wellfleet, Massachusetts from 1881 to 1922. It was dismantled, and reassembled on Point Montara in 1928.

Beside the lighthouse is a squat shiplapped old building that houses the lighthouse museum. A gnarled, windswept cypress stands between the light and an 1863, two-story lighthouse keeper's residence with a distinctive red-shingled roof, three steep gables, and three chimneys. A white picket fence, now faded to ivory, surrounds the perimeter, festooned with colorful crab buoys — white and blue and yellow and day-glow orange, plain and striped — that have washed up on the rocks. The light is automated now and there's no need for a lighthouse keeper, but a couple live on-premises to care for the property and the museum, and to run a youth hostel in one of the outbuildings.

Forty-feet below the light the waves slam into the rocks, retreat, and gather again for another assault, like a ram butting heads with the shore. Gulls ride the air currents at the edge of the cliff. Brown Pelicans glide gracefully, tucked into the lip of peaking swells. And black cormorants skim over the water, furiously beating their wings to stay aloft. In the morning on a sunny day, the fishing fleet can be seen as white flecks upon the blue, and by night the squid boats work under bright lights, standing out like little embers on the vast black surface of the sea.

You can sit at one of the grey weathered picnic tables or benches on the property, and eat or read while listening to the waves. Here, up close, you hear the whoosh of creaming wave tops, the thump of waves as they break, the roar of breakers unrolling like foamy carpets in their rush to the shore, followed by another thump as the rushing water runs headlong into the rocks.

Chapter Thirty-One
Mirada Road

A mile south of the harbor, Mirada Road runs one block along Miramar Beach. A century ago you could cross the wide road and step directly onto the sand. Decades of erosion have dropped the level of the beach by twenty feet, and rip rap now protects the narrow road from the relentless pounding of the surf. Along the road are the Miramar Beach Inn, a former Prohibition roadhouse and brothel that serves an upscale restaurant crowd; two boutique hotels, a couple of private residences; the Bach Dynamite and Dancing Society; an art gallery; and a remarkable compound of small buildings made of wood, driftwood, and rock designed and constructed by adventure photographer Michael Powers. There's an A-frame topped with a carved wooden angel, a geodesic dome, a building that resembles a boat, and a two-story building of shingles and skylights and beach stones. Michael and his Peruvian wife Nonni live on the second floor. Aural Sax Music Studio occupies part of the ground floor, with wrap-around windows that give a wide view of breaking waves. A short stone wall studded with succulents encloses a small courtyard in front of the studio. It's a lovely place to hang out.

Wexler hadn't set foot in the place in at least fifteen years. He let himself in the side gate and walked around to the Dutch door. Inside he saw Mark MacDonald and Henry Hodge. Hodge held up a hand in the universal "wait" signal.

MacDonald stood with his eyes shut, listening to music through headphones, bobbing gently to the beat. When the music ended, he opened his eyes and a smile lit up his face. "Wex! Hey man, how's it hanging?"

Wexler barely recognized his old friend now that he'd cut his hair and gained a few pounds. Henry Hodge, on the other hand, seemed as unchanged and timeless as a rock. He had the same owlish glasses, and tufts of white hair rimed his head like a crown of snow. Hodge was forever humming, seemingly unaware of the jukebox in his head that played a constant stream of music. He had a catholic appreciation of music. His mind might call up The Yellow Rose of Texas one moment, Copland's Appalachian Spring in the next, or Brahms' Lullaby followed by Moon River, and Money for Nothin'. There seemed to be no sense behind the outpouring. He turned an impish smile in Wexler's direction. "We'll be with you in just a minute," he said. "Have a seat on the bench."

Wexler sat on the bench in the courtyard. The sun was warm and a cool ocean breeze carried the scent of brine and iodine from the kelp on the beach. He briefly wondered if Cliff would show up. Then he closed his eyes and listened to the waves rolling shoreward. He might have fallen asleep; it was hard to tell. It was a restful sound like the susurrant whoosh of brushes on a snare drum, punctuated every ten seconds or so by the thump of a breaking wave and the distant beep of the foghorn. Music issued from small speakers tucked under the eaves, and after awhile he became aware of a solo guitar playing in the background, and a shiver went up his spine as he recognized Andy's distinctive riffs. Andy, who'd been dead these twelve years now. Then the pure sound of Morrison's flute joined in. Time seemed to roll backwards. They were playing a haunting instrumental ballad. Wexler stood and opened the Dutch door. Hodge and MacDonald were smiling at him.

"Is that who I think it is?"

Hodge nodded. "They recorded it the weekend before Espinosa overdosed. Nobody ever came back to finish up."

Wexler was stunned. "I had no idea. They didn't tell me."

"They were just messing around, you know, jamming."

The three men stopped talking then and listened to the end. Morrison's flute took the bridge, and Andy, having switched to acoustic guitar, played answering phrases, the two instruments in intimate conversation. It was as though Andy had stepped from the grave in all his youth and glory.

"That's just one tune," Hodge said. "There's more, if you want to hear them."

"You ought to lay down a bass line on top of that," MacDonald recommended. "Give it some drive."

"Did they sing?" Wexler asked Henry Hodge. "I mean, are there lyrics to anything they recorded?"

"Not that I remember. I haven't listened to those sessions in a long time."

"There was more than one?"

"Oh sure. They'd drop by just to gab and try out new material. And drink Jack Daniels. I'd just turn on the mics and lay back and listen. Some of it was pretty awful, particularly when they were tanked, but some of it — well, you heard — some of it is pretty cool."

Wexler wondered how many other jam-sessions he'd been excluded from.

MacDonald chuckled. "Man, sometimes I thought they were trying too hard to live up to the name of the group — they really *were* totally wrecked. I don't know how they played some nights."

"It's sad, really," Hodge said. "Funny at first, and then just sad. Too many young musicians fall into that trap. I've lost patience with them. Give me a seasoned professional every time."

MacDonald addressed Wexler. "You remember when I was still with Loaded and we shared a bill in Sacramento? Morrison collapsed on stage."

"Yeah, but that was more from exhaustion than drugs. We were staying up all night, driving to the next bill, and starting all over again. And they partied hard. I could never keep up with them. Not that I was trying. I didn't have the tolerance for drugs."

"That's an understatement," Clifford Cook said as he let himself in through the Dutch door.

Wexler turned around to greet his old bandmate and had to do a mental reconciliation. Cliff had put on thirty-five pounds, shaved his head and grown a mustache. Only his eyes gave a hint of the boy he'd been.

"I remember one night in particular," Cliff went on. "We were playing Rude Awakening — it's a song with a strong bass line that doesn't change through the whole thing, which is like six minutes long, and Wexler here goes into a trance."

"It wasn't a trance, I just fell asleep while playing. My fingers just kept going even though I'd checked out mentally. It was like I tapped into something."

"So the song ended," Cliff took over, "and Wexler here kept playing, and after about a minute I joined in, and then Andy and Noah stepped in just improvising around the bass."

155

"I woke up about twenty minutes into it," Wexler finished, "and saw this mesmerized audience, and then it all fell apart. I lost the rhythm when I woke up, but then Noah picked it up with a drum solo, and we finished without stumbling too badly. The crowd went wild. That was a weird night."

Cliff bumped fists with Wexler and MacDonald. Wexler turned to Hodge. "Has Cliff heard this yet?"

"Heard what?" Cliff asked.

"Play it," said Wexler.

When it was over Cliff said, "That was Andy on guitar, wasn't it? That was eerie. I don't remember the tune."

"I never heard it before either," Wexler said. "Not until this morning. Do you still play?"

"I play banjo now with a little neighborhood group, but I haven't played guitar in years. An ex-girlfriend threw my guitar out a three-story window."

"Not the Martin!"

"Yeah, bummer. I couldn't afford to replace it at the time, and then I got busy with school. How about you? What have you been up to?"

It was the very question Wexler had hoped to avoid. He shrugged noncommittally. "Not much." Then with a jerk of his thumb toward MacDonald he said, "Nothing like this guy. He's been busy."

"Don't I know it? I do his taxes."

"Right, you mentioned that."

Hodge said, "We weren't quite finished when you dropped in. There's coffee and tea on the sideboard. Cups are in the cupboard. Take a seat while we finish up."

Hodge pulled the shades down and sat in front of three monitors. The center monitor was paused on a video documentary on human trafficking. He put on headphones. "Clarinet this time. Slow and sleazy. "

MacDonald stepped into the glass-fronted recording booth, standing before his own monitors, while Hodge cued up the video and gave the signal to begin. Cliff and Wexler visited quietly in the corner while Hodge and MacDonald finished their session.

Then the four of them strolled down Mirada Road to Miramar Beach Inn for lunch.

Wexler asked MacDonald what he was listening to these days.

"Ah, well, the answer to that question would be misleading. I can't listen to what I want. My girls only allow me to listen to Disney anthems — anything from Frozen; Moana; Brave, Pocahontas."

"Oh god," Cliff said, "at least you don't have to listen to rap. My son is into that crap. That's not singing; that's performance doggerel."

"We sound old," Wexler said.

"We *are* old," said Cliff.

"Don't make me laugh," Hodge said.

They sat at one of the outdoor tables where they could listen to the rhythm of the breaking waves. Wexler did his best to avoid talking about himself for a change, and instead listened intently to these relics of his past who seemed to have made successful transitions to the present. They seemed comfortable in their new personas, in a way that he was not.

Over lunch, MacDonald asked Wexler, "Do you remember Zack Farrell? He was our bass player after Ralph Mankiewicz left?"

"The guy with the mohawk and ear studs?"

"That's him. He was always copying your riffs."

Wexler was surprised and secretly pleased.

Hodge asked curiously, "You don't by any chance play stand-up bass?"

"I do, yeah," Wexler said.

"Can you bow?"

"Sure."

"Great! Can you record a few tracks for me next week?"

Chapter Thirty-Two
The Silence of Music

There were few people on the terrace at the Seal Cove Brewpub when Wexler and Buddy arrived a little before the usual dinner crowd, and the blustering wind kept all but the hardy indoors. The few who sat outside huddled under blankets around the fire pit. Wexler sat by the fire, warmed by a cup of coffee, an Irish sweater, and a sock cap that also served to hide his bald spot.

A golden retriever strained against her leash to say hello to Buddy. The two dogs tentatively sniffed each other's butts, scent mysteriously determining the level of threat, and having passed these preliminaries they wagged their tails companionably. The woman on the other end of the retriever's leash said, "Don't worry; she's friendly."

"What's her name?"

"Rosalind. It's Latin for..."

"Pretty rose," he finished for her. "This is Buddy."

"I've seen you out here before."

"I live on the other side of those trees," he said, pointing vaguely toward the cypress grove.

"Near the Marine Reserve?"

"On Seacliff."

It was a strange phenomenon, but Wexler had found that dog owners often felt free to introduce their dogs, without ever introducing themselves. He was on a first-name basis with a lot of dogs, and while he recognized their owners, he often didn't know their names. This woman was a little older than he, perhaps forty or forty-two, with light crow's feet at the corners of her eyes, but nice looking in a sturdy, athletic sort of way. He noticed she wore no wedding band on her finger, but two gold rings hung on a chain around her neck, which often denoted widowhood.

"So, Rosalind's owner, what's your name?"

"Rosalind."

"You named your dog after yourself?"

She smiled. "I thought it was funny."

"It is," Wexler nodded appreciatively. "Very droll."

"And what is Buddy's owner's name?"

"Well, it's not Buddy. His name is Tom. But that's not me. My..." He usually introduced himself by saying *My friends call me Wexler.* This woman, however, was older and he had no interest in picking her up. So this time he said simply, "I'm Steve."

"What do you do, Steve?"

He might have gone into his falsely modest spiel about Totally Wrecked, or let it be dragged out of him slowly, but with a gig in the offing, he said the unexpected. "I'm a studio musician." He said it to try it on for size. It felt good to say he was working again, even if it was just a few tracks to be laid down in a studio.

"What do you play?"

"Bass, mostly. A little piano. I can fake it on guitar. But mostly bass." Then uncharacteristically he changed the subject by asking her about herself. "Do you play?"

"I played clarinet in our high school jazz band, but I wouldn't say I play."

"What *do* you do?"

Rosalind looked embarrassed. "Nothing at the moment, I'm afraid. My husband and I worked for an internet startup that went public a couple of years ago. There was plenty of money and the first thing he did was buy a Porsche. A month later he was driving down Highway One around Big Sur and took a curve too fast. End of story. I'd rather not talk about it."

"Sorry."

She shrugged. "That's okay, everybody has some baggage. What's the story with Buddy? Why are you walking someone else's dog?"

# # #

"I've had an interesting afternoon," Wexler said when he brought Buddy back home.

"Interesting good, or interesting bad?"

"I've been asked to do some studio work."

"That's good. What kind of work?"

"Playing stand-up bass. I've never played stand-up professionally."

"But you do play?"

"Oh yeah."

"So that's good."

"I guess. It's been a long time."

"Do you play any *real* instruments?"

"What's that supposed to mean?"

"Never mind, I just remembered you play piano."'

"Is piano somehow more real than bass?"

"I just meant an instrument that carries the melody."

"A song is as much about the beat and the spaces between the notes, as the notes themselves," Wexler said.

"Oh, I know, I get it. Bass and drums provide a framework for the music, but it's still not music in the sense that melody is music, a tune you can whistle. That's all I meant."

"But you still don't get it. Not really. Now listen." Wexler crossed to Tom's out-of-tune piano and plunked several notes of equal duration, giving no more emphasis to one note than another. "Can you name the tune?"

"There is no tune."

"How about this? Same notes." He played the notes again. "Recognize it now?"

"Of course — *Tequila*."

"And this?" He plunked out a couple dozen notes with a samba beat.

Tom cocked an ear and following along said, "Nope. No...wait. Oh, I think I got it. No. Nope. It's on the tip of my tongue." Wexler raised his eyebrows and waited for an answer. "Play it again," Tom requested. But after listening a second time he had to shake his head. "No, no idea."

Wexler played it once again, reinstating the familiar rhythm.

"The opening stanza of Beethoven's fifth?" Tom asked incredulously.

"See, music is as much or more about the spaces between the notes, and the emphasis on certain notes. The spaces make the tune work. The spaces and the emphasis are what give the tune its style and rhythm. Can you imagine classic rock-and-roll without the base?" Then he played the baselines of *Willow Weep For Me*; *Day Tripper*; and The Animals version of *The House of the Rising Sun*. "See what I mean?"

"I do," Tom said, surprised to find his neighbor so passionate about something that wasn't female. "I do see."

Chapter Thirty-Three
Reading in the Rain

Driving back from viewing the apartment, Gary wondered how they'd pass the time. It wasn't easy keeping a twelve-year-old entertained. "Have you finished *Ready Player One*?"

"Almost."

"Let's pick out some new books before dinner."

Instead of turning toward the harbor, they drove up the hill into El Granada until they came to the first Little Free Library. Gary left a couple of paperbacks and took a Robert Cole book called *The Spirit of the Law*. He opened it to the title page. It was signed. "Here's another one by that local writer. The last one was pretty good."

"What was it called?"

"*Law's Justice.* It was about a reporter named Derek Law, who lives by his own code of ethics."

"What's a code of ethics?"

"A personal point-of-view about what's right or wrong."

Kyle picked out a Goosebumps book.

"I read some of those when I was your age. You ever read Stephen King?"

"Mom had a book of stories. I only read one. It was called *The Langoliers*. I remember because I kept having nightmares, and she wouldn't let me read any others."

Raindrops were already spotting the windshield when Gary pulled the old truck to a stop in one of the permitted spaces in the harbor parking lot. The street lights blinked on one by one. Lights were also coming on in the hotel windows and restaurants. They walked across the street to the Sandpiper for fish tacos. The place was redolent of cooking oil, freshly grilled fish, sourdough bread, and beer. While they waited for their orders, Gary had a coffee, and Kyle a hot chocolate.

"So you've been on-board a week now," Gary said. "When is your mom coming to pick you up?"

"Dad didn't say."

"I'll bet you'll be happy to get back to television."

"I didn't miss anything. Dad has cable, so everything is recorded."

"Do you miss video games?"

Kyle shrugged. "A little, I guess. I like Civilization."

"What is it about?"

"You build houses and cities and countries and stuff like that."

"I hope you haven't been too bored on the boat."

"I'm fine, Uncle Gary."

Gary couldn't help thinking that his nephew was unnaturally accommodating. It wasn't normal for a boy to go a week without complaining about something. He thought it probably stemmed from trying to please two parents with opposing viewpoints. "Okay," Gary said, "but now that you've had a taste of it, what do you think of crabbing? What stands out?"

"It's hard work."

"It is that. Is it something you'd like to do for a living?"

Kyle shrugged. It was better to be noncommittal when an adult asked a direct question. That way you wouldn't come out with the wrong answer. But Gary persisted. "What do you like and what don't you like?"

"I like steering the boat. I like the view of the land when we're out."

"And what don't you like? Be honest now."

"Well..." Kyle hesitated, reluctant to voice a real opinion.

"Go on," Gary urged.

"Well, it's cold, and I don't like getting up so early."

"I won't argue with you there."

"And no offense, Uncle Gary, but you snore."

"I do?"

"Every night, big time."

"Sorry. Poke me next time."

"And Uncle Gary? — You also talk in your sleep."

"Me? No. What do I say?"

"It's mostly gibberish. But last night you said, 'No, I got it. Get away.'"

"I hardly ever remember my dreams."

The waiter came with a basket of bread and butter and took their orders.

Still thinking about sleep Gary said, "It seems a waste that we live a third of our lives unconscious or dreaming, but it's unavoidable. We all need to recharge."

A southerly wind drove a fine drizzle into their faces as they left the restaurant. By the time they ducked into the tiny cabin they were dripping. They tossed their damp clothes into a plastic crate and changed into dry clothes. A noisome fug permeated the cabin, a combination of wet clothes, bilge water, kerosene, and stale breath. The wind had picked up, coming in gusts now and howling through the masts, jangling halyards and rocking the boat. They settled down on their bunks and began to read by the dim light of electric lanterns.

Half an hour passed before Kyle said, "I have to go to the bathroom."

"Take a whiz over the side."

"It's too windy."

"You can use the head," Gary suggested. But the head had no door for privacy, and the smell emanating from that alcove was unpleasant.

"I can't," Kyle said. "I want to go to the restroom."

Gary helped his nephew into the anorak he wore on the foulest of days, and sent him on his way. The last thing he said was, "Don't run, the dock gets slippery."

Kyle was back in ten minutes with wet, torn jeans and a scraped knee. "We ought to put a bandaid on that," Gary said. "How'd it happen?"

"I slipped going up the ramp. And getting on the boat."

"You're not the first," Gary said, and then made the mistake of saying, "I told you to be careful."

It was an observation guaranteed to provoke resentment and Kyle snapped back defensively, "It's not my fault!"

Gary wondered whose fault it was then, but placing blame was beside the point. "Do you have any dry pants?"

"One pair."

"Let's make sure they stay dry."

"I had to go in the girls' bathroom; there was a dog in the men's room."

"What dog?"

"Just a dog."

"Was it aggressive?"

"He didn't growl, but he barked. He was dirty. I think he was a stray."

That night the wind came howling in ferocious gusts, rocking the boat and driving torrents of rain that beat on the deck above. Inside the cabin was relatively dry, but the maelstrom outside kept them on edge. Deep sleep was impossible. Gary had never felt so claustrophobic on the boat before.

In the morning the gale warning pennants were snapping above the Harbor Master's office. Most storms blew themselves out in a day. This one continued into the late morning, and the NOAA forecast called for more to come by the evening. There would be no crabbing that day.

With all the boats in port, The Careless Crab was crowded and the room alive with the chatter of conversation. The woodstove radiated warmth. Gary said hello to a couple of erstwhile colleagues, and stopped when George Stavros held up his hand for a high five. "Who do we have here?" George asked.

"This is my nephew Kyle. He's been crewing for me."

George turned his eye on the young man. "Don't let him turn you into a fisherman, kid; it's a rotten profession. You're always just a bad season away from bankruptcy!"

"Don't listen to him," Gary said. "His family has been at it for three generations."

"And where has it got us, eh? Go into computers, kid; it's the future."

"He wants to grow lavender."

"Not a farmer! The only thing worse than a fisherman is a farmer. Droughts, hail, floods, pests, disease. Nope, you can have all that. I'd rather fish." Then George turned to Gary. "Oh, hey, I'm glad I ran into you. Word has it you're not satisfied with your bathtub. Are you looking to sell?"

"I really haven't thought about it."

"Because I have a cousin who's interested in starting small, and I heard through the grapevine that you might be in the market for a bigger boat."

"Maybe. It all depends."

"Well, if you are in the market, rumor has it that Bill Whittaker is going to retire at the end of this season."

"Whittaker, he owns the Barbara Anne."

"That's the one."

"I crewed for him for — must be eight, nine years ago."

"I don't know what he might be asking for her, but I thought I'd pass it on, and if you're interested in selling — like I said, I've got a cousin."

"Thanks, George. I'll look into it."

There was plenty to think about. Sometimes opportunities opened up and you just had to make a leap of faith. But the first order of business was to determine if he would continue living on the boat, or move into an apartment.

Over lunch he made calculations on a paper napkin, weighing the cost of the live-aboard permit, a self-storage unit, eating out, and the time and expense of the coin-op laundry, against the comfort of having his own apartment, access to a washer and dryer, and a real bed again. When all was said and done, the deal Emily Abbott was offering was just too good to turn down. He felt he was probably taking advantage of her, but if she was foolish enough to ask so low a rent, who was he to alert her to the error of her ways?

That afternoon Gary and Kyle gathered all their laundry and a few personal items and drove to Emily Abbott's to take possession of the bottom floor of the duplex.

Chapter Thirty-Four
Roscoe is Miserable

At first, Roscoe had been a happy dog. He'd arrived the second week of February during an uncharacteristic heatwave. The rainy season, which usually starts in November, is usually over by March. His home behind the dumpster was sheltered by the eaves, and for the first month he had been comfortable enough. Red Ramsey, the day bartender, brought him scraps of delicious food and even made him a pallet of an old woolen blanket. Roscoe wished Red Ramsey would take him home, but Ramsey's wife would never have allowed it. Jesus, the waiter, advised Red to call the SPCA, but Red was afraid they'd put the poor dog to sleep, a euphemism if ever there was one. So Roscoe remained in his place behind the dumpster, daily dining on such an abundance of table scraps that he'd packed on a nice layer of fat to insulate him from the cold nights.

But now Roscoe was miserable. This late-season storm had come with wind that swept the rain sideways, stealing in under the eaves. As the light blinked on above the back door, Ramsey came out under an umbrella, bringing with him the tantalizing scent of food. He gave Roscoe a quarter of a hamburger and a crab carapace, and rubbed him dry with kitchen towels. He folded the blanket so that Roscoe could lie on the driest side. Then he said a few kind words and walked to his car and drove off. Roscoe watched him go with a sinking heart. Nathan Chan, the night bartender, never gave him so much as a crust. He lay in a circle with his paws drawn in and his tail covering his nose and the fine rain swept in and coated his fur again. After an hour a waiter came out with a plastic bag of trash. Roscoe raised his head in hopeful anticipation, but the waiter merely glared at him, threw the trash into the dumpster, and went back inside, turning off the outside light as he slammed the door.

As much as Roscoe loved the smells and the food, his coat was becoming matted, and he'd picked up fleas that made him itch terribly. He missed having an owner who could scratch the places he couldn't reach, and he missed a warm home to sleep in, even if his last owner had been stingy with food.

When he was thoroughly wet and the cold wind bit so that he shivered, he got up to look for better shelter. He shook the water off and slunk along the backside of the building and around the corner. The north side was slightly sheltered from the wind, but the rain had puddled and there was no place to lie down. He peeked around the front corner. The surf shop and bait shop were dark, but light spilled out of the windows of The Careless Crab and Harbor Bar, illuminating the cars parked in front. Parked side-by-side the cars blocked some of the wind. Roscoe got down on his belly and scooted under the front of an SUV. The engine was still ticking with heat and he lay between the front wheels, sheltered and warm and soon fell asleep to the smell of oil and gasoline, rubber and hot metal.

He dreamed of a blue heron that stood like a statue in a field of tall green grass. The predator's instincts took hold of him as he glided stealthily through the grass toward the unsuspecting bird. Overhead he heard two jarring thumps. He froze, unsure of what he'd heard, and suddenly the engine came to life, roaring and whirring and startling him awake so that he bumped his head on the bottom of the engine. He flattened himself to the pavement, wishing it to stop. Then the headlights came on. A moment later the transmission engaged with a jerk, and the car began to roll backwards. As soon as he could stand Roscoe bolted, sprinting into the dark cold rain, fear gripping his heart. The headlights swept over him; he tripped and banged his nose into something hard, and then he was off again, running toward a lighted doorway.

The doorway was open and he could smell it now. It was the place where humans left their scent. Hundreds of them. He approached cautiously but could hear nothing over the howl of the wind and the clanking of loose halyards. A ferocious gust of cold decided him. In the vestibule he could smell the reek of male urine on one side, and the fainter scent of females on the left. The brighter light was to the right and he shook the water from his coat as he entered. There were bowls of water and two overhead lights. The tile was cold, but it was dry and sheltered from the wind. He drank some water and curled up on the floor to sleep.

Sometime later a boy came in. Roscoe sat up, wagged his tail and barked a greeting, hoping for some company and perhaps a bite of food, or at least a scratch on the back. Instead, the boy hesitated, backed up, and went around to the female side. Puzzled, Roscoe lay down again, wondering if anyone would come to his aid, and soon fell into a deep sleep where the world was full of warm days, with birds and rabbits to chase and things to smell.

Chapter Thirty-Five
Moving In

Sometimes watershed moments come with pomp and circumstance — a graduation, a marriage, a change of scene, a new job, a chance meeting, a fight. Other times they come with no fanfare at all. Our lives are filled with such moments when we went left, when we might have gone right. If the storm had not kept him up all night, if he had been alone on the boat, Gary might not have been tempted to move into the Abbott duplex just then, and his life would have taken another trajectory. As it was, Gary and Kyle Myron showed up on Emily's doorstep slightly damp and carrying their belongings in plastic trash bags.

Luxury is a relative concept. For Gary, after living several months in the cramped quarters of his boat, having a queen bed, easy access to laundry and hot water, a shower, a dishwasher and a refrigerator constituted almost unspeakable luxury, and came as an immense relief. It was three times the size of his old studio apartment and for less money. His only worry was that Emily Abbott might realize her mistake and raise the rent.

"When can I sign the lease?" he asked as soon as Emily had let them in.

"I haven't got one yet. I'm sure there's a boilerplate lease on the internet. We can do that later."

But Gary didn't want to wait. He was afraid she'd pull out of the deal.

"Can I at least write you a check?" he asked. He knew that when money changes hands there's a change of relationship as well. With money comes obligation and expectations, power and hierarchy, give and take.

"Later," Emily said. "I have to figure out the prorated amount. You wouldn't want to pay a full month's rent if you're not here a full month."

"I never asked — how much is the cleaning deposit?"

"Oh, uh, would two hundred be too much?"

"No, I can do that."

He knew that most rentals demanded a cleaning deposit and first and last months' rent in advance, references, and proof of employment. Some even included an administrative fee. He just hoped his new landlord wouldn't turn out to be as crazy as she was naive.

The two bedrooms downstairs were connected by a common bathroom. Gary took the back bedroom, formerly Mary's sewing room, where the corner window afforded an oblique view of purple, cone-like Pride of Madeira flowers and a sliver of ocean beyond.

While Kyle parked himself in front of the TV, Gary did laundry and took a long, hot shower, mentally making a note to relinquish his live-aboard permit, buy groceries, and call Maria.

However, his first call was to Kyle's mom, to tell her where to pick up her son. There was a long silence at the end of the line before she said, "You mean your son-of-a-bitch brother isn't picking him up? He was supposed to pick him up. This is his week with Kyle. What the hell? I made plans. We're not going to be here."

"But Dave said..."

"I don't give a shit what Dave said. He didn't say anything to me. I'll be in Las Vegas with Lyle. I'm not taking a kid to Vegas!"

"But..."

The line went dead.

"Oh, that lying bitch!" Dave said when he was informed. "I left a message on her machine. She knows we've extended our stay. I don't know what to say. I don't know, I'll just...I'll make it worth your while, man. So sorry."

"When are you coming back?"

"Late Friday."

"How late?"

"Hold on." Gary could hear mumbling on the other end. He glanced at Kyle, wondering why people had children, if they didn't want the responsibility. "Flight gets in around 10:30. Then we gotta get our baggage and take the shuttle to our car. Probably won't get home until midnight. I can pick him up first thing Saturday."

Gary knew that *first thing Saturday* really meant late morning. "Do you want me to tell him, or will you?"

"I guess I better."

Gary handed the phone to Kyle and stood back to watch and listen to a one-sided conversation. By his glum expression, Gary could see that Kyle was unhappy, if reconciled to the situation. When Kyle handed the phone back, Gary said, "Look on the bright side — now that I've got this new apartment you won't have to go out on the boat if you don't want to; you can sleep in." He realized immediately that this was the wrong thing to say to a boy who had just been rejected by both of his parents, and quickly added, "But I could sure use your help."

"Can I steer?"

"You bet."

# # #

A small craft advisory was still in effect the following day, as wind tore the tops off each swell and littered a cobalt ocean with white caps. Gary was anxious. When the trapped crabs finished the bait, they would turn on their brethren. They were equal opportunity omnivores.

Mid-morning Emily heard a knock at her door — shave-and-a-haircut, two-bits. She went to the top of the stairs and yelled, "Come in, it's open!" Gary opened the door and before he could say anything she laid down the loose rules. "My door is always unlocked. Just open it up and call for me. My mother always did." Her mother's frequent interruptions had always been irritating, and only now did she realize she had traded her familial obligations for the obligations of a landlord. Still, her tenants were unlikely to interrupt as often, or as rudely or critically.

Gary looked up the steep stairway, and said, "We can't take the boat out in this weather, so I thought I'd go to the market. Is there anything I can get you?"

Emily smiled. Instead of making demands, this interruption came with an offer to do something for *her*. What a pleasant change of pace. "Come on up. I have a list."

At the top of the stairs he took in the layout. "Nice view from up here."

"It is when I remember to clean the windows." It was, in fact, a million-dollar view, but her parents had paid a fraction of that, as they'd bought before the emergence of Silicon Valley and its attendant increase in population. "I'm sorry, the Birminghams' back fence isn't much of view for you."

"Oh, I'm not complaining. I see enough of the ocean every day." He walked to the sliding glass door and looked down on the little red bungalow. "Isn't that where the guy was waving when we scattered the ashes?"

"It is. Tom lost his wife in an auto accident in February."

"I remember because it's the only red house in Seal Cove. It's awful small."

"It was one of the first built after the railroad came through."

"The lot must be worth a fortune."

"I expect it is, but Tom's not planning on moving."

"What's he do?"

"Wine importer, I believe."

"Isn't that a bit like bringing coals to Newcastle?"

"I guess. I think he only imports white wine. At least that's what he drinks."

"Have you been neighbors long?"

"Since I was nine. You met their son; he was on the boat. He lives in Washington state now."

She took the grocery list from under a magnet on the side of the refrigerator, added a couple of items and handed it over. "Keep track of what I owe you. I'll write you a check."

"I still have to write *you* a check," he said, "and sign the lease."

She promised to have the lease ready when he returned.

As he started down the stairs he said, "Kyle's staying, so don't be alarmed if you hear someone downstairs."

He's so considerate, she thought. "Leave the door open," she called after him.

She went back to reading. Ever since the success of Diana Gabaldon's Outlander series there had been dozens of copy-cat time-travel historical romances set in Scotland, most with Highlander in the title, virtually all with a cover that featured a long-haired, tartan-clad warrior with washboard abs.

Margaret Pennypacker, her alter-ego, could never write like that herself. She didn't know the country, she knew no Gaelic, and she couldn't conjure up believable 18th-century dialogue. But she could imagine running her fingers over rock hard abs and bulging biceps, and there was plenty of that in *At the Laird's Pleasure*. And if that was unrealistic, she judged it was no worse than young men drooling over airbrushed beauties in Playboy. *What's good for the goose is good for the gander,* she thought.

Not long after Gary left, Kyle called from the bottom of the stairway. "Mrs. Abbott?"

Emily put down her book. "Come upstairs!" she cried, feeling far too young to be called Mrs. "You can call me Emily." He paused at the top of the stairs, looking tentative. She waited.

"I was just wondering..."

Chapter Thirty-Six
The Theoretical Society

Emily was pleased with herself. She had secured a tenant who seemed a safe bet to be no trouble. She knew she could have charged more, but she would have had to interview prospective tenants and take the luck of the draw. Who knew what might happen? As her best friend in high school had been fond of saying, "The peeps be crazy, and we be peeps." They might turn out to be drug dealers, or addicts, Trumpists, conspiracy theorists, sour curmudgeons, partiers, political cranks, or sanctimonious Bible thumpers. You had to be careful who you shared your house with. She didn't know much about this young man and his nephew, but she did know he seemed sane, he was responsible and he wasn't intimidating. She had to admit that wasn't much to go on, but she was confident she'd made a safe choice. With the house owned free-and-clear, she didn't need much to get along — just enough to cover medical insurance, groceries, property taxes and utilities.

Almost immediately she noticed a difference. The character of the white noise changed. Pipes hissed in the walls, and the washer and dryer in the garage sent out an almost imperceptible thrum that reached all the way upstairs. It was good to have life in the house again, to know there was someone to turn to if she needed help with something.

An idea had been forming in the back of her mind ever since scattering the ashes and passing Smuggler's Cove on the way back to the harbor. She'd been reminded of her fictional sketch of rum runners, and wondered how she could bring a story of smugglers into the present day without making them into anti-heroes. The modern equivalent of rum runners were drug smugglers, but there was nothing romantic about smuggling drugs. It seemed a venal enterprise, lacking a noble purpose. Of course, since her character, Derek Law, was a reporter, he might be investigating smuggling, and perhaps he could progress from admiring smugglers like his rum-running great-grandfather, to seeing them as common criminals. She wasn't sure where to go with it, and until she found her story, she decided to switch to writing a Margaret Pennypacker romance.

Just before sunset the low clouds scudded off to the northeast, revealing a pale moon and Venus. Silt from the coastside streams had turned the inshore water milk chocolate, and further out the wind-scoured sea was a dark blue edging to purple as the sun set behind a bank of cumulus. Emily went downstairs to see how her tenants were settling in and was surprised to see Maria at the stove. Kyle was in the living room watching TV.

"Hello," Emily said tentatively. She hadn't thought to ask if there would be another tenant. "Are you moving in too?"

Maria turned around and eyed Emily with an arched brow and a frown. "Who are you? I've seen you before."

"I don't think we've been introduced. I'm Emily."

"You were on the boat."

"The boat? Oh, when we scattered the ashes. Yes. I'm sorry, I don't remember meeting you."

On hearing their voices, Gary got up and made awkward introductions, awkward only because of Maria's skeptical distrust of a potential rival. "Maria is just making us dinner," he said.

Maria smirked, thinking that the way he'd said it made her sound like the cook. She clarified the situation by staking her claim. "I'm his girlfriend," she said.

"Nice to meet you," Emily replied, because she had been raised to always be polite. Of course, there was no reason why she should have assumed it would be only Gary and Kyle moving in. There were two bedrooms, after all. But she wished she had asked. She wasn't sure how she felt about it. She hadn't really thought about renting to a woman. It wasn't a conscious thought; it was just contrary to her expectations.

Then Gary said, "She's not moving in."

Maria looked from Gary to Emily. "Yet," she added.

Emily was relieved. Not that she had anything against Maria, whom she did not know. It was just that, given the choice, she would rather not have another female presence in the house. She couldn't imagine a woman as an ally. In her limited experience, women were adversaries, or at best members of the same club jockeying for a higher post in the hierarchy. She didn't want to relinquish her new-found authority, or be subject to criticism, however tacit. It reminded her too much of her mother and the exhausting tension of wills.

Later that evening she heard a rhythmic tapping. She put down the romance she was reading. The tapping was slow at first, then faster, and she realized it was the sound of the bedstead bumping against the wall in the bedroom below her study. Tap, tap, tap. She held her breath, feeling like a voyeur. Her heart raced. They were making love, and she felt a painful longing. Down below, down in the dark, like creatures under the sea, they were playing out a scene from one of her own racy romances, a scene Emily could only imagine.

Later the front door closed. Emily switched off the upstairs lights and moved over to the window. She watched Maria get into her car and leave. She wanted what Maria had. She wanted a real life.

# # #

Gary returned with two bags of groceries and stopped at the top of the stairs, surprised to see Kyle and Emily sitting on the floor. "What are you doing up here?"

"Playing scrabble," Kyle said.

"I can see that. I mean *why* are you upstairs?"

"I was hungry and I cut myself opening a can of tuna. Emily gave me a bandaid."

"Oh." He looked to Emily and her smile reassured him that she wasn't annoyed. To Kyle he said, "You can help with the groceries. The bags are in the truck. I'll be down in a minute to help you put things away."

Kyle bounded down the stairs. Emily called after him, "We can finish our game later!"

Gary set the bags on the counter and took out a long receipt. "I kept all of your stuff separate. It's all at the end of the tape."

"I'll write you a check."

"I'll write you one for the cleaning deposit. Do you have the lease ready? How much do I owe you for this month?"

"I'm sorry, I didn't get around to it; Kyle came up and..."

"I'll tell him not to bother you."

"No, it was a pleasure. He's good company."

"Are you sure?"

"Yes, really."

He's a good kid, Gary thought. *His parents don't deserve him.*

They exchanged checks.

Emily said, "Are you free around six?"

"Do you need help with something?"

"No, I thought you might like to come meet our neighbor. I've been looking in on him since the accident, while Steve, (our other neighbor, two doors down) walks Tom's dog."

So that evening they left Kyle watching television and stepped outside into the blow. It was only a few steps to Tom's front door but they arrived looking like vagabonds, with watery eyes and cold noses. Emily smoothed her hair back into place and introduced Gary. This is Gary..." She stopped. "I'm sorry, Gary, I forget your last name."

"Myron," Gary said, shaking Tom's hand.

"I know you from someplace," Tom said. "I've seen you before."

"You look familiar, too."

"He's the captain of the boat we chartered to scatter the ashes," Emily explained.

"No, that's not it," Tom said, "I didn't go out on the boat. I'll figure it out."

Not long after, Wexler returned with Buddy, eyes and nose running. He found a box of tissues in the kitchen, and after a minute of dabbing at his eyes and blowing his nose, he said, "Oh, my god, it's brutal out there." It was theatrical hyperbole, but it did explain his early return. "I thought I was going to be blown off my feet."

Tail wagging, Buddy sniffed Gary's crotch.

Emily caught Wexler's eye and said, "Gary here is my new tenant."

The two men greeted each other with the same laconic, "Hey," and shook hands.

For Wexler's benefit she added, "Gary's a fisherman."

"What kind of fish?" Wexler asked.

"Crab, this time of year," Gary clarified. "I'll be trolling for salmon when the season starts in June."

"I went out on a charter boat once. Got seasick," Wexler said. "Hey Tom, I almost forgot." He reached into his jacket pocket and withdrew a CD in a jewel case. "Here's one of our albums. Just listen to that and you'll see what I mean about the spaces between the notes. Once you start listening you'll see why bass is as much about the tune as piano or guitar."

Tom took the CD and glanced at the cover. "I'll give it a listen. By the way, your piano tuner showed up yesterday. Thanks. It sounds great, even if I don't play myself."

Wexler sat down and played a few chords and a blues riff.

Gary's interest was piqued. "What band are you with?"

"I'm not in a band anymore; I'm..." He was about to say *I'm retired*, but caught himself. He might not be in a band currently, but he did have a gig coming up, and instead he said, "I'm working in the studio now, but I played bass with Totally Wrecked."

Gary was momentarily struck dumb. He had very little interest in celebrities, having never before met one, but he had always imagined that the famous would be somehow bigger than life in person. Wexler didn't seem particularly different from anyone else.

Wexler suddenly perked up. "Oh Tom, I just remembered a quote. It's not about music, but it's kind of the same thing. Twain once said something to the effect that 'It's not what you put into a novel that makes it great; it's what you leave out.'"

Gary asked what he was working on now.

Over the years, it was a question Wexler had usually shrugged off with a noncommittal *This and that*. Now, he was ready to move on. Accomplishments were nice to look back on, but polishing trophies wasn't as satisfying as earning them. It had been fun while it lasted, exhilarating, a tad unreal, and it was nice to have those memories, but it had ended badly, it was long gone, and he wanted to make new memories. It was so much more satisfying to have something new to say. "Just a little something for a documentary."

"Cool."

Emily, who sensed that this conversation could devolve into the Steve Wexler show, steered the discussion in another direction. "Tom has an interesting tale to tell."

Tom eyed her sternly. "That's private."

"You told *me*. How private can it be?"

"I'm not ready to share that."

"Oh, come on," she coaxed, "we're all friends here. Besides, it's fascinating."

Wexler looked amused and curious. "Yeah, come on Tom, let's hear it."

"Let it go."

"No one will judge you," Emily said.

Which was just plain dumb in Tom's view. Everyone would judge him, for better or worse, because they all had their own beliefs.

"We're waiting," Wexler said.

Tom ignored them and offered Gary a glass of wine.

"Make that two," Emily said.

"Three," Wexler added, "but you sit down, I'll get it."

Once the drinks were handed out, Tom and Emily sat in the wingback chairs, Wexler knelt by Buddy in front of the fire, and Gary sat on the piano bench, as they toasted with raised glasses all around.

Tom addressed Emily. "I'm getting my cast off tomorrow. Could you, by any chance, drive? I'll take you out to lunch afterwards."

From there the conversation meandered, as conversations do, from broken bones to modern medicine, to crabbing, to the wine they were drinking. Glasses were refilled before Wexler insisted Tom share the interesting tale that Emily had earlier alluded to.

"You'll laugh," Tom said. "Even my doctor thinks I'm crazy."

"Join the club," Wexler said. "We're all a little crazy one way or another."

"I believe in ghosts," Gary said matter-of-factly. "Some people think that's crazy, but I think you'd be crazy not to believe in them."

"See," Wexler offered, "a case in point."

Tom surveyed his audience, then sat back and began to tell the story of his Near-Death-Experience. No one laughed, because death had touched this house lately. It was like the elephant in the room that no one wanted to acknowledge, but everyone knew was there. They each weighed in with their interpretations.

"It's a big mystery," Emily said, "and I believe that you believe what you saw. But it might have been something your conscious mind conjured in a state of oxygen deprivation. I don't think I can accept a world run by Fates. I'd rather believe we have free will."

"It fits with some of the Eastern religions," Wexler said. "Don't Hindus believe in reincarnation?"

Gary said, "My grandmother is Catholic, and she believes in reincarnation."

"I don't think that's sanctioned by the church," Tom said.

Wexler asked, "Did you have a religious viewpoint before this happened?"

"No. I've always been a skeptic."

"It doesn't make any difference," Emily said. "I read that Christians and Atheists have the same experience, although they might interpret it differently. What you saw as Fate, someone else might see as God, or an angel."

"I didn't expect to get into a theological discussion over it," Tom said.

Gary piped up. "It's not theological if it's not religious, and I don't think Fates are covered by religion."

"Unless you believe in the Greek gods," Emily said.

"It's more theoretical," Gary said.

"Yes," said Tom. "I can only tell you what I saw. You can make up your own theory about whether it was real or not."

"Okay," Gary said, feeling a convivial camaraderie as the level in his glass diminished, a glass he now raised again in toast. "Then I hereby call to order The Seal Cove Theoretical Society."

"That has a nice ring to it," Tom said.

"To the Society," Wexler proclaimed with mock solemnity.

"To the Society," they all chimed in, and all leaned forward to clink glasses.

And thus was born The Seal Cove Theoretical Society, devoted to chit-chat, observation, current events, gossip, philosophical debate, and the occasional profound speculation, and bound together by friendship and forgiveness, which we all need, even if we deny it.

Chapter Thirty-Seven
Tom's Cast Comes Off

The day Tom was to get his cast off, dawn broke on a glassy sea. There wasn't a cloud in the sky, and flags hung limply on their poles. Gary made coffee and sandwiches and he and Kyle left the harbor shortly after the sun cleared the eastern peaks. They had a long day in front of them, pulling up crab, logging in the haul taken from each trap, and replacing bait.

Tom's doctor's appointment wasn't until 11:00 AM. From the mullioned window in his bedroom he looked out on a short garden of Aloe Vera, Echeveria, Pride of Madeira, and Sea Lavender, to the edge of the cliff and the tide pools beyond. He was missing Daisy and irritated by an itch under his cast that he could only reach with a chopstick, when Buddy's ears pricked up. The dog barked, jumped off the bed, and trotted out of the room to investigate. A moment later a knock sounded on the front door. Tom had left it unlocked (there was no need for locks in Seal Cove) and bellowed, "Come in!"

A second later he heard Wexler greeting Buddy. "In here!" Tom called.

Wexler looked in from the doorway. "I thought you'd be up by now."

"It's only 8:00."

"I have to be at the studio at 9:00. I thought I'd walk Buddy early."

"Be my guest."

"Looking forward to getting your cast off?"

"Like the last day of school. I can't wait."

Wexler snapped the leash on Buddy's collar. "I'll keep walking Buddy. I know you're going to want to take it easy on that leg for a while."

Tom cleared his throat. "Actually, I've been looking forward to walking him. I need the exercise. Laying around all day makes me stir-crazy."

"But he'll need longer walks. We walk all the way out to the brewpub and back, or even farther."

Tom was amused. "I may be old, but I'm not decrepit. I think walking might be just what I need."

"You'll want to build up to it slowly," Wexler suggested.

"We'll see."

That morning Wexler walked Buddy to the frog pond by the Seal Cove Inn. There was a spot under a cypress festooned with Spanish Moss, where Buddy liked to do his business, well off the path and away from spying eyes. After delivering Buddy back to Tom, Wexler packed up his standup bass, propped it in the passenger seat of the Corvette, and drove to Aural Sax to add his tracks to Henry Hodge's documentary composition. He was a little nervous at first, but the process of recording tracks hadn't changed much, even if the equipment had.

Emily slept in and was ready to go at ten past ten. Tom hobbled to his car, carrying one shoe. He handed Emily the keys. She repeated Wexler's question. "The sooner the better," Tom said. "I've had an itch that's driving me crazy."

As they passed Montara State Beach he said, "Do me a favor — poke me if I ever start talking about operations or broken bones. I don't want to be one of those old geezers who share every gory detail."

"You're not that old, Mr. B," she said.

"I'm not that young, either." In truth, the accident, subsequent surgery, sedentary recovery, and lonely days without Daisy had made him feel older by decades. Before the accident, he had rarely felt his age. As the years passed, he'd been continually surprised by the older man gazing back at him from the mirror, that man with bags under his eyes, wrinkled brow, and white hair. That wasn't him. He had awakened each morning expecting to see his 40-year-old face because he didn't feel any older inside. The accident had changed all that. Now he felt haggard and diminished. "I may not have said it yet, but I want you to know how grateful I am to have neighbors to help out. I don't know what I would have done without you."

"No problem," Emily said. "That's what neighbors are for."

"Not every neighbor would agree."

A little smile played around the edges of Emily's lips. It felt good to be needed. "It's what I do," she said. "It's what I'm good at." As they passed Rockaway Beach she realized something important. She'd looked forward to not having to take care of anyone, but helping Tom was no burden, just as helping her father had never been a sacrifice. She was happy to do it, because they appreciated her. It was as simple as that. Caring for others gave life purpose and the payment for such service was appreciation. Her mother had made that service a chore by the simple expedient of being ungrateful. It all came down to attitude.

At the hospital, a medical assistant removed the cast and washed Tom's leg, and gave him instructions on exercises to rebuild the strength. "Don't expect to be running around like before," she said. "It'll take some time to build your strength back in that leg. Your muscle has atrophied a bit." She gave him a cane, "Just to help while you're recovering."

He sized it up. "No offense, but that cane has no style. I have some walking sticks that will suit the purpose." He might limp for a while, but he didn't want to look feeble. A man who leaned on a four-prong cane was treated differently than a man with a jaunty walking stick.

Afterwards, they went to lunch at a Thai restaurant in Westlake. The lunch was fine, but he couldn't help remembering the last lunch he'd shared with Daisy before the accident. It reminded him of the empty home he would return to. He looked at the young woman across the table and said, "You shouldn't be here with an old man. You should be here with a boy your own age." He believed it, but it was an observation better left unsaid, as it set Emily to thinking of all she'd missed in life while taking care of her parents, and longing for a love she could only imagine. A melancholy pall settled over them both as they drove home in silence.

# # #

Tom had never felt the want of conversation when Daisy was alive. But now that he was a solo act, he welcomed the companionship. Watching the sun descend over a glass or two of wine with friends, fortified him to face the night alone in a silent house.

The Theoretical Society was an informal, loose-knit group. There were no rules, by-laws, dues, or requirements, and no set time to get together. They gathered on most days in late afternoon on Tom's porch or around the fireplace, depending on the weather. Occasionally the gathering would migrate to Emily's deck or Wexler's deck, but it was tacitly understood that its heart and hearth was Tom's house. It was not unlike the Lyceum or the Algonquin Round Table. Its membership was fluid. Sometimes one or another of them would bring a guest, and sometimes one or another of them had other things to do. Attendance wasn't mandatory nor even expected. It just happened, most days. The only constant was Tom, the undeclared leader of the pack, de facto patriarch by age, if not by temperament. That he was the glue that held them together was apparent when he was away on an errand at the (unofficial) hour. Others might show up bearing a bottle of wine, or food to share, or something to read aloud. Then they'd knock on the door and peer through the front window, and look for Tom's car on the street. And when they determined he was gone, they would go back to their own homes, quietly disappointed.

That first week they discussed what Fate might have in store for Tom. He put the question directly to his young neighbors. "Assuming for sake of argument that I'm not crazy and my encounter with Fate wasn't just a hallucination, I have to wonder why I was brought back. What loose ends was he talking about?"

"He? I thought you said Fate was genderless," Emily pointed out.

"You're right. It really wasn't human in any sense. But it did speak in my voice, so I think of it as male."

"Fair enough."

Wexler asked, "Do you have any regrets? Anything to atone for?"

"I could have been kinder, more understanding at times, but nothing I could remedy at this remove. And I did the best I could at the time. I was young and stupid."

"Maybe you were sent back to help someone," Emily offered.

"Or rescue someone from a burning building," Gary added.

But nothing obvious came to mind.

"Maybe," said Emily, "you weren't sent back to do something. Maybe you were sent back to learn something." That took the discussion in a new direction.

Talk of Fate, of course, sparked a debate on the possibility of an afterlife, the concept of the soul, and free will.

Also that week, they talked of Gary's unshakable belief in ghosts. Steve and Emily held that ghosts didn't exist. Given his recent experience, Tom thought they were probable, though he'd never seen one.

"There are two things I won't believe unless I see them with my own eyes," Wexler said. "Ghosts and levitation. Even then I'd have my doubts. It could just be a magician's illusion."

"You don't believe in magic?" Gary asked.

"Of course not," Wexler scoffed.

"Well explain this then — I saw a lady on the street in San Francisco pull a six-foot staff from a paper lunch bag. If that's not magic, I don't know what is."

"Don't be so gullible."

"I know what I see."

Tom detected a note of condescension in Wexler's dismissal and said, "Let's try to be civil here, Steve."

"What? I can't have an opinion?"

"Sure, you can have an opinion, but let's not trade insults."

Wexler faced Gary. "Were you insulted?"

"Not really."

"See," Wexler said turning back to Tom, "we're all friends here. You can call me crazy anytime. I won't mind."

"Okay," Tom said, "I think you're crazy."

"How am I crazy?"

"Let's drop it."

"No, tell me, how am I crazy?"

"Uh oh," Emily said.

"Okay. I think it's crazy to live a life without purpose. It's no wonder women aren't drawn to you. What do you have to offer? A few tales of a lurid past. Who cares?" The moment he said it he would have taken it back, but it was too late.

Wexler was slow on the uptake and had no response ready, which was just as well, as it took a moment for the truth of the words to hit home. He looked pensive, then he smiled and issued a loud guffaw. "You know, Tom, you can be a cruel bastard sometimes. On the mark, but cruel."

Tom was immediately apologetic. "Sorry, that was uncalled for. I've probably had too much to drink. But if I can give you any advice it's this: Don't wait for the perfect time to go after your dreams. There is never a perfect time. Just get on with it, and when you achieve one dream, always have another waiting in the wings. There's nothing worse than having no goal, nothing to strive for." It was a situation he found himself in at the moment.

"The voice of experience speaks," Wexler said sarcastically. "Okay, you may be right, you're probably right." Still, Wexler wouldn't be coerced into agreeing with his companions just to placate their odd beliefs. Neither did he want to sow discord. "Whatever, we can all agree to disagree, can't we? I might think ghosts and magic and out-of-body-experiences are just magical thinking, but that doesn't mean you have to think the same."

"It doesn't make any difference what each of us believes," Emily said. "It's enough that Tom believes in his near-death-experience, and Gary believes in magic, and I believe in *them*. So what can we do to help?"

That elicited a long discussion on empirical evidence and the nature of belief, all conducted in the spirit of friendly discourse, with no rancor or ill will, which was what set the Theoretical Society apart in this age of acrimony.

When the gathering broke up Tom took Wexler by the elbow. "I didn't mean to jump on you there, it's just that you apparently have talent, and I hate to see anyone waste talent. If you've got it, use it. Not everyone is so lucky."

Chapter Thirty-Eight
Of Dogs and Boats

At Aural Sax, Wexler and Henry Hodge worked until one. Recording music for a documentary was a new experience for Wexler. He'd always recorded with the band, and even if they were laying down separate tracks in a studio it had always been with members of the band present. Here he was in a booth, with headphones, listening to tracks that anonymous musicians had played before him, musicians he would never meet, but with whom he jammed as if they were in the booth beside him. One he knew only by reputation. First Hodge wanted a jazzy bassline to add to violin, piano and flute. Then he wanted the bass bowed like a cello, with long, sonorous notes that lay in the background, building layer after layer of sound. Hodge synced the music to the images, raising the volume at certain points, dialing it back at others, bringing out the piano or the flute as needed. It was meticulous work, even if the people watching the documentary would never appreciate what they heard. If done properly, the music would serve to enhance the emotional impact of the images, without ever taking center stage. The music, though vital to the impression of the whole, remained in the background where it contributed to the spirit of the images and narration.

When they were done Hodge asked, "Would you like to play bass over that jam session we listened to the other day?" — referring to the tracks laid down by Andy Espinosa and Bill Morrison so long ago.

"I don't have my electric bass with me."

"You can borrow mine. It might be interesting to do it with a standup bass, too. Just for interest sake."

So they recorded electric and acoustic basslines to play along with the guitar and flute. Listening to the combined instruments was both comfortingly familiar and a little eerie. He could play with his erstwhile bandmates again, as if they'd stepped out of the past. Time was no barrier.

Returning home close to the time he usually walked Buddy, he walked around the corner to Tom's. Tom answered the door in a herringbone tweed suit, trilby hat, and a dark blue tie with white polka dots. "Wow," Wexler said, "what's the occasion?"

"I got rid of that godamn cast. I can wear my old clothes again," Tom said, though he was reminded that his ivory-colored flannel suit had been lost to the accident and he'd have to buy another.

"I'll walk Buddy, if you want," Wexler offered.

"I'm about to go out with him now, but you can tag along, if you'd like."

Wexler agreed. "Besides, you might get tired, or Buddy might want to go farther."

So they walked down Sea Cliff to the Marine Reserve. There Wexler usually took the footbridge over San Vicente Creek and out the path that followed the edge of the cypress forest to the brewpub. But when Tom continued past the bridge and started to turn up Virginia Avenue, Wexler said, "He likes to take a dump up the hill by the frog pond. Then we usually go to the brewpub."

"I'm not going that far."

"I could take him," Wexler offered hopefully.

"No thanks. We'll just go up this way."

"But he might *go* in someone's front yard."

"I have a plastic bag," Tom said, firm in his resolution to be the one to walk his dog again. "I need the exercise, Steve. You go on, if you want. We'll be fine."

Wexler stopped and watched them go. He debated for a moment whether to follow or not, then shoved his hands in his pockets and crossed the bridge. A hundred yards up the path he saw two figures off the path under a cypress hung with Spanish Moss. The woman gazed nonchalantly eastward, as the dog humped its back in the familiar squat of peristalsis. As he drew closer he recognized them. Rosalind the dog finished her business and the pair tramped back through the weeds to the path. "She likes to go there," Rosalind the woman explained.

"So does Buddy."

"I mean, it's not like anyone is going to step in it over there."

"You don't have to convince *me,*" Wexler said. "Nobody *likes* to pick up poop."

"Last time I got caught an old lady yelled at me. But where does it go if you pick it up? It goes in a plastic bag in a trash can, which just ends up adding more plastic to the landfill."

"And it makes your trash smell," he commiserated.

"Right. And out there in the weeds it just turns back into soil. You know?"

"I know." They walked a little ways in silence. "Going to the brewpub?" he asked.

"In that direction, at least. Where's Buddy?"

"Tom (he's the owner) got his cast off today. He's walking him."

"You should get a dog of your own."

"I might."

"You're good with dogs, I can tell."

"Buddy is easy."

They came to the end of the path and the cypress forest and walked down Beach Street toward Smuggler's Cove. "What kind of dog would you get?"

And so it went. Pets were an entrée to a whole new strata of society. As they approached the brewpub Wexler said casually, "I'm going to stop in here for dinner. Can I buy you a drink?" It was a cliché and had always been offered as a loaded question, with the expectation of the drink leading to a more intimate relationship. He'd used the line so often it was threadbare. But this time he hadn't meant it that way. She didn't fit any of the usual categories. She didn't stir his libido, though she wasn't entirely unattractive. She was mature, unadorned with makeup, sure of herself. She might be his sister, he thought.

She politely declined the invitation.

"All right, then," Wexler said with a good-natured wave of the hand. "I'll see you around."

"But you could buy me a clam chowder."

At the reception desk he addressed the maitre d' by name. "Fernando, could you just tell whoever is serving on the terrace tonight to bring us a bowl of clam chowder and a fish sandwich?" On the way through the bar, he caught Gene Price's attention. "Could I have my usual sparkling?" He turned to Rosalind. "Anything to drink?"

"Iced tea?"

"And an iced tea," he added.

Gene smiled and gave him a nod.

On the way downstairs to the terrace, Rosalind said, "You don't by any chance own this place, do you?"

"No, but I eat here a lot."

At the fire pit she said, "I have a question, and I know it's an imposition, so feel free to say no, I just thought I'd ask. So next month I have to go to San Diego for a couple days, and I was wondering if you could take Rosalind. I'd pay you. She just hates the kennel is all. Of course, I don't know your schedule or anything."

The expression of eager hopefulness with which she waited for an answer hinted at a younger version of herself, without the crow's feet.

"My schedule is flexible. You should bring her over to get acquainted with the space before you go."

"That would be so wonderful. That takes a load off my mind. I wasn't looking forward to boarding her again."

"What's up in San Diego?"

Thursday evening they were all sitting on Tom Birmingham's porch. Kyle sat on the top step petting Buddy.

"I wish I had a dog," he said.

Wexler regarded them from a rocker. "I was thinking of getting a dog."

"What kind of dog?" Gary asked.

"A Lab, or poodle, I think."

"We had a poodle mix when I was a kid, " Gary said. "He was a water dog, loved to swim."

"I've never had a dog," Emily said. "My mom was allergic."

Tom sat up straight, snapped his fingers and pointed at Gary. "That's where I know you from! You were at the back door of The Careless Crab, the day of my accident." Gary shrugged. Tom persisted. "There was a dog."

Now the light of recognition shone in Gary's eyes. "Oh. Right. By the dumpster."

"That's it!" Tom, pleased with himself, sniffed his wine and took a sip. "Is he still there?"

"He was there last week," Gary said.

Kyle added, "I saw a dog in the restroom at the harbor. It might be the same one."

Tom turned to Wexler. "There you go, Steve. A free dog."

"I don't know."

"Of course he might not want to go with you. Red Ramsey was keeping him well-fed."

"Who?"

"Red Ramsey, the day bartender at the Harbor Bar. He was giving the dog restaurant scraps."

They were silent awhile, sipping their wine and watching the sun sink, and the clouds turn pink on the Marin headlands, faintly visible through the sea haze.

"What kind of dog is it?" Wexler asked.

"I don't know," Tom said. "A mutt."

"I think it's got curly hair," Gary added.

"He's awful dirty, though," Kyle said.

High cirrocumulus clouds caught the last light, flaring yellow and pink.

"It's going to be a calm day tomorrow," Gary observed. Addressing Kyle he added, "We should try to recover those lost pots tomorrow."

"What kind of pots?" Emily asked. "You can always borrow some of mine."

"Not cooking pots — crab pots."

"Oh."

"How did you lose them?" Tom asked.

Gary explained his suspicions.

"Bummer," Wexler said.

"Maybe Emily could go with us," Kyle said.

"I don't think she'd like it. We'll be out for hours."

"Let me speak for myself," Emily said. In truth, she didn't think she'd enjoy a whole day on the ocean. But she didn't like people putting words in her mouth, or thinking she was incapable because she was a girl. She had nothing better to do. Besides, if she were to write a book about smugglers on the coast, it might be worthwhile to tag along and take detailed notes — she hadn't paid much attention when they'd scattered the ashes; her mind had been elsewhere. "I would, actually, if there's room."

"It's not a pleasure boat. We'll be crabbing as we go north, and I don't know how long it might take to find the lost pots. We could be out eight or nine hours."

"It's up to you," Emily said, "but I'm game."

Now Gary found himself in a pickle. He wished Kyle hadn't taken it upon himself to offer. It was an awkward situation. He really didn't want anyone riding along as an observer. It was a small boat, there were liability issues, and it could be disruptive. At the same time, refusing his new landlord might create tension on land. The others all looked at him expectantly. "You'd have to work," he said.

"I wouldn't learn anything if I didn't."

Gary felt the trap spring shut. "You'll have to set your alarm. We leave the harbor at 6:00 a.m."

Chapter Thirty-Nine
Unanswered Questions

Tom missed Daisy. Before the accident he couldn't have imagined life without her, and yet here he was all alone. He'd taken for granted that she would always be there to talk to, and he would always be there to listen. It didn't have to be about anything important. She might chat about her students, or read him interesting passages from a book she was reading. They might speculate on politics, or technology, or their concerns for Douglas, or make plans for the future. And when all the words had been said she was always there to hold and share an affectionate kiss and a tender touch. She was his best friend, the object of his affection and appreciation. They'd known each other for almost fifty years, and though they'd grown old together, when he looked at her he still saw shades of her younger self peeking out from beneath the wrinkles, the graying hair and thinning skin. Her brown eyes still sparkled. Her smile still melted his heart. It had never occurred to him that he might outlive her. He'd never prepared himself.

In the hospital the nurse had told him his heart had stopped beating three times. "You were very lucky. You must have a guardian angel watching over you." Perhaps he did, but he didn't feel lucky. He would rather have gone with Daisy. How would he ever find her again? Why was he sent back? What loose ends was Fate talking about? And if Fate pulled the strings, why didn't he/she/it know this was going to happen? How much control did the Fates exert? How much free will did a man actually have? Tom wondered.

The house was too quiet. He reached down and stroked Buddy's fur. The dog beat his tail on the floor. "I'll bet you wonder where Daisy is, don't you Buddy? I wish I knew, but I don't. It's a mystery. I hope dogs are there. I wouldn't like it if there were no dogs in heaven, or wherever we go next."

He'd begun to doubt his near-death-experience. It had seemed real at the time. How else could he recall the memory of it, if it didn't happen? But he'd seen the indulgent expression of his grief counselor, and the way Douglas had immediately changed the subject when he mentioned floating above his body. He hadn't even got to the part about Fate and his past lives.

He could see that his son was afraid he'd lost his mind. Still, he remembered all of it so clearly, and why should he question his own senses? He fervently hoped it was all true; it was comforting to think he wouldn't just blink out of existence, that Daisy was out there somewhere waiting for him, and that they'd meet again in the next life. But how would he find her?

He remembered just vague snatches of the previous lives he'd been shown — a nomad, a rustic sheepherder, a simple sailor, a pig farmer, a French aristocrat, a fallen soldier. What was the purpose of living multiple lives if you couldn't remember each life in detail? He wondered if Fate would have gotten around to telling him if he hadn't been pulled back to life when he was.

"So many questions, Buddy; so many questions. Maybe dogs have it right. Dogs don't ask impossible questions. People are never content to let a mystery lie. I think that's why we invented religion and science, to answer the big questions. You're not religious, are you Buddy? Dogs are content to just be." Buddy thumped the floor again with his tail. "All you need is some food in your bowl and someone to scratch where you can't reach. You don't let big questions get in the way of enjoying each day, do you boy? Dogs and kids just run and have fun. That's what life's all about."

Then Tom remembered Fate asking him if he wanted to be reincarnated as a human or another species. Every species on the planet experienced life differently. Ask a dog to describe his life and he might describe it in terms of smell. "You know, it's funny," Tom said scratching behind Buddy's ear, "we call this planet earth, when most of it is water. Creatures deep in the ocean spend their lives under great pressure in pitch darkness, eating and trying not to be eaten. People wonder about aliens from other planets, but what could be more alien to us than a deep-sea creature? Even our fellow mammals." *What do whales and dolphins and seals think about?* He wondered. For all their assumed intelligence, whales and dolphins and even seals would have a completely different, and to us foreign, impression of what the world and life are all about.

Tom talked to Buddy, but Buddy didn't talk back. Buddy couldn't replace Daisy, but at least he could listen, and Tom was grateful for the company.

Chapter Forty
One Wonderful Day

Soon after daybreak on what was to become one wonderful day, Miss Behavin' slipped out of Pillar Point harbor. Once they were clear of the breakwater Gary handed the helm to Kyle. The engine purred. The prow creased the glassy green water and left a wake of bubbles to mark the boat's progress. The morning commute of gulls caught the first light over the mountains. It was one of those remarkably calm days when the swells peter out before reaching the shore.

Bundled in a sweater, anorak, and sock hat that hid most of her hair, Emily sat on the port storage locker, a small smile on her lips.

Observing her ease, Gary asked if she'd spent a lot of time on boats.

"Not a lot. My dad used to take me into The City and we'd take the ferry to Sausalito. And once we took a Blue-and-White Fleet boat out to the Golden Gate bridge. Have you ever done that? The bridge looks so much bigger from below."

"It's also pretty treacherous. The current there is fast and strong, and the fog can be so thick you can't see ten feet. We almost ran into a container ship coming into the Gate in the fog."

"We went out on a sunny day. It was beautiful."

"Well, you won't find this so much fun. We have a lot of work to do today." He surveyed their position. "Kyle, keep well outside that buoy. Aim for the Ritz." He turned back to Emily. "Coffee?"

"Sure."

Gary poured two mugs from a thermos bottle. "Sorry, I don't have any milk or sugar."

"Black is fine."

Kyle had the helm until they were upon the first set of pots at the southern end of Miramar beach. Then Gary took over to swing Miss Behavin' into position. Addressing Emily, he said, "If you want to make yourself useful, you can help Kyle with the winch."

196

It was a challenge she took willingly. She caught on fast, helping bring the pots up and sorting the crab without a complaint or show of squeamishness.

Then they headed out around Pillar Point, named after one of the offshore rocks that once sported a pillar-like projection — until the Navy used it for target practice during World War II. They gave Sail Rock a wide berth before stopping again off Whaleman Harbor.

All that morning they worked their way northward, pulling up the pots, sorting crab, replenishing the bait, and dropping the pots again. In between the drop zones, Kyle took the helm, while Emily peppered Gary with a continuous stream of questions, and jotted in a small notebook.

"What are you writing?" Gary asked.

"Just notes."

"Why?"

"Curiosity. I don't want to forget any of the details."

Gary voiced a thought before thinking. "Weird." He hadn't meant to blurt it out.

She only smiled and said, "Thanks."

He quickly backpedaled. "I don't mean that in a bad way, but you're not like other girls I know."

"Is it a competition?"

"No, sorry."

There was an awkward silence before she shook her head and said, "No need to apologize; I probably am weird."

"But in an interesting way," Gary said, trying his best to recover from his earlier gaff. "If you don't mind my asking, what do you do with the notes?"

"Sometimes I make up stories to entertain myself."

"Like a role-playing game?" Kyle asked. "Like Dungeons and Dragons?"

"I guess. I don't know. I've never played Dungeons and Dragons, but if you mean you make it up as you go, then I suppose it's a kind of role-playing game."

"What's the story about?"

"I've had this story in mind about smugglers on a boat."

"Present-day, or past?" Gary asked.

"Present, I think."

Kyle asked, "Is your avatar a man or a woman?"

197

"My what?"

"Avatar. You know, your character. Is your avatar a man or a woman?"

"A man," she said, thinking of her protagonist, dashing reporter Derek Law.

"What's he smuggling?" Gary asked.

"Oh, I don't think he's smuggling anything. I think he must be trying to defeat the smugglers."

"That could work. Sounds like a good game."

She almost said *It's not a game; it's a story*, but she didn't want to discuss it further. It was still too amorphous in its embryonic state. "You've given me a lot to think about."

Gary was pleased with himself. "Glad to be of service."

"Now, how far can this boat go on a tank of gas?"

"Including the reserve tank, at cruising speed she'll go about sixty nautical miles. We're a small boat. We only range about twenty-two nautical miles a day."

"How far is a nautical mile?"

"1.15 miles."

She made notes and watched Gary instruct Kyle out of the corner of her eye. Her father had never had the boyish energy and enthusiasm that this fisherman projected; he'd always been quiet, authoritative, and cerebral. But they both possessed an equanimity of spirit that she found reassuring.

At the same time, Gary exuded a youthful physicality that excited her. He was short and wiry, with tanned features and strong hands bearing the scars of a decade on boats. She'd always assumed she would be more attracted to someone like her father, a professor perhaps. She viewed herself as more intellectual than physical. And yet she couldn't dismiss the attraction of a man of action, simple, forthright, stalwart. A man like Derek Law. She wondered which kind of man she would find to share her life, or if she would find anyone at all. It left her pondering what Gary saw in Maria. They seemed polar opposites. He was so relaxed, Maria was wound tight. What did such disparate people see in each other?

"Does Maria like boats too?" she wondered aloud.

"God no," Gary chuffed, "she gets seasick."

#

And so the questions continued until they reached Gray Whale Cove. It was getting on toward noon.

"I'll take the helm," Gary said. "Kyle, get the logbook from the chart table. Emily, could you get the grappling hook from the transom locker?" She knew where to go because she'd been taking notes. "Attach the carabiner to the eye hook on the starboard gunnel, and thread the line into the winch."

He issued the challenge, never expecting her to follow through. It wasn't that difficult for her because she'd watched Kyle doing a similar operation with the crab lines all day. It was somewhat like threading the old movie projector she'd been in charge of one semester in high school.

"Now swing the arm out so the grappling hook can clear the side. Wait for my signal." He motored slowly into place. "Kyle, give me the GPS coordinates."

At the precise place they'd dropped the trap, he gave the order to drop the hook. "Watch the line," he called out to Emily. "When there's slack, you'll know it hit bottom. We're in about seventy feet of water."

"It's on the bottom," she called back.

"Lock it. Now I'm going to back up slowly." He backed away at scarcely more than idle, watching for the line to go taut. When it did, he cut the throttle and left the helm. "I'll take it from here." He pushed the button to start the winch. The line came in slowly as the hook dragged the bottom, then faster when it broke free. "Nope. We'll have to try that again."

On the third try, the grappling hook snagged something heavy enough to make the winch motor labor a little. It came up steadily until the pot broke the surface. Gary swung the arm over the side and lowered the pot to the deck. Inside were four live crabs and the carcasses of several more. "There's one trap. Now we have five more to bring up. Kyle, pull in the crab line and coil it on the deck. I'm not going to drop any pots back in this cove. We'll have to attach buoys and measure the salvaged line back in port. Sort the crab. I'm moving to the next position."

They were an efficient crew. The second pot came up with less effort. On the third, however, they were in for a surprise. Gary knew at once from the sound of the winch that they'd grappled something heavier than a crab pot, but the line kept coming in. The pot became visible at about thirty feet. Something had snagged on the pot, and as it broke the surface he saw that two pots had become entangled, and neither were his. They were old pots. The frames were mostly intact, but the wire screens had entirely rusted away. Inside the pots, a tangle of weed and barnacle-encrusted cargo nets enveloped two wooden cases so waterlogged that they fell to pieces the moment he swung the load onto the deck. Several bottles were broken, but among the shards of glass Emily found eight unbroken bottles wrapped in straw and four black bottles.

"What is it, Uncle Gary?"

"Junk."

What were the odds? Emily wondered. How could she be on this boat on this day? Most of us never recognize the moment when the pieces fall into place. We chalk it up to luck or coincidence. Emily stood dumbstruck and marveling. She knew it for what it was and felt Fate tap her on the shoulder.

Trolling the bottom for the last two pots proved fruitless. "They must've been dragged from their original positions," Gary said, "but it's getting late. We can try again another day."

Gary picked up one of the cargo nets and was about to throw it overboard when Emily intervened.

"Don't throw that."

He paused. "Yeah, okay, I know what you're going to say — it's littering — but I'm just returning it to the sea. I'm not carting it back to the harbor."

"It might be valuable."

He looked skeptically at the nets and rotten boxes. "Looks like junk to me."

She knelt and peeled back the straw to reveal a green bottle filled with liquid. "They're bottles."

"Yeah, I can see that. Is there a label?"

"No."

"So you don't know what's in it. It could be anything."

"Indulge me."

"Whatever it is can't be any good."

"I have a hunch."

He lowered the net to the deck. "I'm not hauling it back to the truck."

"I'll do it for you, then," she insisted.

He shook his head. "Fine, keep the bottles, but the rest of this stuff goes overboard."

She pulled a smartphone from her pocket, an extravagance her mother had allowed so that her daughter would be reachable at all times. "Let me take a few photos first. Hold up the net again. Smile."

From Emily Abbott's Notebooks
The Process is the Product

Steve was pontificating on the creative process tonight. Pontificating — good word. Puffed up as a Pope. Proud as a Peacock. Pompous as a prick? We were talking about favorite songs, and Gary asked him the usual question non-creative people ask creatives — "Where do you get your ideas?"

So, Steve strutted around like he was giving a lecture. I don't remember all of it, but I remember this much — "You can't force it into a mold. You have to trust your intuition, step aside and let the music flow through you. You have to let it take you where it wants to go. The process is the product."

That phrase stuck with me — The process is the product.

But going through the process, whether it's playing notes, putting paint to canvas, or words on a blank page, doesn't make it art, either. He says you can't force it into a mold, but I don't agree. You need structure. Without it, music is just noise, and carefully crafted sentences are just blather. The trick is in matching the form to the content.

And I don't agree that trusting your intuition is enough either. Intuition might inspire a haiku, or maybe a jazz improvisation, but when it comes to writing a novel, the idea that story will miraculously emerge from process is specious. It takes planning. You have to have an understanding of where you're going. Whether you're following a formal outline or carrying a general blueprint in your head, you have to know where you're headed, and the longer the form, the more planning it takes. Like a symphony, a novel is too long and too intricate to improvise. It's like a museum filled with paintings and exhibits designed to lead the consumer through the rooms in a somewhat logical order for a satisfying experience. Even then, it may not be art. What makes one song, or one story resonate, while another falls flat? What makes one book literature and another just cheap escapism? What makes one song or one story last, while another is quickly forgotten? If I only knew the answer to that question, I might do something worthwhile.

Chapter Forty-One
Dogs and Boats and Booze

Back in the harbor, they delivered crab to the wholesaler at the end of the pier, before tying up in their appointed slip. Gary saw the Barbara Anne backed into her slip on the next fairway. "I need to talk to somebody," he announced. "Kyle, help Emily. Then hose off the deck."

Emily liberated several empty cardboard boxes from The Harbor Bar. She and Kyle loaded them with the sandy, straw-wrapped bottles, as well as four black bottles with stenciled labels, and carried them up the ramp to the pier. There were twelve bottles in all. Emily sighed. The carton was too heavy to carry all the way to the truck. "Stay with the bottles. I'm going to get the keys and bring the truck to us."

She walked down the next ramp to the Barbara Anne, where Gary was talking to an older man marked by years of working outside. His deeply tanned face was grooved with wrinkle lines at his eyes and mouth, his nose was red, and white stubble sprouted on his cheeks and chin. He wore a long-billed cap with an embroidered medallion that read, "Aged to Perfection."

They were talking about fuel capacity, range, electronics and diesel engines. Emily waited for a gap in the conversation before politely interrupting and asking Gary for the keys. So intent was he on his conversation that it took a moment for the request to register. He hardly looked at her as he dug in his pocket and dropped the keys into the palm of her outstretched hand.

By the time he returned, Emily had loaded the bottles into the truck, and Kyle had hosed off the deck. Once Gary was satisfied that Miss Behavin' was shipshape they loaded the recovered crab pots into the truck bed and piled into the cab, Kyle in the middle.

As they unloaded the recovered pots at the staging area in the corner of the parking lot Emily asked, "Who was the old man?"

"Bill Whittaker. I was asking him about the Barbara Anne. She's a good size boat, not too big, but big enough to handle twice the number of pots I can in one go, and she's set up to trawl for salmon. You could make a good living with a boat like that."

"I take it you want to buy it?"

"Turns out he's not selling, and even if he was, I couldn't afford it. Besides, I still owe the bank for Miss Behavin'."

"How much is a boat like that worth?"

"It depends, but I'd say between 160 and 200,000. Some of the bigger boats go for half a million or more."

"How much is Miss Behavin' worth?" Kyle asked.

"Are you always so nosy?" said Gary.

"Just curious."

"Curiosity killed the cat."

"Kyle is not a cat," Emily persisted. "Are you going to answer his question?"

"I paid 75,000 for her."

Emily calculated. "So if you sold Miss Behavin', you'd still need over a hundred grand, give or take."

Gary thought about this for a moment. "I'd have to come up with another 20 to 30,000 to qualify for a bigger loan. My parents won't cosign, and I don't think I'll have enough by the time the crab season ends. It's nice to dream, though. Listen, I'm dropping you two off. I have some errands to run."

"What errands?" Kyle asked.

"I'd like to find a deckhand for tomorrow. I have to refuel. Then I have to paint a few buoys and measure more line for the recovered pots."

"I can help paint," Kyle said.

"No, you need to pack. Your father is coming in the morning."

Emily, who had been listening, was curious. "This is your dad from Hawaii?"

"Yeah," Kyle said. "I have to go back to school on Monday."

Emily was confused. "He's coming to visit?"

"No," Gary said, "he's coming back from vacation. They should be arriving around midnight."

"Oh, he lives here?"

"Over the hill — San Bruno."

Emily looked to Kyle. "So you go to school in San Bruno?"

Kyle nodded. "Cowell Middle School."

"And you live with your dad?"

"And my mom. I stay with Mom one week, and Dad the next."

"I see." Emily said. "But you've been on the boat for a while, haven't you?"

"For all of spring break."

"He's been a great help," Gary said appreciatively, ruffling the youngster's hair. "By the way, Kyle, don't let me forget to pay you before you go."

"What time is Dad coming?"

"Knowing your father, later rather than sooner. I still have to go out to tend the pots, so I hope he's not too late."

"Can I come again in the summer?"

"If I'm still in business."

Emily was dismayed. She'd made erroneous assumptions and now had to rearrange her expectations. "I'll be sorry to see you go," she told Kyle sincerely. She'd so looked forward to having young energy in the house. "I was hoping to play more games with you."

"We could play tonight."

"Do you know quarto? I think you'd like it."

In truth, she had envisioned a different dynamic in the household, Kyle acting as a kind of buffer between the adults. One of the reasons she'd picked Gary as a tenant was her perception that he was a kind and responsible young man, who showed as much by taking in his abandoned nephew. The reality was somewhat different. Although it didn't diminish her estimation of his character, living in a house (even if it was a duplex) with a young bachelor would never meet with her mother's approval. She could hear her mother's indignant protestation. The emphasized word would have been, "unseemly." Immediately she chided herself for conjuring up that nagging voice. She could do as she wished now and only hoped that in time her mother's voice would die to a whisper.

# # #

Tom needed a respite from thinking. He couldn't get over the feeling that he shouldn't be here. It was a mistake. Human beings can believe anything, no matter how it deviates from the laws of nature, no matter how nonsensical, no matter how it defies logic. A man will believe anything that serves to succor his psyche. But Tom couldn't believe he had "loose ends" to tie up, as Fate had suggested. After all, Fate had been ready for him to move on. His story was ostensibly complete. So how could he have loose ends? What did it mean? How would he recognize these loose ends when he saw them? For that matter, how was it that Fate hadn't seen this coming? Didn't Fate say their story had been hijacked by a colleague? And if his personal Fate wasn't the provocateur here, who was? It was far from clear. He was left guessing, and it was driving him crazy.

All the while he wondered, where was Daisy? How would he find her? He had too many questions without answers.

At night he dreamed he was there again in that nexus between life and death. But in his dreams, Fate remained silent. During the day he brooded and stared out to sea, his mind blank but troubled. He talked to Buddy and Buddy listened sympathetically. But it wasn't the same as talking to another human being. He tried talking to Daisy but had no sense that Daisy's spirit was close or listening. She had moved on.

So it was only natural that he looked forward to the daily meeting of The Seal Cove Theoretical Society. At first, this gathering seemed unremarkable. It was just a spontaneous congregation of neighbors who came, in the beginning, to help out with Buddy and to commiserate with his recent loss and recovery from his injuries. They'd been extraordinarily solicitous in his misfortune and that wasn't something he took for granted. He had, however, expected them to fade away as he recovered. So it lifted his spirits each day as they continued to drop by before sunset for a glass or two of wine and a bit of conversation. It was the one time of the day he looked forward to.

# # #

Wexler's Ford F150 pickup needed to be driven about once a week to keep the bearings lubricated and the battery charged. On the morning that Miss Behavin' set out to recover the lost crab pots, Wexler drove the pickup to the small parking lot behind the Careless Crab, where the employees parked. Sure enough, a dog was resting on a pallet behind the dumpster. As Wexler slowly approached, the dog perked up. Wexler crouched down and put the back of his hand out in supplication. The dog wagged his tail. Wexler turned his hand over to reveal a dog biscuit. The dog sniffed and took the treat. Wexler scratched him behind the ears. He was a healthy-looking dog, though his curly hair was dirty and matted.

Wexler tried the back door but found it locked. The bar didn't open until eleven-thirty. So he walked around the building and entered The Careless Crab, which opened early to accommodate the fishermen. There he ordered coffee, an artichoke omelet and hash browns for himself, and a hamburger and French fries to go. He ate slowly and read a few pages of the new Margaret Pennypacker novel to kill the time until the bar opened.

Red Ramsey was the only person in the bar when he entered at 11:30. Ramsey was lining up a few Bloody Marys, Screwdrivers, Mimosas, and Ramos Fizzes for patrons of The Careless Crab. Ramsey put his hands on the far. "What can I do you for?"

"I'm interested in the dog out back."

Ramsey brightened. "Lookin' for a pet?"

"Maybe."

Then Ramsey laid out the story. "I'd love to take him myself, but the Mrs. won't allow it. You live near here?"

"Seal Cove."

"You know he'll probably run back here at some point."

"That's okay, as long as I know where to find him. You can call me and I'll pick him up." He gave Ramsey a card with his contact information.

So Wexler went out the back door and used the extra hamburger to lure Roscoe into the cab of the truck. Roscoe was ecstatic. He may have preferred a crab sandwich, but this was no dried up scrap. It was big and juicy and it tantalized his nose for the five seconds it took to wolf it down. Then Wexler rolled down the passenger side window enough that Roscoe could stick his head out. From the first moment the truck started to roll, Roscoe was in heaven. He had almost forgotten how wonderful it was to fly down the road. The parade of smells was heady!

In Half Moon Bay they stopped at Pretty Pets. While Roscoe was given the full spa treatment — wash, blow-dry, coat and nails trimmed — Wexler bought a collar and leash, a large, padded dog bed, chew toys, dog treats, kibble, a comb, and a book on how to properly train a dog.

Back home, Roscoe sniffed his way around the house and the backyard. Clearly, there had been another dog here, but there was no dog here now. At the edge of the cliff, he lifted his leg to add his own scent. This new man was good. He was free with the food, and he could scratch those inaccessible spots between his shoulder blades and his tail. What a good thing it was to have a human to anticipate his needs.

Wexler dragged the new dog bed into the music room, where Roscoe lay contentedly listening to Wexler play the piano, until he fell asleep.

Chapter Forty-Two

Karma

Wexler and Roscoe were the first to arrive on Tom's porch. As soon as Tom opened the door, Buddy bounded out to take stock of the newcomer. Roscoe stood nervously still until Buddy had sniffed his butt and was satisfied they were of the same political persuasion. Roscoe returned the favor. Then both dogs wagged their tails and padded from one human to the next, garnering a scratch behind the ears, a vigorous rub between the shoulder blades, and a dog biscuit each for good behavior. Emily arrived with Kyle, a quarter of an hour later.

Wexler proudly introduced them to Roscoe.

"He's so soft," Emily said.

"He doesn't look like the same dog," said Kyle.

"I took him to a groomer."

"He seems to get along with Buddy," Tom observed. Then he looked around and asked, "Where's Gary? I thought you were going out on his boat today."

"We did," Kyle said. "We got a lot of crab, and we found some of the lost pots."

"And something elsc," Emily said.

"Uncle Gary dropped us off. He had some stuff to do on the boat."

"What stuff?" Tom asked.

Emily was fascinated by how Tom made everyone around him feel at ease. He was old enough to be Kyle's grandfather, but Kyle conversed with him as a peer because Tom didn't talk down to him.

Emily waited for an opening, then asked Tom how much he knew about hard liquor.

"In my business, you tend to know about everything that's behind the bar. The first distributor I worked for imported Canadian Whisky, Sambuca, Tuaca, and rum. Why do you ask?"

Emily related the story of how they found the bottles.

"They're probably filled with seawater," he said.

"How can you tell?"

"Let's take a look."

So Emily went next door and brought back two bottles, one green, and one black. "I have eight of these green bottles, and four of the black ones."

The moment Tom laid eyes on them he said, "Well, that puts a different spin on things."

"What does?" Emily asked.

"The necks are dipped in sealing wax, which should have kept the water out. They used to use wax to protect bottles from being adulterated. These days a few producers use wax as a matter of style, Maker's Mark being the most notable."

He picked up the green bottle and held it up to the light to inspect the contents. "There's no ullage."

"No *what*?"

"Ullage. Evaporation. The liquid is still into the neck of the bottle. The wax probably kept water out. Of course, with no label there's no way to tell what's in the bottle. The shape and color of the bottle suggests whisky of some sort. Scotch, or Canadian, or Irish, even Bourbon. Or it could be cheap moonshine. Assuming no seawater got in, it should still be drinkable because liquor doesn't age in the bottle."

"How much would a bar pay for it?"

"Sorry to rain on your parade, but you have to have a wholesale liquor license to sell to a retailer."

"Couldn't *you* sell it? *You* have a liquor license."

"No, I have a wholesale wine license. You'd have to get a liquor license and enter the bottles into a bonded warehouse. There would be taxes to pay and storage fees, and you'd have to account where it came from. You don't want to open up that can of worms. No, they're really more of a curiosity than anything. Shall we open a bottle?"

"How do you know it's not poison, or solvent or something?" Wexler asked.

"There's only one way to tell for sure." Tom turned a hopeful expression toward Emily.

"Might as well," she said.

Tom used the tiny knife on a sommelier's corkscrew to etch a line around the neck of the bottle. The wax, being brittle, chipped off easily, exposing the stopper, a wooden disk attached to a short cork. Trying to ease it out, the wooden disk tore free from the cork. The corkscrew fared no better, breaking the cork into small pieces that fell into the bottle. He went to the kitchen and returned with a tumbler, a sieve, and a glass of water. The sieve caught the cork pieces as he poured a couple of shots into the tumbler. He smelled it and passed it around.

"I want to smell it," Kyle said.

Tom raised an eyebrow, but held the tumbler under Kyle's nose. Kyle took a deep whiff, his head kicked back, his eyes went wide, and he sneezed. "People drink that?"

"It's an acquired taste," Tom said. He brought the tumbler to his chin and inhaled. "It's got a nice nose." He took a drop on his tongue and let it evaporate. Then he added a splash of water to the tumbler. The nose blossomed, revealing a fragrance of vanilla and spice. This time he took a sip. "That's nice and smooth. Definitely not moonshine. Probably Canadian rye."

He poured tumblers for Emily and Wexler and added a dollop of water to each.

"I'm not much of a drinker," Emily said.

"Then you have a lifetime supply. How many bottles did you say you had?"

"They're not really mine. Technically they're Gary Myron's. But in answer to your question, eight."

Wexler picked up the black bottle and turned it around. "This one has writing on it." He rotated it so Tom could read the simple label stenciled in white paint on the side of the black bottle.

"Holy...!" Tom began and, in deference to Kyle, held the vulgar expletive in check.

"What is it?" Emily asked.

"How many of these did you say you have?"

"The black ones? Just four. What is it?"

"Fonseca 1918 vintage port," he said. "*Pre*-Prohibition. It would have been aged a few years in barrel, or pipe as they call them, and bottled in the early 1920s."

"Could you sell that one?" Emily asked. "Port is wine, isn't it?"

"It is, but you wouldn't sell something like this to a retailer." Tom felt a thrill of excitement. "I think this could be worth quite a lot to a collector though. It's hard to tell. Old wine, like art, is often sold at auction, and it all depends on who does the bidding."

"How much? Take a guess."

Tom shrugged. "I don't know. Four or five hundred dollars a bottle, I should think. Maybe more."

"If it's a hundred-years-old," Wexler felt compelled to point out, "wouldn't it have turned to vinegar?"

"No, probably not," Tom replied, "since ports are fortified with spirits they can last for decades. When I was just starting out in the business I had a hundred-year-old Ramos Pinto that was amazing, and about five years ago a collector friend of mine treated me to a taste of the 1927 Quinta do Noval that was equally stunning."

"Let's taste it," Wexler said.

Emily took the bottle back from Tom. "If it's worth a lot, we should ask Gary before we taste it."

"Emily's right," Tom said as he fitted the whiskey bottle with a stopper. "Would you mind if I shared this whiskey? I have a friend who might find this interesting."

"Is he a collector?"

"No, he's a bartender, but he knows a lot of collectors."

"Could Gary sell the whiskey to a collector?"

"Maybe, though old whiskey isn't very valuable because spirits don't age in the bottle. The only real interest would be to compare it to a modern bottling to see if the recipe has changed, but you can't do that because you don't even know who made it. As to the port, I do know another colleague who haunts the auction houses. He might be able to tell you what the port is worth. I'll put feelers out this week."

Wexler and Roscoe were the first to leave. The sky was twilight blue and the squid boats roamed the dark ocean with yellow sodium lights to draw their prey to the surface like moths to a flame.

Emily turned to Kyle. "You ought to get packing. I'll make us some dinner in a little while."

When he was gone she asked Tom, "How do you suppose those bottles ended up there?"

"Who knows? Smugglers were creative, but there were always losses. Sometimes they'd be forced to dump it overboard if revenuers were closing in. Other times it was just bad luck — overturned boats and the like. I'll bet a lot of the sea glass you find on the beach dates from the Prohibition era. But I don't think your bottles ended up on the bottom by mistake. I suspect they were meant to be submerged. Why else would they be sealed with wax? If the cases were lowered to the bottom, connected to buoys on the surface, they'd look just like any other crab buoys and they could be picked up later whenever it was safe. If I had to speculate, I'd say the buoys were torn free in a storm."

"That makes sense."

#

Gary found Emily and Kyle upstairs playing quarto at the dining table.

"Don't you have to pack?" he asked his nephew.

"Done," Kyle said.

"There's dinner on the stove," Emily said. "You'll have to reheat it in the microwave." She wrinkled her nose. "What's that smell?" Then she looked embarrassed. "Oh."

"What?"

"You smell like crab."

"Yeah, pretty nice, huh? They ought to bottle this scent."

"We took showers already," Kyle said.

Gary peered at the concoction in the skillet. "What is this?"

"Israeli couscous, onions, mushrooms, basil pesto, and cheddar cheese."

Gary heated a bowl of the stuff and sat down at the table. "What's the game?" he asked.

"Quarto," Kyle said. "It's really easy to play, but it's hard not to make mistakes."

Emily asked about Gary's errands.

"The pots and buoys are ready, but I didn't have any luck finding a deckhand. There was one guy, but I couldn't give him a definite time, because I can't leave until Dave picks up Kyle."

"Sorry, Uncle Gary."

"It's not your fault. It's my brother's."

"I could do it," Emily said, "on one condition."

A month before he would have rejected the offer out of hand, but he'd learned a thing or two since then. It was true that experienced deckhands made the work go faster, and they didn't require instruction. On the other hand, he'd worked with a twelve-year-old boy for two weeks, and what Kyle lacked in strength and experience, he'd made up for with enthusiasm and a willingness to learn. He'd made it fun again. Emily had shown a similar temperament, and she was one of the few people he'd met, man or woman, who was not intimidated by crabs. Not only could crabs pinch, they also had sharp points on the ends of their legs and on the edge of their carapace. And crabs were surprisingly strong.

"What condition?"

"That we go back and drag the bottom for more bottles."

"What do you want with old bottles?"

So she told him what Tom suspected about the vintage port.

"Really? You'd have to be crazy to pay that kind of money for one bottle. Are you sure?"

"That's what Tom says."

"Lucky you," Gary said.

The discovery had left her with a moral quandary that didn't take long to resolve. As a child, she'd found a wallet stuffed with what seemed a fortune at the time. The term *finder's keeper's* kept running through her mind, though she'd been quite sure her parents would disapprove. She kept it five long days, her conscience growing heavier with each hour before she guiltily showed it to her father. He'd made it simple. "Did you earn this money?" No. "Is your name on that driver's license?" No. "Do you have food to eat, clothes on your back, and a roof over your head?" Yes. "Then you know what to do." So they tracked down the owner, who had given Emily a twenty dollar reward for returning the wallet, and she'd felt so unburdened that her heart sang with joy for days.

So when Gary said, "Lucky you," she naturally replied, "No, lucky you."

"I would have thrown them out," Gary said.

"But it took your boat and equipment to bring them up."

He couldn't argue with her sense of morality, but he had his own set of principles. "I usually don't look a gift horse in the mouth, but those bottles would still be sitting on the bottom if I'd had my way. Why don't we split any profits?"

"Are you sure?"

"It's only fair."

"Okay then, partner."

"But I'm still not spending the whole day dragging the bottom. I'll be trying to find my missing pots. If we happen to snag something else, so be it. Is it a deal?"

"It's a deal."

"We opened a bottle of the whisky."

"Was it any good?"

"I guess, if you like whisky. I let Tom take the open bottle to share it with somebody. I hope you don't mind."

Kyle made a move. Emily moved a piece of her own to block him.

"You know," she said, "you should thank whoever cut your lines."

Gary smiled at the irony. "I suppose so. If that stuff is really worth what you think it is, I must have a guardian angel looking over my shoulder. How many bottles do we have?"

Chapter Forty-Three
Wexler & Rosalind

The first time Wexler took Roscoe on a walk up the path that skirted the cypress grove, he was looking forward to introducing Roscoe to the other dogs that frequented the Seal Cove Brewpub. That he was also hoping to make the acquaintance of a young woman was beyond question. He didn't have a particular woman in mind. It wasn't even the foremost thing in his mind; it had simply become the subtext of any social outing. He approached the eternal quest with a hopeful heart. Whether or not anything came of the unspoken pursuit, today he was filled with a strong appreciation for womankind. He was, after all, a male of the species, driven by nature to compete for the attention of females. The undercurrent of sexual desire gave life its zing. He yearned for the approval and admiration of women. He was captivated by their joy, their vibrancy, and ineffable beauty. And yet, he did not understand them at all.

There was, too, a growing fear that he was past his prime. He'd seen the signs. It was getting progressively harder to pick up women, even for a casual conversation. As he aged, the pool of prospective candidates diminished. All the good ones had been snapped up by younger, better-looking men than he, men who had more to offer than an interesting past. Men like Cliff and MacDonald. He remembered Tom saying *Anyone can get laid.... Have you ever been in love?* And when he admitted he'd never figured out what women want, Tom's response had been brutal — *One thing is for sure, you must not be giving it to them, or one of them would have stayed.* That thought kept looping in his mind, "...or one of them would have stayed." What was wrong with him? He obviously wasn't giving women what they wanted, or one of them would have stayed. Did he want someone to stay, someone permanent, someone he couldn't live without and who couldn't live without him? Someone to love? Of course he did. But it seemed a pipe dream. *Have you ever been in love?* Tom had asked. What was love, anyway? It was such an amorphous term. To hear some tell it, love was what living was all about. But one "loved" in so many different ways. There should be different words for different kinds of love. Love for a pet, for instance, or for your parents, your siblings, a friend, an experience, an object. Love for the opposite sex in general. Love for a particular person. Love in all it's degrees from mild appreciation to obsession. Had he ever been in love? Of course he'd been in love. Half a dozen times, though others might dismiss those moments of bright and joyful insanity as infatuation. But just because his infatuations had never grown into long term relationships didn't diminish their power and effect. It saddened him that his loves, or infatuations had faded with time. On reflection, the objects of his desire had usually been the first to lose interest. Perhaps they just grew bored. *"One thing is for sure, you must not be giving it to them, or one of them would have stayed."*

What did women want? To judge from the covers of the dozens of romance novels he'd read, novels written by women, for women, it was all about money and muscles. Those book covers featured washboard abs, bulging biceps, and sweat. Rarely a face. Sometimes a faceless stud in a tuxedo. Sometimes a cowboy, his hat obscuring his face, his shirt unbuttoned to display improbable musculature. Why were women so obsessed with muscles? What did muscles signify? Protection. Power. Animal magnetism. Decisive action. All of that and then some, he realized. It was a depressing thought, as his physique was neither robust, nor was he physically capable of defending himself against a determined attacker. For a brief moment, he considered joining a gym. If only he could bulk up, things might be different. Of course, muscles weren't the only attraction. Money was an attraction that few women could discount, as reflected in titles like *The Billionaire Boys Club; The Billionaire Banker; The Secretary and the Billionaire; Billionaire's Bargain; Billionaire's Baby; No Ordinary Billionaire;* and *Knocked Up By a Billionaire.* Wexler had plenty of money, but he was no billionaire. Celebrity was an attraction, though his erstwhile celebrity had worn thin with time. What did he have to offer?

He found a place to sit on the terrace at the brewpub, and scanned the crowd. There were Hubert and his owner, Speedy and his owner, Bella and her owner, Lilly and her owner, Colin and his owner, Rosalind and Rosalind. He caught the latter's eyes and held up a hand in greeting. At the far end of the terrace, he saw a young woman with a German Shepard. She was perhaps ten years younger than himself. Not jailbait, but not his type, either. There were a few couples, and a dogless woman who looked appealing, though she was frankly out of his league, and besides, he thought he saw a ring on her finger. He was still assessing the female contingent when Rosalind and Rosalind came over and sat opposite.

"Who is *this*?" she asked with real interest.

"This is my new dog, Roscoe. Roscoe, meet Rosalind and Rosalind."

Roscoe wagged his tail and sniffed his canine counterpart. Rosalind wagged her tail. Everything was copasetic.

Wexler watched the interaction and smiled. If only human relations were so simple. He looked at Rosalind, the woman, and felt none of the usual desire. She was not his "type" — too tall, too old, too strong. He was reminded of a photo he'd once seen of a sturdy milkmaid carrying wooden buckets suspended from a yolk that lay across her shoulders. Like that milkmaid, there was nothing delicate or frilly about Rosalind. But she was friendly. And if he wanted to know what women wanted, why not go to the source? Not the object of his desire, but a friend who could just tell him outright how he could improve his chances of attracting and keeping a woman without resorting to trickery. So many problems could be avoided, he thought, if only people were honest and direct. Of course, in hindsight he could see that he had neither been particularly honest nor direct with the women he'd picked up. Not really. Though they surely knew his ulterior motives.

A waitress came by and asked if they'd like to order. Wexler looked to Rosalind. "My treat," he said.

"That's not necessary."

"My pleasure."

"In that case, a bowl of clam chowder and a glass of white wine."

"Make that a bottle of Sauvignon Blanc for the two of us," he said, "and I'll have two hamburgers."

When the waitress was gone Rosalind said, "Two?"

"One is for Roscoe. Although, now that I think about it, I guess I should divide it between the dogs."

"That might be better."

"Right. I wouldn't want Rosalind to think Roscoe was stingy."

"No, not on their first date."

"Are you match-making?"

"Just coming to a natural conclusion. Come to think of it, since you're paying for dinner, are *we* on *our* first date?"

"Oh no, actually, I'm hoping to pick your brain."

"About?"

"What women want."

"I can't speak for other women."

"But you're representative. So tell me — what am I lacking? What's my problem?"

"I don't think I know you well enough to say. Why do you think you have a problem?"

"Because I can't get a woman to stay. I mean, I've had a number of relationships, but none of them have stuck."

Rosalind looked at him for a long moment, then smiled. "That's adorable," she said.

"What?"

"Your honesty! It's refreshing."

Wexler ignored the comment. "A friend of mine, who was married for a long time, said I must not be giving women what they want, or one of them would have stayed."

"Have there been many?"

He looked up, started to count, and gave up. "Well, let's just say I haven't been celibate."

"That's good to know."

"I don't try to chase them away. They just leave."

She was silent for a long moment as she considered. "I'd like to help, but I'd have to see you in action to venture an opinion."

"Never mind. Forget it. Let's change the subject."

"Have you introduced Roscoe to Buddy?"

"Oh sure, they get along fine."

"It was sweet of you to walk him."

"Buddy is a good dog."

"Where did you find Roscoe?"

Wexler recounted the story.

"Our dogs seem to be getting along," Rosalind observed.

Wexler divided the second hamburger and parceled it out.

They finished the bottle of wine and left at the same time. They walked to the corner under the streetlamp, where their destinations diverged. Rosalind the dog pulled toward Roscoe.

"I don't think she's ready to call it a night," Rosalind the woman said.

"Why is that?"

"I think she wants to get to know Roscoe better. And didn't you say she should get acquainted with your place before I go to San Diego?"

"You're welcome to come over, if you want. Do you like champagne?"

Chapter Forty-Four
Unused to Being Used

In company, Tom put on a brave and cheerful face. Left alone, he deflated. What was he doing here? What was the point? Buddy regarded him with doleful eyes. "If it weren't for you, Buddy, I'd check out of this motel. I'd go upstairs and find Daisy. And I'd give Fate a piece of my mind. I have a lot of questions for that..." He refrained from uttering the epithet on the tip of his tongue, in case Fate was listening. "I don't want to be here anymore." Buddy whined, as though he understood. Tom knelt and scratched behind both of the dog's ears. "I just want it to be the way it was."

He fell asleep watching the Giants and Padres, and dreamt he was in that sterile white space with Fate once more.

"What are you doing back here?" Fate asked.

"I should ask you the same thing," Tom said. "Why are *you* here? Why don't you have more lives to live?"

"This is my appointed work," Fate said defensively.

"Who appointed you?"

"I don't remember. I've been doing this for..."

"Were you ever human?"

"Not as such."

"What does that mean?"

"Look, Life is a mystery. Death is a mystery. You and I are just layers of that mystery."

"Who do you answer to?"

"I don't understand the question."

"Who tells you what to do? Who makes up *your* story?"

"I don't know."

"You said my grandmother was a...a...an intern or something — a Fate in training."

"Yes."

"So what were you, before you were a Fate?"

There was a long silence before Fate replied. "I've lived so many lives I can't begin to explain. We're just the energy that drives the universe. You, me, your grandmother. It's a mystery. Why can't you be content with the mystery?"

"I like to think there's a reason for every action."

"Don't kid yourself."

"You're saying it's all random chance?"

"I'm not saying that."

"What are you saying then?"

Fate struggled to develop an analogy. "We're each like an atom in fission. We burn bright for a millisecond, and as we do we power the universe. We are part of the universe, and we feed the universe, and we *are* the universe. Does that make sense?"

Tom reflected for a moment. "You mean we make a collective reality?"

There followed a silence so long that he thought Fate may have fallen asleep. Then Fate spoke once more.

"I suppose that's one way to look at it. No one really knows. I've given this much thought, and it's my opinion that our purpose is to be conscious. To be cognoscente. To give meaning to the void. A universe without consciousness has no meaning, no reason to exist. We give existence a purpose. In our awareness, we are existence itself. I could be wrong, of course, but that's what I've come to understand after an almost infinite series of lifetimes."

Once again there followed a long interval of silence as Tom digested this bit of news. Finally, Fate spoke up. "I probably shouldn't have said any of this. It's only an opinion. What do I know?"

Tom was incensed. How disturbing it was to find that the force that animated him, that informed his life's choices, was as clueless as himself. Mysteries beyond mysteries. But then the very ability to think, to suppose, to theorize, seemed a great gift. "Existence is rather wonderful, isn't it?" he said.

"It's heaven."

"It's all we have."

"It's what we make of it."

Tom could almost get his mind around that. We each design our own lives with every decision we make. "So what am I supposed to do with what's left of this life? You said I could help tie up loose ends. What loose ends?"

"Your influence is yet to be exhausted."

Somewhere on a nearby beach a sea lion barked and Tom startled awake. For a moment he was caught between worlds, before awareness of his surroundings pulled him out of the dream. *Wait*, he thought, *I have more questions*. Even as he thought it, he knew the oracle was suspect. This Fate, the Fate he'd been addressing in his dream, the Fate that had answered his questions, however ambiguously, was just a figment of his imagination. This Fate was within him.

# # #

Wexler awoke to the drone of a small plane passing overhead. His mouth was dry, his head felt like it was stuffed with cotton, and a dull ache pulsed behind his eyeballs. He rolled onto his side and found himself staring into the eyes of Rosalind, the woman.

"I didn't think you'd ever wake up," she said. "Do you want breakfast?"

"What time is it?"

"Almost eleven."

He groaned, thinking about the previous evening. How had he let himself do it? He liked this woman well enough, but he didn't want to complicate their friendship with sex. "About last night," he began.

"You're *not* going to claim you don't remember?"

He let out a deep breath. Amnesia would have been a convenient conceit. "No, of course not. It's just...I just didn't plan it that way. You know, too much alcohol and inhibitions go out the window, and..."

"Don't worry, I don't blame you for taking advantage. I'm the one who should be apologizing (except that I don't believe in apologizing for anything). I seduced you."

"You did?"

"Of course I did. You were snockered and I took advantage."

"You're not angry then?"

"Why would I be angry? I got what I wanted."

"What was that?"

"Physical intimacy, skin to skin action, a pleasant way to pass the time."

"You weren't disappointed?"

"No. Whatever problem you think you have with the ladies, it's not in the bedroom. I mean, you're not the best I've had, but you'll do."

"Thanks, I guess."

"I'll whip us up some omelets, and then I have to get home. Things to do, people to see."

Chapter Forty-Five
More Treasure

Dave showed up earlier than anticipated on Saturday morning. He hugged Kyle and shook his brother's hand. "Thanks, bro. We had a great time, and we couldn't have done it without you."

"Not a problem. Kyle has been a great help. Speaking of which...." He took a money clip from his pocket and peeled off some bills. "Here you go, Kyle. You earned it."

Kyle was flabbergasted. No one had told him that he'd be paid.

"Now, your dad and I have some business to discuss." Gary led Dave inside to settle their accounts.

"Jesus, that's expensive," Dave said.

"It's what we agreed on."

"I know, but it's a lot of money."

"You didn't have to stay longer."

"Okay, I get it. It just seems a lot for babysitting."

"I wasn't babysitting. Kyle did a lot of work. He was a great help."

"So, what am I paying for?"

"Don't go there, Dave. We had a deal. Pay up."

Dave grudgingly wrote a check.

"He's welcome back, anytime," Gary said.

Dave sighed. "Sure, 'til next time."

# # #

Overnight the fog had moved in, smothering the coast like a wet blanket. The sea and the sky were a uniform gray. There was no horizon. Gary and Emily motored from spot to spot aboard Miss Behavin', pulling up pots, sorting, baiting, and lowering the pots to the bottom again, moving from one to another in numbing repetition.

Emily wondered how she'd gotten herself into this. Why had she volunteered? Certainly, there was the excitement of a treasure hunt, the thrill of anticipation, like panning for gold, or fishing, or now that she thought about it, pulling up crab. You never knew how many there might be. But she'd also wanted to spend a day alone with Gary. Not, she told herself, that she was attracted to him. She was just curious. She hadn't been alone with anyone close to her age, male or female, since she'd left college to care for her mother.

"I have to admit, even *I* get a little green around the gills in this kind of weather," Gary admitted.

Emily was fighting a tinge of nausea. "My hands are freezing and I smell like crab," she said.

"Welcome to *my* world."

"Doesn't the cold bother you?"

"You get used to it."

Emily snugged down her sock hat. "I don't think I ever could."

"Warm your hands on a coffee mug. There's a thermos down below."

"I used to watch fishing boats going by and it looked so romantic out here in the sun and fresh air, but this weather ruins my fantasy. This is cold, hard work!"

"Some days are better than others, but I like it. It's honest work, and I'd rather do this than push paper across a desk all day."

They traversed the waters of the marine reserve at speed, leaving a long white wake until they found themselves off Gray Whale Cove. They found the first lost pot on the second try, then spent the better part of an hour dragging the bottom for the last lost pot. They came up with seaweed, rocks, rusted fragments of old pots, rotten cordage, ruined binoculars, a cellphone, another grappling hook, a plastic milk crate, empty beer bottles, cans, and plastic bags. Once the grappling hook got stuck and required careful maneuvering to dislodge it. Finally, their search was rewarded with a disintegrating cargo net containing two wooden cases. Permeated with salt water, the nails had rusted away and the cases collapsed under their own weight as they were lowered onto the deck. One case yielded eleven unbroken barnacle-encrusted bottles of champagne, the labels of which had long since dissolved. The other case contained a dozen green bottles of whisky. The last lost crab pot was nowhere to be found.

# # #

Emily started for the Harbor Bar to requisition some empty liquor cartons, while Gary hosed off the deck. She was in a good mood, so when she passed Maria on the ramp she greeted her with a smile and a cheerful hello. Maria did a double-take and stopped in her tracks. Emily continued on, intent on her task.

Returning with two cardboard boxes, she passed Maria once again at the foot of the pier. This time Maria scowled and muttered, "Bitch."

Emily was taken aback. "Excuse me?"

"You heard me. Stay away from my boyfriend."

"What? I wasn't.... We were just crabbing."

"Just stay away."

"How am I supposed to do that? We live in the same house!"

"Stay away, or you'll be sorry."

Emily watched her go, feeling more than a little guilty for her thoughts, for even if it had been idle fantasizing, she had wondered what it would be like to take Gary as a lover.

"Maria's unhappy," Emily said as she stepped aboard.

"Don't worry about her. She has a jealous streak."

"Jealous people do stupid things."

"She's not violent; she's just loud." He began coiling the hose on the dock.

"Why would she be jealous?" Emily asked.

"Because she can't imagine a man and a woman being in close proximity without some hanky panky going on."

I wish, Emily thought but didn't say. She was a little disappointed he hadn't even tried to flirt.

"She's been a little tense since Trump was elected," Gary said. "She and her parents are illegal. Technically she's DACA (you know, Deferred Action for Childhood Arrivals?). She's been here since she was two. Her brother and two younger sisters were born here."

Just then Bill Whittaker came strolling down the dock, hands in his pockets, and stopped in front of Miss Behavin'.

"Myron," he said, "I've been thinking about our conversation. Do you have a minute?"

Gary finished coiling the hose and straightened. "What do you have in mind?"

"I don't know how this rumor about me retiring got out. I was probably bitching about the weather or some equipment failure. You know how it is — you say something like 'I hate this business' or 'this shit makes me want to quit,' and a deckhand overhears, and the next thing you know word gets out that you mean to retire. I really hadn't thought about it. But since you brought it up, it got me to thinking. I've been at this thirty-six years. In another ten I'll be sixty-five. I don't know if I'll have the energy to keep going that long. I got a bad back and some arthritis in my hip. Anyway, I discussed it with the wife, she handles the books, and she was saying I ought to find a way to cut back, maybe take on a partner (a minority partner), someone younger, who still has the drive and experience to get the job done. That way I could still keep my hand in it, have an income. What do you think? Would you be interested in an arrangement like that?"

"I might be, sure, but I don't know if I can afford it. How much are you asking?"

"I can't tell you exactly, she hasn't figured that out yet. I just wanted to know if you'd be interested."

"Yeah, yeah I would be. Can't hurt to talk about it. I'd have to see if the numbers work, you know, but yeah, I would be interested."

"Good, that's good. So, I'll get back to you with more details after she's come up with something more concrete." He paused glancing up at the cenotaph to lost fishermen at the foot of the pier, nodded slowly, took a few steps down the dock, then turned back. "I don't want to rush into anything, understand. I just want to explore the possibilities. Even if I decide to do this, it might not be for a while."

"Okay. Sounds...sensible," Gary said.

Whittaker nodded to Emily and gave Gary a casual salute, then headed toward the ramp. Gary watched him go.

Emily began carefully loading the old bottles into cardboard boxes. "I must bring good luck," she said.

"How do you figure?"

"First we find treasure, and now you have a business opportunity fall into your lap."

"Don't get too excited. Your so-called treasure could turn out to be seawater, and Whittaker's offer might not pencil out."

"Don't be so negative."

"I won't, but I won't count my chickens just yet either."

He did, however, have to admit that opportunities were suddenly opening up all around him, opportunities he might seize if only he kept his eyes open.

Chapter Forty-Six
Consulting with Tom

When Wexler, Roscoe, Rosalind, and Rosalind came around the corner they saw Emily and Gary standing in the street staring intently at Tom's house. Emily saw them and held a finger to her lips.

"What's up?" Wexler whispered.

Emily gestured toward Tom's front porch. The old man sat, chin to chest, asleep in his Adirondack chair, a bottle of cognac on the little table, a half-full snifter cupped in his right hand.

"How long has he been like that?" Wexler asked.

"We arrived about five minutes ago," Gary said, sotto voce.

"We've been wondering if he'll spill his drink before he wakes up," Emily said. "Care to wager a bet?"

Wexler considered. "Five bucks he doesn't spill."

"You're on."

Wexler bent down and unleashed Roscoe, who wagged his tail at Buddy. Buddy then sniffed at the two Rosalinds. The dogs seemed copasetic.

"Why are we standing out here?" Wexler asked.

"We don't want to startle him," Gary said.

After a short consultation, they padded quietly up the walk to the porch and gingerly took their accustomed chairs. Short a chair, Rosalind sat on the top step wondering if Wexler would be gallant enough to offer her his chair, but he was oblivious. No one spoke. Wexler's rocking chair squeaked rhythmically. Gary, who was carrying two bottles, placed them at his feet. The two dogs shuffled from person to person looking to be scratched or petted. When a few minutes had passed, Buddy brushed against Tom's legs. He stirred, brought the snifter to his lips, sipped without opening his eyes, and in a minute was snoring.

Wexler had been eyeing the cognac covetously. He arose quietly and let himself into the house, returning with two wine glasses, a juice-glass and another snifter. He eased himself back into the chair, unstoppered the XO cognac, and poured a round. Emily took hers, stuck her nose into the glass and immediately stifled a sneeze. Tom's eyes opened slowly. He brought the snifter back to his lips.

Wexler turned to Emily. "You owe me five bucks." Then he leaned toward Tom. "I see what you mean; this really is smooth. I'll have another splash. How much did you say this goes for?"

Tom took a deep breath and looked sleepily around him. "Sixty dollars at Costco," he mumbled. He picked up the bottle and poured a dollop into each extended glass. "It's getting cold out here. We should go inside."

Tom tossed off the rest of his own snifter and ushered them into the house. "Come in, come in," Tom said. "I'll stoke the fire. It's been a dreary day. And who is this enchanting creature?" he asked as Rosalind stepped over the threshold.

"Which creature?" Wexler asked.

"Young lady," Tom said, ignoring his long-haired neighbor, "I'm Tom Birmingham, and you are...?"

"Rosalind. Rosalind Kenway."

"Welcome to The Seal Cove Theoretical Society."

Emily and Gary shed their coats. The dogs sniffed at the garments with interest.

"We found more bottles today!" Emily announced brightly.

"Tell me about it," Tom said with a yawn.

"We found eleven bottles of these, and a case each of these two," Gary said, handing him three bottles. Tom examined the green bottle. "I'd say it's more whisky, based on the shape and color of the bottle, but without a label, we can't know exactly what kind it is. This other is obviously champagne. Again, without a label, we can't know which champagne house. Unless, of course, it's written on the cork. He held the bottle up to a lamp. "Who knows? It could be flat. It could be seawater. But the cork seems intact, and there's still a little air in the neck, so I suspect it's water-tight. Champagne isn't known for its longevity, but it might be worth something as a curiosity. The black bottle looks like more port. I put out some feelers yesterday to a couple of colleagues. They might have a better handle on what all of these bottles are worth. They'd couldn't offer an opinion without tasting it first, of course, but I wouldn't get my hopes up. It would make an interesting story though. I'll bet Bob Hammer at the Review would write about it."

Emily looked puzzled. "I thought you said a bottle could be worth hundreds of dollars."

"If no water got into it, the Fonseca port would be valuable, because it's identifiable. These other bottles remain a mystery, although under the circumstances we can probably assume the unlabeled bottles are of a similar age. Keep in mind, collectibles like this don't really have an intrinsic value. They're worth whatever someone is willing to pay. That could be fifty dollars, or a thousand dollars, or nothing."

"But the four with labels are worth a lot, right?"

"Like I said, you might get five or six hundred a bottle or more. I don't know for sure — they're rarities."

"Oh," Emily said disconsolately. "That's something. I was just hoping all the bottles.... I guess I was getting ahead of myself."

"It's a fantastic historical find," Tom said.

"It's not exactly the fortune I thought it was though."

"We have four bottles of the Fonseca," Gary reminded her. "We might get a couple of grand for that, and that's nothing to sneeze at. And who knows what we'll get for the others."

"No, you're right."

"What did you think they were worth?" Tom asked.

"Never mind. I was just hoping."

"Lottery fever," Wexler said.

"What?" Emily asked.

"Lottery fever. You know, you start thinking about what you can buy with it before you've won it."

"Oh, I don't need anything."

Needs were one thing. Wants were another. She wanted to live a real life that matched her fictional romances. She wanted to find the treasure and tame the handsome rogue. She wanted to be the heroine of her own story.

Wexler thought her response odd. "If you don't need anything, why would you care how much it was worth? What could you do that you can't do now?"

Gary was still thinking about Bill Whittaker's offer. "I'd buy a bigger boat," Gary said, thinking aloud. With enough money, he could buy into that opportunity.

"I suppose the first thing I'd do is travel," Emily said. "I've always wanted to see Paris, and Rome, and Switzerland."

"If that day ever comes," Tom said, "I have a friend who rents out an apartment in Paris. It's a lot cheaper than a hotel."

Gary couldn't imagine why anyone would want to visit a city. He found the bustle and crowds claustrophobic.

Wexler, who had the money to travel well, had never been bitten by wanderlust, and in any case, what he wanted couldn't be bought. He couldn't have told them what he wanted if they'd asked, because he didn't understand it himself. He had all of the physical comforts. It was only since Tom had pointed it out that he'd been plagued by a niggling sense of purposelessness, like a constant headache that stole his verve.

"Paris is beautiful in the Fall," Tom added.

"Oh, I wouldn't want to travel in the Fall. It's my favorite time of year here. I'd travel in the summer and get away from the fog."

They all concurred that fog season on the coast was a dreary time of year.

"If you want to get away from the fog you can come stay with me," Rosalind said. "I have a small place on Maui."

"Really?" Emily exclaimed, thinking *How lucky I am to have wealthy friends.* "I may take you up on that."

"It's just a little condo I rent out most of the year, but I always take some time for myself in August or September."

Rosalind's revelation set them all to thinking. Emily hoped she was serious. Gary wondered what kind of fish could be caught in the warm waters off Hawaii, and if Miss Behavin' was seaworthy enough for an ocean voyage. Wexler imagined himself lying in a hammock strung between coconut palms on a beach, watching bikini-clad women parade temptingly past. Contemplating a lonely retirement, Tom saw himself like solitary Prufrock, walking at the edge of the warm sea with his flannel trousers rolled to his knees, and stifled a tear of self-pity.

From Emily Abbott's Notebooks
Boat Names

Every boat reflects the dreams and personality of its owner. As you stroll the docks you'll find all manner of names, fanciful names, no-nonsense names; humorous names, boats named for wives and lovers, poetic names, wishful names, philosophical names, names that play on words, and clever puns.

Pleasure boats lean toward the humorous. Names like Tax Refund; The Office; Independent Claws; Escape Claws; Episode Won; Booty Calls; Duty Calls. There are names like Gone Fishin'; Lost Bet; Full House; Topsy Turvey; Ketch 22; Bad Juju; Grand Gesture; Hang Loose; Knot Again; Knot at Work; Knot Too Shabby; Pain Killer; Yabba Dabba Do; Wanderlust; and Whimsey.

Working boats tend to sport more dignified names. Names like Grateful Spirit; Ghost Rider; Marauder; Moriah; Barbara Jo; Mary Jane; Martha Grey; Katie Lee; Miss Behavin'; and Second Wind. There are Serenity; Lost Dreams; Sweet Dreams; Windsong Warrior; Gypsy Dancer; Western Flyer; and Carpe Diem; Pale Horse; Pacific Star; Polaris; and Necessity.

Below the name on the transom, the boats declare their home ports. Most are from the home port of Half Moon Bay, but there are always a few boats from northern ports — San Francisco; Alameda; Sausalito; Bodega Bay; Fort Bragg; Eureka; Crescent City, and from the southern ports of Santa Cruz; and Moss Landing; Monterey; and Morro Bay.

Chapter Forty-Seven
Real Treasures

Gary and Emily were the last to leave. Stepping into their common entry Gary said, "I'm starving, I haven't had a thing to eat since this morning."

"If you want leftovers, I have a refrigerator full," Emily said. "I can't get used to cooking for one; I'm always making too much."

"What have you got?"

She looked up as though reading a menu on the ceiling. "Mushroom risotto, mac and cheese, chicken fettuccini, curried prawns, cauliflower, roasted potatoes, Italian sausage..."

"Stop! Okay, I get the picture. Yeah, that would be great. I'll take a shower and be up in fifteen. Thanks!"

So began a pattern. Over a glass of wine at Tom's, followed by dinner at Emily's, they developed a pleasant routine that suited them both. For her part, she really did find it easier to cook for two, and after a lifetime of geriatric conversation, she welcomed the company of someone closer to her own age. Besides, having spent so much time in casual banter at the putative Seal Cove Theoretical Society, there was no pressure to make a good first impression, as there would have been on a date. She reasoned that if nothing else, dinner with Gary was good practice for the future. So, more often than not, they ate together at Emily's table, except on Thursdays and Sundays when Maria was off work. Now, you can only spend so much time across a table, looking into one another's eyes, before a certain rapport develops. Gary came to feel a brotherly warmth and relaxed camaraderie for Emily. She, in turn, daydreamed about something more intimate, hoping he would make a move.

One Wednesday when Gary failed to show up at Tom's, Emily returned home and opened his door saying, "Are you coming up...?" She stopped mid-sentence at the sight of Gary and Maria eating pizza at the kitchen table. She looked disconcertedly from one to the other, then smiled brightly and finished with "...to pay you your rent?"

Looking from one woman to the next, it took a moment for him to reply. "Uh — I'll slip a check under your door, if that's okay."

"Sure, no problem, sorry to interrupt," Emily said, perfectly aware of the blush rising in her face.

She hurried back upstairs, but Maria's raised voice and the sound of breaking china left no doubt as to the ensuing argument below. Soon after the front door slammed Gary came upstairs to sheepishly report two broken glasses, a broken plate, and a scarred cabinet door. He offered to replace the broken items and repair the cabinet.

Emily took a shaky breath. "I didn't expect her..."

"No, it was a surprise to me, too. She switched shifts today."

"Well, then...."

"She brought a pizza. Want some?"

Emily didn't even have to think a second. "Why not?"

# # #

If hope of a valuable treasure had dissolved, the germ of an idea had begun to grow. She'd started her new story with a flashback of Grampa Ed telling a six-year-old Derek Law about his great-grandfathers, who had been on opposite sides of the law during Prohibition. The moral gray area between personal freedom, the letter-of-the-law, and the spirit-of-the-law appealed to her.

However, it was only when Gary mentioned Maria's predicament, that Emily found the same kind of moral ambiguity in the present. Should "the sins of the fathers" be extended to their children? It set her to wondering. If Maria and her parents were deported back to Mexico, they would be separated from Maria's siblings, who were U.S. Citizens. What mother wouldn't do her utmost to be reunited with her children? And what of Maria, who had no memory of a country she'd left as an infant? Wouldn't she try to reenter the U.S. to reclaim the only life she'd ever known? It was a compelling premise for a drama.

Writing as Robert Cole, Emily had to build the stakes and present Derek Law with a moral conundrum. Could he be sympathetic to both illegal immigration and the rule of law? How far would he bend? Would he remain law-abiding, choose to look the other way, or scoff at the law, and at what price? It was a fertile field for fiction. The story came plodding along like a dog on a mission, sniffing the ground, pausing here and there to ferret out a missing piece of the puzzle, lifting a leg to leave its own scent, then wandering across the road to explore the detritus of an empty lot.

Muriel Davis, a professor of creative writing at the College of San Mateo, had once told her to trust her instincts. "If you get lost, let your characters tell you where the story is going. Don't force them to do things they wouldn't feel comfortable doing. Let them lead the way." It was honest advice, but it wasn't working. Derek Law wasn't talking. *If Miss Davis knew my characters, she might not have the same opinion*, Emily thought. *My characters couldn't write a novel if their lives depended on it. And their lives do depend on it.*

Some days bits and pieces of the story coalesced. Other days nothing new came of her ruminations. Emily sat in her wingback chair, one leg tucked under the other, chin resting in the palm of her hand, looking blankly out to sea, and allowed her mind to wander where it would. She wrote random notes, character sketches, backstories, snatches of dialogue. It was slowly coming together. She started with the handsome investigative reporter, Derek Law, remembering Grampa Ed's stories about his great-grandfathers' exploits during Prohibition. When the lady who cleans Derek's house is deported back to El Salvador, her daughter Gloria who, like Maria, is in the DACA program, comes to Derek for help. Some of his contacts lead him to Hector, a fisherman suspected of smuggling women into the country. Meanwhile, Immigration and Customs Enforcement officer, Paul Overstreet, is tracking a racketeer named Earl "Domino" Jackson, who is suspected of selling women into prostitution. Somehow Derek Law and Paul Overstreet would combine forces and — but that was as far as her story had progressed. So it was that Emily, in the guise of Robert Cole, began to build a story out of thin air.

# # #

Most evenings before dinner Emily would go next door for a glass of wine and a little human contact, for though she did not miss her mother's demands, she did miss hearing a real human voice. She'd tried leaving the television on in the background just to hear the chatter, but found the frantic pace and artificial gaiety too distracting. She treasured her time with Tom. Most days they were joined by Wexler and Roscoe, often Gary, and sometimes by the two Rosalinds. Even Maria, whose time was governed by work schedules and familial obligations, managed to drop by a day or two a week. On those days Gary studiously avoided looking at Emily and seemed a little more reticent to join the conversation. Maria would sit next to him if there was a free chair, or at his feet if there wasn't, patting him on the knee or squeezing his hand proprietarily, sanguine in her position. Towards Emily she remained aloof, her dislike always simmering just below the surface. Emily tried to observe the couple with the detachment of an anthropologist studying the mating rituals of a previously undiscovered tribe.

Later in the evening, as Emily sat quietly reading upstairs, she was attentive to other sounds in the house, and when the downstairs bed creaked and the headboard tapped its breathtakingly primal rhythm on the wall, her heart would race, and she would think how absurd it was that Maria could have seen her as a threat, she who was so laughably inexperienced. Other twenty-six-year-olds had been on their own for years. They had taken entry-level jobs after high school, or had graduated from college and were becoming established in their careers. They had had boyfriends. They had had sex. Some even were married and had children. They had experience. They'd made mistakes. They were taking their place in adult society. Emily saw herself being left behind, an outsider.

One cold afternoon, having come to a roadblock in her storyline, she decided to visit Tom earlier than usual. He was sitting at the kitchen table in front of a tall bottle of Alsatian Pinot Gris that was already half gone. He saw her look and said, "I know, I know, you don't have to say it."

"I didn't say anything," Emily said.

"But you were thinking it."

"Maybe I was, maybe I wasn't."

"I don't want a lecture right now. I know I'm drinking too much, but screw it, it eases the tension."

"Mind if I have one?"

"Help yourself."

She knew the routine. She fetched a glass and poured it half full.

"I'm probably a bad influence," Tom said morosely.

She studied him as she sat down across from him. "Probably."

"Just don't follow my example. You have to take care of your health at your age. Me, I don't give a damn anymore. What's the worse that could happen? I could die (again) and maybe find out what I was sent back to do, or learn, or whatever the hell it is Fate has in mind. I hate not knowing. I feel like he's — sorry, *it's* — playing games with me. Sometimes I think I'm dead and all of this is just a dream. A bad dream."

She regarded him a moment. "I think you should go back to work."

"Out of the mouths of babes."

"You need something to occupy your time and keep your mind off your troubles."

He nodded his head and smacked his lips. "Maybe you're right. Maybe I will. What about you? Have you given any thought to going back to school?"

"What? No. Why?"

"Now that your mom is gone, you have the time. Daisy always felt bad about your having to interrupt your education."

"She did?"

"Not many kids would take on a responsibility like that these days — not to say my generation was any better. We were only too happy to put our parents in nursing homes."

"What did they do, your parents?"

"Diplomatic Service, the pair of them. They did consular work. I was born in Brazil. Lived in Switzerland until I was eleven. They ended up as government liaisons in San Francisco."

"I had no idea."

"Worked out for me, because it gave me a smattering of languages, which helped in the importing business."

"Which languages?"

"French and German, a little Italian."

"No Portuguese?"

"No, we left Brazil when I was an infant." Tom added a splash of wine to his glass. "Anyway, I don't think you answered my original question."

"Which was...?"

"Have you considered going back to school?"

"I always thought I would, but now I think being thrown together with a bunch of eighteen and nineteen-year-olds would be strange; I don't have anything in common with them." *Except for inexperience,* she thought. *Then again, I never have had the same touchstones, the same cultural references as my classmates.* "I don't think I'd fit in."

Tom offered the familiar platitudes.

They were silent for a time as Emily thought about it. She was twenty-six, and though she had no practical experience, reading had given her experience beyond her years, and the decline and death of her parents had given her a mature perspective. "Study is fun, but it's something you do to prepare for life, and right now I'd rather live it."

"Do you have plans then?" Tom persisted.

"I'm working on a couple of projects."

"What kind of projects?"

"Just some stuff for myself," she said evasively. She didn't want to talk about her creative work; she had a fear that talking about it might jinx or dilute it somehow.

Tom didn't ask her to elaborate. "What about longterm goals?"

"I don't know. Anything could happen." *Maybe I'll write a bestseller,* she thought. "Maybe I'll be a housewife," she said. "I know it's not exactly P.C., but...." *I can always dream,* she thought. *A Prince Charming would be nice. Maybe a devoted patron of the arts.* Where did she see herself in five years? She wanted her freedom for a while. She wanted to see the world, if only she could afford it. Then, in the long run, she thought she'd welcome a family. She could write and still have a real life, couldn't she?

"Daisy always wanted to teach," Tom continued. "She loved kids. But after thirty-five years..." His voice caught in his throat. "Damn, she was so looking forward to...." Then, with no warning, he covered his face with his hands and wept. "Sorry, sorry," he kept repeating. "Sorry, sorry, must be the wine."

Emily got up and put her hand on his shoulder. "It's okay. It's expected. It's normal. Just let it out."

Buddy jumped up, alert, and a bark sounded outside. They heard steps on the porch and Wexler came in with Roscoe and a bottle of Barbera. Tom rose quickly, said he had something in his eye and hurried off to the bathroom. Wexler looked after him with concern. "What's with...?"

"He was talking about Daisy."

"Ah," Wexler said knowingly, nodding his head. He went to the cupboard and came back with a glass and a corkscrew. "You got a head start on me. Would you like some Barbera?"

Chapter Forty-Eight
Time Passes

Tom returned composed though bleary-eyed. Soon Rosalind and Rosalind arrived. Roscoe and Buddy got up to welcome their canine cohort.

The conversation wandered from dogs to politics, and then on to science and recent DNA analyses in Australia that were upending theories of early human migration. The sun set and they were getting ready to break up when Gary arrived in a grumpy mood, still smelling of salt water and crabs.

"Engine crapped out on me again. I damn near ended up on the jetty."

"Tell us about it," Tom said.

Gary paced the floor, hands in the back pockets of his jeans. "I was out about three miles and the main outboard quit. The first time I managed to get it going again, but the second time it was just dead. I had to fit the auxiliary, and almost dropped it in the water. Which wasn't all bad, because I learned an important lesson — always secure a safety line before dangling anything over the side." He ran fingers through his hair, and his eyes grew wider at the recollection. "Anyway, I was coming in around two o'clock. I was almost at the harbor mouth when the auxiliary started coughing and quit. Then the swells were pushing me toward the rocks. I had to throw out an anchor and call the harbor patrol to get towed in. It was a close thing. I spent the rest of the afternoon working on the engine."

"You need a drink," Wexler concluded and poured him the last of the Barbera.

Chapter Forty-Nine
Gary Spills the Beans

One evening, while Emily was drinking a second glass of wine and cooking dinner, Gary wandered into her study and came out with a copy *Lawless*, the new Robert Cole thriller.

"What's with all the Robert Cole books?"

Emily looked over her shoulder, saw what he held, and turned back to sautéing onions. "What about it?"

"Why so many?"

"I give them as gifts. Do you want one?"

"Sure, thanks. I liked the last one."

"Really?" She asked. "Which one was that?"

"*Lawless.*"

"Where'd you find it?"

"A Little Free Library in El Granada. Have you read it?"

"I have. It's not my favorite, but it was fun."

"I didn't think a girl would like his books."

"Why not?"

"Well, for one thing, Derek Law is a man's man — he's smart, but he doesn't say much. He understands women, but he doesn't fall for the women who throw themselves at him. Not your typical chick-lit. And he's amoral."

"Amoral? How is he amoral?"

"For one thing, in *The Spirit of the Law* Derek Law lets Palmer die when he could have saved him. And he let Palmer's associate get away. What about that?"

Emily sighed. "What would you have done if you were in his place?"

Gary shrugged. "Hell, I'm not a good example; I'd probably have shot them both."

"But that makes no sense. By your own standards, Derek Law is more moral than you are."

"Yeah, but I'm a guy. We were talking about why girls wouldn't like Robert Cole books."

"So, you think women are morally superior to men?"

"Absolutely."

"Then you're holding women to a different standard."

"What's wrong with that?"

There was so much wrong with that, she didn't know where to start. That was the kind of double-standard that allowed men in some cultures to get away with murder, both figuratively and literally, to enforce strictures on women and overlook the same behavior in men.

When she didn't reply he said, "Did you know he's local? Robert Cole, I mean."

"The writer? Really? Do you know him?"

"No, but I'd like to meet him."

"I wouldn't have pegged you for a literary groupie," she teased. "Or a reader, for that matter."

"Why? Do I look illiterate?"

She shrugged. "Blue-collar workers aren't known for being readers."

Gary wondered if she was being serious or satiric. "What *are* we known for?"

Emily leaned her back against the stove and counted the fingers of her left hand. "Drinking beer, watching television, wearing sloppy clothes, making lewd jokes, and driving pickups."

"My, aren't we a hotbed of prejudice tonight? Anything else?"

She counted the fingers of her right hand. "Poor education, conservative politics, religious intolerance, vulgar language, and a love of cheeseburgers."

"Do you always resort to stereotypes?"

"Whenever possible; it makes things so much easier."

"Well, I do drive a pickup, I like cheeseburgers, and beer, and especially lewd jokes (though I can never remember them), but I also like to read. How do you account for that?"

"Maybe you're not truly blue-collar. Maybe you're more of a turquoise."

Gary smiled crookedly. "You're funny."

"It's all in the delivery. Let me know what you think of the book when you're done."

Later, propped up in bed, he opened *Lawless*. The title page carried the same handwritten request as on his copy of *The Spirit of the Law*:

245

Dear fellow Coastsider,

If you enjoyed this book please do me the favor of leaving an honest review online. If you find any typos, or if you have any criticism, questions, or suggestions, feel free to email me at SealCove2@comcast.net.

Happy reading,

He didn't have any questions or suggestions, but he thought he might email Robert Cole to say how much he enjoyed the last book. Then he saw the signature.

Margaret Pennypacker

Had he picked up the wrong book? He checked the cover again. *Lawless* by Robert Cole. He checked the interior pages, and there, as expected, found reporter Derek Law. He didn't keep many books after reading them, but he had saved his signed copy of *The Spirit of the Law*. The message and the handwriting were identical on the title page in every detail but the signature. So who was this Margaret Pennypacker, and how was it that she'd signed a book by Robert Cole? The two inscriptions were clearly written by the same person. It was a puzzle. He checked the time. It was too late to disturb Emily, and he was already in bed. He made a mental note to ask her if she had an explanation, then settled down to read the first chapter. After a couple of pages he put the book aside. The mystery of the wrong signature bothered him.

He didn't own a laptop computer, but an online search on his phone brought up three Robert Cole books on Amazon. The page for *The Spirit of the Law* was linked to Robert Cole's author page, which in turn had a link to Robert Cole's blog. One of the blog entries, entitled "Margaret Pennypacker," caught his attention. In it, Robert Cole expressed his admiration for her romance novels. It included a link to her blog, where she returned the compliment in turn. Skipping ahead, he saw that Robert and Margaret had become an item, and finally that they were engaged and vacationing on Majorca — the latter entry posted ten months earlier. That the inscriptions began with the salutation "Dear fellow Coastsider," bore witness to these being local authors. Which still didn't answer the question as to why the inscriptions were written in the same hand but signed with different names. He thought it possible that Margaret had taken it upon herself to write an inscription for her fiancé's book, and that she'd mistakenly signed her name. It was the only thing he could think of that made sense. But how did Emily fit in? Why did she have so many copies of Cole's books? Did she know the couple? Was she handling public relations for them?

The problem ate him all the next day. He went over and over it in his mind. It was the shelf of Robert Cole books that had piqued his interest, as he'd just read *The Spirit of the Law*. He remembered thinking it was odd that she had so many duplicates (she must have had ten copies each of the three Robert Cole titles). He had picked up a random copy of the new book, and only later noticed the inscription on the flyleaf. What were the odds that he'd pick up the only signed copy? He wondered if perhaps all of the copies were signed, and if so, did they all contain the same mistake?

That evening Emily was stepping out the front door just as he was returning.

"I'm going to Tom's," she said. "I have to pick up some ingredients at the little market, so dinner will be a little later than usual. Are you coming to Tom's?"

"Later maybe, I want to take a shower first. What are you making?"

"Tacos. We need cilantro, cumin and some other stuff."

"I could go over and pick it up now, if you want."

"There's a list on the refrigerator upstairs."

She turned and started for Tom's. Gary watched longer than he had to, appreciating the sway of her hips. Then he went upstairs for the list. He plucked it off the refrigerator and noticed the door to the study was open. Here was a chance to answer some of the questions that had been needling him all day.

On the top shelf above the small desk were an old dictionary, a thesaurus, the Cambridge book of quotations, and how-to books on the mechanics of story structure and outlining. Below that was a shelf filled with copies of the four Robert Cole volumes, while the bottom shelf was devoted to three Margaret Pennypacker novels. He picked one at random, then another and another. He saw they were all inscribed and signed in the same hand, and then something clicked. He pulled the grocery list from his pocket and caught his breath. The handwriting was also the same. So Emily was responsible for the inscriptions and signatures of both authors. What was her game? Then he remembered their conversation about role-playing games on-board Miss Behavin'. Only she hadn't exactly said it was a role-playing game. She had said she made up stories "to entertain herself."

He mulled it over as he showered and made a quick run to the Coastside Market. He could think of no reason why she would sign the books, unless...unless she'd written them, and if what he supposed was true, he would now read them with an eye to what they revealed about her character. So when he took a chair on Tom's porch, he listened to the conversation while watching Emily with new interest.

They were discussing homelessness and the encampment under Pilarcitos Creek bridge in Half Moon Bay. "In the old days they had vagrancy laws," Wexler said. "They'd be arrested and transported over the county line with a warning not to come back."

"That didn't solve anything, did it?" Tom said. "All it did was pass the problem onto the next jurisdiction."

"I don't like to be uncharitable," Emily said, "but you can't just let people sleep anywhere. They have no fresh water, no toilets. It's not sanitary."

"It's not safe," Wexler said.

"It's a huge problem," Tom agreed. "But you can't force a man to work, or to rent an apartment."

"Of course a lot of them are addicts, or mental cases," Emily said. "They should be in rehab, or mental hospitals."

Looking straight at Emily to enjoy her reaction, Gary said, "Maybe Margaret Pennypacker would have a solution."

She froze, and felt heat begin moving up her throat.

"Who?" Tom asked.

"The writer?" Wexler asked, perplexed.

"You know her?" Gary asked, surprised.

"I've read a couple of her books. She's local, you know."

"I know, her fiancé is a local writer too — Robert Cole. Have you heard of him?"

Wexler shook his head. "Nope."

"Mystery writer. Not bad."

Tom asked, "Who is Margaret Pennypacker, and why would she have a solution to homelessness?"

In the meantime, the men didn't seem to notice Emily's face flushing deep red.

"She's just a local writer," Gary answered nonchalantly. "I just thought it would take someone with excessive imagination to come up with a new solution. Ask an artist instead of a politician."

Tom shrugged at the suggestion and was about to speak when he saw Emily and was brought up short. "Are you all right?"

"Wine went down the wrong way," she croaked. "I think I'll go home."

"I'll go with you," Gary said. He had meant it all as a joke, but he could tell she didn't find it at all funny and was sorry to have brought it up.

"No, you stay. Have your wine. I'll make dinner."

"Groceries are on the table."

"She looked like she was about to choke," Wexler said when she had gone.

Chapter Fifty

The Assessment

No sooner had Emily disappeared around the corner than Rosalind came up the walk. "What's wrong with Emily? She didn't look good."

"Who didn't look good?" Rosalind asked, coming up the walk.

"She inhaled some wine," Wexler said.

"At least it wasn't brandy."

Gary then put down his drink. "I think I'll go check on her."

He found her sautéing onions and ground beef with cumin and chili powder.

She didn't turn around. "Did you all have a good laugh at my expense?"

"I didn't tell them anything," Gary said, and added, "I wouldn't tell them."

Thinking about the racier parts in the Margaret Pennypacker books Emily was mortified. "How did you find out?"

Gary explained about the mistaken signature, and how he'd discovered the blogs.

She turned around to face him. "Promise me you'll never tell."

He stood with a hangdog look and promised.

She looked at him a long moment, trying to judge his sincerity. "No, actually, your promise won't do. I'll make it simple. If you tell anyone...ANYONE...I'll throw you out."

Surprised at her vehemence he said, "What's the big deal?"

"It's private."

"How private can it be? You put it all in books, for heaven's sake! Anyone can buy it online."

"I didn't put anything in a book. Margaret Pennypacker and Robert Cole put stuff in books."

Thinking about the couple of Robert Cole books he'd read, he couldn't imagine what her objection was. Although he had to admit the Dereck Law stories showed questionable morality, as well as a masculine sensibility.

"And stay out of my study. I don't want you anywhere near my books."

Gary felt gut-punched. "Sorry, I didn't mean to upset you, but don't be such a hypocrite."

"How am I a hypocrite?"

"You didn't mind outing Tom when he wanted to keep his out-of-body experience private. I seem to remember you saying no one would judge him, we're all friends."

"That was different."

"How is it different?"

"I don't want to talk about it."

Emily turned back to her cooking.

He waited. "Do you want me to go?" He felt dejected, like a kid who'd just received a dressing-down.

"No. Why don't you make some salsa? Tomatoes and cilantro are in the fridge, onions, and limes in the bowl there."

"Do you have any sweet peppers?"

The next day Emily bought a locking doorknob at Ocean Shore Hardware and installed it on the study door, just in case. As it turned out, it didn't matter. Gary downloaded all of her books to his phone and began reading avidly, hoping to find what could possibly be deemed private and yet shared with the world at large, albeit pseudonymously.

That night Emily lay awake giving voice to her self-doubts. Admitting her authorship would have meant taking responsibility for her failings. As long as Margaret Pennypacker and Robert Cole were the authors, the onus was on them. Any criticism fell on their shoulders. The truth was that Emily Abbott felt like an imposter, a poseur, a wannabe. She wasn't ready for the scrutiny that came with ownership.

She avoided Tom's porch for the rest of the week, and when she returned she watched and listened closely to see if anyone betrayed signs of knowing her secret, but nothing more was ever spoken of Margaret Pennypacker and Robert Cole at the Theoretical Society, even though Gary now viewed her through a different window.

# # #

Tom had already informed his clients that the spring delivery was canceled. Now he had to think what he wanted to do with the rest of his life. Would he retire, or continue working? He had never been all that keen to retire in the first place, but Daisy was so happy at the prospect of their spending more time together that he'd relented. His bookcases were filled with volumes on wine. The subject had always interested him because it was multi-disciplinary, encompassing history, geography, meteorology, geology, chemistry, viticulture and viniculture — all of the combinations that made one wine distinct from another. Wineries and wine caves had their own mystique and fascination, from mom-and-pop operations, to lavish estates.

He stood now in front of his bookcase filled with ampelographies, atlases, encyclopedias, histories, crop reports, books exploring different wine regions, and memoirs. In addition there were more than a dozen cookbooks, as food and wine were intertwined. It had been a passion his entire adult life. It had afforded him many friends, and many memories of convivial meals spent over bottles of wine in cellars, and vineyards, and fine restaurants around the world. Now, however, he wasn't sure if he wanted to go back to work. After all that had happened, he felt less inclined to make the effort.

Then one day he awoke feeling better than he had since the day of the accident. Daisy's loss still lay heavy on his heart, but on this day he was in no hurry to follow her. It was one of those achingly beautiful days that one can't help but savor. Each element — the pale cloudless sky, the cobalt blue ocean, the dark, twisted cypresses, a bracing sea breeze, and the continuous roar of breaking waves rolling into shore — combined to lift his spirits.

He and Buddy walked the bluffs as far as the radar tower, and on the way back he stopped at the Seal Cove Brewpub for the first time since that fateful day. It was during the lull between lunch and dinner, but there were still a few patrons at the bar. Gene Price, the bartender, greeted Tom warmly and offered his condolences. "We were all so sorry about Mrs. B." He shook his head. "Ain't life a bitch?"

Tom frowned and made a sweeping gesture to indicate all they could see. "Don't tell me life is a bitch when you get to look at this view all day. Life is not a bitch, Gene. Mortality is a bitch."

Gene grinned. "You're right. When you're right, you're right."

"Besides, Mrs. B wouldn't want to be the cause of such morbid thoughts."

Gene attended to another customer, then looked expectantly at Tom. "Can I get you something to drink?"

"No, thanks, Gene. Listen, I was remembering that on the day of the accident you made a comment about learning the import business. I don't know if it was just idle conversation, or if you were serious, but if you are, I was wondering if you'd like to get together and talk it over."

"Sorry, Mr. B., I really haven't given it much thought. But sure, I'm always open to hearing more. Why don't you come by tomorrow before we open. Say ten-thirty?"

"Works for me."

Tom and Buddy walked home through the cypress forest above Smuggler's Cove and came out of the trees overlooking the Marine Reserve. From that high vantage, he counted seventy-three grey harbor seals silently sunning themselves on the beach below. He bent down to pet Buddy, glad to be granted this day, even if he didn't understand why he was still here.

# # #

Back at the brewpub the next morning, Gene said, "Let's sit, I have to stand all day on the job."

Tom hoisted his daypack onto a table in the bar and pulled out a sheaf of papers that he slid in front of Gene. "I knew you'd want real numbers, so I ran these reports to give you an idea of the potential. The problem, of course, is that you have to compete with the big guns, the corporate distributors, which is why I've specialized in a niche market. There's less chance of stepping on their toes. It's not the most lucrative business, but it is scalable."

They talked business for half an hour. Then Tom pulled a stoppered liquor bottle from the pack. "I thought you might appreciate tasting this."

"What is it?"

"Taste it first. I'm interested in your opinion."

Gene went behind the bar and returned with two glasses and a small pitcher of water. "It's not homemade, is it?"

"Don't fish for clues. Just taste it and tell me what you think."

Gene poured a shot into each glass. He sniffed, put a drop on his tongue, and let it evaporate. Then he added a dollop of water, sniffed again, and closed his eyes before taking a swig. "Well, I'm no expert," he said modestly, "but I'd say it's a Canadian rye. Am I right?"

"Could be."

"Why doesn't it have a label?"

"Funny you should ask," said Tom, and launched into the story.

When he finished Gene said, "Intriguing. Have you contacted The Half Moon Bay Review? I'll betcha Bob Hammer would jump on a story like this."

"I was thinking the same thing."

"And you say there's port and champagne. What are your friends going to do with it?"

"Can they do anything without getting the ABC involved?"

Being on the wrong side of the Department of Alcoholic Beverage Control was asking for trouble.

"That's the problem, isn't it? Government bureaucracy. You don't want to stir up a hornet's nest."

"No, that's what I told them. I'm afraid they had high hopes of making a pile of money, but I don't see how they can do it without alerting the authorities."

"Let me think about it. I'll talk to my boss, and I'll ask Bob, too. There must be some way to capitalize on this. If nothing else, we could have one hell of a party!"

A couple days later Bob Hammer stopped by Tom's to taste the booze and interview Emily.

When he was done, he took a photo of Emily holding a bottle. Then he said, "I'd also like to get a picture of you and your boyfriend on the boat."

Flustered, it took her a moment to answer. "Gary? No, he's not my boyfriend. We're just friends. Actually, he's my tenant. And we're friends. I guess."

Tom looked at his watch. "There's no time like the present. He should be back in the harbor by now. Let's go see."

The photo that appeared in the following week's paper showed Gary and Emily standing shoulder to shoulder on Miss Behavin', holding up identical bottles. The headline accompanying the article read Local Couple Finds Treasure.

Emily was thrilled. Maria was furious. That evening Emily closed her door and put on a Sarah Vaughn album to drown out the argument going on below.

No sooner had Maria stormed out than Gary's phone rang. His parents had seen the paper and were excited to know more details.

"There's nothing much to add," Gary said.

"What do you think it's worth?" his father asked.

"Not as much as we'd hoped."

"Tell us about your new girlfriend," his mother said.

"She's not my girlfriend, Mom, she's my landlord."

"Oh, we thought..."

"No, Mom."

"You're not still seeing that Mexican gal, are you?" his father asked, suddenly gruffer than he'd been a minute before.

"Yes, I'm still seeing Maria," Gary said, though he wasn't one hundred percent sure after this latest fight.

"Don't be suckered into doing something foolish. She could just be using you as a road to citizenship."

"She's not like that, Dad."

"Just be careful. Use a condom."

"William!" his mother exclaimed.

"Just sayin'."

The next day on his porch, Tom commiserated with Gary and apologized for setting the wheels in motion. "My fault, sorry, I should have talked to you before talking to Bob Hammer. I didn't mean to start a fight."

Remembering his own misunderstandings with women Wexler said, "It's not your fault, it's Maria's."

"No," Gary sighed, "if it's anyone's fault it's mine. I should have nixed this before it ever got into the paper."

Rosalind weighed in then. "You can blame it on whoever came up with that headline. He —"

"Or she," Wexler reminded her.

"Or she," Rosalind corrected herself, "should have said: Couple Finds Local Treasure, not Local Couple Finds Treasure."

"Or: Fisherman Dredges Up Past," Gary suggested.

"Fisherman Uncovers Local Mystery," Tom amended.

"Or," said Emily, "Foolish Fisherman Finds Fragile Flotsam."

"My dad called to see if I had a new girlfriend," Gary said.

Emily smiled to herself. It was a role she wouldn't mind trying on for size — for a while. Girlfriend had a nice ring to it. There was a physical attraction that exited her, and while she didn't see Gary as husband material, he was refreshingly uncomplicated and conveniently close by. And she had to start somewhere.

From Emily Abbott's Notebooks

Lost

Had a good laugh today. The lost-and-found section of the Half Moon Bay Review had the following entry:

LOST: MIND — Sometime in 2004-05 when pregnant with first or second child. Not chipped. If found please message me.

After I stopped laughing, I wondered what might have inspired this woman to take out such an outlandish ad. Was there a note of desperation here? Did she mean it as a cry for help? Or was she just in a mood? Being flippant, finding humor in pathos? Maybe she'd had a drink or two before noon. Who is this lost woman?

Sometimes I feel lost myself. Where am I headed? I have a hard time imagining where I'll be in five or ten years. I put my own desires on hold for so long, and now that my time is my own I don't know quite what to do with it, what direction to take. I'm reminded of that Yogi Berra quote — "If you don't know where you are going, you might wind up someplace else." I'm of two minds about it. I yearn for adventure, and at the same time long for a normal life — a relationship, love, a husband, children, career. How do I reconcile competing desires? How do I find direction? If I can invent stories and people, I ought to be able to invent myself. Shouldn't I?

Chapter Fifty-One
The Snowball Effect

The publication of their story put other wheels in motion. First Larry Lu, co-owner of the Seal Cove Brewpub, knocked on Emily's door begging for a taste and more details. He was a tall, slim Eurasian with black eyes and a small nose. It was the middle of the day and Gary was out on the boat. Leery of Mr. Lu's wide-eyed enthusiasm, Emily led him next door, where Tom was writing an email to his European suppliers. He invited them in and poured Lu a small sample from the only open bottle, which was now two-thirds empty.

Lu tasted it with a satisfied glint in his eye. He addressed Emily. "Where did you say you found this?"

"We didn't say. That's the one part of the story we're not telling."

"Smart girl." He gazed at the horizon. Dark clouds scudded south above a celadon sea. "The thing is, this would be such a publicity coup. You know the brewpub was a Prohibition roadhouse back in the day."

"Everyone knows that," Tom said. It would be hard to forget, as the story was printed on the back of every menu, and immortalized by a bronze plaque beside the front door.

"I can see it now," Lu said excitedly, with a sweeping gesture taking in the imagined scene. "We'd have a grand party, everyone dressed in period clothing, the liquor arriving by antique car. It would be the reuniting of the lost stash with it's intended destination, arriving a hundred years late, but arriving nonetheless. What do you think?"

"I think the liquor belongs to Emily," Tom reminded him. "Emily and Gary."

Lu ignored Tom and flashed a bright smile at Emily. "How much do you want for it?"

"You know they can't sell it to you," Tom cautioned. "You'd lose your retail license. You can only buy from a wholesaler."

"I know," Lu said, "I wasn't born yesterday. But there's a loophole: individuals can sell alcoholic beverages to other individuals. You can thank Andy Wong for that."

"Who's Andy Wong?"

"Counsel to the State Senate Judiciary Committee, and an ardent wine collector." Lu chuckled. "It helps to know people in high places. So Emily, you could sell it to my brother-in-law, for instance, and then we'd have a private party. Of course, you'd all be invited."

Emily eyed him warily. He seemed too eager by half. She was tempted to dismiss him out of hand but didn't want to close the door completely. "I'd have to talk to Gary first, but I don't think we'd be interested unless you could make us an offer we can't refuse."

Next, Tommy Roberts, the mayor who had run on the slogan "a crab in every pot," sat down with Gary and Emily in Gary's living room to discuss ways that the town could capitalize on the discovery. "To put the town on the map, so to speak."

"It's already on the map," Emily said.

Beaming, Roberts accepted that observation as a compliment. "It is, isn't it? But it doesn't hurt to remind others of how special our little town is."

Neither Emily nor Gary said anything, but they were both thinking the same thing — they didn't want to remind others of how special their little town was, as it only invited day-trippers from San Francisco who clogged the roads each weekend.

Of course, the mayor talked in terms of a donation. "...a great tax write-off," he said. Emily and Gary looked at one another with perfect understanding, before Emily turned to the mayor and said, "We're not in a tax bracket that makes a donation attractive."

Gary nodded enthusiastically, marveling at her elegant turn of phrase. "In other words," he said, "what's in it for us?"

The mayor went away disappointed, but not discouraged. He said he'd talk it over with others and get back to them. "I'm confident we can come to an arrangement that will satisfy everyone," he said.

"What do think?" Gary asked when the mayor Roberts had gone.

"I think he's a politician who promises what he can't deliver. I'm not giving up anything."

Gary smiled in admiration. No one was going to push this woman around. On the other hand, politicians did have connections, and who knew what he might offer? "Keep an open mind," he said.

"Don't give in."

"Never — without your approval, of course."

It soon became clear that they were losing control of the narrative. Everyone had competing views of what should be done with their treasure, such as it was.

The Coastside Chamber of Commerce heard about it from the mayor and jumped on board, offering several suggestions from an auction, to a raffle, to a surfing contest.

The San Mateo County Historical Society asked if they could meet to discuss using their story in an exhibit to illustrate the rich history of the coastside.

The youth hostel at Point Montara lighthouse proposed a party and silent auction to be held at the century-old shiplap building that housed the lighthouse museum.

The mayor of Half Moon Bay offered the I.D.E.S. Hall as a venue, but was turned down for the obvious reason that the mayor of Seal Cove wasn't interested in playing second fiddle to the mayor of Half Moon Bay.

In the end, with the aid of Mayor Roberts, the Chamber of Commerce, and the lighthouse museum, a plan began to take shape.

"Why a silent auction?" Emily asked. "Why not a regular auction?"

"We think you'd get more bang for your buck with a silent auction," said Mayor Roberts. "For a regular auction, you'd have to go through an auction house and hire an auctioneer and pay them a commission. And you'd have to combine like bottles into a single lot. It would be over in five minutes. With a silent auction you could offer each bottle as a separate lot."

Emily and Gary both liked the idea of an auction, but they weren't so sure if a party was worth the trouble.

"Oh no," the mayor said, "you have to have a party."

"Why?" Gary wanted to know.

"If you want people to bid at your silent auction, it needs to be an event. You can't just invite people to bid and give them nothing else to do. They'd either stay home or stand around staring at each other. No, you want to create a festive atmosphere, get people happy and excited, build anticipation. You might have music, a DJ, catered hors d'oeuvres, and a bar."

"This is starting to sound expensive," Emily said. "How much is this going to cost us?"

"Nothing, it'll all be covered by the gate."

"What gate?"

"If you want a good turnout, make it exclusive; sell a limited number of tickets, say one hundred. There's no sense in giving away anything for free."

"What kind of party would it be?" Emily wanted to know. "Who would we invite?"

"It's your discovery and your party," the mayor said.

"How would we get the word out?" Gary asked.

"Leave that to me; I'm just here to facilitate. You tell me what you need, and I'll see what I can do."

# # #

The Seal Cove Theoretical Society was in the thick of it. As the sun glinted blindingly on the water, they all sat on Tom's porch and debated the proposals. Tom rocked in his chair, chin in hand. "Just take care, don't let them rope you into something you don't want to do."

"I won't," Emily said, "but a Prohibition party does make sense."

"We could wear flapper outfits," Rosalind said, "and learn some 1920s dances. It would be fun."

"What kind of dances did they do back then?" Gary asked.

"The Charleston," Tom said, "and the Black Bottom."

"The Lindy Hop," Emily offered.

"Then there were the trots," Tom said. "The Turkey Trot and the Fox Trot."

"Tango," Rosalind said. "Didn't Rudolph Valentino dance the Tango?"

"Who's Rudolph Valentino?" Gary asked.

Tom raised his eyebrows in dismay. "Who's Rudolph Valentino? Are you serious?"

Gary shrugged. "Never heard of him."

"Film star of the silent era," Rosalind explained. To Emily she said, "I know the perfect place in the city, on Union street. They have period costumes and vintage clothes."

"I don't think I could afford that. This is all starting to sound too expensive, what with a caterer and a DJ and all."

"You can't have a DJ," Tom said. "They didn't have DJs in the 1920s."

"It wouldn't be much of a party without music," Wexler said.

"So hire a band," Tom said.

"Musicians don't work for free."

"You're the musician," Tom said; "you've got contacts. Figure it out."

The next afternoon Wexler and Roscoe walked a mile north to the lighthouse. A cold, arctic wind tore the tops off of swells, driving the angry green sea southward. It was the kind of weather that made his cheeks turn red, his eyes water and his nose run.

On his way back he saw smoke rising from Tom's chimney, borne away on the wind like smoke from a steam engine. He decided to stop in, despite the early hour. Gene Price was there, this being a Monday when the restaurant was closed. He and Tom were talking about the wine importing business. Buddy and Roscoe settled down by the fire.

Wexler poured himself a glass of dry Riesling.

"Steve, you know Gene, of course."

Wexler raised his glass in salute and said, "We've known each other over the bar for years, but I think this is the first time I've seen your feet."

"There's a first time for everything," Gene said. "Feet, meet Mr. Wexler. Mr. Wexler, my feet."

Rosalind and Rosalind were the next to arrive. Introductions were made. The conversation drifted to the outrageous political headlines of the day, which reminded Rosalind of the movie *The Manchurian Candidate,* that in turn reminded Tom of the movie *Seven Days in May*, which led them on digressions about movies starring Kirk Douglas and Burt Lancaster, and back to Rod Serling, the screenwriter for the latter movie, who had also produced *The Twilight Zone*, and then on to favorite episodes of *The Twilight Zone*.

Emily arrived, followed shortly thereafter by Gary, at which time Wexler delivered the news. "This morning I did some digging. It's not easy finding a local band that plays authentic 1920s jazz. There's a group in the City called Felix and the Jazz Cats. They play Gatsby parties at the Julia Morgan

Ballroom in San Francisco. But they don't come cheap." Counting off on his fingers he said, "There's a vocalist, drums, bass, piano, clarinet, trumpet, sax, trombone, banjo, and guitar. We're talking at least three thousand, easy, maybe closer to five."

"I hate to heap on the bad news," Tom added, "but I also heard from Mayor Roberts today. He's lined up a caterer. For a party of a hundred, it'll cost another four or five grand. And the lighthouse hostel wants a three-hundred-dollar cleaning fee."

Wexler said, "I went by the lighthouse today, and it's a nice, open room, but there's not much there. Certainly no piano."

They compared expenses against what they might expect from the gate and the silent auction. Emily despaired. "We can't possibly afford this. I'm all for having fun, but it's getting out of hand. Between the caterer, costumes, advertising, and the band, we'd be lucky to turn any profit at all. What's the point of putting on a party to attract bidders if we're going to lose money doing it? We need to call this off."

Each of them looked to the others for suggestions. It was Rosalind who weighed in first. "The silent auction is still a good idea."

"The mayor was right," Wexler said. "You can't have a silent auction and give the bidders nothing to do."

Tom rocked forward, hands clasped between his knees. "The party was a good idea too. It just got too big."

Emily brightened. "So why don't we have a small party, just for ourselves and a few friends? No caterer, no band."

"I liked the idea of a band," Rosalind said. "I want to dance."

"We need bidders," Emily said.

"I was hoping to make enough to buy a new engine," Gary said.

Tom brought steepled fingers up to his chin and cocked his head in thought. "How much would this engine cost?"

"Five to six thousand," Gary said.

"Yikes," Emily exclaimed, "I had no idea they were so expensive."

"That's not expensive for an engine. The guy in the next slip has two 250 horsepower Evenrudes that cost him fifty grand."

Emily shook her head in disappointment. "I wanted to make enough to go on a trip, but if it comes down to a choice, then you should have your engine. You need an engine. I don't need a trip."

"Okay," Tom said, "let's just proceed with that goal in mind. We want to make at least enough to get Gary his engine, and hopefully have something left over for Emily. Let's all put on our thinking caps and reconvene tomorrow."

"I have to work tomorrow," Gene said.

"If you come up with any bright ideas, phone them in," Tom said.

"Who's going to tell the mayor his big party is off?" Emily asked. "I hate confrontations."

Chapter Fifty-Two
Planning the Party

The next day Emily received a call from Larry Lu. "Gene told me you've decided to call off the party. I think I can help."

It seemed to Emily as though everyone thought they could help — themselves. She decided to lay down some ground rules.

"Before you get started, let me stop you right there. First, we're not interested in anything that's going to cost us money. Second, I'm not the only one involved; you'll have to talk with Gary Myron, too, and he won't be back until late afternoon. So if you want to talk to us together, we should both be at Tom Birmingham's around 6:00." In truth, she wanted Tom to hear what Lu had to say. She trusted Tom's judgment.

It was a glorious spring evening, warm in the late sun, cool in the shadows, and it happened that Tom and Emily and Gary and Wexler and Rosalind were all present, as were Buddy, Rosalind, and Roscoe, when Larry Lu showed up bearing a bottle of northern Italian Arneis. "Gene said you might like to taste this," he said, handing the bottle to Tom, who passed it to Wexler, who opened it while a dining room chair was brought out for Larry Lu. The wine was poured and tasted and commented upon.

Then Lu got down to business. Addressing Emily and Gary he said, "Okay now, so, as you know, I said before what a great publicity opportunity this could be for the brewpub, and that hasn't changed. But now that I know where you're coming from, I have an offer I don't think you can refuse. As Gene explained it, as I understand it (correct me if I'm wrong), you're looking to make some money from your find, so you like the idea of a silent auction, but the party was getting too expensive. Am I right so far?" Heads nodded in agreement. "So here's what I'm offering. I propose we hold a private party at the brewpub on a Monday, when we're closed to the public. We'll provide the space, the hors d'oeuvres, and better yet — our mailing list. We keep a database of our best customers and their preferences. That should help winnow out the wheat from the chaff. We'll only invite those who will be likely bidders."

Emily was wary. "How much is this going to cost us?"

"Nothing."

"Then what are you getting out of it?" Gary asked.

Lu leaned forward, a glint of excitement in his eyes. "I'm glad you asked. Now here's what I want..." Then he laid out his plans for a grand Prohibition themed costume party. He'd invite the local TV Stations, food editors from the San Francisco Chronicle, the Half Moon Bay Review, Pescadero Pebble, Sunset magazine, and Epicurean magazine, and he would hire a photographer and videographer to capture it all to use for publicity. "If we can get even one local TV Spot, and a one or two page spread in a magazine, it will be more than worthwhile. And we can write it off on our taxes as a business expense."

They kicked the idea around for a while, most of the questions and suggestions coming from Emily and Gary, with input from Tom. Wexler was silent through it all, until the meeting seemed on the verge of breaking up. Then he asked, "What about music?"

Lu brightened at the reminder. "I have an old Victrola with a big brass horn and a few 78s. Does anyone else have 78s?"

"Can't we have a live band?" Rosalind asked. "We want to dance." She glanced at the others for support and seeing reluctant faces amended her statement. "Well, I want to dance, anyway."

"A band *would* be nice," Tom said.

"Hold on," Emily objected, "if it's going to cost more money, I'm nixing it."

"Musicians don't work for free," Wexler reminded her.

"That's what I was afraid of," Emily said.

"I'll throw in a couple hundred bucks, if that'll help," Rosalind offered.

Wexler asked Lu if he had a budget for a band.

"I can supply a pianist," Lu said. "Gordan Pierce plays in the bar on Friday and Saturday nights. I'm sure he wouldn't mind."

"Steve here plays bass," Tom pointed out in return.

Wexler might have protested, but for the way Tom had worded it. He hadn't volunteered Wexler's services for free. He hadn't even asked if he would play for money. He had simply presented a fact — Steve plays bass. Yes, he did. And while he was, ostensibly, a professional, to ask for payment among friends at a party to which he was invited would seem mercenary. He imagined a scene in which he played his standup bass beside a piano, and in his vision he saw Cliff playing banjo, while Rosalind, dressed in flapper garb, danced the Charleston. A piano, bass, and banjo would have a chance of creating a credible 1920s ambiance. He looked to Larry Lu. "Does your pianist know any tunes from the '20s?"

# # #

By the time Larry Lu left, they'd agreed to the preliminaries and a tentative date at the end of June. Then Tom brought out a Pinot Noir and a plate of salami, cheese, and olives. As the sun descended in the west, they sat on the porch, pleasantly inebriated, basking in the warm glow of friendship, a common goal, and something fun to look forward to together.

Wexler, Rosalind, and their canine companions left a few minutes before sunset. When they came to the corner they stopped.

Wexler didn't want the evening to end. "My place? I'll cook."

"No, I want to get home before dark."

Wexler couldn't help looking disappointed.

"Besides," she added, "you cooked last time. It's my turn. Do you like prawns and wild rice?"

"I don't have any prawns."

"No, I'm offering to cook at *my* house."

"Your house?"

"Yes, is that a problem?"

"No, no problem." They continued walking. He hated to admit it, but he didn't even know where she lived. He asked.

"Beach Way."

"Beach Way?" he repeated, furrowing his brow. That didn't make sense. They'd walked right past her house on the way to and from the brewpub several times and she'd never said a thing, implying she had further to go, or that they were going in the same direction. "You mean you live near the brewpub?"

"Third house."

He took a deep breath and exhaled slowly. It was a puzzle, but then women were by nature inscrutable. Perhaps he could figure it out if he knew more about her. So instead of trying to sell himself, as he might have done had he been trying to seduce her, he decided to probe for answers. "Tell me, where did you grow up, and what brought you to Seal Cove?"

They walked down Seacliff to the Marine Reserve parking lot, crossed the bridge over the creek, and took the winding path up to the bluff into the dark, twisted cypress grove. Almost touching the horizon, the sun laid down a shimmering gold path on the water, casting long tree shadows and bathing the trees in an orange light. While they walked, Wexler peppered her with questions about herself for a change.

They came out of the grove just a hundred yards from her front door. She lived in a newly renovated, historic beach bungalow with a white picket fence, mullioned windows, and a stone chimney. Old cypress loomed over the street at the edge of the cliff. She had a lovely view of the ocean between the grey trunks of the old trees.

While she prepped for dinner, he excused himself to find the bathroom. On the walls of the hallway were historic photos of the house, as well as a wedding photo of Rosalind, her husband, and the wedding party. They looked to be in their late twenties. There was another of her and her husband looking happy atop a mountain, obviously taken either early in the morning or late in the afternoon, as the mountain threw a cone-shaped shadow across the top of a layer of clouds far below. There was another of her husband grinning on a beach, with a facemask pushed up on his forehead, fins in one hand and a fish on the end of a spear in the other. A third photo showed the two of them standing by a black helicopter in front of a waterfall somewhere in the tropics. They looked like they owned the world.

Coming back down the hall from the bathroom he glanced through an open doorway into her bedroom. A framed photo of her husband stood on the nightstand beside the bed. It was a picture of a handsome man exuding confidence and a zest for life. He would be a hard act for any man to follow.

Wexler sat on a stool at the center island and watched Rosalind peel shrimp. "You sure you don't want any help?" he asked.

"There's not enough room; we'd be bumping into each other."

He wondered how she could adjust to being alone after such an eventful life. He had never been particularly good at being alone, though he'd had plenty of practice.

"Would you like a glass of wine?" she asked.

"No, thanks, I had enough at Tom's."

"He's a nice man."

"Nice? I would say brutally honest is closer to the mark."

"Does that bother you?"

Wexler rolled his eyes. "There are times I'd like to kick him. He's a little too free with his opinions."

"He's just trying to offer advice. At the very least, he makes you think."

"He could be more tactful."

"Give him some slack; he's been through a lot," she said irritably. "It isn't easy losing your spouse."

Wexler was about to retort when he remembered her own loss and, chastened, held his tongue.

"Did you know his wife?" she asked.

"Just to say hi to. I don't think we exchanged a dozen words in all the years I've lived here. They were a lot older. I didn't really get to know Tom until I had to take care of Buddy."

"That was good of you."

Wexler didn't know what to do with the compliment. His mind was elsewhere and he was on unfamiliar ground. The women (girls, really) he'd had relationships with had been too young to have had a life yet. Nothing interesting had happened to them, unless one counted cheating boyfriends, fleeting crushes, and flirting with drug addiction interesting. Rosalind was different. He was suddenly curious to know what made this woman tick.

"What was your husband's name?"

"Ronnie."

"Tell me about him. Where did you meet?"

Ronnie had been an alpha male with an MBA, a philandering workaholic. Confident. Energetic. Egotistical. Opinionated. Exciting. He strove for excellence and expected everyone else to follow his lead.

"He was a handful, but damn he was fun! So full of plans. He always joked, 'He who dies with the most toys wins.' And by that measure, I guess he won. But he had the bad taste to die on me, the son-of-a-bitch. Men can be such dicks."

"He sounds insufferable."

"Quite the opposite. Everyone in his orbit felt energized. We all put up with his faults because he was bigger-than-life. It was like he was the star of the movie, and those of us lucky enough to be in his orbit were bit-players."

Later, after dinner, she asked if he wanted to spend the night. It pained him to decline, but with tales of her husband fresh on his mind and Ronnie's photo propped up beside her bed, Wexler didn't think he wanted to compete with the memory. He feigned a headache and stood to go.

"Oh, don't go yet," she implored in a tone of such exaggerated emotion that it was evident she'd had a glass or two too many. "It's too quiet when I'm alone."

So they talked on, or rather she talked and Wexler listened. Eventually, his bladder insisted on a visit to the toilet. On his return, he found her slumped into a corner of the couch, snoring. He covered her with an afghan, woke Roscoe, and walked fearlessly home through the dark cypress forest, spooked only once when Roscoe took after a wild turkey.

# # #

As he set about making a pot of tea and washing glasses, Tom thought of Daisy. If she'd been there they would have been cooking dinner together, engaged in conversation. There was never much quiet time in their house, even after Douglas had gone to college and moved to Bellingham. They never ran out of things to talk about. Now the house was deathly quiet, or rather it lacked the rhythm of human speech. Of course, the coast itself had an eternal resonance made up of the crash and rumble of advancing combers, wind soughing through cypress boughs, and the pulse of the foghorn. As he dried the glasses, he spoke to Buddy to fill the space with words.

"What do you dream about, Buddy? Are you chasing rabbits in your dreams? You must not dream in color, because you can't see much color. That's hard for me to imagine. The world would seem so bland without color. But then, I suppose you smell in color, in a way. Did you know butterflies can see the ultraviolet spectrum?"

Buddy lay on the kitchen floor. He understood his master's tone as a question, but he had no idea what the man was saying. Buddy was thinking *how can he be so smart and yet be unable to learn dog language?* Buddy had tried to teach him, but every time he barked he was reprimanded. How would his master learn if he was unwilling to listen?

"I wonder if you miss Daisy as much as I do. I'll bet you wonder where she is, don't you boy? So do I. I'd follow her in an instant, but I'm afraid speeding things along might be against the rules, and then I'd never find her. What do think?"

Buddy groaned and turned sad eyes on his master. He wished the man would stop prattling and scratch his back, or give him some food.

"We're lucky though," Tom continued. "We have friends and neighbors. The funny thing is that they were there all along and we didn't know it. We never needed anybody else. We had each other, and Douglas, and you of course. But now it's different. It's good to have friends. You see, people need human contact, just like you need canine contact. You can't deny it. I've seen you and Rosalind together. She's quite a bitch, and that's a compliment for a dog."

Chapter Fifty-Three
Forming a Band

The following Friday evening found Wexler at the Seal Cove Brewpub accompanying Gordan Pierce on piano, with Clifford Cook on banjo. They were an odd-looking trio. Pierce, a chunky, middle-aged man with a mahogany complexion and receding hairline, wore a tuxedo, while Wexler, hair pulled back in a ponytail, wore jeans and a t-shirt, and Clifford, whose only hair consisted of bushy eyebrows and a matching mustache, wore slacks and a dress shirt.

Pierce had a limited repertoire of tunes from the 1920s, but the trio didn't sound half bad. Cliff's banjo worked well with "Sweet Georgia Brown," "Blue Skies," and "Mack the Knife," though he couldn't figure out how to contribute to ballads like "Someone To Watch Over Me." Once they'd exhausted Pierce's shortlist of '20s tunes they progressed to the standards of the 1930s and '40s. They played for half an hour before taking a break. Their effort was rewarded by a lone drinker at the bar who put her drink down long enough to clap and make eye contact with Pierce.

"That was fun," Pierce said. "I usually play alone and nobody notices. It can be depressing. But if we're supposed to play only 1920s tunes at this party, I'll have to brush up on my song selection."

Cliff swung around on his stool. "If we want a really authentic sound, we'd need a trumpet, and maybe a clarinet or sax."

"Don't forget drums," Wexler said, thinking about the price of putting together a full band. He knew Emily and Gary would balk at the expense. That was why he'd recruited Cliff, who was happy to play for free, for old-time's sake. But Cliff was right — to achieve an authentic 1920s sound, they needed a horn section. It might be just a silly private event, of little import to anyone, but in that moment it was important to Wexler that he get it right, even if it meant coming out of pocket himself. His friends were counting on it.

They played again on Saturday night, and on Sunday they were joined by Larry Lu's nephew, Ryan Miller, on drums. It was obvious from the first song that the kid needed to go lighter on the drums. By the third song, he was driving people out of the bar and onto the terrace. Gene Price gave Pierce a signal, and Pierce said, "This isn't working."

"Yeah," Miller said. "What's with the banjo?"

Wexler looked at Miller, who was all of eighteen. "It's not the banjo, kid. Take a walk with me." He led Miller out to the parking lot. "Let me guess, you've played in some kind of high school rock band."

"So?"

"So first of all, we're playing jazz standards. This isn't a rock band. You have to tailor your playing to the music."

Miller rolled his eyes. "I don't play elevator music."

"If you're ever lucky enough to hear your music in an elevator, count yourself blessed. Second, it's a small room where people are trying to carry on a conversation. You don't want to drown them out. It's why we're playing acoustically. Dial back the volume. Use the brushes."

"You're going to tell me how to play drums now?" Miller retorted.

Wexler ignored the rhetorical question. "You also don't want to overpower whatever instrument is taking the melody. You're part of the rhythm section. You're supposed to stay in the background unless you're called on to solo."

Miller smirked.

"And the last thing is, you don't criticize your bandmate's instrument. Banjo was an integral part of early jazz bands, which is what we're trying to play here. Show some respect."

Miller rolled his eyes again. "Just because you're old, doesn't mean you know anything."

Wexler couldn't believe this brat was arguing with him. It made him feel mature in a good way. He'd learned a thing or two since he was a teenager. "Pack up your drums."

"You can't tell me what to do. My uncle owns this place."

"Honestly," Wexler exclaimed, "you're out past your bedtime, kid. The adults don't want to play with you." Then he went back inside. Ryan Miller didn't return.

The next day Wexler drove to Aural Sax for advice. From the small courtyard he could see Hodge seated intently at his desk, eyes on his computer screen, while a mandolinist played in the glass-fronted sound booth behind him.

Wexler sat on the bench and listened to waves crashing into the riprap at the foot of the crumbling cliff. He was remembering one of the first things Tom had said to him that had resonated and kept popping into his consciousness. Tom had said, "You call yourself a musician, but you're not really a musician. You're a former musician. You were lucky, you had success, and I'm happy for you, but you need to ask yourself — was it all about the acclaim and the women that came with it, or was it about the music? If you're really a serious musician forget about the past, forget about fame or the lack of it, and just get on with your craft. Practice it. Hone it. It's enough to just do it, and do it consistently. Make it a habit. Then you can call yourself a musician and mean it."

The lecture had bothered him because there was more than a grain of truth to it. His music was the source of his pride and self-worth. If he wanted to continue calling himself a musician, he had to get back to it, and this was as good a place to start as any. Otherwise, he would be no different than the one-time high school quarterback whose only claim to fame, whose very self-identity, revolved around a game played a lifetime ago.

"Hey man!" Hodge peeked his smiling face around the door to the courtyard. "Come on in. We're just taking a break."

Wexler was introduced to the mandolinist, who needed no introduction, and asked what they were working on.

"It's a PBS documentary on the lasting impact of presidents no one can remember. It's actually pretty fascinating. What brings you by?"

Wexler briefly explained his need for a drummer and horn section on a limited budget. "I was hoping you could point me in the right direction."

Hodge looked puzzled. "Don't tell me MacDonald turned down a gig?"

"I haven't asked him."

"Why not?"

"He'd be too expensive."

"Between guitar and woodwinds, you wouldn't need anyone else. And you could always trade him your time for his."

"You should call Max Vandoorne," the mandolinist said. "He's a local drummer trying to break into the business. Here, I've got his contact info on my phone."

So Wexler called MacDonald, who said, "If you really want an authentic '20s sound, you'll need a trumpet. I know a guy..."

And that's how it played out. The quintet was composed of Gordan Pierce on piano, Max Vandoorne on drums, Steve Wexler on standup bass, Clifford Cook on banjo, Scott Dewar on trumpet, and Mark MacDonald on sax, clarinet, and guitar. Larry Lu agreed to pay Pierce and Vandoorne, Cliff was playing for free, and Wexler quietly came to terms to pay MacDonald and Dewar out of his own pocket, because he wanted a certain sound and was willing to pay for it.

# # #

Not everyone ended up at Tom's on any given day or at any given time; the mix was fluid, with people arriving early and leaving early, people arriving early and leaving late, people arriving late and leaving late. One day when Wexler didn't show up, Tom asked Rosalind if she knew where he was.

"He's home, jamming with the guys who're playing at our party."

"What are they gonna play?" Emily asked

"Let's go see," Gary suggested.

So they all decamped to Wexler's house. The musicians were playing in the music room. Rosalind led the group into the living room, and when the music stopped, they all peeked around the corner. "Mind if we listen in?" she asked.

"Sure," Wexler said, "as long as you do it from the living room. We're kind of cramped in here."

The quintet, which would practice on Tuesdays and Thursdays until the night of the event, launched into *Bye, Bye Blackbird*.

When they were done Rosalind asked, "Does your band have a name?"

"I don't know," Wexler said, looking to other members of the band. "Do we have a name?"

MacDonald said, "How about 'Beiderbeck's Boys'? After Bix Beiderbeck?"

Wexler shrugged. The others nodded agreement.

MacDonald said, "Wex, why don't we do that again. I'll take lead guitar this time."

"It's better suited to clarinet."

"I can't play both at the same time."

"Stick with the clarinet."

"Uhhh," Rosalind interrupted, "I'm not exactly a professional, but I do play clarinet, in case you need both."

The band turned as one to Rosalind. Wexler was nonplussed. "You play clarinet?"

"I told you I played in high school band."

"But this is jazz."

"I may not be up to your standards, but I can play...a little...in case you wanted...." Rosalind read Wexler's confounded expression. "Never mind."

"No," MacDonald insisted, "I want to hear it. Take my stick."

They played "Bye, Bye Blackbird" again, with the addition of MacDonald's guitar and Rosalind on clarinet.

"Sweet," Pierce said.

"Not bad," Wexler agreed.

"What's your name?" MacDonald asked with interest.

"Rosalind."

"Well, Roz, do you know 'Ain't Misbehavin'?"

"I think so."

When they finished, Wexler said, "That was a bit rocky."

"Sorry," Rosalind said. "I sucked on that one."

"It wasn't that bad," Max Vandoorne said. "How about "Blue Skies" next?"

"I'll take the clarinet back for that one," MacDonald said.

Later Rosalind declared that she wanted to learn some of the old dances. "Can you play the Charleston?"

While Gordan Pierce searched through his binder of sheet music, Rosalind called up dance instruction on YouTube. She invited Emily to join her. They practiced the steps for a couple of minutes, then Rosalind cajoled Gary into joining them. Tom declined. "I'm here strictly as an observer. I never could dance, and I'm too old to learn now."

Before the band broke up for the night they came up with a firm playlist, all hit songs in their day, but barely known to members of the band.

"We ought to have some vocals," MacDonald said.

Pierce played soft chords and said, "I could take "Ain't Misbehavin'", and "Blue Skies." What about you, Wex?"

Wexler took a deep breath and looked skeptical. "I'm more of a backup singer, but I'll look at the list and see what I can do."

"Some of these tunes call for a female voice," MacDonald said. He looked toward the living room. "Do we have any volunteers?"

Emily looked abashed and turned to Rosalind. "Oh, I couldn't. I only sing in the shower," Emily confessed. "I've never sung in front of people."

Rosalind shrugged. "Well, I'm no Mariah Carey, but I can carry a tune, no pun intended."

Thereafter, on Tuesdays and Thursdays when the band was practicing, Rosalind hung out at Wexler's and practiced her two clarinet parts and sang her two numbers.

The first time she set foot in the music room, she was both surprised and impressed. She looked at the photos, and at the gold records, and realized that Steve Wexler was more accomplished than she'd imagined. She remembered Totally Wrecked. She had bought their second album when she was in college. The fact that he'd never mentioned his association was a source of amazement. It gave her a whole new perspective from which to judge this man. For all his swagger, he now impressed her by his humility. Had she known that he'd only refrained from mentioning the band because he wasn't trying to pick her up, she would have come to another conclusion entirely. As it was, she saw him in a new light, a man who was not only successful but humble. It was an attractive quality.

Rosalind enjoyed the practice sessions. There was something liberating about putting her ego on the line. She had a beautiful singing voice, which was somehow sweeter than her speaking voice, or perhaps it was just that "Someone To Watch Over Me" brought out a sweetness that wasn't really there. She gave the impression of believing the lyrics. She sang it so plaintively that Wexler would have been compelled to wrap his arms around her, had he not been playing upright bass at the time. But her voice was as versatile as the material demanded, and singing "There Ain't No Sweet Man Worth the Salt of My Tears" brought out a bitter growl with each chorus.

It was during these sessions that MacDonald took to referring to Rosalind as Roz, and he'd always called Wexler Wex. The nicknames stuck. There was a brashness about Rosalind that seemed better represented by Roz, and Wex was so much more interesting than Steve, and less of a mouthful than Wexler. Roz and Wex took their new names to the Theoretical Society, where they were picked up within the group, though Tom resisted calling Wexler by anything other than "Steve."

# # #

At the end of the second week, as the band was gathering in the music room, Wexler glanced over his shoulder and saw Nicole enter the room ahead of her father. In the few seconds before Cliff stepped out from behind her, Wexler's mind flew ahead to weigh the consequences. He fully expected to see a scowling face and clenched fists. There would be an unpleasant altercation, and what could he say in his defense? Then, unexpectedly, Cliff grinned and said, "I hope you don't mind, but my daughter is a fan, so I brought her along. Nicole, this is Steve Wexler, my old bandmate."

Wexler smiled his brightest smile, gave a slight bow, and said, "Pleased to meet you," as they shook hands. She winked. He gestured toward the photos on the wall. "Your dad is in some of these. Take a look around. I hope you won't be bored. I'm afraid we won't be playing rock-and-roll tonight."

"We're playing songs from the Roaring Twenties," Cliff explained, "a century old, but classics."

Nicole locked eyes with Wexler, and smiled a most beguiling smile.

"Make yourself at home," Wexler said.

She made pretense of discovering the photos for the first time.

Cliff leaned toward Wexler and muttered, "Sorry, she really wanted to meet you."

"No problem. She's beautiful."

Cliff smiled proudly. "She is, isn't she?"

Later, after everyone had left, Rosalind couldn't help teasing. "I think you made a big impression tonight. She was star-struck."

"I doubt it. Kids these days don't remember. She wouldn't even know who we were if it weren't for her parents."

"Really? I remember you were really big my second year of college. My roommate had a crush on your lead singer."

"No surprise there. Everyone fell for Andy."

"She's very pretty."

"Nicole? Yeah, she is," he sighed wistfully, "and very young. Reminds me how old I am."

"You don't look old to me."

"You're very kind."

"Just telling the truth. You're not even middle-aged."

"Do you want to stay the night?"

"I was hoping you'd ask. I wasn't looking forward to walking home in the dark. Besides, the dogs are asleep."

"Nightcap?"

"Now, there's a word no one uses anymore. Do you have champagne?"

"Always. Champagne is a staple."

Chapter Fifty-Four
Learning to Dance

Twice a week, after stopping by Tom's for a drink and conversation, Gary, Emily, Rosalind, and Wexler would extend the party by stopping at Emily's for half an hour or so, to watch instructional dance videos on YouTube, and practice dancing to the playlist they had planned for the party.

Being more adept, Rosalind and Wexler took to repeating the steps for Emily and Gary to follow. It wasn't long before Gary began to get the hang of it, but Emily remained stiff and reserved, embarrassed that she had no aptitude for dance. Nothing seemed to work. Even Rosalind was beginning to wonder if they could ever teach her how to feel the music. Everyone was frustrated until Wexler brought some magic brownies to the party. He sat beside Emily and said, "Do you remember in *Dumbo*, how the mouse told Dumbo that the magic feather could make him fly? Now just imagine that this brownie is like that feather. These are dancing brownies. They have magical properties that will make you feel the music."

"I thought you didn't believe in magic."

"It doesn't matter if I believe it. It only matters if you believe it. It's kind of like the placebo effect — if you believe it, you can make it be true. Like Dumbo, in the end you may find that you don't really need the magic, but it can't hurt. Now, close your eyes and repeat after me: "I give myself permission to be silly."

She repeated the words.

"Dancing is fun."

She repeated the words without conviction.

"I will let the music flow through me and become part of me."

"Oh, this is just silly," Emily said. But she repeated the words nonetheless. They sat around the kitchen table, over a bottle of white wine, listening to old-time jazz, making small talk and letting the conversation follow its logical course. Emily munched her brownie and chased it with the last of the Pinot Gris. Then she closed her eyes, and without visual distraction she let her other senses expand. She immersed herself in the music. Her fingers tapped the table in rhythm. Soon she was anticipating the notes, almost as if her fingers were drawing the melody out of thin air. *I feel a little tipsy*, she thought. *I've had too much to drink.* Whether she'd had too much, or just enough, she felt unusually happy and at a remove from herself.

Wexler's whisper came out of the darkness behind her eyelids. "Believe in the magic."

Her feet unconsciously tapped the floor, and with her eyes closed her head began to rock to the rhythm.

Rosalind tapped her on the shoulder. Emily rose and followed with a bounce to her step. She seemed to float above the floor as they stood side by side kicking their heels out to the infectious beat of The Charleston. And though Emily sometimes lost the beat, she was no longer self-conscious of her mistakes. She knew her friends would not judge her harshly, and when she was in sync with the music it really was fun. It would only take practice. Soon they all joined in and kicked and shimmied to a non-stop loop of The Charleston until, one by one they dropped out, breathless.

Rosalind was the last to stop. Sweating and exhausted, she audibly exhaled, "Whoohoo, that was a workout!" They sat down for a minute to catch their collective breath. "I read that the Fox Trot was the most common dance of the '20s and '30s. Let's try that." So, they watched an instructional video, then paired up to try it out, Rosalind and Wexler, Gary and Emily.

Now, consciously or unconsciously dance has always been a courtship ritual. Yet it had been more than sixty years since the sexes had danced together. Sometime in the middle of the last century dancing had evolved from an activity where one was in physical contact with the opposite sex, dancing prescribed steps, to one in which two people faced each other and jerked and shrugged in a freeform style of self-expression. The few who were good at it were blessedly lewd and fairly took one's breath away. The rest looked as though they were having epileptic seizures. Thus the Fox Trot was a new sensation to the couples now gathered at Emily's house. This was a tactile experience. Of course, Wexler and Rosalind had already danced another kind of tactile dance between the sheets, so this was nothing new, but Emily had never so much as held a boy's hand. She might as well have come straight out of a convent, for all the experience she lacked. So when Gary took her right hand with his left and placed his right hand against her back, the effect was electric. Emily was transported to another world strikingly similar to the world in her books, with a heightened sexual tension that made her hair stand on end and sent a shiver up her spine. They stood close to one another, gazing into each other's eyes, and waited for the song to come around to the beginning again. Reality and imagination blurred. It was awkward at first. Gary worked on how to guide her with his left hand and refrain from stepping on her toes. Emily worked on following his lead and dancing backwards. They tried their best to emulate the couple in the instructional video, but it wasn't easy.

"This is going to take some practice," Gary said.

"We've got six weeks," Emily replied with hopeful excitement.

By the end of the next week they were becoming proficient at the Fox Trot, navigating the room without bumping into things, or stepping (too often) on one another's toes. Then they returned to the Charleston, which had the unusual quality of being a dance you could dance either alone, or face-to-face in loose contact with one another while jigging in place.

There is an intimacy in formal dance, something magical happens when a man and a woman hold hands, gazing into one another's eyes, while concentrating on the music and anticipating their partner's moves. For Emily, it was an accelerated path to becoming accustomed to the physical proximity of another person. With repetition, the awkward tension of the first few days soon gave way to familiarity, confidence and ease.

Curiously, it had a somewhat opposite effect on Gary. The more time he spent in Emily's orbit the more tension he felt. He noticed details he'd never noticed before — the sparkle in her eyes, her lopsided grin when they moved as one, the delightful sound of her laughter. She seemed to come alive when they danced. The scope of his perspective narrowed incrementally with each repetition. When he was dancing with Emily, Rosalind and Wexler seemed to recede into the background.

Then, too, ever since he'd discovered the true identities of Robert Cole and Margaret Pennypacker, this hitherto ordinary girl had taken on a mysterious allure. Now that he'd read the Robert Cole books and begun the Margaret Pennypacker series, he felt compelled to explore the three sides of Emily Abbott — the public Emily, her two pseudonymous alter-egos, and their fictional alter-egos. Her fiction provided a window into her mind that made her all the more interesting. Attitude, aspirations, philosophy, politics, desires, concerns, insecurities, and prejudices all bubbled to the surface of the stories. He found it fascinating to uncover the intersection between artifice and reality, to reconcile the different sides of her personality. No wonder she felt protective of her identity. Who, he wondered, had inspired the character of Derek Law, and might he one day find himself in the pages of one of her stories? Who was Emily Abbott?

Chapter Fifty-Five
Territory Reclaimed

A motley group continued to show up on Tom's porch for pre-prandial libations. One of the core group sometimes brought along a guest. Early one evening Rosalind and Rosalind arrived first, followed half an hour later by Wexler and Roscoe, with Max Vandoorne in tow. Then came Emily, and finally Gary, who announced, "I can only stay a minute. Maria's next door."

"Bring her over," Tom said, handing him a glass of German Pinot Blanc.

"No, she's too rattled. There was an ICE raid at the restaurant this morning, before her shift. They arrested some of the staff, so she's steering clear for a while."

"What's ICE?" Vandoorne asked.

"Immigration and Customs Enforcement."

"I thought she was DACA," Emily said.

"Kids of illegals," Gary explained. "The government hasn't figured out what to do with them. Maria's been here since she was two. She doesn't even remember Mexico."

Emily, who had researched the subject for her latest Robert Cole book said, "I thought DACA were protected."

Gary shook his head. "The guidelines are loose. It really comes down to the individual ICE officer. This morning they arrested three of the staff, including another DACA who's been here over twenty years, which has Maria freaked out."

"I'm from Canada," Vandoorne said, "and I was shocked by how many illegals there are in California. And homeless people."

"Now that's a national embarrassment," Tom said.

When the subject turned to homelessness, Gary excused himself, and in the desultory manner of these gatherings the theme meandered like a boat drifting downstream and stopping at various towns along the way. The current pulled them from homelessness to addiction, drug cartels, corrupt and inept politicians, ineffective policies, and the shameful vitriol in public discourse.

In replaying some of the arguments later that evening Tom pondered Maria's situation. There was a large illegal immigrant population on the coast. They formed an integral part of the workforce. They picked crops, washed dishes, bussed tables, cleaned houses. They were gardeners, and tree trimmers, and nurserymen. Like so many problems, immigration was a polarizing subject, and as with all social problems, there were no simple solutions.

# # #

When the bottle was empty and the last glasses drunk, the rest of the party broke up. The dogs stretched, and shook, and stood up, and yawned, and looked expectedly at the humans for their cue. Vandoorne left them in front of Emily's front door.

"Shall we dance tonight?" Emily asked.

"I'm famished," Wexler said.

"Let's order a pizza" Rosalind suggested.

"Pepperoni?" Wexler asked.

"And mushroom," Rosalind said. "I suppose we should ask Gary and Maria if they want some."

"We can get an extra-large."

With a little coaxing, Gary and Maria came upstairs. Rosalind, whose natural inclination was to take charge, said, "Let's dance while we wait for the pizza. We can burn off some calories before we eat."

Emily led the way upstairs thinking *it's my house now. I can do what I want. I can play loud music. I can read trashy novels. I can even let dogs have the run of the house.*

Maria asked Emily if they could dance Salsa.

"I'm not much of a dancer. I only know what we're practicing for the party."

"What party?"

There was an awkward silence as all eyes turned to Gary for an explanation. He was clearly put on the spot.

"I hadn't got around to mentioning it."

"What party?" Maria asked again.

"Just a party at the brewpub in June. You're probably working that night anyway."

"Okay, but what kind of music?"

"Just some songs from the 1920s. Nothing you'd know." To the others he said, "Maria's a great Salsa dancer."

"Gary is hopeless," she chided.

Rosalind's eyebrows shot up. "Gary, hopeless? You should see him do the Charleston. You could do it with us. If you're good at Salsa, the Charleston will be a cinch. We'll teach you."

"Okay," Maria said. "Show me."

They moved the table and chairs out of the way. Then they lined up and Emily turned on the music. Maria watched and copied. She was a good mimic and had the steps down by the time the pizza arrived.

"That was so much fun," Maria said appreciatively. "Gary, I'm proud of you. You did good. I didn't know you could dance like that."

"He's been practicing," Rosalind said.

"What other dances do you do?"

"Just the Fox Trot. Come on gang, let's show her how it's done."

Emily had her reservations and looked to Gary for a cue as to what to do, but he was getting up to put on the music. Then Rosalind took her hand and Emily allowed herself to be pulled to her feet, thinking *oh, that will be okay, Roz will dance with me,* which on later reflection was a foolish assumption, as she knew the men wouldn't be caught dead ballroom dancing with each other. Rosalind turned to Wexler, leaving Emily paired with Gary, who seemed utterly oblivious to the situation. As they rotated counter-clockwise around the floor, smooth steps flowing with the graceful ease of long practice, Emily was peripherally aware of Maria's building ire and tried to affect a disinterested expression as she looked over Gary's shoulder. Then he smiled and she couldn't help smiling back.

Maria fumed. "How long has this been going on?"

Rosalind was too busy listening to the music and concentrating on her steps to pick up on Maria's tone. "Three weeks, but you'll catch up really quick, I can tell."

"Oh, hell no!" Maria exclaimed. She strode forward and grabbed Emily's arm. "Get your hands off my boyfriend! I told you before!"

"We're just dancing," Emily declared, sounding more innocent than she felt.

"Just dancing?" Maria scoffed. "You little bitch."

Maria had one hand on Gary's chest, the other on Emily's throat in an effort to push them apart.

"Hey!" Rosalind spoke sharply, as if reprimanding a dog. "Hey, hey, hey!"

Maria kicked Rosalind in the shin.

Emily pried Maria's hand away.

Gary stepped between them and pushed Maria back a step. "That's enough, Maria. Don't, please don't."

Then Maria went for his face with her fingernails, but he caught her hand and twisted her wrist until she yelped and stopped struggling. He let go. She swore at him, red-faced and furious and shrieked, "Downstairs now!"

As she stormed out she could be heard muttering, "Slut."

Gary called after her, "Wait, Maria, wait, you've got this all wrong."

He paused at the top of the stairs, looked apologetic, and said lamely, "She didn't mean it. Sometimes she just overreacts."

Emily watched him go and said quietly, "Oh, I think she meant it all right."

"That was interesting," said Wexler, who had watched the whole altercation with detached interest.

The door at the bottom of the stairs slammed, then another.

"I hate drama queens," Rosalind said reproachfully, "Are you all right, Emily?"

"A bit shaky, but I'm okay."

"You have a nasty scratch on your neck. You should disinfect that."

They went off to the bathroom to look for a bandaid, and came back in five minutes. Wexler stood in the middle of the room, arms crossed, looking uncomfortable. From downstairs they heard raised voices and the tinkle of broken glass. Emily was thinking she should have asked for a security deposit. Wexler put on an energetic Fats Waller tune and turned up the volume to drown out the commotion downstairs. "Let's dance," he said.

Since Emily had no partner, they danced the Charleston in a line, shoulder to shoulder. Waller sang, "Ain't misbehavin', savin' all my love for you."

When they put on a Fox Trot, Emily sat down and watched until Rosalind stepped aside and said, "You two dance together. I'm going to sit out for a couple of rounds."

Wexler wasn't a bad dancer, Emily thought, but he wasn't Gary either. For one thing, she felt clumsy trying to match his longer stride. It was like trying to ride a bike that was a little too big, and she had to crane her neck just to look into his face. Even then he seemed to be looking at a spot over her right shoulder. What's more, dancing with Wexler was like dancing with an older brother; it lacked that peculiar zing she felt with Gary, the promise of future intimacy. Perhaps, she thought, the intimation of pleasure was only as exciting or as mundane as the imagination allowed.

Chapter Fifty-Six
Territory Lost

Anyone observing Gary for a few hours might come to the conclusion that he was either very simple or very wise. He was utterly unconcerned with the touchstones of popular culture. In this respect, if in no other, he was perfectly in tune with Emily Abbott. He did not have time for social media, keeping up with the latest music, or taking part in the nation's passion for celebrity. So when Maria made frequent pop culture references Gary had a hard time following the conversation. It was in the nature of his vocation to be more concerned with weather, tides, equipment maintenance, and local fisheries, than what celebrity couple was getting divorced, what song was up for a Grammy, or who would win an Oscar. His one passion, beyond fishing, was baseball. He was an avid San Francisco Giants fan and watched or listened whenever he had the chance. There was nothing more beautiful, he thought, than a well-turned double play. Maria found the game tedious.

Yet for all of their differences, Gary admired her work ethic, and he was strongly attracted to her physically. Her delicate features, sweet smile, and puppy dog eyes made it impossible to deny her whims, at least when she was happy. But when she was angry her lips drew back in a snarl and her eyes became fierce with bitter contempt. Then he would try to deflect her anger until she cooled down enough to listen. Usually her invective was aimed at *him*. This time it was aimed squarely at Emily and, since he thought it unwarranted, he felt compelled to defend Emily, which only made Maria more furious.

"Calm down, you're being ridiculous," he said.

"She had her hands all over you!"

"We were dancing!"

"If you want to dance with someone, dance with *me*."

"I wish you'd try to get along. Emily's not only my landlord, she's a friend."

"Men and women are never just friends."

"That's baloney. I like Emily, but I am not attracted to her like that. She's not half as pretty as you."

"You might not be attracted to *her*, but she's attracted to *you*. She's trying to steal you away."

They'd been keeping company for about a year now, and he hadn't dated anyone else — didn't want to, for that matter — but he took exception to her choice of words. After all, he couldn't be stolen unless he was owned, and he didn't like the idea of being owned. He was glad they had a close relationship, but there were limits to how much he was willing to bend to please her. He would not allow her to dictate who could or could not be his friend. This so-called Theoretical Society was as close as he'd come to having a circle of friends since high school.

For the next week Gary stayed away from Tom's, and he stopped having dinner with Emily. As Rosalind commented, "I would stay away, too, if I were him. I'd be embarrassed for putting up with that shit." When he did finally show up on Tom's porch, tail between his legs, neither Tom nor Wexler had the temerity to ask about Maria. They were curious, of course, but they were also discreet. Rosalind, on the other hand, was just biding her time. She sat back and watched first Gary, then Emily, waiting for one or the other of them to broach the subject.

Tom, who had not been privy to the altercation, was oblivious to the tension, and offhandedly mentioned the Planning Department's proposal to install roundabouts on the coast highway, which opened the door for both he and Rosalind to swap personal stories, harrowing and humorous, of roundabouts they'd come across in their travels. The subject led to a discussion of traffic problems and solutions, road erosion, the tunnels through Montara Mountain that connected them to the north, coastal history, smuggling, roadhouses, and eventually the Seal Cove Brewpub, which brought them around to the party.

"Speaking of the party," Rosalind said, focusing her attention on Gary, "we're going to practice another dance tonight. Are you coming?"

"I can't, Maria's coming over."

Rosalind stared at him from under an arched eyebrow and cocked her head as if assessing him. No one else spoke. The silent scrutiny made him uncomfortable until he finally asked, "What?"

Rosalind said, "You do realize we're putting on this party for *your* benefit?"

He did know that. He didn't understand why, exactly, but he did know it. He looked sheepishly around the porch. "What am I supposed to do?"

"Jesus, grow some backbone."

"Easy for you to say, I'm trying to keep the peace."

"We all know the piece you're trying to keep."

"I lose either way," Gary lamented. "Either I disappoint you guys, or I piss off Maria."

"You might start by trying to get her to apologize."

Gary was the first to leave, and he left disgruntled.

When Wexler thought Gary was out of earshot he looked to Rosalind and said, "That was a bit harsh, don't you think?"

She shrugged. "Sorry, but I don't have any patience for drama queens or their enablers. The same goes for the male version, only we don't call them queens, or even kings. We just call them jerks. She's one of those people who throw a tantrum whenever they want attention. His problem is that he falls for it. He should just tell her to fuck off."

"Tell us what you *really* think," Wexler said sarcastically.

Tom was smiling. This was better than reality television.

Gary, who was around the corner but *not* out of earshot, paused long enough to take in the exchange. He didn't appreciate Rosalind's abrasive comments, but it set him to thinking. He was damned if he did, and damned if he didn't. Maybe Rosalind was right. Maybe mollifying Maria was just enabling her misbehavior.

# # #

It set him to thinking about their relationship and what he wanted in a girlfriend. She was beautiful. The sex was great. She was fun to be with. But she was young, just twenty, and she lacked emotional maturity, which could be trying at times.

She'd been working at The Careless Crab for three years, and while he'd taken notice of her, they hadn't spoken until early one morning the previous fall. A bunch of the deckhands were sitting around a horseshoe-shaped booth singing "La Bamba." They sang boisterously, "Yo no soy marinero, Yo no soy marinero, soy capitan, soy capitan, soy capitan"— *I am not a sailor, I am not a sailor, I'm a captain, I'm a captain, I'm a captain."*

Maria, who arrived to refill their coffees, scoffed, "Ha! In your dreams. You are all just lowly deckhands."

"Not this one," Ray Pacheco said, pointing to a beaming Gary Myron. "He just bought a boat! He is a captain now."

"It's only a small boat," Gary said humbly.

"But he is the captain of his own destiny," Pacheco said, raising his coffee mug. "May we all be captains one day."

After that, she'd been more attentive. They started dating before Thanksgiving.

# # #

Rosalind turned to Emily. "You do realize we both need new dancing partners for the party."

Wexler took exception. "What am I, chopped liver?"

"Think about it," Rosalind said, swinging back to Wexler. "You're in the band. You can't play bass and dance at the same time."

"I hadn't thought of that."

"Well, I thought about it, but I figured Emily and I would trade places dancing with Gary. Now that Maria has stepped in and monopolized him, we both need new partners."

All eyes slid toward Tom.

"Not me," he said. "I don't dance. Find somebody younger."

Rosalind looked to Emily. "You don't happen to have a mysterious boyfriend, do you?"

"No, sorry."

"Maybe someone you met at work? What *do* you *do*, by the way? I've never asked."

Emily shook her head. "I don't have a job. I've never had a job. I was going to school, then I was taking care of my mother."

"A classmate then?"

"No boys, I'm afraid."

"You poor thing. That puts things in a different light. We'll have to fix you up, won't we Wex?"

"With who?" Wexler asked.

"One of the guys in the band maybe."

"I don't think so. Vandoorne has a girlfriend, and the others are married."

Rosalind took a sip of wine, thinking. "If worse comes to worst, I know a guy I used to work with who could be persuaded, if I put him up for the night."

The thought of an interloper distressed Wexler. He had been looking forward to being with Rosalind at the party. "What about me?" he said softly.

"What *about* you?"

"What do I do between sets when you're hanging on some other guy's arm?"

"You might start by introducing yourself."

"I don't want to meet your boyfriends."

"No one is forcing you. And he's not my boyfriend. He's just a friend. Do what you would do if I wasn't there."

"What fun is that?"

"You want me to hold your hand?"

That was, of course, exactly what he wanted, but he wasn't about to admit it. Nor would he do what he usually did when she wasn't there, which was trying to pick up another woman. For some reason that no longer appealed. He wasn't interested in one-night stands, not when he had a best friend with privileges. His head knew they didn't have an exclusive relationship, but his heart didn't want to share her either.

Chapter Fifty-Seven
Angels and Demons

Later that night Emily could hear music coming from the downstairs suite. She crept downstairs and pressed her ear to the door. The music was an old jazz standard they'd been dancing to, and she could hear Gary's voice, too indistinct to make out the words, but in the lilt and tone of an instructor. Then came Maria's laughter. They were dancing! Emily pulled back, a sudden pang of disappointment and jealousy gripping her heart. She ran upstairs, her stomach in knots, kicked a stray shoe and flopped onto her bed.

It was while she was working on her latest Robert Cole adventure/ mystery the next day that a thought came to her. A terrible, diabolical, wicked thought. Just as in her story, she could eliminate Maria from the picture with one anonymous phone call to ICE. It would be so easy. She went as far as to look up the number for ICE and dial the number. The line was answered by an automated voice. "You have reached the office of Immigration and Customs Enforcement. To continue in English, press one. *Para continuar en español, pressione el número dos.*" She would inform the authorities and then — then she realized she didn't know Maria's address. She ended the call. Her heart was racing. It was a minor hiccup. It shouldn't be too difficult to find. A check of the internet found three Maria Hernandez on the coastside, along with their ages, but they were all a decade or more too old. So Emily slept on it.

The following day a stiff wind kicked up white caps on a choppy, slate-gray sea, and set cypress branches to creaking. She took a long walk under the leaden sky, angels and devils dancing on her shoulders the whole time.

What was wrong with following the law? Maria would get what she deserved. But what would happen to the rest of the Hernandez family in the maw of government bureaucracy? She brooded about the consequences for three days, during which time she came to write the scene in which Derek Law's cleaning lady, Gloria, asks for help after her mother is deported. By the end of the scene, Emily had managed to vent her anger with no real-life consequences.

Still, a specter of malevolence festered beneath the surface. Why should she always be the one to do the right thing? People who got ahead were people who took what they wanted and damned the collateral damage.

Then she heard her father's voice. "You know better than that. It's not like you to hurt someone out of spite."

And her mother piped in. "She always was a selfish girl."

"No," her father countered, "don't listen, Emily. You're a good girl, a kind girl. You know this train of thought will only bring you sadness and emptiness. Envy doesn't serve you. Jealousy only hurts you. Forgive her and move on, for your own sake, if not for hers."

As usual, her father was right, but that didn't stop her mother from sniping from the sidelines. "She's a Daddy's Girl. She always does what Daddy wants. You're pulling her strings, John. Just leave her alone and see what a little snip she really is."

Her mother was wrong, of course, but not entirely wrong. If not for her father, Emily would not have been so selfless. *To hell with Maria,* she thought. *She's not worth a troubled conscience. And to hell with you, mother.* For a moment she was satisfied that she still held power over her rival, even if she chose not to use it. But the thought was not comforting. Holding a weapon in check was not the same as forgiveness.

"Let it go," her father said. "Move on. Remember they're doing the best they can, given their circumstances, and be grateful you're not in their shoes."

She realized then that she would never be entirely free of her parents, that they would always be there telling her what to do, guiding her path through life. And perhaps that was as it should be.

# # #

All morning the fog moved in and out like a tidal wave, rolling forward and swallowing the town, giving it back up, and swallowing it again. Thick ghosts flew past Emily's window, dimming the light, until the sun beat the wraiths back. The fog bank retreated to a mile offshore, where it sat gathering forces for another assault on the land. Then shortly after noon, the fog bank shrank back toward the horizon. It was one of those days where it was warm in the sun and cool in the shade, and a fresh breeze came off the water.

Emily was making good progress on her story. Gloria and her mother had both been deported and were trying to smuggle themselves back into the United States. Of course, it was never so simple, for Derek Law was once again confronted by a moral conundrum. Not only was the question about illegal immigration, but about human trafficking and women unknowingly destined for sweatshops or sexual servitude. The only thing the story lacked was a romance. Derek needed a love interest.

It was a Saturday and Rosalind had promised to bring their new dance partners around in the afternoon. She arrived well after lunch with a pizza, a bottle of rosé, and two well-groomed young men. She first introduced Emily to Jay Broderick, a former colleague from Silicon Valley in his early thirties. The way his muscles rippled under his t-shirt made it plain that he frequented a gym. He reminded Emily of Gene Kelly in "An American in Paris" — short, compact, graceful, with a dazzling smile, and winning confidence.

Behind him was Martin Torgenrud, about Emily's age, tall, more reserved, with owlish spectacles, his head topped with a mop of dark hair that was shaved close on the sides and back. He wore a white suit, white buck shoes, a baby blue dress shirt with French cuffs and white collar, and a thin, cream-colored tie. He held up a straw boater and wiggled it in greeting. "I thought I'd dress the part," he said with an embarrassed smile.

Upstairs, Rosalind put the pizza on the kitchen counter and handed the rosé to Emily.

"I can't drink this early; it'll put me to sleep," Emily said.

"I can't either," Jay said. "I'm flying tomorrow. I could lose my license."

Rosalind looked at them archly. "I'll take one glass now, thank you very much. It puts a spring in my step. How about you, Marty?"

"Just a splash to counter pepperoni breath."

Emily asked if Rosalind had explained the kind of songs they'd be dancing to.

"We're your guys," Jay said enthusiastically and winked at Martin.

"They could be dance instructors," Rosalind said.

"And you can come to the party?" Emily asked.

"Of course, we wouldn't miss it. Martin is a huge fan of the Roaring Twenties."

"And Jay's looking forward to bidding on your hooch," Martin said.

The former friends and colleagues got caught up-to-date over pizza. Then they danced to the setlist that would be played at the party, switching from Charleston to Fox Trot, and switching partners every few tunes. The men were superb dancers and were soon teaching the women several variations in both dances.

They were gliding through a Fox Trot when Gary and Maria came to the top of the stairs. Maria looked uneasy, if contrite. Emily noticed them first and stopped dancing. Unmindful of the dancers, the music played on until Rosalind turned it off.

Gary was surprised by the newcomers. He caught Emily's attention. "Sorry for interrupting. Maria has something to say."

Maria stepped out from behind him. "I want to apologize. I lost control. I thought...I thought you were trying to steal my boyfriend."

"We were just dancing, Maria," Emily said, though she knew it was a little more than that — for her, at least.

"I'm sorry I lost my temper."

It had been easier to forgive Maria in absentia. Then it had all been theoretical, forgiveness just a concept. Seeing her now with Gary brought back some of the visceral envy that had sparked her interest in the first place. She really did like Gary. He was easy to be with. So easy. Gary's appeal lay in his wonderful simplicity, but it also prescribed his limitations. His frame of reference was narrow, and she didn't think he was likely to expand his horizons as time went on. She didn't want to lose his friendship, but she had to admit to herself that she didn't envisage him as a life partner. She would have welcomed a romantic relationship, but she didn't see him as her one and only. In the long run, she wanted a partner with whom she could grow. And just maybe he was Maria's one and only.

Her father whispered in her ear, *You know what to do*. She smiled and said, "Apology accepted. Would you like to join us?"

"Oh, no," Maria said at the same time as Gary said, "Sure." They laughed.

"Maybe just a song or two," Maria said.

Gary had already taught her the basics, and after they'd all danced the Charleston to "Somebody Stole My Gal," and a Fox Trot to "Bye, Bye, Blackbird," Rosalind wanted to take a break.

"We just got started," Maria complained.

"You just got started. We've been at it awhile."

"Is anyone up for Salsa dancing? I downloaded some on my phone."

"I could try," Gary said. Maria had tried to teach him before, but he had two left feet when it came to Salsa.

Maria ignored him.

Jay stepped in instead. "I love Salsa."

Maria called up a tune on her iPhone, and for the next five minutes they put on a show. Jay was a perfect partner and Maria was sexy, sultry, and flirtatious as she pranced and wiggled and tossed her hair around, intent on giving Gary an anxious moment.

Emily had a fleeting impulse to ask Gary to dance, just to see how Maria would react, but the steps were beyond her expertise.

When the exhibition was over, Gary and Maria went downstairs promising to see them later at Tom's.

The door had only just shut, when Jay wanted to know the scoop. "You could've cut the tension with a knife. Dish the dirt."

Chapter Fifty-Eight
Flying High

They found Tom on his front porch. He was dressed in a new cream-colored flannel suit, a blue shirt open at the collar, and a Panama hat cocked jauntily over his left eye. He sat in his rocking chair, an open book on his knee, staring out to sea.

"Have a seat," he said. "Who do we have here?"

Rosalind introduced the newcomers as their new dance partners. Seeing Martin, a smile spread across Tom's face and he pointed a finger. "A man after my own tastes. Nice suit!" Martin grinned shyly and tipped his boater.

"Jay and I used to work together," Rosalind explained. "We brought a rosé."

"You know where everything is. Bring me a glass of the Pinot Gris in the fridge."

When they were settled, Jay asked Tom what he was reading.

"Kristin Hannah, one of my wife's favorite authors. It's called *The Great Alone*, all about pernicious jealousy and growing up in isolation in Alaska."

Jay's face lit up. "Ooo, we just heard a tale of jealousy."

"Don't go there," Emily warned.

Tom smiled mischievously, looking to Jay for the gossip. "Tell me more."

"Nothing you don't already know about," Rosalind assured him. "Gary and Maria came by."

"Ah, poor Gary."

Emily had mixed feelings. The first voice she heard was her mother's. *He made his bed, now let him sleep in it.* Then her father spoke up. *Be charitable. Ill feelings don't serve you.*

"Speak of the devil," Rosalind said as Gary and Maria came up the walk.

"Who's the devil?" Gary asked.

Never one to prevaricate, Rosalind said, "We were just talking about you. Nothing too bad. Wine is in the kitchen."

Gary shrugged and went inside to pour a couple of glasses.

Gesturing toward the book set in Alaska, Jay said he'd spent a season working in a cannery in Anchorage, and was regaling them with stories of the land where the summer sun never sets, when Wexler showed up. All of the chairs were taken, so he sat on the top step of the porch, glancing sideways at Rosalind and Martin, and listening to Jay's animated narrative. Jay finished his Alaskan tale by saying, "I always thought it would be fun to be a bush pilot in Alaska, but the weather is too brutal."

"Do you fly?" Tom asked.

Rosalind piped in. "They flew down from Santa Rosa."

"Honestly," Jay said, "we could almost have driven down in the same time, but we like to fly. Or maybe I should say, *I* like to fly. Marty's not so keen."

Martin spoke for himself. "I like the view; I just don't like the noise. Gives me a headache."

Tom asked Jay if they were flying back that evening.

"Oh, no, we're staying at Roz's."

"What kind of plane do you fly?" Tom asked.

"Piper Cherokee."

"Can I beg a ride? I love to fly."

"We're going to Monterey for lunch tomorrow. You're welcome to come with us."

"I know a place on Cannery Row with an excellent wine list. My treat."

"Tom imports wine," Rosalind explained.

Jay looked interested. "Really? You'll have to tell us all about it over lunch. I can't drink though, because I'm flying. But don't let that stop the rest of you."

"Oh, it won't," said Rosalind cheerfully, "I'll drink your share."

"I've always liked small planes," Tom said. "My dad flew sailplanes when we lived in Switzerland."

"I love Switzerland."

And so, for the next three-quarters of an hour Jay and Tom, both extroverts, held center court trading stories about a variety of subjects. Meanwhile, Wexler kept trying to get Rosalind's attention, but she was sitting between Jay and Martin, attentively listening to the two raconteurs, and barely glanced his way. The one time she saw him looking at her she smiled and quickly turned away before he could signal her. Gary and Maria listened for a while, then had a conversation of their own at the other end of the porch.

The summer sun was still high when Rosalind glanced at her watch and said, "Time to be going. I'm taking these boys out to dinner."

Jay and Martin both got up to leave. Jay shook Tom's hand. "We'll pick you up around 10:00 to 10:30."

As they started down the walk, Wexler finally got Rosalind's attention. "You want to go into The City tomorrow? There's a new exhibition at the Legion of Honor."

Rosalind looked puzzled. "Weren't you listening? We're going to Monterey tomorrow."

"Oh," Wexler sighed, realizing his mistake. "I didn't know you were going, too." He looked from Rosalind to Jay and back. "Any chance of tagging along?"

"Sorry," Jay said. "It's a four-passenger plane."

Wexler tried to look as if he didn't care. "Ah, right, okay then. I'll see you all when you get back. Have a smooth flight."

Rosalind and her friends departed. Wexler took a seat next to Emily. "Who were those guys? No one ever introduced me."

"Those are our new dance partners — old friends of Roz's."

Wexler was troubled as he saw in his mind's eye a lurid threesome taking place at Rosalind's later that evening.

# # #

The next morning the little plane flew down the coast at two thousand feet following the dark, redwood-covered spine of the mountains. The single-engine Cherokee was loud, too loud for comfortable conversation. They wore headsets equipped with microphones, and Jay pointed out the landmarks when he wasn't talking to air traffic control. At Santa Cruz, they descended to a thousand feet, skirting the old brick lighthouse and the beach boardwalk. Just south of Capitola the mountains ended. They crossed the twenty-five-mile wide Salinas floodplain until, at the northern end of the Santa Lucia Mountains, they turned onto final approach into the Monterey Regional Airport.

Rosalind called for a car and they drove to Pacific Grove. Cannery Row was already busy with tourists. They stopped into a couple of art galleries before lunch. The restaurant was built on pilings at the edge of the water. It was still a little early for lunch, so they were able to secure a window table with a north view across the deep blue bay. Tom dropped a couple of samples with the Wine Manager, who in turn comped them to a New Zealand Sauvignon Blanc. Jay ordered a virgin margarita.

Over a lunch of fresh fish, Martin said, "I want to go to the aquarium after we eat. I've never been."

"It's great," Rosalind said. "Especially the jellies and the kelp forest."

Tom said, "Speaking of jellies, did you know there are huge jellyfish in this bay? A few years ago the Lady Washington came into Pillar Point. She's a square-rigger used in the movie *Pirates of the Caribbean*. I booked a day sail from Half Moon Bay to Moss Landing, and when we reached Monterey Bay I climbed to the top of the mainmast. From up there you can see deep into the water, and we passed dozens of jellies that were at least six to eight feet long. I've never seen anything like it anywhere else."

Jay topped that with a story of a personal encounter with a harbor seal in a kelp forest off of Point Lobos. The mention of Point Lobos reminded Tom of the photographer Edward Weston, which in turn reminded Jay of Ansel Adams who, as it turned out, Tom had met in his youth. One story sparked another as the two men found connections. Martin even got in a word or two. After a time the conversation turned more to speculation on the intelligence of cetaceans and cephalopods, and the nature of reality as perceived by other animals.

Catching Rosalind's eye, Tom raised his glass to toast. "I believe we have two new recruits for the Theoretical Society."

Which, of course, required an explanation and a recounting of the conversation that led to the naming of their little group, followed by a further discussion on the nature of Tom's near-death experience.

Jay steepled his fingers in thought. "You say you have unfinished business. Forget about that for a minute. Ask yourself what business you've already finished. What have you accomplished? What do you see as your life's mission?"

It was a sobering question from the only truly sober person at the table. It was the central question of existence. Tom was stymied. "My life's mission? You know, I don't think I've ever given it much thought. I'll have to get back to you on that." If he could figure out the answer to that question, he might figure out what "loose ends" needed tying up.

After lunch, they walked down to the aquarium. There Tom excused himself. "You go ahead. I'm going to take a walk down to Lovers Point and back. Call me when you're out."

He walked uphill a block to the coastal trail that was built on the path of the old rail line. There Rosalind caught up with him.

"You don't have to come," he said.

"I know, I wanted to."

Along the path, wind-twisted cypresses stood watch over frothy waves assaulting granite crags.

"You and Steve getting along?" Tom asked.

Rosalind laughed. "Well enough. He's easy to please."

"He seems fond of you."

"He likes the sex." She smiled wickedly at Tom. "Do I shock you?"

"You can't shock me; my generation invented sex. Not that I benefitted. I met Daisy early on in college."

"How long were you married?"

"Forty-four years."

"And how many girlfriends did you have while you were married?"

Now Tom did look shocked. "None."

"Hmm. You weren't tempted?"

"I won't say I've never been tempted. But I never trusted anyone enough to take that chance. And I never fell out of love with my wife."

"Lucky you."

"You didn't love your husband?"

"I did. He had a roving eye, and he could be a selfish prick, but I loved him."

303

"I detect a note of resentment."

"No, we just went through phases where one or the other of us was more in love than the other."

"That's normal."

Rosalind frowned. "Yeah, well, the thing is — there was a passenger in the car when he drove off a cliff. She was in sales at Oracle. I doubt she was hitchhiking." Tom made a guttural sound of understanding. "And I'm just so..." She paused a moment, trying to find the right word, but all she could say was, "...pissed. I should be able to mourn him. Instead, I have questions that will never be answered. Questions, doubts, accusations. The son-of-a-bitch didn't even have the decency to leave me with regrets."

Tom could only imagine the dismay she must have felt. He said, "At least you can move on without feeling guilty for betraying his memory."

"Guilty? Hell, no. Why should I feel guilty? Anyway, I'm not interested in going through that again."

"Through what?"

"Marriage. That kind of emotional rollercoaster."

"Does Steve feel the same way?"

She shrugged. "I don't think he's interested in long-term relationships."

"Oh, I think he might surprise you. Beneath the bravado, there's a lot of insecurity. He looked awfully uncomfortable when you went off with your boyfriends last night."

"I'm sure he's not worried about my friends. You and Jay seemed to hit it off."

"I like him, he's interesting, we have a lot in common. Although I feel sorry for his wife."

"His wife?"

"Martin's too. I could never tolerate an open marriage myself, but to each his own. Not that I'm judging."

"What makes you think they have wives?"

"Oh come on, I'm not blind. They both have rings."

"Because they're married."

"That's what I'm saying."

Rosalind rolled her eyes. "To each other."

Tom stopped. "To each.... O-o-o-oh!" he exclaimed as the light went on. He chuckled. "I never would have guessed. You should tell Steve."

"It's none of his business, and anyway I'm sure he already knows. It's obvious."

"Not to me."

They walked in silence for a minute. Then it was Rosalind's turn to stop in her tracks.

"Wait! You thought I was screwing those guys?"

"Well, you are rather cavalier about your sex life."

"Not *that* cavalier."

"Sorry."

"You're such a dinosaur."

"Guilty as charged."

They walked on toward Lovers Point, Tom pointing out bed-and-breakfast inns where he and Daisy had stayed. Rosalind had her own anecdotes. At Lovers Point they sat on a bench on the grass, in the shadow of a tall cypress overlooking the little sandy beach.

Tom said, "Every time I come down here, I lament that I didn't bring a swimming suit. It always looks so inviting."

"You'd need a wetsuit; the water is so cold, you'd freeze your nuts."

Tom smiled. The quip was obviously calculated to provoke, but he wasn't such a prude that he didn't find it amusing. Daisy would have disapproved of the vulgarity, but to be truthful, it was just the kind of thing that a male friend might offer as a humorous aside. It was just unexpected coming from a woman, though maybe it shouldn't have been unexpected coming from Rosalind. "Speaking of nuts, since you've concluded that Steve is only in it for the sex, I have to wonder what you're getting out of it."

"Sex."

"Joking aside, if you don't think he's in it for the long haul, why do you hang out with him?"

She took so long to answer, that it was apparent she was giving it serious thought. "He doesn't impose expectations. I feel like I don't have to go out of my way to please him. And he's a good listener."

"Well, that's something."

"That accounts for a lot, in my book."

Chapter Fifty-Nine
Behind the Scenes

Over the next few days, Tom thought about how mundane Daisy's last words had been — "We should stop at the market and pick something up for dinner." What would his own last words be when his time came? He didn't expect they would be anything profound or quotable. If he ended up dying in a hospital, he would likely say nothing so memorable as, "Nurse, can I have some juice?" Or," Let me sleep." He just hoped his last words were positive. He didn't want to go out with a complaint.

His best chum from high school, who had cultivated a cynical, world-weary view in adulthood, had been fond of saying, "Life's a bitch and then you die." He had died at 32 in a collision with a tree while skiing. For some, life was a sentence, a burden to be endured. And certainly, there were those whose existence was little more than a trial.

Tom counted himself one of the lucky ones. He'd been born into relative affluence and had spent his life in comfort. He'd always had food and shelter, parents who loved him, an interesting occupation, freedom from need, if not want, and Daisy. It was important to find someone to love. To be the object of love was a fine and comforting thing, but it was just as important to find one on whom to bestow love. Otherwise, he felt, a person would burst. His father had offered a toast at their wedding: "As Lao Tzu wrote 'To love strongly gives you strength. To be loved strongly gives you courage.' So may you both grow stronger and more courageous with each passing year." And so it had been. He had nothing but good memories, and for that he felt both grateful and unworthy. What had he done to deserve such luck? It seemed that there was no way to repay it but to pass it on to others, as best he could, and now that Daisy was gone, and Douglas had moved away to start his own adult life, he was left with this motley group of neighbors and friends to look after. There was some comfort to be had in community.

# # #

To that end, he worked in the background, reaching out to those who might be interested in bidding on the bottles. His feelers came back with more questions and some positive interest.

The next Monday Gene Price opened the brewpub for a private tasting. He made up a cracker and cheese plate, bowls of olives, bowls of peanuts, and glazed walnuts. Tom arrived early, followed a few minutes later by Steve Skidmore, a collector of his acquaintance; Bob Hammer, from the *Half Moon Bay Review*; Michael Kinney from *Wine & Spirits Tasting Guide,* and finally Mike Temple, a wine buyer for a high-end wine and spirits retailer. Tom had known them all professionally for twenty-five years or more, and yet he knew very little about their private lives.

The six of them sat at a window table with a view of the cove, bottles of sparkling water, champagne, port, whisky, spit buckets, and appropriate glassware between them. Tom put two hands flat on the table. "As Bob pointed out in his article in The Review, Emily Abbott and Gary Myron were dragging the bottom for some lost crab pots, when they came up with a cache of Prohibition Era wine and booze. We assume this, even though the paper labels of most of the bottles have long since dissolved, because four bottles of 1918 Fonseca port were found with paint-stenciled labels. We didn't bring the Fonseca, because we all know that if it's sound, it's worth quite a lot per bottle. We *have* tasted the liquor, and Emily has graciously allowed us another bottle for your evaluation, as well as an unknown champagne, and an unknown port. The purpose of this tasting is first to determine if these bottles are drinkable. If they are, what is their likely age and provenance, and how much are they worth?"

"That's a tall order," Bob Hammer said. "It's like trying to put a value on a painting that isn't signed."

"That's why I brought you all together. You have the experience to make an educated guess."

"Are they for sale?" Skidmore asked.

"We're holding a party and silent auction at the end of June. Let's start with the champagne."

The bottle opened with a satisfying pop. Gene poured the champagne flutes half full. They all sniffed, tasted, spit, made notes, and repeated.

Temple said, "Surprisingly bright and effervescent, all things considered. I would have thought it decades younger."

Kinney tasted and spit. "I get hawthorne blossom on the nose, a bit of caramel and toast on the palate. I didn't have high expectations. I'm amazed at the shape it's in."

Then Gene Price brought out the Stilton cheese and honey glazed almonds, and they tackled the mystery port. Traditionally, Tom knew, decades-old port would be opened with great ceremony by heating port tongs in a fire, clamping them onto the neck of the bottle and cracking the neck off below the cork. However, the liability of leaving a shard of glass in someone's drink was enough to cause him to opt for another method. The neck had been dipped in black sealing wax, which he now chipped off before attempting to extract the cork with a cork puller, which tended to work better than a corkscrew on old corks. This particular cork was saturated with wine and he had difficulty keeping it from sliding down into the neck of the bottle. But with a little coaxing and patience, he was able to pull it out in one piece. He sniffed the cork and passed it around the table. Gene brought out a crystal decanter and a fine sieve. Then he lit a candle and held it beneath the shoulder of the bottle, as Tom poured carefully, watching for the telltale signs of sediment. None came. The gorgeous copper-colored liquid poured out clear to the very bottom. The tannins had sheeted to the side of the bottle.

Smiles and superlatives flew around the table, and there were groans of satisfaction as the wine was tasted. Skidmore swallowed his, saying, "That's too good to spit."

As Bob Hammer would write later that week in the *Half Moon Bay Review*, "A few weeks ago I wrote about the discovery of a cache of Prohibition-era liquor and wine that was recently discovered along our coast. At the time, I had only sampled the whisky, I had not yet tasted the wine. This week I had the privilege of tasting one of the bottles that will be auctioned off at the end of June. I've had some very fine old ports in my time, but nothing quite like this. The bottle, one of a dozen, had risen from nearly a century of slumber at the bottom of the ocean. Lacking provenance, these anonymous bottles may not have the cachet of a famous port house attached to them, but their worth is undeniable. This was as close to perfection as any dessert wine I've experienced in all my years of writing about the subject. The nose was incredibly aromatic and persistent, the balance unbelievable, and the flavors deep and complex. At its core, it tasted of butterscotch and berry syrup, with notes of apricot, tangerine, toasted hazelnuts and nutmeg playing around the edges. The finish lingered for minutes. I've had a few dessert wines that equal it, but none that have bettered it. An auction, which includes all of the bottles recovered (whisky, port, and champagne), will be held at a private event on June 24. A limited number of tickets are available. Serious bidders should contact Lawrence Lu at The Seal Cove Brewpub for more information."

When the port and Stilton and nuts were consumed, Temple said, "That was majestic. I should give Carl Lundquist a call. He's the national Brand Manager for Fonseca. And Al Carreta from Dow. Peter VanGiersbergen from Warre's. The publicity value of these bottles is enormous."

Then they tried the whisky. Hammer said, "I have some contacts at Canadian Club. They might be interested in bidding on this."

"How do I get in on this auction?" Skidmore asked.

Later, Tom recounted the tasting and told Emily, "Don't worry, these guys can get the word out. They have contacts, and their contacts have contacts."

Chapter Sixty
Getting Ready

While sunny summer weather came to the rest of the Bay Area, a June gloom settled on the coast and the little town of Seal Cove. Crab season ended, the humpbacks returned from their wintering in Hawaii, and the pelicans returned from wherever they go in the colder months. Gary switched to trolling for salmon and albacore, but with a temperamental engine, he was forced to fish closer to the harbor than he wanted. Some days the fog was thick enough to add an air of mystery. Most days were merely dreary, as though the atmosphere had leached the color out of the air. Thin fog condensed in the trees and dripped incessantly on rooftops, and blurred the distinction between ocean and sky. Inhabitants of Walnut Creek and Danville in the East Bay, flocked to the coast on weekends to escape the heat. Once or twice a week the afternoon sun burned through and the fog dissipated for a few hours, only to return in the evening.

Most days the Theoretical Society still gathered informally at Tom's, but they sat inside and their collective mood was subdued. Even the upcoming party garnered no enthusiasm.

One evening Rosalind said, "This was supposed to be fun. I'm getting tired of this party and we haven't even had it yet. If I'd known it was going to take this much work, I would've paid for Gary's engine and taken the booze off his hands. I should be in Maui."

"Too late to bail out now," Tom said.

"I've had enough of practicing. I want to have some fun. Emily, I'm taking you shopping tomorrow."

So the next morning they drove into The City. Rosalind was evasive when asked where they were going. Emily welcomed the excursion and the chance to get to know Rosalind a little better, but she worried too. "I can't afford to spend a lot," she said.

"Not to worry. I've got a plan."

At Sears Fine Food on Powell, they bonded, over a brunch of Swedish pancakes and sausages, mimosas, and coffee, in a way that was impossible when men were present and the conversation desultory. Here they could share autobiographical details, though it must be said that Emily had very little of interest to share, and she wasn't yet ready to share her secret passion to be a writer. That was too personal, too like sharing a diary. Her life paled beside Rosalind, who had a rich history and stories to tell, of fortune and misfortune, triumphs and failures, joys and sorrows, career and travel. Emily just wanted to soak it all in and live vicariously through her friend. Her only girlfriend. Rosalind glanced at the time, called for the check and said, "We have to be going, or we'll miss our appointment."

"What appointment?"

"You'll see."

They walked down to the American Conservatory Theatre on Geary. "The theatre rents costumes. We're going to try on flapper outfits."

The costume department had everything they needed, from dresses to shoes, pocketbooks, coats, costume jewelry, cloche hats, headbands, and feather boas. With Emily as her blank slate, a living doll she could dress up and transform, Rosalind had a ball playing big sister. Emily was mesmerized by her own image in the full-length mirror, as each dress conveyed a different mood. For the next hour, they each tried on several outfits, before settling on their favorites.

Emily picked a sleek cream and gold, sleeveless dress accented with sequins, beads, and fringe. Rosalind chose a short dress with geometric patterns in black, coral and ivory. Once they'd made their selections, a seamstress took measurements. Then it was time to pick accessories. There were drawers of jewelry separated by decade and era, much of it original, though none of it expensive — just the sort of thing a girl in the 1920s might wear to a party. When they were done, the accessories were put into boxes to be saved until the dresses, properly altered, were picked up prior to the party.

Emily was bubbling with enthusiasm as they left the theatre. "My god, that was the most fun I've had in forever! How much do I owe you?"

"Oh, don't worry about it. You can pay me back by picking up the dresses after they're altered. Just remember we can only keep them for a week from the time we pick them up."

"I wonder what Jay's wife thinks of his dancing with me. Is she coming to the party?"

Rosalind looked at her closely to see if she was joking, and decided she was as clueless as Tom. "For heaven's sake, is everyone in Seal Cove so dense?"

"What?"

"He's gay."

"Oh," Emily said. "Oh, that makes sense. Ah." They walked half a block. "And Martin?"

"They're a couple."

"Of course."

Rosalind consulted her watch again. "Next stop, Union Square."

"What more do we need?"

"You want to look the part, don't you?"

"Sure."

"Then we need new faces. We have just enough time before our next appointment."

At Macy's, they stopped at the makeover counter. "I'll go first," Rosalind said.

Emily picked up bottles of foundation and eyeliner and turned them over to peek at the prices. She whispered in Rosalind's ear, "I can't afford this stuff!"

"I'll take care of it, I'm getting low on supplies."

Rosalind opened her purse and took out a black-and-white photograph she'd found on the internet. "We're going to a Gatsby party and we want to look like this, only in color."

When the makeup artist was done transforming their faces, Emily looked in the mirror and almost gasped. Her eyes were framed by black eyeliner, mascaraed eyelashes, and blue eye shadow. Her cheeks were rouged, and her lips painted scarlet.

Rosalind bought some perfume and purple eyeliner. On the way out of the store Emily hissed, "I don't look like myself."

"That's the point, isn't it?"

"I feel like I'm wearing a mask."

"She did go a little over the top, didn't she?"

Outside on the sidewalk, Emily felt the eyes of strangers upon her. "People are staring."

"Ye-e-es," Rosalind cooed. "Isn't it fascinating? It's like assuming a new identity. Who are you today, Emily Abbott?"

Emily thought a moment. "I'm not Emily. I'm a mysterious woman with a past. I'm Ester."

"And I'm Madeline. I live in Paris and I'm the mistress of Monsieur Colbert, a powerful financier. Our affair is scandalous because everyone suspects I'm working for the opposition."

Emily, who by nature or nurture was more reserved, wondered if this was the way actresses felt upon taking a new role. When you were yourself, you were naturally more circumspect — any *faux pas* fell squarely on your shoulders. When you put on a new face, the onus fell upon your fictional persona. There was a freedom in adopting a new identity. It was precisely like bringing fictional characters to life. When she wrote, she was no longer just Emily Abbott, she was Robert Cole or Margaret Pennypacker, writing from the point of view of Derek Law or Penelope Stratton. She could pull their strings with impunity. What power! What delicious freedom!

Back at the car, Rosalind said, "Now we have one more stop to make, and you'll have to trust me on this one. You'll love it."

Emily was only too happy to oblige. It was both comforting and liberating to be taken under the wing by a more experienced woman. All she had to do was follow her lead.

In Farallone City they stopped at Maxine's Hair and Nail Salon, where Rosalind once again produced a print from her purse. This was a page from a beauty magazine of the ten most popular hairstyles of 1924. She pointed to one of the styles. "I'm going for this look," she said, pointing to a photo of a blonde sporting a French, center-part bob with marcel waves that rested just above her shoulders. "It should go well with the cloche hat I'll be wearing." Then she stepped back, looking from the page to Emily and back again, critically assessing Emily's thick, dark Dutch Boy that hid most of her face. "For you, I was thinking of something sleek, something that would suit the headband and show off your bone structure. Something like this," she said, pointing to a photo of Louise Brooks with a boyish bob that swept forward just above her jawline.

Later, they found an all-male contingent gathered in Tom's living room. With Gary still out fishing, the group consisted of Tom, Buddy, Wexler, Roscoe, Gene Price, Dave Olney (whom Tom had run into while walking Buddy,) and Dave's Pomeranian, Tiger. They all stared at the women, seeming at a loss for words.

Tom said, "I was just saying, I wonder where the ladies are."

"Ah," Rosalind began, speaking in a dreadful mock-French accent, "and 'ere we are. *Enchanté Messieurs*, I'm sure. My name is Madeline, and ziss charming young lady is Ester. What do you ssink of our new look?" She patted her hair, pursed her lips, and raised an eyebrow.

The men just kept staring.

"It does not meet with your approval?" Madeline asked. "But how can ziss be? Ziss is zee newest look for 1924."

Wexler, Gary, Dave, and Gene all took sips of wine as a prophylactic against foot-in-mouth disease.

"Wow," Tom said. "Just...wow."

Chapter Sixty-One
The Party

The day of the night of the party there was activity on all fronts. Being Monday, the brewpub was closed, leaving Gene Price and a couple of assistants all day to prepare. They rearranged the furniture to make a dance floor of half the dining area. Extra chairs and tables were carried to the storage shed on the side of the building. A room behind the bar, usually reserved for large parties and corporate events, served as the auction room. Stations corresponding to the various auction lots were set up around the perimeter of a long dining table draped with a simple, white table cloth. Gene had fetched the bottles the day before, and now he set them carefully in their allotted spots. There were both single-bottle and multiple-bottle lots. At each station clipboards and pens were set out for the bidders. In the center of the table print-outs of Bob Hammer's article and tasting notes were displayed, along with photos Emily had taken on the deck of Miss Behavin' on the day of their discovery. Bob had instructed that his name be added as the first bidder on each lot, thus establishing a minimum bid. Gene added his own name and bids to several lots, though he held out little hope of winning the bids.

Larry Lu fretted about the details, bustling here and there, removing obvious signs of modernity, and worrying that the money he was spending on photography would be wasted by the intrusion of newfangled gadgets. Plastic beer taps sporting brand logos were replaced with old-fashioned wooden handles. The electronic cash register disappeared under the bar, to be replaced by an antique brass register. At one point he paid a visit to the auction room and raised all of the bids, hopeful of landing a few bottles for future marketing and promotion.

All morning the sun teased and flirted and threatened to win the day. Patches of blue sky shone through rents in the fog. Midday the fog withdrew, and like a chameleon the ocean turned from grey to cobalt blue. The dark cypresses took on more definition.

The mayor had arranged to have an antique car club park period autos in front of the brewpub to give the scene an authentic Prohibition-era atmosphere, and to ferry home anyone who had drunk too much to drive. The club arrived at noon.

The photographer and his assistant began scouting angles and taking photos. A drone operator was just beginning to take aerial video when the fog returned thicker than ever, obscuring the far end of the cove, stealing color and creating a dreary twilight world. The drone made just two quick passes before a heavy mist began to fall. Larry Lu despaired.

That afternoon Tom debated over which suit to wear. He kept looking out at the tide pools bathed one moment in bright sunshine, covered the next in a dense fog. In the end, he decided to be optimistic and selected the three-piece ivory flannel suit, and a paisley tie. He pulled on argyle socks and shined his two-tone spectator shoes.

Emily was both excited and nervous. She tried reading, but she couldn't concentrate. She had only actually been to two parties other than birthday parties. One had been a Halloween party, in high school. The other had been a college party with a lot of alcohol and pot and loud music. She had been a wallflower at both. Now she would be conspicuously on display. The thought made her stomach do flip flops. She just had to remind herself that:

a). She had practiced the dances until she could do them in her sleep, and

b). She would be hiding behind the costume and makeup. She would be Ester.

Martin and Jay, who had spent the weekend with Rosalind, parked at the harbor and walked the coastal trail past the boat ramps to Sam's Chowder House for lunch.

Late in the afternoon, the videographer staged the arrival of the booze under a leaden sky. Three of the staff dressed in gangster garb — black suits, shirts, and fedoras, white ties and spats — arrived at the front steps in an immaculately restored Model A Ford. Two men sat in the cab. A third stood on the running board, brandishing a Tommy Gun. Dummy cases of booze were piled in the rumble seat. Gene Price, wearing a green eyeshade and armband garters directed waiters to rush the "booze" inside. They repeated the scene six times so that the videographer and photographer could document it from different angles.

Back in the kitchen, the cooks were concocting various hors d'oeuvres — buckwheat blinis with crème fraîche and caviar, crab wonton purses, salmon mousse in puff pastry, seafood sliders, oysters on the half shell, petit fours and fruit tarts.

Rosalind helped Emily apply her makeup. An hour before the festivities were scheduled to begin, Emily and Rosalind and Rosalind walked the short block to the brewpub for photographs at the bar. When they were done, Rosalind the woman took Rosalind the dog downstairs to the terrace and left her with a bowl of water and a blanket to lie on.

Bored with the preliminaries, Gordan Pierce sat at the piano playing riffs for his own amusement. The rest of the band filed in soon thereafter. They were all dressed in tuxedos, and had he not been hefting a standup base, neither Rosalind nor Emily would have recognized its owner. Steve Wexler had cut his hair short, doused it with oil, slicked it back, and parted it in the middle. He looked like another person entirely. He looked like he'd stepped out of a black-and-white movie. Rosalind was too dumbfounded to make her usual sarcastic remark.

Steve was heading for the stairs with Roscoe when he glanced toward the bar and did a double-take. It was the first he'd time he'd seen the women in their flapper outfits. He smiled, winked, then pursed his lips and blew an old-time wolf whistle (old habits die hard).

The early birds came, saw that the party had not yet begun, and went back outside to take photos in front of the antique autos. Martin and Jay straggled in. Tom put on his Panama hat, hitched Buddy to a leash, picked out a walking stick, and strolled contentedly up the path that skirted the cypress forest. Sensing their direction, Buddy grew excited. He hadn't been to the brewpub in quite a while, and he remembered the delicious food and the camaraderie of his fellow canines. Before they were halfway there the fog slipped silently out to sea, revealing a sparkling blue ocean and a crescent of white sand. "What a lovely place we live," Tom remarked aloud, thinking that it was useful to have a dog at your side when talking to yourself. At the brewpub, Tom left Buddy with his compatriots on the terrace where, during the course of the evening, the dogs reveled in the attention of kind strangers, and gorged themselves on hors d'ouvres that slipped from human fingers (sometimes even by accident).

317

Finally, the guests began to arrive. Caesar, the *maître d*, handed out raffle tickets. Gary and Maria walked in. Steve Skidmore came early and seeing two familiar faces, he sidled over to the bar to say hello to Gene and Tom, and to examine the labels of old bottles that other collectors had brought to share. He had a sly smile and assessed the crowd like a carnival barker sizing up the rubes. "Are you bidding?" he asked Tom.

"I might."

"Save your money, because I'm prepared to outbid you. I expect to take all the ports and a lot of the liquor. We're passing on the champagne."

"*We're*? You and who else?"

"I put together a little syndicate with Mike Temple, the buyer for Beltramos, and a few other interested collectors. No one else has a chance, I think."

When the majority of expected company had assembled, Larry Lu stood on a chair in the bar and gave a short welcome speech, recounting once again the story of bottles lost, then found, and explaining how the silent auction was set up. "Enter your bids on the clipboards beside each lot. Bidding closes on the stroke of ten. The highest bidders will then be announced. Winning bidders must pay by cash or credit card, and take your bottles with you. If the winning bidder is not present, the next highest bidder will win the lot. Please be out of the restaurant by eleven (we'll have a lot of cleanup to do before we open tomorrow). Now, you've all been given three tickets, two blue and one red, good for any drink. *However*, only the red one will procure a one-ounce pour of genuine Prohibition whisky. If you want more, you'll have to bid!"

Larry Lu stepped down and there was a general push toward the bar. Waiters circulated with trays of hors d'oeuvres. Serious bidders all headed straight for the auction room.

As the din of ordering drinks subsided, the band set the mood with Gordan Pierce taking the first phrase of "Rhapsody in Blue" on solo piano, followed by the rest of the band as the piece progressed toward its crescendo. Next up was "The Charleston," and the couples took to the floor. Jay had come in a well-tailored tux. Martin wore his white suit and straw boater. Gary wore a white dress shirt and pleated black pants with suspenders. Maria had come in her Salsa outfit, a red miniskirt with fringe on the bottom, and red stilettos. They were joined by an older couple also dressed in period clothing. When it ended everyone applauded the band and the dancers. Rosalind left the floor to sing "Someone to Watch Over Me," while flirting with this new version of Steve Wexler. He flushed with pleasure at the attention, but when she returned to the dance floor and swung effortlessly around the room with the dashing Martin, he felt a nasty pang of possessiveness. As "Stardust" ended, he leaned over the piano and asked Gordan to take the next song without him. Then he made a beeline across the room and tapped Martin on the shoulder. "May I?" It was a rhetorical question.

Martin politely bowed out, as Gordan Pierce crooned, "Blue skies, smilin' at me, nothing but blue skies do I see." More couples joined in.

"Aren't you supposed to be playing music?" Rosalind asked.

Wexler was too agitated to answer. Instead, he bluntly asked if she would like to stay the night at his place.

"I have two men to entertain."

"Let them entertain themselves."

"Why would I do that?"

"Because I miss you."

"You do? How sweet." She considered playing hard to get, but there was something endearing in his worried expression, a vulnerability that made her disinclined to play the tease. "Why not?" she said. The relief in his eyes wasn't lost on her. She gave him a peck, playfully running her tongue under his upper lip. He pulled her closer. When the song ended, he floated back to the band for a bouncy rendition of "Sweet Georgia Brown."

They were dancing a spirited Charleston to "Ain't Misbehavin'" when Maria's stiletto heel snapped off and she fell hard to the floor. There was a collective gasp. The band didn't miss a beat as, mortified, her face flushed red, she jumped up and lurched toward the ladies room without looking back. Gary looked lost. He couldn't very well follow her into the ladies' room. Then Jay and Emily, Martin and Rosalind broke apart and they all finished the dance in a line. In the short lull between songs there was polite applause for the music and murmurs of concern for Maria.

Jay left to put in his bids, and Emily turned to Gary as the band launched into "S'Wonderful." She held up her hand, he took it, and they began to Fox Trot. Dancing with Gary came easily, like riding an old bike. They were comfortable together.

"I should go find Maria," Gary said anxiously.

"Give her a minute to compose herself. That was a hard fall."

She thought *This is what I dreamed of when we started planning this party.*

And yet.... And yet as they twirled around the room, moving fluidly with the beat of the music, she was aware that something had changed. The thrill had gone. The chemistry wasn't there. When they'd first been learning to dance, before Maria had intervened, the touch of his hand, the merest brush of his thigh, had sent a spark of electricity up her spine. Now, she realized, that electricity was not something communicated to her by Gary. Instead, it was something trapped within her, yearning for release. Over the past six weeks, dancing with Jay and Martin, she'd become accustomed to the feel of another's touch. The novelty and zing of anticipation were now missing.

Maria came striding barefoot past the bar, alert and disturbed, a wary anger clouding her countenance. Emily saw her coming, smiled, and beckoned her over. She handed Gary off mid-song and, surprised, Maria mouthed a confused, "Thanks."

Emily watched them wheel away, her dreams evaporating as she saw the smiles on both of their faces. When she felt a tap on her shoulder, she swung around expecting Jay, only to find herself looking at a stranger.

"May I have this dance?"

"I'm..." she began to say *not very good*, but bit off the end of the sentence. Why belittle herself? She'd been practicing. She was perfectly capable of dancing a Fox Trot with this ruggedly handsome young man. He wore a stylish herringbone vest and a yellow bow tie. He was, she noted, not much older than herself and he wore no wedding ring.

"I've been watching you dance," he said, struggling to suppress a grin.

There seemed to be nothing to reply to that statement, but it didn't diminish her pleasure at the implied compliment.

"My name's Paul. Paul Kennerly."

"I'm Emily."

"Great outfit. Very convincing."

"It's from A.C.T."

"The theatre? Are you an actress?"

"No."

"What do you do?"

"Not much."

They made a few rotations as she thought, *Don't be so self-effacing. Besides, you'll never see him again anyway.* "I write," she admitted.

"For a magazine?" She shook her head. "A blog?"

"No, just fiction."

Paul was intrigued. "Anything I might've heard of?"

"Not a chance, unless you read obscure romances or mysteries."

There, she'd said it. She couldn't brag about being a bestseller, or proudly declare that her latest novel was being optioned by Hollywood. She might never find acclaim. But finishing each book was a small triumph in itself. It wasn't so bad to be a nobody, if you could do what you loved the most.

"What do *you* do?" she asked in return.

He grimaced. "I'm afraid I'm a writer, too. Nothing so grand as a novel, though. I tried once, but I couldn't seem to find the story. It just sort of petered out. I couldn't finish it."

"Great, then we're both starving artists. I was hoping you were a doctor or a lawyer. What do you write?"

"Travel guides."

"Really? Do you get paid for that?"

"Not much, but I get comped a lot of free room-and-board, and I've been all over the world. So, I guess that's worth something."

"I would love to travel."

"Would you like a drink?" he asked, which was shorthand for, "Would you like to have a conversation and get to know each other?"

They went off to the bar together.

Tom sat against the wall at the edge of the dance floor, nursing a glass of champagne and wondered what Daisy would have made of it all. She was never a party person, but she did like people. *God knows why,* Tom mused. *Humanity is capable of such mindless horror. We embody the worst inclinations of all living things on earth — cruelty, hubris, greed, unspeakable violence, and disregard for consequences. And then we turn around and embody the best of all living things on earth — compassion, music, art, literature, scientific inquiry, invention, and great imagination. What a burden it is to be human. What a privilege.*

Rosalind stood up to the microphone and said, "Here's a sassy tune that was, oddly enough, an early hit for Bing Crosby." Then she sang, "Brokenhearted sisters, aggravatin' misters, lend me your ears, there ain't no sweet man worth the salt of my tears."

Tom tapped his foot to the music and sipped his champagne. This was turning out to be a fine party. As Rosalind sang, he closed his eyes, and soon his head lolled forward, and he fell asleep.

Emily said aloud to herself, "I don't know how he does that."

Paul asked,"Does what?"

She gestured in Tom's direction, "He's asleep but he doesn't drop his drink, doesn't spill a drop."

"Maybe it's narcolepsy. My uncle has a mild case of narcolepsy, he can sleep anywhere.

Tom looked up and saw that Daisy was holding out her hand, asking him to dance. He had always wished he could dance, for her sake, but he'd never figured out how to move his arms and legs and torso to the beat of the music. For Daisy, it came effortlessly. She could shake and shimmy and ripple like a hula dancer, and glide gracefully across the dance floor. She often danced to music she heard on the radio, but Tom had never joined her. Now that she'd come back, though, he had a new confidence. He stood and took her hand. She led him to the dance floor and for once the music seemed to flow through him. His feet obeyed the beat, his hips and shoulders moved in synchrony. Daisy was smiling. When the song ended she led him up to the bar. She said, "This was a fun party, but it's time to go home."

"I'm ready," he said, but stood for a moment looking over the room, feeling that he should tell someone he was leaving. They might be worried if he just left without saying goodbye. But they were all occupied.

"Come on dear," Daisy said. She pulled him through the crowd, and as they approached the door he felt someone else take his other hand.

Someone said, "Here, let me take that before you drop it."

He opened bleary eyes and found himself still in his chair at the edge of the dance floor. Emily was prying the champagne flute from his fingers. Daisy was gone. The band was playing a different song.

"Damn, I was having such a nice dream. I'm tired, I think I'll go home."

Tom retrieved Buddy and they stepped outside. It was near to summer solstice, the sun still above the horizon. The fog bank sat a couple of miles out to sea, biding its time. Daisy was still fresh in his mind. He felt sad, but also grateful for the visit. His soulmate. Some people find their soulmates the moment they set eyes on them. Other couples grow into soulmates over time. Either way, it was a precious thing to find another in sync with one's own worldview. Tom let Buddy lead the way home, as behind them the music faded away until all they could hear was the indistinguishable susurrant whisper of wind in the cypress boughs and waves rolling into shore, the sound of silence.

# # #

Meanwhile, the party rolled on. At one point an amused and boisterous young man came upstairs, bellowing that two dogs were humping on the terrace, causing a tittering through the crowd and a movement of voyeurs toward the windows. Rosalind arched an eyebrow at Wexler. He was tempted to quip, "Like mother, like daughter," but good sense prevailed before he opened his mouth. "Why are you looking at *me*?" he asked instead.

"Tell me you've had Roscoe fixed."

"Fixed is a funny way of putting it. I don't believe in cutting a dog's balls off. It's cruel. Besides, what makes you think it's him? It could be somebody else's dog."

She was tempted to quip, "Like father, like son," but held her tongue.

Rosalind and MacDonald played a clarinet duet on *Tea for Two*, before the band took a break between sets.

Someone commented on the sunset and all heads turned to watched the sky catch fire, ooing and ahhing as the colors morphed toward twilight.

Soon the band began the second set, the dancing continued, and the bidding heated up when Larry Lu announced he'd received unexpected texted bids from representatives of Fonseca port, and Canadian Club whisky.

Wexler was in his element. The crowd and the conversation faded into the background as the band carried on a musical conversation between the instruments that was the global language innately understood by every musician everywhere. It was all about synergy, deconstructing a song and bringing it seamlessly back together again, and it was magical.

Wexler brought the final set to a close singing a Bix Beiderbeck tune in a clear, fluty tenor:

> "What your tomorrow may bring
> don't mean a thing.
> That's why I say
> take your tomorrow
> and give me today."

From Emily Abbott's Notebooks
Party Time

Where to begin? Last night we had the auction party. We netted a boatload of money, way more than we expected. Gary ought to be able to buy his engine now. It was such a fun party! I met a ~~boy~~. ~~Man.~~ Young man. Writer. Paul Kennerly. He writes for a few travel guides. He's been to 26 countries! If I had to come up with a list of dream jobs, that would be high on my list. I would love to travel. There are so many places I'd like to see. He just got back from the Philippines. He has so many stories, and he's funny. I just looked him up online. Not a bad writer, either. Lives in San Mateo with his parents, when he's not traveling.

Come to think of it, a travel writer would make a great profession for a main character — you could set your story anywhere in the world, and he (or she) could meet any number of people from different walks of life. It would be perfect for both mystery and romance genres. Or maybe a husband and wife travel writing team.

I'll probably never see him again, but I'd love to pick his brain. He asked for my number and I gave it to him. I should have asked for his. I didn't want to come off as needy, or pushy. Damn, I should have asked for his number. I hope he calls.

EPILOGUE

Tom loved life, but having already experienced death, he wasn't afraid of it. He hadn't just blinked out of existence. He'd been conscious and present the first time, and this gave him courage. In the days and months after the party, he often wished his dream had been real, that Daisy had come for him, that he'd taken her hand and walked out the door into whatever came next.

But life is rarely so tidy. In life, if accident or disease doesn't claim us in our youth, we just tend to wind down. Tom wouldn't take his last breath for another four years.

The party raised enough money to buy Gary his engine, with enough left over for Emily to take a trip to Vancouver with Paul Kennerly. Kyle returned to work on his uncle's boat for the remainder of the summer. Soon after Roz and Wex returned from Maui, Rosalind (the dog) gave birth to a litter of five rambunctious puppies that looked like white and gold versions of Roscoe. Rosalind (the woman) kept one. Emily took the runt of the litter, a fluffy little scamp she named Mary, after her mother. The rest went to other neighbors and coastside families, and today they and their progeny can be found walking their owners on the coastal bluffs. One is even a frequent visitor to the terrace at the Seal Cove Brewpub, and has a curious penchant for crab.

In the Fall after the party, Tom Birmingham and Gene Price traveled to France and Germany, so that Gene to meet Tom's suppliers and begin forging relationships of his own. And though the transition took a while, Tom did finally turn the reins over to Gene.

Emily finished her Derek Law adventure, *Law Abiding*, her best yet, and started writing a contemporary romance that was, for once, based on personal experience.

Gary and Maria broke up, and got back together, and broke up again. Eventually, he met and married Maria's cousin, Rosa Gomez, and with the help of her family, he was able to buy a share in Bill Whittaker's Barbara Anne.

Steve Wexler and Rosalind Kenway have never married, and see no point, but they've insinuated themselves into each other's lives so thoroughly that they might as well be married. Steve has found his niche playing studio gigs, and the occasional wedding and Gatsby party with Beiderbeck's Boys.

Tom's last day arrived without fanfare, a crisp autumn day when the horizon was sharp and the shadows long. He walked out to the lighthouse alone, Buddy having passed the previous year, and sat down at a picnic table to read *Time Management, a Novel.* He'd just got to the part about old San Francisco when he felt suddenly weak and exhausted. He lay his cheek upon the book and fell asleep, and he dreamt he was young again. Not the youth of his childhood, but his young adulthood. He was at school and a young woman was saying, "Mind if I sit down?"

"Be my guest."

"Do you know me?"

She reached out and took his hand, and it seemed he did know her. She was the embodiment of every girl and woman he'd ever loved. She was his mother, and Marty and Jane and Cathy and Anne and Nola and Lorna, and Julie and Mary and Daisy. They were all of a piece, and they were all Love.

When he awoke from the dream he found himself bathed in a cone of light as everything outside of the cone dimmed. Then he rose like an untethered balloon, rising higher than the lighthouse, higher than the gnarled trees, higher than the mountains, gaining speed as the passage narrowed and he was spat out the other end into that bright space again. The pillar of light that Tom took to be Fate was having a conversation with another soul. Fate caught his eye and spoke in a voice he didn't recognize. "You'll have to wait your turn. It's been one of those days."

Tom looked around the space. There were no walls or horizon. It was as though he floated in the center of a hollow sphere of snow. Kindly spirits he remembered from his last visit still stood silently on the periphery, emanating placid good-will. Then Fate spoke in his mother's voice. "Okay, it's your turn."

Tom moved forward and eyed Fate cautiously. "Why are you speaking in my mother's voice? Are you *my* Fate?"

"Didn't I use your mother's voice last time?" Fate asked in his father's voice.

"No, and you didn't speak in my father's voice either."

"Well, I don't remember. Help me out here."

"You spoke with my own interior voice."

Fate adjusted. "Is this better?"

"Yes, perfect. I mean, now I recognize it's you."

"Any more requests, before we proceed?"

"No, that's fine."

"Okay, where were we? Remind me now."

"Well, you were about to give me a new life when the paramedics pulled me back into my body."

"Ah, right. And how did that go?"

"I survived."

"Did you learn anything?"

"No. You said I had some loose ends to tie up. I never figured out what those loose ends were."

"And I never said they were *your* loose ends. As I recall, I said there were loose ends that you could help me with."

"Did I? Help you out, I mean."

"You did."

"I don't remember doing anything worth writing home about. What could I possibly have done to make any difference at all?"

"For one thing — that so-called Theoretical Society brought together a neighborhood that will continue to impact the lives of everyone around Seal Cove. If you hadn't asked Emily to arrange for a boat to scatter Daisy's ashes, she would never have met Gary Myron. Without Gary, they would never have found the bottles. There would have been no party, so Emily would never have met Paul Kennerly. They'd never have married or had kids."

"They don't have kids."

"They will. Just because you're gone doesn't mean your influence is spent. You've had more impact than you realize. If you'd died with Daisy, Buddy would have gone to the pound, Steve Wexler would never have found Roscoe, or come to appreciate Rosalind, or taken up his music again. Gary Myron wouldn't have had the money to buy a new engine. He would have lost his boat on the rocks, and all the fish he caught would be swimming still."

"Bad news for the fish."

"People who would have eaten those fish, would have eaten artery-clogging beef instead. And who knows the consequences of that! The permutations are nearly endless. You did good. "

"I never knew."

"Are you ready for the next life?"

"I want to find Daisy."

"You know she's not one of my charges. I can't guarantee you'll meet in the next life. I can put you into her vicinity, but the rest is up to you and her."

"Is there any way I can make sure?"

"Her mother is about to give birth to a baby boy. Why don't we make Daisy your older sister this time around. Then you'll be sure to meet."

"I don't want Daisy as a sister."

"Would you rather she was your mother?"

"Oh, now that's just creepy."

"She'll make a good big sister."

"That's not what I bargained for."

"There are limited cards in my deck. Let me check with my colleagues." The pillar of light that was Fate pulsed, and its face, never particularly stable, morphed from a child to a woman to an old man and back again. It asked, "Has anyone taken Molly Mars' next child?" There was a long pause, as though Fate were listening to someone on the other end of a phone connection. "No? Okay, then," Fate said, turning its attention back to Tom. "That position has not yet been filled. I can guarantee you'll meet if you're in the same family. Otherwise, you'll have to take your chances."

"I don't suppose there's any room for discussion?"

"You've got to play the hand you're dealt. Do you want the position, or not?"

"No thanks, she should be easy to find now."

"How do you figure?"

"Now I know her mother's name is Molly Mars."

The pillar of light turned a bright rose. "You tricked me."

"No, I just paid attention."

"You know with each passing year you'll remember less. You might even forget her name before you meet again."

"I'll take my chances."

Fate laughed, if you could call sputtering and spinning laughter.

"You're a handful," Fate said. "A handful, but fun. Now, you're holding up the line."

"The line?" Tom turned and saw another couple of souls waiting diffidently off to the side.

"When it rains, it pours," Fate said. "Now, good luck, and let the next adventure begin!"

& & &

Moss Beach, Feb 6, 2017, to June 10, 2019

Author's Note

Though this is a work of fiction, there is a real Seal Cove, and Seal Cove Inn, and an old roadhouse (called The Distillery) perched on the cliff above the cove, and a Coastside Market, and a lighthouse, and a Marine Reserve, and a Theoretical Society, all in Moss Beach. A few of my fellow inhabitants have wondered why I didn't just call this book The Moss Beach Theoretical Society. The answer is that I wanted the freedom to bend the facts and move things around a little bit, and because the essence of a thing isn't always apparent on its surface. I initially intended to call our town Cypress Cove, as Cypress trees are a distinguishing feature — both short, wind-sculpted cypress, and towering, majestic Monterey cypress that scare the hell out of us when the wind blows hard. However, there is already a mystery series by Carlene O'Neil, set in the fictional town of Cypress Cove, so Seal Cove it is.

Thanks to my Advance Reader Team, whose insights materially changed the arc of the story, especially to Patricia Guy, Robbie Bergerson, Una Willers, and to my wife, Mary Etcheverry.

Special thanks are also due George Jue, captain of Necessity, out of Half Moon Bay, who kindly shared his experience as a crabber.

# # #

If you finished this book, please consider leaving a review online. Reviews, both positive and negative, help other readers discover books they might otherwise have overlooked.

And though I would love for you to read my other books, be forewarned that they have very little in common, save for style and a wry sense of humor:

With Artistic License

Time Management, a Novel

Evelyn Marsh

If you'd like to be informed about new books before they're available to the general public, you can join my Advance Team by filling out the form on my website: www.swclemens.com.

Thanks for reading, S.W.C.

* * *

About the author:

Scott William Clemens has a Masters in English Literature from U.C. Riverside. During a long career as a newspaper columnist, writer, and magazine editor, he visited 29 countries, tasted more than 100,000 wines, published more than 13,000 wine reviews, and wrote more than 500 articles on wine, food, and travel. His photographs have graced the covers of dozens of magazines and books, and illustrated hundreds of articles. He was the publisher of Epicurean magazine and its successor Epicurean-Traveler.com. For the past decade he has concentrated on fiction, authoring the novels *With Artistic License; Time Management, a novel;* and Kindle Scout winner *Evelyn Marsh*. He lives in Moss Beach, California.

Made in the USA
Las Vegas, NV
31 March 2021